W9-CMQ-705

A Tryst of Fate

A Tryst of Fate

A XANTH NOVEL

Piers Anthony

INTEGRATED MEDIA
NEW YORK

978-1-5040-6681-5

Published in 2021 by Open Road Integrated Media, Inc.
180 Maiden Lane
New York, NY 10038
www.openroadmedia.com

A Tryst of Fate

Chapter 1

MURDER

Squid woke alone in her bed to a bright morning. She sat up as her awareness solidified.

For a good moment and a half, she froze in moderate horror. Had it all been an amazing dream? About her being the most important person in the universe, about finding the most awesome boyfriend ever?

No, it was real. But where was Chaos? The imprint of his host's body remained beside hers; he had slept here. Well, Laurelai had slept here, but there must have been an hour of daylight when Chaos took over to join Squid on the bed. Chastely, as they were underage, unfortunately.

She had overslept. Chaos had elected not to disturb her when he was there. Not that anything he could do would disturb her as long as they remained a couple.

She got up, washed her tween-shaped body, swept her hair back into a ponytail—she did have real hair now, rather than a body painting of it—donned a decent dress, and considered herself in the mirror. She was distinctly ordinary, even for age twelve, with dull brown hair, gray eyes, and a turned-up nose. Of course, she could change her appearance, since it was not her natural one, but what was the point? Chaos liked her this way. That was all that really counted.

She left her room and went to the dining room. "Morning, sleepyhead!" It was the pet peeve, as dull for a bird as Squid was for a human.

"Morning, birdbrain," she replied, relieved that at least this one remained on duty. "Where is everyone?"

"Outside enjoying the air, unwinding after the fine mess you got them into."

"The fine mess I got them *out of*," she said, knowing the bird was teasing her. It was the peeve's custom to routinely insult everyone else.

"Eat your swill." The peeve waved a wing at the table where a bowl of cereal awaited her.

She obeyed. Then it hit her: "Am I still the—"

"Yes, you are still the protagonist," the peeve agreed. "I would have thought you'd be tired of it by now."

"I am! I did my time. It is someone else's turn. I just want to go find someone to hug and kiss, then sink into oblivion."

"Lots of luck with that last, as long as you remain the story's main character."

"Grumble," she muttered as she dissolved her teeth, rinsed out her mouth, and reformed them sparklingly clean.

She walked to the wall, gripped the inset ladder, and climbed up toward the upper deck. "Oooo! I can see your legs under that skirt, and your thighs," the peeve called from below. "And that's not all."

"As if you cared, beak-nose," she called back. "My panties wouldn't freak you anyway, even if they had adult power."

Now she stood on the deck. The boat was parked on a hammock, and the ground was actually closer down than the interior. The sail was furled vertically, with only faint wisps of fire around it. It would burst into full flame when spread and blown by wind. Fibot, the Fire Boat, was a marvel, far larger inside than outside, and one of the wonders of Xanth.

"There you are!" Chaos called, reaching up toward her from the ground.

"Here I am," she agreed gladly, doing a little leap-step into his elevated grasp, her skirt flaring wickedly. "I trust you are seeing more than my legs." She kicked her feet invitingly.

"Plaid panties," he agreed as he held her over his head, looking up.

"If you were normal, you'd freak out," she complained.

"I am not normal, and at eleven you are too young for full panty effect."

That was the bleep of it. "Twelve."

"Yesterday you were eleven," he said as he swung her most of the way down.

"Yesterday was a different novel. We all age a year between books, regardless of the actual time passed," she explained. "You are now officially thirteen." Chaos had existed longer than the universe, but he was still learning the nuances of mortal interaction. She was glad to instruct him. "That is, the human body hosting you, Larry, is thirteen. If you use it, you need to honor its limitations."

He nodded. "I am doing so. And we need to be nineteen and eighteen, to graduate from the dread Adult Conspiracy to Keep Interesting Things from Children."

"More's the pity. Now stop teasing me and kiss me. We can at least do that."

He enfolded her and kissed her. Her feet would have floated off the ground had they not already been off. Oh yes, she loved him.

After a timeless moment they separated somewhat, and he set her all the way on the ground. "You have filled out some," he said appreciatively.

"Yes, it's that extra year. A hint of some padding on the hips, bottom and chest, and a little off the waist. Next novel, when I'm a teen, I'll have more. Maybe some real handfuls."

"But is it permissible to grope it yet?"

She considered briefly. He actually wanted to grope her? There had to be a way! "It's against the rule, but we may manage to cheat a bit if we're careful, just as we did when I innocently flashed my panties at you. The Adult Conspiracy has trouble policing every piddling little detail. Pretend you're sniffing my lustrous hair, while virtuously holding my delicate hand. That's two things to distract its snooping interest."

He drew her close again and sniffed her far less than lustrous hair while holding one of her stubby hands in his.

"Meanwhile no attention is being paid to your other hand," she murmured. "So—*Yipe!!* You got it!"

"I certainly did," he agreed, laughing. "And a delightful bit it was."

Bit or butt? She was careful not to say. "Thank you. More anon, when."

"But if this is a story for a future book, what do the readers think?"

"Readers like a little bit of naughtiness. It perks up the dull text." She sighed. "But this business of being the protagonist again is unfair. I deserve some time off. For one thing, we could get away with a lot more if the critical eye of the reader were not on us."

"I could remonstrate with the Demons." He frowned, and for a moment his aspect changed alarmingly as part of a hint of his monstrous power manifested.

Squid suffered a vision of galaxies blinking out of existence as the War of Demons resumed. “No!” Then, seeing his slightly hurt look, “Please?”

He relented. “For you I would do it, but not if you don’t want it. I want only to please you.”

“And I want to please you, too. It smells like love to me.” She wrinkled her nose. “Not that I really know what that smells like. I wish we could suddenly be over eighteen so we could—never mind, we’re not supposed to even know the options at our age. I’ll just have to find someone else to give the Protagonist Role to.”

“Will anyone else take it?”

“Not if they have a choice. Nobody likes being constantly snooped on. So it’s a problem.”

“Oh, I almost forgot. You told me that today we would visit your family.”

Squid clapped her hand to her forehead. “That’s right! That’s why the boat anchored here overnight, near where my folks live. How I dread it!”

Chaos looked confused. “Perhaps I misunderstood. I thought you wanted to see your family again.”

“Oh, I do. But now I must introduce you to them, and that is what I dread. They are halfway conventional. They will not understand about my dating a Demon. But I have to tell them.”

“I could stay clear and let you visit them alone. That way you could avoid telling them about me.”

“No way, Chaos! I love you. It just may be awkward.”

“Whatever you decide.”

“Let me ponder half a moment.” She was briefly silent. In exactly half a moment she spoke again. “Maybe it would help if you gave them something. A token gift that would distract them slightly.”

“A planet? A nebula? A burgeoning hamper of Dark Matter?”

She laughed. “No, no, nothing like that. Something token, maybe amusing, a mere trinket, maybe useful in some simple way, but typical of you.” She paused again, this time only half an instant. “Maybe a mini ball of chaos.”

“A mini ball?”

“A mini ball. A trifling token. Like a mini spell that has only minimal effect. A cute toy. To amuse them for half a moment.”

"Maybe a mini chaos bomb? One that makes only close things chaotic?"

"Yes! They should like that. Let's go there now, before I change my foolish female mind."

"As you wish."

They stood before the little house that Kandy and Ease used. Squid made a mental note to try to become less impulsive when with Chaos: she kept forgetting he could take things literally, and make them happen before she thought them through. Still, they could walk away.

Squid heard a buzz. There was a bee. No, it was a floating eyeball. She reached out to catch it, somehow knowing it wouldn't sting her. What was it doing here? She examined it closely.

"Eye of the bee-holder," Chaos murmured.

"Why is it buzzing around here instead of looking at more important things?" she asked.

"Maybe it's lost."

"Well, I can't help it." Then she got an idea. "But maybe I know who can."

The door opened. Kandy stood there, a completely lovely creature with luxuriant midnight hair dropping down to her slender waist: everything that Squid was not. "Squid!" she cried, sweeping the girl into her embrace. So much for walking away. "Whatever brings you here? We thought you were in a dancing troupe aboard the Fire Boat."

Squid stuffed the eye into a pocket. "I, uh—"

Then Ease was there, too, strong, handsome, smart, with short curly blond hair and a bit of a matching blond beard. Her wonderful parents. "But great to see you, kid," he said. "We missed you."

Squid realized she had better get on with introductions before too much could go wrong. "Uh, I came to have you meet my boyfriend, who—"

"Boyfriend!" Kandy exclaimed, taken aback. "Squid, you're way too young to get into that kind of relationship. You're a child!"

Just so. If dating was left up to parents, their children would be in their forties before they started, if then. That was just part of the awkwardness.

"Come in and we'll get to know each other," Ease said, always the easygoing one. That was his talent: to make things seem easy, even when they weren't.

In most of another moment they were inside, seated facing each other. "Uh," Squid repeated, casting about for the right words when she suspected there were none. "His name is Chaos, and he's—" She broke off to take a nervous breath, then plowed on. "A Demon."

Kandy was still on her original track. "Squid, you're only twelve years old! Way too young to have a—" She broke off. "A . . . What?"

"A demon," Ease said.

"Demon, dear," Kandy murmured. "Capital D. But this is impossible!"

"They do mix with mortals on occasion, sometimes quite compatibly," he said. "I remember a demoness who—" Kandy's glare had cut him off at the knees, so he changed the subject. "Squid, big or little D, does he know your nature?"

Squid was glad to follow this diversion. "Yes, he knows that I am an alien cuttlefish emulating a human girl, a tourist who got trapped in a future Xanth when it ended. That Fornax and Astrid Basilisk rescued me and four other children and brought them here to this reality track of Xanth, and arranged local adoptions for us, for which we are forever grateful. They saved our lives! He doesn't mind."

"She even changed for me," Chaos said. "She became the cuttlefish, with its marvelous mimicking ability, and swam in a lake. She's not human at all. But neither am I. Regardless, it's her mind that interests me."

"Her mind?" Ease asked. "No boy is interested in a girl's *mind*, even if she is said to be the most important person in the universe."

But now Kandy was reorienting. She eyed Chaos in the way only a protective mother could, and that was a warning even a Demon dared not ignore. "Let me introduce myself further," she said with deadly deceptive calm. "Then I will expect similar candor in return."

Squid knew this was mischief. Chaos needed to avoid this poisonous exchange. Squid opened her mouth.

"Of course," Chaos agreed.

Bleep.

"I was a rather ordinary breathtakingly lovely young woman who wanted more than the ordinary," Kandy said. "I was nicknamed I Kandy, and I thought the I stood for Irrelevant. I didn't realize at first that it was actually Eye Candy, no respect intended. I was tired of being constantly eyed by boys who wanted only one thing, which was not my mind. So I made a wish at a wishing well, explaining that I was bored stiff and wanted Adventure, Excitement, and Romance. My wish was granted, but not quite the way I intended. I had misspelled 'bored' in my mind, and got changed into a stiff board."

"And a great board she was," Ease added. He reached toward Kandy and took hold of her ankle. Suddenly, she was a big wooden board, which he wielded like a club. Then he brought it to his face and kissed it, and abruptly Kandy was back and completing the kiss. They clearly understood each other and were hardly bored.

"So we did not have the usual kind of relationship, at first," Kandy concluded. "But we worked it out. So we understand unusual associations. Then we made a home for Squid, a remarkable girl in her own right." Her eyes came to resemble the mouths of Mundane machine guns as they focused on Chaos. "How did you come to make Squid's acquaintance, and what are your intentions toward her?"

Squid opened her mouth again to try desperately to head this off, as the Demon's own candor could permanently alienate her folks. But Chaos was already answering.

"In my time, the universe was without form and void, and darkness covered the firmament. Then other Demons came on the scene and introduced concepts like light and gravity and electromotive force. I was appalled, so I confronted them. But they had been too long entrenched, so I could not immediately destroy them. So we arranged a compromise: a dialogue between representatives of our powers. Three spot contests, and the winner of the majority would govern. If I won, the universe would end. Their selected representative was Squid. We talked and she showed me that without the other Demons and their artifacts I was just a space without definition. That I actually needed them to have any apparent reality myself. I was also curious about this mysterious concept of Love, as nothing of that nature exists in the void. I asked her to explain it to me."

What was there to do except finish it? "I couldn't answer with any authority," Squid said, suppressing her despair of ever getting parental understanding, let alone approval. A twelve-year-old pseudo-girl dating a capital D Demon? Talking of love? She was hardly supposed to know the meaning of the word. "I was too young to comprehend the secrets of the Adult Conspiracy, and I wasn't even human. So I kissed him."

"It was some kiss," Chaos admitted. "After that I was her captive. It was as if without her I was nothing physically, and without her love, I am nothing emotionally."

Ease looked thoughtful. "You spared the universe because you liked Squid?"

"Yes."

Ease spoke to Squid. "And everything might end if you break up with Chaos?"

That was the literal truth, but could she say it? "Uh . . ."

Ease spoke to Kandy. "Is that a good enough reason for you to accept him as her boyfriend?"

She considered dubiously. "Uh . . ."

She was pondering letting the universe end, rather than allow her daughter such a relationship? "Mother, I love him! I know you don't think I'm old enough, but I know how I feel. That was a two-way kiss."

Then both parents laughed. "We're teasing you, dear," Kandy said. "Of course you can date him if that's what you really want."

They were accepting it? This suddenly seemed too easy. "Even though, well—"

"We knew, dear," Ease said.

Squid was shocked. "You knew?!" She actually managed both punctuation marks.

"The peeve told us," Kandy said.

"The peeve! I should have known that ill bird couldn't keep its beak shut!"

"At ease, girl," Kandy said. "All five families have been regularly briefed by the peeve. It was a condition of allowing the children to serve for an extended time on the Fire Boat."

Squid was appalled. "You mean the bird has been ratting on us all along?"

"You're *children*," Kandy said. "We care about you. But we know your judgment isn't always perfect. So we try to stay informed."

"We trust Grania," Ease said. "We know she won't let you stray too far. But we didn't adopt you only to pass you on to someone else. We prefer to *know*."

It did seem to make sense. What would have been the point of adopting the children from the future if they didn't try to take care of them? Squid realized she had no real grounds for complaint.

"It also serves as a relevant example for Chaos," Ease said. "A practical demonstration of what family unity is all about."

"So you'll know when your turn comes," Kandy concluded.

Squid had not thought of it that way—her turn to have children, to become a family. When she was grown and adult. She was awed. But of course a cuttlefish and a Demon could never—

Chaos touched her hand, and she felt a tiny ripple of his immense power.

A cuttlefish and a Demon *could*. If they wanted to.

But that was a matter for another day, far away from now. Time to change the subject. "Um, Chaos, the bomb," she murmured.

He picked right up on it. "I have a small gift for you," he said to the parents. "A token of my appreciation for your courtesy."

"Oh, no gift is necessary," Ease said.

"Especially not a bomb," Kandy agreed.

"Not really a bomb. It's just something cute you might like," Squid said quickly. "He—it's as if he has a talent, to make these little things. He can show you one, so you know how to use it, if you ever need to. But maybe better to demonstrate it outside."

They went outside. Squid looked around and spied a small termite mound that was under siege by an ant army. "Maybe that scene," she told Chaos.

"Those creatures have developed some bad blood," Ease said. "It's termite territory, but the ants are expanding their domain. Now it has come to war."

Chaos nodded. He walked to the mound, and the others followed. In two thirds of a moment they all stood around the mound, just outside the ant platoons. The siege was well advanced, but by no means concluded. The termites were ranged along the upper battlements, about one foot above the ants, armed with miniature spears. On the next deck up their archers were aiming their bows. The ants had filled in one section of the moat and were charging across, pulling a wheeled battering ram, holding their shields over their bodies to fend off the arrows.

But the defenders were ready. As the ram neared the wall, they tilted a relatively huge vat of boiling oil, ready to dump it on the attackers.

Then the ants did something odd. They brought out captive female termites, and put them on a stage in full view of the mound.

"I didn't know termites had ladies," Squid said. "Or ants either. Not like that. I thought they had single queens who laid all their eggs, and the others were just, well, locked into childhood girls."

"You're thinking of dreary Mundania," Ease said. "This is Xanth."

Oh! Of course. Xanth was more advanced, and far less dull.

The lady termites, evidently trained under duress for this purpose, gyrated on the stage. The termites manning the battlement paused to stare. Then the ladies faced away, bent over, and flipped up their skirts to flash their panties.

Termites had skirts and panties? Oh, right: this was Xanth. The lady ants probably had them too. How else were the brute males to be kept under control?

The workers tilting the oil vat froze in place. They had freaked out. Meanwhile the ram rolled ever closer to the wall. The ant legions massed, ready to march double-time into the gap the moment it was smashed open.

"Time for the bomb," Chaos murmured. He held one hand over the mound and dropped something invisible. There was an invisible flash. Squid knew that such a description would be nonsensical anywhere but Xanth.

The termite troops guarding the rampart started running around aimlessly. The bows and arrows fell to the bricks. The ant legions puffed into legends, charging in all directions at once, forward, backwards, and into the moat. The ram bleated and overturned, its mission unaccomplished. Some of the ant soldiers began making out with the termite lovelies, who seemed happy to accommodate them. The regal termite queen came to the rooftop, her jeweled crown flashing in the sunlight, but then she aimlessly wandered back inside. The ants ignored her. Nothing made much sense anymore. The defense had collapsed, but so had the offense. The siege had dissolved into confusion, and little was being accomplished at a great rate.

In fact, it was, well, chaos. Fortunately, its effect was limited, and did not reach as far as the watching human figures.

"That is impressive," Ease said. "But I didn't see the bomb, just its effects."

"It is unseeable," Chaos explained. "Because it *is* an effect. Organization has no chance when chaos rules." Then he gave Ease and Kandy three bombs, which were parked invisibly beside their souls, that they could invoke at any time with a thought and a gesture. If they were ever under military siege by ants or trolls, they would find good use for them. "These are larger, and their range will extend out about fifty feet," he explained. "They also will not affect you, as they belong to you. So if you ever have trouble with robbers, dragons, nicklepedes, or panty-flashing nymphs, you will be able keep your sense and walk away."

Ease nodded, though Squid suspected that he might prefer to handle the nymphs by himself. All men were foolish in such respects. "This is a useful gift. We thank you, Chaos."

"We do indeed," Kandy agreed. If Ease did not use a bomb on the nymphs, she might use it for him. Then she stepped up and kissed Chaos on the cheek. He stood there, frozen in place. He had freaked out!

"Wake," Squid said, snapping her fingers.

Chaos woke. "What happened?"

"Mom kissed your cheek, and made you freak. Bleep, I'm jealous of her adult power. Maybe when I'm grown, I'll be able to do it too."

"But I never saw her panties."

"A really pretty girl can do it without flashing," Squid said. "Mom's the prettiest."

"Even as a board," he agreed faintly.

"You just saved yourself a spanking," Kandy murmured, flashing her board form for barely a quarter of an instant. There was something suggestive about it that did not seem to smack of punishment. More Adult Conspiracy stuff? Bleep, that was annoying!

Then they bid their partings and moved on. The worst chore had been accomplished. The Parents had been Told. Not that it had been necessary, as it turned out.

"Um," Chaos said as they walked through field and glade, holding hands.

"Um?"

"Fornax wants to borrow back the host body, though it is not yet nightfall. She has a message."

The Demoness Fornax, the patron of antimatter, who associated with this host's female aspect, just as Chaos associated with the male aspect. She was also the children's aunt figure, and the adoptive mother of one of them. She was not to be denied.

"Fornax is not one to waste time or attention," Squid said, concerned. "We'd better let her in, even if it's not yet night. It must be important."

"Agreed."

The host had both male and female forms. The male was Larry, whom Chaos had taken over, while the female was Laurelai, with whom the Demoness associated when she chose. They were able to communicate slightly with each other, but only enough to indicate the desire to communicate further.

So it would have to be done. "Kiss me and go," Squid said. "Maybe she won't need to stay long." She had nothing against Fornax, nothing at all, but when it came to Love and Kissing, she preferred Chaos.

He kissed her, and it was delightful as always. Then his body shifted in her embrace and became smartly female. Even at age thirteen, Laurelai was lovely with her glistening blue-black hair and eyes. She would be devastating when she matured.

"What is it?" Squid asked her friend.

Laurelai looked surprised. "I don't know."

"But you asked for the body back."

"Fornax asked. But she's not telling me why. Just that we need to prepare quickly—immediately—for a trip to another reality of a month or more. We have to clear it with Nia and go."

"Another reality! For a month! But Chaos and I wanted to have some time to—you know."

Laurelai nodded understandingly. "I do know. You want to get in some serious flirting and maybe sneak some naughty feels past the Conspiracy." The two girls understood each other pretty well, and Laurelai was capable of some pretty racy behavior herself. She was surely a trial to the Conspiracy. "But Fornax says that will have to wait. This is urgent."

They wasted no further time in dialogue. They were already hurrying toward the Fire Boat. They reached it and clambered aboard, over the rail around the deck, carelessly flashing panties at the sky as they did. A cloud locked in place, until the following cloud bumped into it and snapped it back alert. That had to be Laurelai's relatively mature exposure, not Squid's juvenile effort.

The pet peeve was there, of course; it knew when anyone came or went.

They went straight to Grania's cabin and knocked. Nia opened the door. She was a beautiful adult woman with dark brown hair, gray eyes, and a slender torso. She looked twenty-three, but was actually sixty-three thanks to a confrontation with a pool of youth elixir. She seemed to have no trouble living with her apparent youth. If *she* ever swung over the deck rail in a skirt, the entire welkin would freeze. "Yes?"

Then Squid remembered the eye she had put in a pocket. She took it out. "I found this, I think it's lost. Can you help it? You know about flying eyes." Because Nia's talent was to form a pair of phantom eyes that could go anywhere and look at anything, relaying the images, so that it was hard to keep any secrets from her.

Nia took it. "Why yes. This is an Eye of the Bee-Holder."

"That's what Chaos said. I thought he was joking."

"You're right. This one is lost. I will scout out its hive and see about returning it. Meanwhile it will be safe with me." Her phantom eyes formed and peered at the eyeball. It promptly flew up to join them, evidently finding them compatible.

Nia's natural eyes focused again on Squid. "You didn't come here about that. What is really on your mind, dear?"

"Fornax says we have to travel across the realities," Squid said breathlessly. "We don't know why, but it must be important. For a month or more. Can you spare us?"

"What Fornax wants, Fornax gets," Nia said, sounding her real age. She evinced no surprise at seeing Laurelai by day. Grania effectively ran the Fire Boat, and did not misuse her authority. "We'll be doing a routine dance tour; Fornax or Chaos will be able to locate us when you return. We'll save your cabin. We'll miss you, but we can cope." She glanced at Squid. "The boys are busy elsewhere at the moment. But perhaps you should bid farewell to the girls."

"Win! Myst!" Squid agreed. They were her closest siblings and friends, though they were not related by blood, quite apart from Squid's own difference. Win's talent was to have the wind always at her back, and it had been enhanced so that now she blew at the fire sail of the boat so that it could rapidly travel anywhere. Myst's talent was to become a cloud of mist, and re-form as a ten-year-old girl, so no cords could hold her, and no prison, unless she got sealed up in a corked bottle. She was wary of bottles.

Squid left Laurelai to fill in what few details there were, and ran to find them. But Myst was already coming to find her. The peeve would have told her that something was up. She was in the form of a pudgy red-haired scamp. They hugged.

"Laurelai and I have to go away for a while," Squid said. "We don't know where or why, but Fornax says it's urgent."

"Some folk get all the adventures," Myst complained with a smile. But there was a tear in her eye. She didn't like losing Squid even for a day. "At least you're going together. You can maybe sneak in some hand holding along the way." She, too, knew that Squid's romantic aspirations went way beyond interdigitation.

"We'll return as soon as we can," Squid said. They hugged again.

Win appeared, similarly notified, and they hugged as the breeze blew past Squid. Win looked just as nondescript as Myst or Squid, but was crucial to the operation of the boat. There was another tear or two.

Then Squid went to her own room and efficiently packed whatever she might need. Where *were* they going?

The boat sailed to a new location, which was just a glade in a forest, as Nia followed Fornax's relayed instructions and Win blew the sail just right. Then Squid and Laurelai left the boat and stood in the small clearing as the craft departed, watching the fiery flickering of the sail. They were alone together.

Now Fornax appeared in her own assumed form, a stately older woman. "Take my hands," she said. "We have a distance to go."

She still was not explaining what this was all about?

Squid took her right hand, and Laurelai her left hand. The three of them stood in place. There was no sensation of motion. The sun started moving across the sky, gaining velocity. Then it set, and night closed in. Then came dawn, and day, and night, faster and faster. They were crossing the boundaries of alternate realities, and each was a second or so ahead of its neighbor, so it seemed like time travel. They could have gone backward as readily by crossing to the lagging realities. This was only an aspect of Fornax's Demonly power.

So this was to be an excursion into a virtual future Xanth. Squid understood, because she had come from a future fifty years ahead of the one she lived in now, just like the other siblings. Were they returning there?

But Laurelai was confused. She was special in her own right, but had not been rescued from the future. "What is happening? Are we living faster?"

"No," Squid answered. "We're moving across realities. Each is a bit different in time. It's like drawing pictures on a pad of paper, each slightly different, so when you flip the pages it looks like motion."

"Weird."

Now the changes were so rapid that the days and nights were mere flickers. It seemed that they were not going just next door, as it were.

Then Squad realized something else. They were talking naturally, having no trouble despite the shifting of reality frames. The Demoness must have set up a bubble of personal reality that insulated them, like a diving sphere that kept the air in so folk could breathe. Not that Squid needed to; she could breathe the water.

Okay. "Fornax, now we can talk without being snooped on, because nobody else could be crossing realities at our pace. So what is really happening?"

"We are going to handle a murder mystery," the Demoness replied.

"A murder mystery?" Laurelai exclaimed. "We're not detectives!"

"True."

Squid knew Fornax better than Laurelai did. She phrased her question carefully. "Please give us some necessary details on this case. In some future world there has been a murder. What are we expected to do about it, giving that we have no expertise in crime?"

"First we must cover up the murders, so that no one else knows they have even occurred. Then we shall solve them, identifying the perpetrator. Finally, we will establish justice."

"Why not let the regular authorities handle it?" Squid asked. "The local town mare, maybe, supervising from city hall." A number of towns had mares, lady horses that efficiently saw to the routine operations. Some mares were quite well known, at least in political circles.

"Or an investigator sent by the king or queen," Laurelai said. "A professional. Maybe even someone with relevant magic."

"Because there may be Demon involvement."

There was a heavy silence. Naturally, regular folk could not handle a Demon.

After a significant while, the sheer weight of the silence caused it to sink to the ground and dissolve. "And how are trifling folk like us expected to handle a Demon?" Squid asked. "Surely that is a matter for other Demons. We have some Demon friends, but that's neither here nor there."

"Because you are already involved," Fornax answered. "Only you are in a position to accomplish the three aspects of the case."

"Cover-up, Solution, Justice," Laurelai said. "But we're not even from the reality frame where the murders occur. Apart from that, this is a distinctly odd way of handling it. How can a murder be solved if no one even knows it has happened?"

"That is the only way it can be solved," Fornax said.

"Maybe the problem is that our feeble mortal minds just aren't up to Demon caliber," Squid said. "How does this make any sense at all?"

"Because you are the victims."

They were traversing alternate realities. Suddenly, their own reality crashed down upon them. They were both doomed to die? And they were heading right for that fate?

Squid exchanged a tortured glance with Laurelai. What had they gotten into?

Chapter 2

COVER-UP

"Perhaps you would appreciate a bit more detail," Fornax said as the flickering of changing realities continued. "I regret surprising you in this manner, but I was otherwise occupied with the salvaging of the universe and not paying full attention to the other reality frames, which are myriad. This crime slipped by me. So I acted as soon as I could, hoping to remedy the situation so that further damage does not occur."

"Further damage than our deaths?" Laurelai asked numbly.

"Yes."

"Why didn't you just travel to the time they happened, and prevent it?"

"That would evoke the paradoxes of time travel, a complication generally to be avoided. Now I must act after the fact. Time travel differs from frame travel."

"Yes, thank you, we would appreciate a bit more detail," Squid said, similarly numbly. "About the murders themselves, and why covering them up could possibly help."

"Gladly. The relevant frame is approximately seven years ahead of your normal one. You were about to be married in a double ceremony, Squid having become of age in the past year. First Larry male and Squid female, then Squid male and Laurelai female. So at ages twenty and nineteen you prepared to make the vows. But the night before the wedding day as you walked hand in hand along the pretty path and paused at a romantic pavilion to kiss, something came there and brutally hacked you both to pieces, leaving the parts strewn across the pavilion as perhaps a signal to others. The others do not yet know of this slaughter, but at dawn they surely will, so immediate action is essential."

"To cover it up?" Laurelai asked.

"To make it seem that no such crime occurred, yes."

"*Why*?" both girls cried almost together.

"Because a Demon is surely behind it. He must have sent his minion to do the killing. If it appears that there has been no killing, he will assume the minion was somehow deceived, as by encountering realistic mock-ups. He will send the minion again, to get it right this time."

It was starting to make sense. "And the only way to make it seem the murders failed would be by having us show up as scheduled for the wedding," Squid said. "Only we two could do that truly persuasively." She took a ragged breath. "Except for one detail: we are too young by seven years."

"Um, no," Laurelai said. "Remember my talent. I can age us seven years, at least for a few hours. Enough to get us through the ceremony."

"Enough to get you through the month or more," Fornax said. "Whatever is required."

The two girls exchanged another glance. The Demoness intended to strengthen the talent so that an age change could be made indefinite. This might not be quite according to the normal rules, but as with getting an illicit feel, it could be managed if no one protested. They were not about to protest.

"But that still won't undo the murders themselves," Squid said thoughtfully. "We'll still be dead."

"So thanks for nothing," Laurelai agreed, perhaps a trifle ungraciously.

"Bear in mind that *you* will not be dead," Fornax said. "Only your alternate selves in the other reality. You can at least catch the culprit and bring him to justice. That is a good deal more than nothing. Thereafter you can return to your own frame and live out your lives as planned, knowing that you will not die in seven years."

They exchanged a third glance. What happened in one reality was pretty much echoed in the others nearby, unless something outside interfered. They might indeed be acting to block their personal future selves from murder. If nothing else, knowing who the culprit was could help them save their own lives. It was, indeed, not nothing.

"Uh, I'm not sure I want to see my own slaughtered corpse," Squid said. "I don't think I'd be very good at cleaning up that particular mess."

"Me too," Laurelai agreed with a shudder.

Fornax nodded. "That is a consideration. But that is not your task. You must assume the roles of your future selves and carry on as if nothing has happened. I will arrange another mode of cleanup."

"Thank you," Squid said faintly. Indeed, she feared she was near fainting. "Maybe we can wear safety pins, to keep us safe." She wasn't really joking; such pins existed, and they did keep folk safe from incidental mischief.

"As you wish," the Demoness agreed. "However, I shall be watching you this time. You will not be killed again."

"When—when do we get there?" Laurelai asked.

"Now." The flickering slowed, became discernible days and nights, and finally settled on a single night. "It is about half an hour after the action."

"Half an hour," Laurelai said weakly.

They stood on a pleasant path outlined by glow worms on either side. Ahead they could see the light of the candles of the pavilion, where the recent slaughter was.

"Uh—" Squid quavered.

"You will at least need token confirmation, so you know this is not cruel humor," Fornax said. "Wait here, and I will bring it to you." She faded out.

"Token?" Laurelai raggedly breathed.

Squid shivered. "I have a feeling we are not about to enjoy this."

"We must brace ourselves," Laurelai said, looking distinctly unbraced. "It won't help to get sick."

"We must be strong," Squid agreed weakly.

Fornax returned. "For you," she told Squid, handing her an object.

It was the tip of the torn tentacle of an alien cuttlefish. It had the colors of Squid's own. It was authentic.

"I believe," she said, and quickly handed it back.

The Demoness gave something to Laurelai. It was an eyeball with a blue/black iris the exact shade of her own.

"Ditto." She handed it back.

Fornax faded out. Then something came trotting along the path.

It was an extremely ugly figure of a bear. A grisly bear.

That seemed appropriate. The creature moved on to the pavilion. They heard it chewing on flesh and bone, and slurping up blood.

The Demoness reappeared. “By the time it finishes, there will be no recognizable sign. Now you must assume the roles and proceed as if nothing has happened.”

“Yes,” Laurelai agreed. “Seven years.” She took Squid’s hand and exerted her power. In barely a moment they were straining their clothing at ages twenty and nineteen.

“There’s new clothing in the room,” Fornax said. “Go back the way you came.”

They turned and followed the path away from the pavilion. What else was there to do?

They reached their room, easy enough to locate because it was marked THE LOVING COUPLE. This was evidently a regular site for weddings, so romantic things were there.

But Squid was troubled, apart from the death of her alternate. “Even if this track is almost identical to our own, it is still seven years ahead of us, and a lot could have happened in the interim. How can we be sure we won’t run afoul of something we are expected to know, and don’t?”

“Good point. I have an idea: we crossed myriad alternates getting here. Maybe Fornax could take us across to the next one, where I presume no murder occurred, and we can see what the ordinary course is, and make notes or something.”

“Yes, indeed. Except that if anyone sees us there, there could be mischief.”

“Unless Fornax could make a Mundane type video recording we could watch without running the risk of interfering.”

“Yes! Let’s call Fornax now. We don’t have much time.”

The Demoness appeared. “I am here. And here is your recording.” She gestured, and a magic mirror appeared, propped up on the table. It was playing a scene of the path they had just traversed. They were immediately absorbed in its detail.

Their older selves walked the path, holding hands and smiling at each other. Squid was her mature self, surprisingly pretty at age nineteen, wearing a dress with a décolletage that showed that beyond doubt she had indeed matured physically. Her front was remarkably curvaceous with more than a hint of cleavage, and her skirt flashed legs that were marvels of firm rondure. A mischievous gust of wind flipped up the hem and flashed a tantalizing hint of a mature black panty. She loved it!

Laurelai was in her male Larry form, tall and handsome. Then as they rounded a bend in the path, his hand sneaked down and briefly cupped her pert bottom from outside the skirt. "Yipe!" she protested with complete insincerity.

They continued walking. They came to the dread pavilion. There, slightly masked, they kissed—and shifted genders, coming out of it as Squid male and Laurelai female. Now it was Squid's turn to sneak a feel, which Laurelai pretended not to notice. But Squid saw how she teasingly flexed her buttock under his hand.

"Bleep! I'm jealous," Squid muttered. "Look at what they're getting away with!"

There was no attack. It was indeed limited to the single reality frame. That was in its fashion good to know.

"I have a question," Laurelai said. "Why can't we just make a similar recording of *this* track we're on now and see the murders take place? Mystery solved."

"Wow!" Squid exclaimed. "I dread watching it, but it is exactly what we need."

"Negative," Fornax said, appearing. "It cannot be accomplished."

"Why not? What's a little thing like time travel to a Demon?"

"You confuse time travel with frame travel," the Demoness explained patiently, as she had mentioned before. "Time travel has paradoxical complications, which is why we discourage it. Frame travel is safer and versatile in its own right. It enabled us to save you five children from doom in the frame fifty years ahead of the one where you now reside. Had true time travel been feasible, we could have saved your entire original frame."

"Um, yes," Squid agreed soberly. "But then, this parallel track we're watching—"

"It is an emulation rather than reality. I assembled it from myriad adjacent frames. Each frame is a fraction of a second ahead or behind its neighbors. Each is fixed in its own time, but by viewing them in rapid order we can generate the illusion of seeing into the past or the future. I recorded them in sequence to make a composite that resembles a single frame."

"That works for me," Laurelai said.

"Like the way the Mundanes watch a series of still pictures on a screen," Squid said. "When they are shown fast enough, they seem almost like reality."

"Exactly. They call them Movies."

They resumed watching the emulation. Soon the two adults returned to the shelter. But Squid was still not quite satisfied. "This doesn't tell us of their customs. We need to see the last day or so."

Immediately, the mirror showed the day before, as the two conversed with well-wishing friends and made last-day preparations for the morrow. Both Squid and Laurelai made hasty notes.

"Were the murders a natural occurrence," Fornax remarked, "they would be echoed in all the adjacent frames. The fact that they aren't means an external force is involved, likely of Demon nature. That of course requires investigation."

Apart from the incidental additional fact that it was Squid herself being murdered.

"Demons do on occasion participate in mortal events," Laurelai said. "Such as Chaos using my male aspect to date Squid."

"Chaos!" Squid repeated. "How will *he* react to this news?"

"It will be up to you to see that he takes it in stride," Fornax said. "Clearly, he was not involved in this, or it would not have been possible."

And Chaos in a fit of grief or rage could destroy the universe. "Don't rush to change," Squid told Laurelai. "I have to consider my phrasing."

"We can't wait too long, lest he become impatient," Laurelai said.

"Don't I know it!"

Then they viewed the coming day, and saw themselves getting married, with all their friends attending. All of them were seven years older, but recognizable. Squid felt an almost painful nostalgia for the wonderful occasion that their two selves of this frame would never experience. Instead it would in effect be faked. By themselves.

They played the sequences over repeatedly, getting things as straight as they could. Because an error could generate suspicion, and they couldn't afford that. They had to be perfect.

Finally, they ended it. They had learned as much as they could, and now had a clear notion of the coming event and their parts in it. They needed to rest and sleep, because they had a big day coming. Bigger than their friend would know.

Squid took a shaky breath. "I guess it's time to tell Chaos."

"Remind him that *you* still live," Laurelai said. "The murders are on another track."

"Yes. I hope that's enough."

"It wouldn't make sense for him to abolish you, along with the universe, just because one of your myriad other selves died."

"If only he sees it that way."

They kissed, consoling each other. Then Laurelai shifted, and Squid was embracing her Larry form, and Chaos.

She kissed him avidly. "I've got nasty news," she said when she could no longer prolong it. "Just remember that I love you, and that will never change."

He tensed. "We can't be together?"

"That's not it. In fact, in time we can be married. It's that I'm dead, in another frame of reality. We have to catch and punish the perpetrator."

He stared at her. "I know that there are an infinite number of you spread across the realities. But this is the one that counts for me. I regret that any of you may not survive, but illness and accidents happen in the mortal realm. As long as you, here, remain, I am satisfied."

So far so good. But it wasn't settled yet. "I was murdered."

He stiffened. "Then I will destroy the murderer."

"When the time comes." She took a breath. "You can read my mind, right? I have nothing to hide from you. Read me. Then you'll know everything I know." Including her hope that his anger over the murder would not destroy the universe.

He took her hand. She knew he had monstrous power that he normally held in check, but sometimes its presence was felt, like the rumble of a boulder rolling down a mountain and crashing onto her head. It was as if she exploded into a macroscopic dust nebula and imploded into a microscopic mote at the same time. He possessed all of her mind, in the most intimate sense.

Thereafter the normal realm emerged from the chaos. "I will destroy him," he repeated, and the firmament quaked.

Then he vacated the host, and Laurelai returned. "How did it go?" she asked. "I'm still here, so it can't be too bad."

"Not too bad," Squid agreed tremulously. "I think."

Then they went to bed, hugged each other, and slept. It had been a formidable day. Squid was amazed again that she, now at age nineteen, was fully fleshed in the adult woman manner, as was Laurelai. When they hugged, their fronts pressed against each other in a way that had not occurred when they were younger. Which was another reason they matched genders at night; if one of them were male, sleep would be impossible.

In the morning they reviewed the coming sequence in the mirror once more, then dressed exactly as their alternates did. They had a wedding to accomplish.

"I will cast a quiet acceptance spell," Fornax said. "So that there will be no suspicions unless you make a truly egregious error. Such magic is traditional for weddings anyway."

It proceeded. The process was continuous, but Squid's somewhat distracted awareness focused on particular scenes.

They had seen it in the mirror, but the reality was still awesome. All the siblings were there, all significantly older. For example, her Magician brother Santo, now an impressive twenty-one, together with his partner Noe, now twenty and in male guise. All of the siblings and their associates were able to assume male or female forms, just as Laurelai and Squid could, because of the gender spells they carried. Noe loved Santo, and was happy to be with him, whatever way satisfied him.

Then they were in the wedding, with King Ivy officiating. They spoke the key words and were pronounced married. They kissed in public.

It would have been so great if only it had been real. But they were faking it, impersonating the real couple. The dead couple. Were it not for that, Squid would have loved finally kissing as adults.

They stood side by side to receive the guests, Larry (they did not know of the presence of Chaos in this frame) in a nicely tailored suit, Squid in her wedding gown complete with tiara and very special white gloves. Several of the men insisted on kissing the bride. She remained bemused that she, never any beauty as a child, was suddenly in such demand as a new adult. Maybe it was the formidable bosom she now carried.

Then came Piton Bone and Myst, ages twenty and seventeen. Myst had been a pudgy red-haired scamp, but now was a breathtaking auburn beauty. She grasped Larry and drew him down for a passionate kiss. Squid had to stifle her slightly unkind reaction, just as she knew Chaos was stifling his as she kissed the men.

Meanwhile Piton was taking hold of Squid. But she was prepared. As his errant hand moved toward her bottom for a grope, her magically gloved hand reached to and into his trousers, passing through the cloth as if it were illusion. She grasped his hidden anatomy with a warning squeeze.

Astonished, he hesitated, then withdrew his hand, grope unaccomplished. She withdrew her hand, the warning having served its purpose.

He kissed her, and this she allowed. The two moved on. "You didn't know about the gloves?" Myst asked Piton as they departed. Squid had to smile. Myst had made her those gloves long ago, from her own hair, and they shared her nature. How nice it was that her this-frame self had kept them all those years.

There was a banquet following the main event, and Squid got to chat with all her friends. None of them suspected that there was anything out of line except possibly Santo, who was hideously smart and knew her entirely too well. He kept his peace, of course. How she wished she could tell him the truth!

Nia, now age thirty physically, proffered a toast. "We all cherish Larry and Squid," she said. "Ever since Caprice Castle was stolen by the Dwarf Demons and held hostage so that they could also acquire the key children who operated it, Piton and Data, who had been away at the time. But Larry and Squid proffered a choice that was simply too tempting for the Demons to ignore. That was Fibot, the Fire Sail Boat, together with its crew of the pet peeve, Tata the robot dogfish, Dell, myself, and the five visiting children from the future."

Nia paused to nod at Squid. "One of whom is now getting married. So the Demons foolishly focused on that, while Squid and Larry quietly freed the hostages in Caprice Castle and enabled them to spirit the castle away and out of the Demons' reach. Then when the Demons returned to discover the absence, Squid and Larry took advantage of their second distraction to get Fibot out of there too. It was a bold and amazing accomplishment for which we, and especially I, will forever be grateful."

The hall burst into applause. Squid readjusted. So that was what had happened in this frame! No Chaos, no battle of the Demons, only the salvation of Caprice Castle and Fibot and their personnel. Well worth doing, of course. But—

Squid had never met the Demon Chaos. She was marrying Larry, not Chaos. There was of course nothing wrong with that, and perhaps she loved Larry in this frame. But she would never, ever, exchange that for Chaos! He was her truest love.

Beside her, Chaos squeezed her hand. He knew and appreciated her thought.

The frames seemed quite similar, superficially, but what a difference emotionally!

Nia completed her toast, which here was a drink rather than a piece of slightly burned bread, and the others raised their glasses similarly, then drank their doses of boot rear, grunting in unison as the drinks connected. Boot rear was always fun.

Then it was evening, and they were retiring to their marital chamber. They had done it! They had successfully emulated their older selves so that no one knew they had been murdered. The cover-up was complete.

Then Squid realized something else. "We're of age!" she exclaimed. "And married! It's doubly legal. No more dread Adult Conspiracy to poke its formidable finger in our eye, or wherever! Now at last we can do it!"

"We can do it," Chaos agreed. There was no need to identify "it" further. They intended to send the stork a signal that would blast it off its nest.

But immediately she suffered an equal and opposite counter reaction. "We can't do it."

"We can't? I thought age and marriage sufficed." Chaos had existed for ten billion years, but was still learning about local mortal details.

"They normally do. But we, I mean mostly me, are still underage inside. And worse . . ." She trailed off, pained.

"Worse?" He was genuinely perplexed.

"We can't let our future adult deaths promote our present juvenile gratification. It's as if we are profiting from their tragedy. That's wrong."

Chaos considered. "I will honor the nuances as you perceive them. I want only to please you. But given that we are here to conceal those deaths so that we may in due course identify and punish the killer, we need to emulate the parallel tracks as closely as possible. They show Larry joyously doing it with Squid female, then Squid male doing it with Laurelai. It is one seductively wild night, wearing them blissfully out. If we differ from that course, it will become evident, at least to any Demon observer, that something is amiss. Am I correct?"

She nodded. "You are correct. We dare not differ from the tracks, especially in that detail. And I do want to do it. Oh, do I ever! But right now, knowing what I know, I just *can't*. Do you understand?"

"No. But I love you and will wait on your decision."

Squid smiled somewhat lopsidedly. "I'm not really sure I understand either. But bleep, let's take a walk while I sort this out in my confused conscience. Each frame does differ slightly from its neighbors, so I think we can differ in this small respect without triggering an alarm."

"We will walk," he agreed.

"As two girls, so that temptation doesn't spoil whatever I'm struggling with."

He became Laurelai. "Already my turn?" she asked expectantly. Then she paused. "Oops, Fornax is updating me. I think you're right, Squid. We need to think about this. We don't want this joyous occasion to be marred by personal guilt, even if no one else here knows of it."

"Thank you." Squid was relieved that the other woman understood.

They walked hand in hand down the path to the pavilion in the forest glade. As girls they weren't lovers, but they were closest friends. They understood each other in a way that few others did. They looked around, picking up on the scenery. It was a beautiful path through wonderful terrain, by no accident, but Squid still hated it because it was also the scene of their brutal deaths. That tentacle tip . . .

"I know what you're thinking," Laurelai murmured. "Because I'm thinking it too. This will always be a place of horror to me. That eyeball . . ."

They reached the pavilion. "Killer, if you're nearby, here we are," Squid muttered.

"I just thought," Laurelai said softly. "If he comes, how will we stop him?"

"Fornax will smash him to smithereens."

No, the Demoness thought to them both.

"No?" they both thought back.

He is in the vicinity. His ugly thoughts suggest that he has been sent again to complete the job he evidently messed up before. He doesn't know who sent him, just that he is obliged to do it. If I destroy him, I will not learn who the real culprit is.

Squid had an inspiration. "The two Dwarf Demons, what's-their-names. The ones we foiled seven years back, so they didn't get the castle or the boat. They must be the true culprits!"

"Demon NA and Robot NA," Laurelai said. "The initials being for Not Announced."

"They are the obvious suspects," Squid agreed. "But knowing it and proving it are different things."

Even for Demons, Fornax agreed. *A Demon trial is never about mere suspicion.*

Squid had another thought. "So maybe we made the DDs mad back then in our own reality. Maybe mad enough to kill us for revenge. Why would they murder us seven years later in a random alternate frame we never heard of before? Why not do it right there where we messed them up?"

Several reasons. One is that the Dwarf Demons in that frame are in no condition to hurt anyone else. They were given a Demon trial and will be on probation ever after. So it had to be other Demons, angry about what happened to their friends. They did not wait seven years; they crossed the frames, as we did, arriving here perhaps only minutes after they departed, though in other respects it seems like seven years. It may also be the closest frame they could reach that wasn't being observed by Demons who could stop them. Then, once here, they decided to strike at the most hurtful time, just before the two of you married. So it is hardly random.

It made painful sense. "They certainly found a way to hurt us," Squid said soberly.

"So we don't smash the killer," Laurelai said. "But how do we stop him without warning the Dwarf Demons that we're onto them?"

"Because they'll be suspicious that *we're* suspicious," Squid said.

Nicely phrased. I have a notion. There is a cloud of empathy-enhanced conscience vapor that formed when the Good Magician accidentally dropped and broke an obscure bottle of elixir. He is a hundred years old; he fumbles things. The mist is drifting this way. It will dissipate in due course, but remains a threat to local creatures for now. We may be able to use it. It would hardly affect the two of you, because you are already conscience-burdened.

"How is conscience a threat?" Laurelai asked.

If a dragon goes after a harmless deer, it can't afford to feel guilty for killing an innocent creature. An outright villain would be ruined.

"Ah, I see," Laurelai said. "I can suffer grievous guilt just for accidentally stepping on a bug. But how would the acquisition of a conscience help, when the killings have already been done?"

It would nullify the killer for any future killings and make him largely harmless to others.

"But that's not punishment," Squid objected. "I want to see that killer suffer!"

He will suffer severely for what he did before he obtained the conscience. He might even be driven to suicide.

Squid thought of some of the mean things she had done as a child, before she knew better. They still bothered her, and she wished she could undo them. If she had killed someone, well, maybe she wouldn't want to keep on living herself.

"And if he suicided," Laurelai said thoughtfully, "that would not implicate us. Well, except in the sense of being the source of his guilt."

"So the Dwarf Demons might be confused," Squid concluded.

"And maybe give themselves away," Laurelai agreed. "Trying to find out exactly what went wrong this time."

The killer is getting close. He is orienting on the two of you, knowing your personal signals from his prior attempt. The cloud is that direction. Move!

There was a flicker of light, as from a candle, beyond the pavilion. They hurried toward it, but like a will-o'-the-wisp it teasingly moved away.

Meanwhile, behind them came a crashing as if something heavy or clumsy was charging in pursuit. They knew Fornax would protect them from any direct attack, but it was nervous business regardless. Now they did some unladylike crashing through the brush themselves, desperate to stay clear of whatever it was.

They burst into what would otherwise have been a pleasant glade. It was lighted by glowing lantern flowers so that the darkness of night was held off. There was something else about it, more of a feeling than an appearance. Squid knew that Laurelai felt it too. What was it?

Then Squid caught on. "The conscience cloud! We are experiencing twinges of conscience. But we're used to it, so we're not suffering."

"It remains eerie," Laurelai said.

Wait here.

They halted and turned to face their nemesis, their pulses racing, and not from any delightful expectations. They expected something horrible.

It burst into the glade. It was worse than what they had feared. It was roughly man-shaped in outline, but had cruel spikes for knees, the kind that could rip limb from limb. Its feet were caterpillar treads on stout wheels. It had a black metallic torso clearly invulnerable to attack. Its arms terminated in circular saws evidently capable of cutting through wood or bones. Its head was a bald dome with a blank face-plate.

This was a transcendentally ugly killing machine.

A pair of eyes appeared on the thing's face-plate, seemingly painted there. They gazed at the two girls. Then a mouth appeared, similarly drawn. "I killed you," it said. "I sawed you asunder. How did you reconstitute?"

The thing could see and talk! "Yes, you did," Squid replied grimly. "And you are going to pay for that crime."

"Who the bleep are you, anyway?" Laurelai asked.

"I am Goar Golem, gifted killer."

"Gifted?" Laurelai asked. "You are a foul slaughterer of innocent girls."

"Enough chit-chat. This time I will make better sure of you." The creature charged forward on its crunching treads, hand-saws whirling viciously.

"Uh, Fornax," Squid murmured. "Now might be a good time."

Not yet.

Laurelai threw down a handful of seeds. Was she trying to sprout a garden? No, they looked more like teeth, of all things. Fornax must have generated them and given them to the girl. What possible use could they be at a desperate time like this?

The teeth hit the ground and instantly took root. They grew at a blistering pace, becoming thorny bushes. No, man forms. No, soldiers, who formed a line and faced the charging golem with swords drawn. These were dragon's teeth!

Goar didn't hesitate. He plowed right into the line, saws squealing. Fragments of soldiers flew out. There was no blood; these were not living creatures, but robotic machines. The first line was quickly decimated, but already a second line was attacking, and a third.

The whine of the saws ground to a halt. There were swords jammed in, clogging the circular blades.

The golem tried to back off, surely to charge again at a weaker spot. But pieces of robot were jammed into the treads, and they, too, were stalled. Dozens of robots had been killed, in their fashion, but they were winning the battle.

A cloaked figure appeared behind the golem, then another. One stepped into the melee, and the soldiers dissipated like blown steam. The other touched the golem, and it was instantly restored to full fighting efficiency.

"Foolish girls!" the first figure said. "You thought to save your fleshly hides with dragon's teeth? From Demon vengeance? Now we will make sure of you!"

Then Fornax appeared. "Got you!" she exclaimed with deep satisfaction, reaching out to grasp each Dwarf Demon by the scruff. "There's a Demon trial awaiting you."

The two Dwarf Demons disappeared.

Goar Golem, restored, did not attack. "What am I doing? This is not right!"

The conscience cloud had taken hold.

Fornax oriented on it. "Now for you, killer. Have you anything to say before oblivion?"

The thing pondered half a moment. "Only that I am sorry. I was governed by a directive I could not oppose, and I am indeed a crafted killer. Oblivion is too kind. I deserve torture."

Fornax glanced at the girls. "Oblivion or torture?"

Laurelai winced. "Oblivion."

But Squid suffered another siege of contrary reaction. "The golem is awful, and may deserve the most savage punishment. But he was not in control of his actions. The will of the DDDDs governed him."

"DDDDs?"

"Damned Dreadful Dwarf Demons. It's not entirely right to punish him for what they made him do."

"Even though he brutally killed us, and meant to do it again?"

"He is sorry about that. He said so."

Laurelai shook her head. "Sometimes you have unhumanly weird takes on things. That's one of the things I love about you."

"Well, I am a weird unhuman. But even so—"

Say no more aloud, Fornax's thought came to them. The Demoness still stood beside them, but seemed only to be listening. *There is something else.*

They both waited. There had to be good reason for not saying more aloud.

I remained hidden in order to trap the Dwarf Demons, Fornax continued. *Now it occurs to me that something else may be hidden in order to expose Chaos.*

Chaos! Squid exclaimed mentally.

Should I transition so that he can take the body? Laurelai asked.

No. Chaos must not manifest openly until we know that this is not a trap for him. Perhaps I am mistaken, but it seems best to be cautious.

What could threaten the most powerful Demon of them all? Squid asked nervously.

Possibly a secret coalition of Demons who resent that power. They might scheme to provoke him to manifest here in an out of the way reality so they can somehow trap or nullify him. A threat to Laurelai or Larry could be the device he could not ignore.

Squid shuddered mentally. *I will warn him, mentally, when he returns.* She was grateful that Fornax was clearly no part of any such scheme. *Thank you.*

A threat to Chaos is in return a threat to Larry and Laurelai, who are under my protection, Fornax thought. *Not to mention the security of the universe. Regardless, the Demons made a deal with Chaos, and we will not dishonor that. Meanwhile it seems best to have me keep track, until we know what's what. When he is with you, Squid, treat him as a lover, not a Demon.*

A lover! Squid exclaimed mentally. *Now we are old enough!* Except for that tacit guilt she had expressed before.

And your hosts are married. Now continue the verbal dialogue.

"Torture," Squid said, suffering a bright flash of inspiration as they returned to the open subject. "And I know the fitting kind. Make Goar the protagonist of this story."

"The protagonist?" the Demoness asked aloud, surprised. "But that's normally an honor."

"Not in this case. He must get to know us, so he appreciates what he has done."

"Until he atones for the crimes he has committed," Laurelai said. "Only then can he be released."

Goar Golem looked at them. "I don't understand."

Squid looked back. "You will in due course. You have a conscience now."

"Genius!" Laurelai breathed, catching on. Of course, conscience was the key.

"But this smells more like mercy, which I don't deserve."

"It's not mercy. It is what you must handle."

"I have no idea how to proceed."

"Then go see the Good Magician. He will tell you what to do. It will cost you a year's service or the equivalent, but you'll be in service to your conscience anyway."

Goar bowed his metallic head. "So be it."

"We will keep an eye on you," Squid said. "Until you earn our forgiveness." *Or until the plot against Chaos is exposed and resolved*, she thought but did not say. They were in it for the long haul.

Meanwhile Chaos, in the guise of her husband, Larry, would have all the private time with her they both desired. And she did mean desire.

Chapter 3

GOAR GOLEM

Goar Golem blinked his face-drawn eyes as the two pretty girls walked away, and not just because their rear views were as interesting as their front views. How could he have slaughtered such lovely creatures, even knowing that their bodies were not exactly what they appeared to be? One was an alien cuttlefish wearing the semblance of a human girl; the other had no fixed age. But of course he had been under foreign control then. Also, one of them had been a man at the time, but it seemed it made no difference because they were gender changers. It hardly mattered; he should not have killed them, and would not have, had he but had a choice.

There was the rub. He had never in his dubious life had real choices, and had made bad decisions that just kept driving him deeper into doom. Now the cuttlefish girl had cursed him into yet another round of evil, as the protagonist of this story. Until he somehow earned her forgiveness for killing her.

He paused. Did that mean it was possible to gain forgiveness? That there was some devious route to actually make up for the evil he had done? It seemed unlikely, but there was a faint hope. He would cling to that, because that was all there was between him and eternal damnation.

Protagonist: that meant the main character, the one who saw everything happen. The viewpoint person. But who was also the object of universal cynosure, because anyone and everyone could read the story. He would have no secrets at all, and would be constantly judged. That was indeed a kind of torture.

What now? She had told him that too: go ask the Good Magician.

He focused, and the necessary direction came to him. He had been able to orient on his assigned prey; now he found that he could orient on whomever else he needed. That helped. *That* way.

He started walking that way, forging through the brush and foliage, heedless of the plants and wildlife he might crush underfoot.

Until this moment when he thought of it. Now suddenly he had a conscience, and it forbade him from hurting anything without good reason. That was a significant inconvenience he had never suffered before. Sure, he had wanted to avoid going to Hell, because he understood that it was an uncomfortable and tedious place, but that was common sense, not conscience. The idea of not being able to do anything without considering whether it might in some devious manner harm another creature was appalling. How could he ever get anything done efficiently with that being the case? He had never been bothered by such foolish restrictions in the past.

But he was bothered now. So he did what he had to do. He stopped and looked about until he found a path. He made his way carefully to that, and followed it, because there were no plants or bugs to be stepped on there. It did not lead directly to the Good Magician's Castle, but it would get him closer until he found another path to correct the deviance. Efficiency simply had to be sacrificed, unfortunately.

The Good Magician's castle turned out to be some distance away. He needed to find a place to spend the night, because he could not see to avoid stepping on innocent things in the darkness. He spied a path-side shelter and approached it.

A young woman emerged from it, coincidentally, as he came close. She took three quarters of a look at him and screamed in terror. "There's a bare-naked robot man out here with spinning saws for hands!" An apt description.

A man came out, maybe her boyfriend. He took a look and a half, then grimly lifted a club. "Get out of here, you bleeping freak, before I knock your bleeping block off!" The nearby foliage wilted in the heat of his expletives.

Goar had no fear of the man. One sweep of a spinning saw hand would lop off the man's threatening arm, and maybe also his head. But that would be unkind, as the man was only trying to protect his girlfriend, and Goar now preferred to avoid unkindness. So he did the humiliating thing, and retreated.

"And don't come back, you bleeping pervert!" the man yelled after him.

Goar had never been concerned about clothing before: he didn't need it. But now he realized that nakedness was another kind of harm, because it seemed it bothered regular folk. So if he was going to go among people, he needed to put on some clothing.

That was a problem. He had no idea where to find clothing, or what would be appropriate. He stood bemused. This was not as simple as tackling a path to a castle.

"Do you have a problem, sir?" It was a cute young woman who looked slightly angelic and slightly demonic, an odd combination.

"Yes. I think I need to find clothing, but I don't know how."

"That's easy to fix. There's a grove of clothing trees not far from here. I'll show you where it is. Right this way."

This was evidently a favor. Goar researched in his dim memory for the proper response, and managed to find it: "Thank you."

"You're welcome. I like helping folk, when I can."

What was the next proper response? There were a number, and he could not expeditiously choose between them. So he took the closest one. "You are not afraid of me."

"Should I be?"

"No."

A silence overtook them as they walked. "You're not much of a conversationalist," she remarked.

"No, I'm a killer, or at least I was. Dialogue was not much of a necessity."

"A killer! Why did you change?"

"I entered a conscience cloud. That changed my perspective."

"Ah. I suppose it would. Very well, let's introduce each other. I'm Misty."

This response was more readily available. "I am Goar Golem."

"I'm the daughter of Beauregard Demon and Angela Angel. That makes me a demangan. I have a bit of trouble deciding exactly what my nature is, because there are pulls in both directions. So I rotate between Bad, Good, and Neutral. Showing you where the clothing grove is is neutral, because there's no telling whether you have any taste in clothing. Ah, there it is now."

Indeed, there was the grove, replete with shirts and pants galore. Goar gazed at it, having no idea what to take.

"I see you are in doubt," Misty said. "So I'll do my good deed and find you a Housewife."

"A what?"

"It's a soldier's mending kit. It will show you how to dress." She looked about. "Ah, here is one." She picked up a small bag from a round pedestal and handed it to him. "I must go."

She had abruptly changed her mind about associating with him? He needed to fathom this, so as not to do it again. "Why? Have I offended you?"

"Not at all. I think you're nice, for a killer golem. It's that now I'm due for my bad act and I don't want to do it to you, so I must go find someone or something else to do it to. Someone who deserves ill. Bye." She hurried away.

Someone who deserved ill? Had she stayed a moment more he would have told her that he was the ill-deserving one. She had completely misjudged him. Yet he was foolishly pleased.

Goar looked at the kit. It was just a tied bag containing things. "And how do I use you?" he asked, bemused.

The bag expanded into a middle-aged or even older woman. An old bag. "I'm so glad you asked. You definitely need help."

"You're a person?"

"I'm a magic mending kit. By day I can be invoked as a wife. By night I'm a house. House wife. Get it? Now let's get you dressed."

She took him into the grove and expertly selected shirt and trousers. Soon he was properly garbed. She even found magic gloves to cover his circular saws, so that now they looked like gauntleted hands. The fit was not perfect, but she brought out scissors, needle, and thread, and expertly remade the junctures to perfect it. She stood him before a mirror hanging from a branch, and he saw that he now looked less like a metallic robot and more like a garden variety man.

Goar's memory of human ways was returning with practice. Regular people generally made exchanges of favors or services. "What do you want?"

She smiled, "I thought you'd never ask. You have saw blades for hands. Can you use them effectively?"

"Yes."

"I need new furniture for my house stage. Saw me up some deadwood to the proper specifications."

"Yes."

She took him to a pile of deadwood, and he removed the gloves and sawed up numerous pieces exactly as she directed. Soon there was a fair pile of it.

The sun was descending. "At sunset I will convert. It's my nature. When I do, tote the pieces inside. Then I will instruct you on assembling the furniture."

How would she do that, if she was no longer a woman? He would surely find out. "I will do so."

She glanced around. "That will happen in about half an hour. Fetch in some food also so you can eat. There's a pie patch just beyond this grove. And just beyond that is a toilet tree. Go poop there, because I don't have internal facilities."

Goar obeyed. It was easy to get things done when someone told him what to do. Within half an hour he was back with a bag of freshly harvested pies and milkweed pods. The magic gloves enabled him to hold and carry things in the manner of real ones.

He returned just in time, because the housewife abruptly converted to the house. The door was open, so he ferried the wood and food inside.

Then he looked around. It was a compact four-room house, with a bedroom, living room, kitchen, and storage room. Just right for an overnight stay.

"Turn me on." It was a box with a front windowpane sitting in the living room.

He found a button and pressed it. The box illuminated. A picture appeared on the pane. It was the face of the housewife. "Now eat," she said.

He swung open his face-plate and stuffed in two pies and squeezed milk from a pod. His innards would process the nourishment. The box face watched without comment.

"Now to assemble the furniture." She gave detailed instructions on what went where and how it was fastened in place, and his emulated hands enabled him to do it. In due course there were three new wooden chairs and a wooden table. "That will do. Toss out the old furniture." He tossed.

"Now go to bed and sleep," the face said. "Turn me on again in the morning." The screen clicked off.

The bed was comfortable. He didn't need the pillow or sheet or blanket, but used them anyway because it was easier than setting them aside. He doffed his shirt and trousers and lay down. He slept.

In the morning he woke, got up, dressed, and turned on the face-box. "Good morning, Goar," the face said. "The weather outside is nice, and no nasty creatures are patrolling the area. Complete your meal within half an hour."

"Thank you." He shoved in another pie and pod.

"A word or three to the wise," the face said. "You need to improve your table manners, lest you alienate regular folk. See if you can get instruction along the way."

There was something wrong with the way he ate? "I will," he agreed.

Goar closed his face panel and was ready to depart. "You have been a good house-guest," the face said. "Now please step outside before I change. Dawn is incipient and you wouldn't want to be caught inside."

He stepped out of the house. It changed to the woman. "Thank you for using me," she said.

He knew the proper response. "You're welcome. You were just what I needed."

"Now set me on the pedestal, so I am ready for the next user." She paused. "Unless you prefer to keep me."

"Keep you?"

"I can't stay long in woman form unless a man takes me as a wife, but I can be useful as a kit when your clothing tears or when there is no convenient shelter during rain. All I ask is that you pass me along in due course to someone else who needs my services."

He considered briefly. "I would like to keep you, at least for now."

"Thank you." She took his hand and shifted to the mending kit form, now in his hand.

"You're welcome," he repeated, and put her bag in a shirt pocket. If this was what regular mortal life was like, he could learn to like it.

He resumed his walk along the paths, and by midday he arrived at the Good Magician's Castle.

It was surely a scenic sight, but Goar did not care about the view. He just wanted to talk to the Good Magician and find out what to do next. If he had to perform a year's service for that advice, very well, *that* was what he would do next.

There was a winding path leading toward the castle. He followed it. In less than two moments he came to a fat horned creature grazing beside the route. "Aha," said the beast. "You must be today's Challenger."

That was right, Goar remembered. There were supposed to be three Challenges before a person could get in to see the Good Magician. "Yes."

"Well, first you have to get past me." The creature moved to block the path with its considerable bulk, bearing its horned nose menacingly.

"No problem." Goar moved to draw off his gloves and expose his saws. The horn was no threat to him.

Except that his gloves did not pull off. They were stuck on the ends of his limbs. Then he remembered: folk could not use their special powers when trying for access to this castle. He was stuck with what might as well be real hands. Bleep!

"So how do I get past you?" he inquired, not expecting an answer. Why would a Challenge tell him the solution?

To his surprise, the beast answered. "You will find what you want in next to no time."

A fast solution? That didn't seem likely. Where was the catch?

Goar gazed around, and saw a building to the side. Words were printed on it: NO TIME. A big help that was!

Then an idea flashed, illuminating the landscape for almost half of a split second. That was the name of the building! So the answer must be in there.

Or was it? The cunning beast might be trying to trick him into leaving the path to enter the building, forfeiting the real answer. In fact, now he recognized it. "You're a Hornswoggle! You're too lazy to do much of anything yourself, so you try to swindle others instead."

The creature blew such an angry blast through its horn that a small cloud of smoke emerged.

"And I think you're not really a Challenge," Goar continued. "You're faking that, too, just for the notoriety. You're just a wandering brute out to mess up others."

There was another blast of smoke. Goar knew he was scoring.

Then he got another flash. "And there's nothing in that building. NO TIME is too obvious a hint. What I want is *next* to it, maybe in that adjacent shed. Except that I don't want anything here anyway. Now get out of my way, you paunchy faker!"

He marched up to the animal, and this time it moved out of his way, clearing the path. He surely had enough of a challenge just getting through the legitimate Challenges, without getting distracted by fake ones.

He rounded a curve and passed through a patch of thick mist. It clung to him like spiderwebs. He brushed it off impatiently and marched on. But now he had to push past thickly intruding foliage that stuck leaves and burrs and chips of wood to his body because of the sticky moisture. He brushed these off, too, but wasn't sure he was getting them all. It was a nuisance. He emerged into the light as a swarm of odd flies scattered into the air. He must have disturbed their nest, or whatever.

He paused to look at it. Not a nest, but an arrow hovering in midair. There was a sign below it: TIME FLIES LIKE AN ARROW.

Oh. Of course. They had been perching on it before he blundered into it. "Sorry, flies," he said apologetically. "I didn't see you." He had heard that time flies could make time fly backward or forward, so it was best to avoid them.

Just beyond it was a floating banana. More flies were perching on it. Their bodies were shaped like little cherries, apples, peaches, pears, and plums. What were they? Then he saw the sign beneath them: FRUIT FLIES LIKE A BANANA.

Now he understood. They were fruit flies. He was careful not to jog the big banana.

He resumed the path. There ahead was a pool. Around the pool were maybe a dozen lovely young women in scanty swimsuits. "Ooooo!" they exclaimed, spying him. "A handsome man!"

A what? Goar was about as un-handsome as a male humanoid could get. Golems were not generally appealing in appearance, and the modifications he had suffered made him worse.

The girls clustered around him. "Ooo," one ooohed as she stroked an arm. Her tight suit was red, as was her hair and lips. "Oooo'" another cooed as she stroked his hair. Her suit was green, matching her hair and lips.

Hair? Goar was bald. It was part of his ugliness.

"OoOo!" It was a third girl whose suit was blue, echoed by her hair and lips. "And that manly beard!"

Goar lacked a beard also. It was part of his hairlessness. "Stop pretending, and let me get on to the Challenge."

The three girls seemed taken aback. "Who's pretending?" Red asked, taking a breath that threatened to snap some threads on her suit. "Not me," Green said. stretching some threads of her own. "Or me, handsome," Blue said as her suit started to tear.

There was something interesting about those suits, but Goar had other thoughts to process. "Then you must be blind, because I am ugly as sin."

"He doesn't know," another girl said. Her suit, hair, and lips were yellow.

"We must show him," a golden girl said. Her whole body was a golden tan, making her suit seem to disappear in a surprisingly intriguing way.

"You do that, Goldilocks," Yellow called.

They clustered closer about him, pressing their remarkably soft torsos against him as they drew him toward the pool. In half an instant he was staring into the water, seeing his own reflection.

He couldn't believe it. He was completely handsome, with shining armor and manly locks of hair that trailed into a perfectly manicured short black beard. How had that happened?

Then he realized that it must have been the sticky mist, followed by the thick brush. Reverse wood! Burrs and seeds and leaves and chips, all rendering him into the opposite of what he really was.

"Girls, I'm not really—" he started

"OoOoOo!!" they exclaimed as they shoved so forcefully against him that they all toppled into the pool with a mighty splash.

Now he was buried in lithe bodies. Firm young arms cuddled his head, while firmer young legs clasped his torso. He opened his mouth to protest, but a soft young bosom pillowed his face so that he couldn't get the protest out. He tried to swim to the edge, but his hands encountered endless softness and couldn't get anywhere. He tried to stand on the bottom of the pool, but his feet were stuck on bottoms of another nature that flexed enticingly under his treads. What was he into?

Then he saw letters along the rim of the pool. UFA.

"What is UFA?" he asked.

"Unwanted Female Attention," the girls still on the deck chorused.

That was certainly the case! It wasn't that Goar was anti-girl, but he had never had cause to trust them, since none were ever attracted to him.

He finally managed to clamber out of the pool, dragging several suits filled with girls along with him. Smears of color decorated his torso where the girls had rubbed against him.

And still they came, scrambling out of the pool with flashes of slender limbs and curvaceous wet torsos. The UFA remained in full force. How could he get out of this?

Then he realized that this must be the First Challenge. He had to escape the attentions of the multicolored girls before they had their nefarious way with him, whatever that might be. But how?

He remembered that the Good Magician's Challenges were supposed always to have their solutions conveniently nearby. The challenge was to figure out how the solutions could be applied. He needed to think.

The girls gave him no time for that. They were converging on him in much the manner their frontal curves converged on each other, leading to a crevice that dived under their dripping suits. "First girl who gets him wins the pool!" Red cried as she charged.

"Me first!" Green exclaimed as she leaped to follow.

"Me too!" Goldilocks called from the throng. Or maybe that was thong.

Win the pool? But they had just scrambled out of the pool! Did they mean to haul him back into it?

Goar backed away from them. He tripped over something behind him and fell on his back. Immediately, the girls were on him in a softly heaving pile. Strangely, they were not trying to hold him down so much as to get out of their clingingly tight suits. What did they have in mind? He certainly didn't trust it. He wished he had never blundered into this mess.

Then his desperate gaze saw the floating banana he had passed on the way here, with the fruit flies. Beyond it was the floating arrow, with its time flies.

Time flies. That made time fly backward or forward. If he could use them to go back just a little bit—

He heaved himself up, along with his burden of feminine flesh. An empty blue swimsuit was covering one eye, and a green one was aiming for the other eye, while a yellow one was entangling his feet, but he managed to stagger the short distance to the arrow. He reached out and grasped it, making the flies buzz up again. "Time Flies!" he shouted. "Take me back ten minutes!" Would it work?

Then he was just emerging from the thicket of reverse wood, about to spy the pool with its cluster of colored girls. They were just looking up to spy him. The flies were buzzing around.

"Five more minutes!" he gasped.

He was just pushing past the Hornswoggle, about to round the curve that concealed the thicket. Good enough! He jumped to the side, found an alternate path, and hastily followed that. He had escaped the pool.

Now green foliage pressed in from either side. In fact, they were two hedges with oddly oblong leaves, green on one side, gray on the other, marked with figures. ONE DOLLAR, FIVE DOLLARS, TWENTY DOLLARS. There were also little pictures of faces on them. What kind of plants were these?

Then he remembered another obscure oddity. In drear Mundania they used something called money, that came in paper pieces like these. Instead of harvesting food, clothing, or shelter, in the sensible Xanthian manner, they got hold of these papers and somehow used them to obtain the things they wanted. It didn't seem to make a lot of sense, but they were Mundanes, who had never been noted for sense, common or rarefied. Indeed, they seemed to possess an unsatisfiable craving for greenish paper, hoarding it rather than spending it. They called it funds. So hedges like these must be where they obtained it. Hedge funds.

But Goar knew that neither hedge funds nor green money itself were much protection against losses. Mundanes were forever running out of funds, and losing things they valued, like their houses or the strange moving boxes they called cars. So he wanted nothing to do with these hedges; they were not safe.

Yet he seemed to be trapped between them. He had to go where they channeled him, or back out of this, well, surely it was another Challenge.

He turned around, and saw that more hedges had grown in behind him. He was trapped, just like a foolish Mundane. He had nowhere to go but forward, wherever that might lead.

He screeched to a halt. He wasn't going that fast, but he heard the screech. What was he to do?

Worse, a storm was coming. He saw the clouds massing in the sky, ready to bank into each other and make the booms that generated dangerous sparks. Soon he would be soaked, and perhaps electrocuted. That might be the Challenge's way of goosing him into action; staying in place could quickly wash him out, especially if the rain were heavy enough.

Then it started. Two clouds collided, with a fearsome booming sound. Then a lightning bolt crashed into the path just behind him. It bounced, rolled, and came to rest almost beside his feet, its heat steaming up as it cooled. That was a close call, surely warning enough. Suppose it had landed on his head? His head was hard, but not *that* hard. He *had* to get moving.

Or did he? These Challenges were fashioned to spook folk into acting foolishly. Those who kept their wits reasonably close could often get safely through. Was the bolt a coincidence, or was it a hint?

He reached down to pick it up, as it was no longer burningly hot. It was surprisingly light. It hardly seemed metallic.

In fact Goar himself felt lighter now. He set down the bolt, and felt heavier. It was affecting him. Was that good or bad? Or did it depend on how he saw it? So it made him weigh less: What was the point? Could it make him so light he could float away from all this?

Float away. No, float *toward*. Toward the castle. That was how he could get out of the Hedge Fund bind.

He picked up the bolt again. "Do your thing," he told it.

He felt himself getting lighter and lighter, until he did indeed float. He flapped his arms to give himself some motion, and flew slowly over the hedges. Challenge #2 was being navigated.

Soon he drifted down to a rocky slope. A girl was there, digging in the sand with her hands. "Darn!" she swore in ladylike fashion.

"What's the matter?"

She jumped. "Oh, sorry, I didn't hear you coming."

"That may be because I wasn't walking. I floated over the hedge and landed here."

"Oh, you're a querent!"

"A what?"

"A querent. Someone who comes to see the Good Magician about a Query. A question. To get an Answer."

"Oh. Yes."

"I know how it is. I am serving my year's service by working here for my Answer. It's boring, but I'm getting through it." She glanced more directly at him. "I'm Jemma."

This required a return name, but not extra detail. "I'm Goar Golem."

She smiled. "Hello, Goar. I would offer to shake hands, but mine are covered in dirt."

He put a smile on his face-plate. Best not to describe his digits. "What was your question?"

"I asked him what my talent was, because I didn't know. He told me it was dragging gems out of the ground, here in Xanth or in Mundania, if I ever went there. So now I'm doing it for him. I'm looking for a good one for Sofia, because her birthday is coming up and he wants her to have something nice."

"Sofia?"

"Sofia Socksorter, his Designated Wife of the Month."

Goar's memory did not relate to this. "Designated Wife?"

"It's a long story, but the essence is that he had five wives who aged and died in the normal manner, before he thought to use Youth Elixir on them. When he went to Hell to recover the last one, he wound up with all of them. Hell likes to make things difficult. Since only one wife at a time is permitted, they now take turns. This month it's Sofia, the Mundane. He married her because she's good with socks, and he has a real problem tracking his socks."

This seemed an odd reason to marry a person, but Goar was not much familiar with the nuances of human life. "Thank you. You seem frustrated."

"I am. I need to see closely what I am doing, but that darned mountain keeps getting in the way, casting a shadow so the details aren't clear. It's called Sneak Peak. When I move, it moves. It's most frustrating. I'm likely to dig out a dinosaur turd instead of a gem. I think the mountain got the idea that I'm a querent, so it's messing me up."

"Perhaps it is my presence that confuses it."

"That must be it. Mountains are big, but they aren't smart. Usually, this one is trying to use its height to see down into my dressing room when I'm changing. It's annoying, but I can close the curtains. But I need to get that gem in the next hour, so I can polish it and have it ready in time. Bleep."

Goar realized that she must be really upset, because she had progressed to an unladylike epithet. "The Challenge must be meant for me. If I get it done promptly, then you should be able to work unhampered."

"That must be it! Let me get out of your way." She stood and moved to the side.

Goar considered. So the Sneak Peak moved about to mess people up. It was probably supposed to block his path to the Castle, but got distracted by the girl. It might be a male mountain, as males generally liked to catch sneak glimpses of girls. Maybe it was frustrated by not being able to see the colored girls of the pool; they had plenty to glimpse. What he needed to do was somehow anchor it in place so it couldn't move. Then he would be able to proceed unimpeded, and Jemma would be able to get her job done.

But how could he anchor a mountain? He gazed about, hoping for some hint, but all he saw were some guy wires holding a boulder in place. They looked quite thin, but were surely magical, able to hold anything without snapping.

No, they weren't attached to the boulder. They just seemed to be there, using the boulder as a pretense. Just hanging about.

Guy wires. They, too, were trying to see the colored pool maidens next glade! Because they were guys, and guys looked. But again, the girls weren't in sight. So why were the guys still here?

Where there were guys, there were generally gals. Goar looked, and saw the Gal Wires, lounging during their slack time, unaware that they were being seen. Or maybe just pretending to be unaware. The Guy Wires were ramrod straight, while the Gal Wires were marvelously curvaceous.

And there was his answer. Wires to anchor the mountain!

He walked to the Guy Wires, but they twanged away as soon as he got close. Maybe they felt guilty about gazing.

Now what? Well, if the Guys could do it, surely so could the Gals.

Goar marched to the Gal Wires and gathered a bunch of them in his arms. They hummed with appreciation for the attention.

He carried them to the nearest foot of the mountain and fastened one to its big toe. He fastened the other end to some exposed bedrock. The bed wasn't even made, but it was firm. Then he went to each of the mountain's other feet and anchored them similarly. He was able to circle it; fortunately, it was not a large one. This mountain wasn't going anywhere fast.

"If I have figured this correctly, that mountain will no longer bother you," he told Gemma as he completed the circuit.

She clapped her hands in girlish glee. "Goody!"

"Once you get your gem, maybe you should release those Gal wires. It wouldn't be nice to anchor the mountain too long."

"I will. Thank you. Please don't tell Sofia; it's supposed to be a surprise."

"I won't," he promised.

She kissed him on the side of his face-plate. "I hope you get a good Answer."

He was discovering that living an ordinary life could be surprisingly pleasant. Especially, getting kissed by a girl.

Goar walked on along the path, circling the mountain. The mountain strained at the wires, but the Gals held it firm.

He had completed the third Challenge.

The path led on to the castle moat and its drawbridge, which was down. He crossed to the outer wall. On the way he glanced down, and discovered that the effect of the reverse wood had worn off. He was ugly again.

Gemma had kissed him when he was ugly. He didn't know what that meant, but he liked it.

He came to the front gate. A woman was waiting for him there. "Do come in, Goar. I am Wira, the Good Magician's daughter-in-law. I will take you to him in due course."

"Thank you."

She led him through the murky halls and passages of the castle until they came to what appeared to be a sewing room. A rather plain older woman was there, sitting on a pile of hosiery, darning a sock.

"Mother Sofia, this is the Querent Goar Golem," Wira said, and departed.

"To be sure," Sofia said. She finished the sock, then looked at Goar. "It will be a little while before Humfrey is ready to see you. Lift your foot."

Goar lifted one foot, showing its treads.

"Just as I thought. You could use a sock. Also a shoe."

"My treads have served me well enough, hitherto."

"Appearance is important when among the human kind," she said with certainty. "We'll need to cover those knee-spikes also." She rummaged in the pile and came up with a pair of long stockings. "These."

Goar put them on. They covered his treads, lower legs, and the knee spikes, which seemed to disappear. She stood him before a full-length mirror. It was surprising how well they fit, and now his legs and feet looked like those of a normal human person.

"These are old stockings Humfrey has no further need of," Sofia said. "But in the old days he wore them for some time, so they have picked up some of his magic. I have washed them three times, but that magic has become embedded in the fabric itself, and can't be cleaned out. You will just have to live with it. However, one advantage is that they do fit perfectly, and will adapt to the shoes." She dug out an old pair of men's shoes. "Put these on."

"They are too small."

"Pshaw. They will fit."

He tried a shoe, and lo, it fitted comfortably. It seemed that the socks accounted for this too. Now his legs and feet looked completely human in the mirror.

"You know what you're doing," he said.

"It's a survival trait, in this establishment. When you need to use your treads and spikes, simply remove the shoes and socks and they will be there and serviceable."

"Thank you."

She eyed him speculatively. "You can use a head sock, too. It won't make you look handsome, but it will make you look human."

"Why should I need to look human?"

"I'm sure I don't know, but Humfrey said you needed to, so I am seeing to it." She rummaged some more and came up with a single off-white sock. "Over your head."

He pulled the sock over his dome and face-plate, then looked again in the mirror. And was amazed.

His whole head looked human, with a shaped nose, mouth, and chin. He now had eyebrows over dark eyes. And—

And a head of hair.

"Have a fresh cookie," Sofia said. "Wira harvested some from the banks of the With-A-Cookie River this morning. Also some Tsoda Pop, from Lake Tsoda Popka. They are very good."

Goar accepted them. He bit into the cookie, and it was delicious. Then he gulped the tsoda pop, and it was tangy and tasty too.

Sofia stood there, watching him. What was on her mind?

Then it came to him. He had just eaten and drunk without removing his face-plate! The head-sock covered the plate, but the plate was still there.

"It's another magic sock," Sofia explained. "Now you can talk normally too."

He had been talking by generating sounds from a diaphragm inside his head, while his painted mask-mouth moved to match it. "I am amazed," he said, watching his mouth move in the mirror.

"You can even kiss with it, should you ever want to."

"Who would want to kiss me?" he asked. Because while he now looked distinctly human, he remained homely.

"You never can tell. Let's try it now." She stepped up to him, took his head between her hands, angled it just so, and put her mouth to his mouth, her lips to his lips. She kissed him, hard and long. Pleasure radiated from his mouth back through his face and coursed down across his body. He felt as if he were slowly floating off the floor. Then she released him and stepped back. "It will be proportionately better when you kiss a real girl, instead of another man's old wife. This was just a demonstration."

"I am amazed," he repeated as he feet returned to the floor.

"You should be. Humfrey is not always so free with his magic."

"But why? I am just a singularly undeserving killer golem."

"The ways of the Good Magician are typically obscure. But they always make excellent sense in the end. You just have to play it through properly."

"I will try to do so."

"Oh, one more thing. Squid and Laurelai have a token for you that we agreed to relay after they met with Humfrey." She held forth what looked like a sparkling bracelet.

"But I killed them! They can't give me a gift."

"It is not a gift. It is a tracking device, so they will always know exactly where you are and what you are doing. It is formed from platinum plated antimatter, invulnerable to any ordinary tool. Put it on your ankle."

Oh. Of course. Why should they trust him on his own? He drew the anklet over his socked foot and onto his right ankle, where it tightened snugly and disappeared. But he could still feel the slight tingle of its presence. Antimatter!

"If you should need to contact them, merely touch it with a finger and think *PLEASE.*"

"But if they already know my whereabouts, why do that?"

"To ask for help."

"Help! Why should they ever want to help me?"

Sofia shrugged. "I'm sure I don't know. But if the occasion comes, now you know how to invoke it."

Wira returned. "The Good Magician will see you now."

"Good fortune, Goar."

He paused half a moment. "You are some woman."

"Thank you. I do my best." She returned to her pile of socks.

Wira led him up a tightly winding staircase to a gloomy little chamber on the second floor. Within it an ancient old gnome pored over a giant open tome. This had to be the fabled grumpy Good Magician, whom Goar remembered kept his age at an even one hundred years.

"Father, this is Goar Golem, here to ask you what to do with his life." She faded back.

Goar was surprised again. He had never mentioned his mission, in fact had hardly formulated it coherently in his mind. But she had it right.

"You will join the Oma Incident and her three companions. She is approximately human. You will assist them to the best of your abilities."

Who and who? "Uh, sir, is this my Answer or my Service?"

The Magician looked up at him with evident annoyance. "Both."

"How will I know when my Service is done?"

"When Larry and Squid forgive you for killing them."

Goar opened his mouth for another question, but Wira took his elbow. "Your interview is done. I will take you to them now." Indeed, the Good Magician's attention was locked on the tome. He had tuned them out.

Then he was following her back down the staircase and to the ground floor. She led him not back to the sewing room or the front gate, but into the central courtyard and its garden. They halted at the trunk of a large tree. A small door was painted on its bark.

"They await you here," Wira said.

"Inside the tree?"

She smiled. "Not exactly." She put a hand to the painted doorknob, turned it, and drew open the door. Inside was a short hall with a door at its far end.

"This is ridiculous," he protested. "That has to lead out the other side of the trunk, and I can see that no one is standing there."

She smiled. "Do I have to kiss you to make you believe?"

He looked at her. She was not a beauty, but neither was she plain. Kisses had power he had not imagined. After his experience with Sofia he knew better than to risk it. "No."

"Oh, I almost forgot. I must give you this note." She dug in her shirt pocket and brought out a tiny envelope. "It's very important."

"What is it?"

"I do not know. He said you will understand it when the time comes." She handed it to him.

Another minor mystery. He was getting tired of these. Goar took the envelope and tucked it in the top of his sock next to the anklet. Then he ducked his head and stepped into the hall. She gently closed the door after him.

There was faint illumination here that seemed to come on when the door shut. A thought paused him. He brought out the envelope. If it contained something confusing, it was not too late to turn back and demand a clarification. He opened it and read the folded note inside.

It was simply a list of four names. Hack. Gloria. Moxie. Xylia. He had never heard of any of them. What use were they to him?

He shrugged. He would just have to trust that he would indeed understand when the time came.

He took the few steps down the hall, put his hand on the far knob, turned it, and the door swung open. He stepped out.

It was not the far side of the tree. It was a completely different scene, a glade in a forest. He shut the door behind him and turned around to face the forest.

Chapter 4

INCIDENT

"Hello."

The voice startled him. There before him stood an ugly girl. Behind her were three ugly animals: a bird, a rabbit, and a turtle. The girl was unclothed, but it didn't matter because she was not at all attractive. Her face was worse than plain, her hair was dirty brown, and her proportions were so gnarled that he would have doubted that she was human, had not the Good Magician identified her as such. These were the folk he was supposed to work with?

"Uh, hello," he said. "The—the Good Magician sent me. You are the Aloma?"

"Yes. I am Incident, and these are my three companion animals, Bird, Rabbit, and Turtle. I am an Oma, and they are my companions and assistants."

"What's an Oma?"

"That's complicated to explain, but in essence, we deliver nasty tumors to undeserving folk, some of whom die from them."

He was appalled. "You like this work?"

"No. But we are locked into it. We will die and go to Hell if we stop, and Hell is not much fun."

"I am supposed to work with you. I am supposed to assist you to the best of my abilities. Only in that manner will I ever win redemption."

She smiled tiredly. It was not a pretty sight. "Lots of luck there."

"It is as least theoretically possible. It is all I have to go on. I can't continue my old ways, since I got caught in the conscience cloud."

"The conscience cloud!"

"You know of it?"

"Yes. We passed through it unawares. It did not change us physically or mentally, exactly, but emotionally it was devastating. We could no longer do evil. So we went to the Good Magician for help, and he told us that in due course that would come in the form of a golem. You must be that golem."

"But I have no idea what I am supposed to do!" he protested. "I thought you were supposed to know."

Incident sighed. "It seems we have a problem."

"Maybe there was a mistake," he said. "Maybe we should go back and ask him again.

"How?"

"The way I came. Through the tree."

"The tree?"

"The door in the tree, yes."

She grimaced, which she did effectively. "What door?"

He turned to point it out. And paused. The tree was there, but the bark was unmarked. He felt it with his gloved fingers, but there was nothing.

There was no door.

Now he sighed. "It seems it was a one-way trip."

"We were warned that the Good Magician's Answers could be obscure. It seems that was no exaggeration."

"Yes. But I understand also that they always make devious sense in the end."

She shrugged. "It seems we are stuck with each other. We have a temporary den near here that we made so we could stay near the tree until you came. Maybe we can figure it out." She did not sound hopeful.

"Maybe," he agreed, with no real hope to add.

They went to the den. This was a lean-to lined with fur and feathers. It was reasonably comfortable. They had collected a few pies and milkweed pods, so they settled down to eat while they got to know each other.

"You are not as ugly as we are," Incident said. "So you must have been in some other line of business."

That was a change. Goar was used to being the ugliest of those he encountered. "I did not deliver tumors, no. But what has that to do with appearance?"

"Each time we do a bad deed, we get slightly uglier. After several years we became—" She shrugged. "As we are now."

He nodded. "Let me show you my own ugliness." He stood, pulled off his head-sock to reveal his metallic dome and plate, then started pulling down his trousers.

"You don't need to show us that," Incident said quickly. She was naked, but too gnarled to show anything interesting. Goar was less gnarled. A man's bare anatomy could have a freaking effect on a woman. Women, oddly, did not enjoy getting freaked the way men did; it was one of the mysteries of their gender.

"Yes, I do." He pulled them off, revealing the plate that covered his groin. If she had expected more humanoid anatomy, this alleviated that. Then he showed them his uncovered feet.

"Caterpillar treads!" Incident exclaimed. "You *are* different."

"I am a golem," he agreed. "Armor-plated."

"And I am an Oma, as you know. Why is your state significant?"

"I was crafted to be an efficient killer, as were you." Now he removed his gloves and revealed his circular saw digits. "To saw up living flesh and bone. But now I have a conscience, and can no longer pursue my old mission. So unless you need a killer in a good cause, I can't help you."

"We don't want more killing," Incident said.

"I am not surprised. The obscurity of the Good Magician's Answer is beyond me to fathom."

"All that we have in common is doing much evil and encountering the conscience cloud," she said. "Maybe he thought that made us compatible."

"But how does it solve our problems?"

Incident shook her head. "That is beyond me too."

They lapsed into an uncomfortable silence. Then Goar put his clothing back on, becoming more humanoid. "Maybe we need to get to know each other better, in case there is some other way we can help each other."

"Maybe," she agreed unhappily.

"I was once a human child, but I was always a bad boy. I got away with my mischief because folk did not really believe that a young child could be truly evil. Then I went too far."

"You got caught?"

"No. I lived near a railroad track, a sort of Mundane artifact in my area of Xanth, and each day I saw the powerful trains pass with their many following cars. Sometimes other children put pennies on the track, and the metal wheel of the train squished them flat, making them interesting. But that wasn't enough for me. I wanted to see a train wreck. So instead of a coin, I put a metal bar calculated to derail the train. It worked! The train ran off its rails and wrecked. Several adults and six children were killed." He paused, remembering.

"So that was when you got caught?"

"Not exactly. In the confusion they never noticed the little boy watching with relish. The people killed became ghosts. The adults focused on making their way to Heaven, but the children ghosts were more alert. They spied me and read my nasty little mind and knew what I had done. That I had killed them. They were angry, so they haunted me. I could not escape them, and finally they drove me to suicide."

"So you paid for your crime."

"No. Even my death did not appease the little brats. They still harassed me as ghosts, because as another ghost I could not escape them. They blocked the way to Heaven and Hell so that I could not get there. They got their jollies from tormenting me. I was desperate."

"But you are alive now," Incident pointed out.

"Two Dwarf Demons needed a ruthless killer. So they assembled a killer body from junk parts, here an arm, there a leg, and buttressed them with metal spikes and springs."

"And spinning saws!" Incident said, catching on.

"And caterpillar treads," he agreed. "The result was a composite golem, technically alive but not pretty. But they needed a soul to animate it, and I was the most evil one available, so they grabbed me and put me in the body. Thereafter I was required to do their bidding, though it darkened my soiled soul yet more."

"Until you blundered into the conscience cloud."

"Yes. It was a routine mission until then."

"My turn now," Incident said. "Originally, I was Elle, a lovely but naughty Sylph, a nymph of the air, without a conscience. All I cared about was having fun, and much of it was mischievous. I entered a contest among my kind to see which of us could lure the handsomest mortal man to his death. I won! I was thrilled." She grimaced. "Now that horrifies me, because of my conscience."

"I know how that is," Goar said.

The two exchanged a glance of mutual understanding.

“Then later, bored, I discovered that I actually did have a soul, but it was in a rudimentary state, having received no exercise at all. Beautiful sylphs don’t really need souls. I went to apologize to my victim’s girlfriend, and learned that she had been about to break with the man anyway, because he chased after any pretty girl he spied, including, as it turned out, a sylph. She did not wish him dead, but her grief for him was limited. Still, as my soul got a bit of practice, I was sorry for the other unkind things I had done to mortals, and wished I could somehow make up for it. But I saw no way.”

“That, too, I understand,” Goar said.

They exchanged another look. “You know, if you were handsome and I were pretty, those looks we’re generating would mean something,” Incident said. “But as it is—”

“Nobody wants an ugly person,” Goar agreed. “Even though the ugly one might like to have a relationship.”

“That’s why getting ugly is such a punishment. If I put on panties and flashed them at you, you would be disgusted, because a wart hog has a better bottom than I do now in the disaster of my discontent. And if you tried to kiss me, I would snatch my face away, involuntarily, because of course I want *only* a handsome man.”

He liked her apt phrasing. “And I desire only a pretty woman.”

“Yet we are coming to understand each other well enough so that we might indeed make a satisfying couple. We know that intellectually, but not emotionally.”

“We understand each other’s grief,” he agreed. “And share it.”

“Yes, I think we do. Traditionally, in the kind of fantasy we live in, a boy meets a girl early on, and by the end of the story they fall in love and become a permanent couple. It is standard operating procedure. But the boy has to be handsome and strong and decent, and the girl has to be lovely and nice and accommodating. We are none of these things, so it’s a mismatch. The fact that we seem to be compatible is irrelevant.”

“Irrelevant,” he agreed regretfully. “Were I those boy things, and you those girl things, we might be perfect together. But we are not.”

Incident scowled. Her features were perfect for that. “We are not. So back to my story. One day, basking in my own depression, I came across a park honoring mundane poets. One plaque was about one William Ernest Henley, listing his assorted poem titles. One was 'Invictus.' I did not know the word, so I approached the separate plaque that dealt with it. When I came close not only did the words show in lighted print, the poet's voice sounded, speaking it aloud. I was entranced. 'Out of the night that covers me,' and darkness descended. 'Black as the Pit from pole to pole.' And there was a giant pit I cautiously skirted. Yes, I was an immortal air spirit, but I was wary of the mood of this pit, that might have magic and be hard to escape if I fell into it. 'It matters not how strait the gate, / How charged with punishment the scroll.' I thought the words were 'straight the gait,' so I walked a perfectly straight line through the open gate I came to. I was so ignorant, back then! Not that my stunted soul was worth mastering. 'I am the master of my fate: I am the captain of my soul.'"

Incident paused, smiling deprecatingly. "I thrilled to the sentiment, but it was illusory for me. I was not even the mistress of my fate, let alone the master. I was the captive of the realm of the Oma. It happened when I walked through the gate, distracted by the poem. The whole park was a trap to lure in unsuspecting travelers. And so I became Incident Oma, compelled to do deeds I detested, that made me ever-uglier, but I had no choice. I was no longer Elle Sylph, but a dark creature, virtually immortal and invulnerable. I could retire at any time, but then I would lose those benefits, so there really wasn't a choice. I was locked in."

"Yes!" he agreed. "Continue your history."

"I was assigned a territory. The designations started with AA and went through AZ, with the B alphabet and others elsewhere. My district bordered the lots of the A group, all of them being Omas. Mine was AL. I learned that to do my new job properly I would need the assistance of three animals: one flying, one racing, one crawling. So I went looking for them. I discovered that I had been given the ability to sense what I wanted, or at least to know the direction of it. So I focused on flying and before long came across a small bird, a sparrow, caught in a trap meant for something else. A hungry snake was approaching. So I touched the bird, and found that it understood me via a sort of contact telepathy I now possessed. I sprang the trap and freed it, but its leg was broken, its wings battered and it was in no condition to fly. So I healed it, finding that I could do that too. And I said to it, 'Join me, little bird, and I will give you the ability to assume any bird form, small or great, and like me you will become invulnerable and immortal and have near human intelligence as long as you stay with me.' Then the snake struck, biting down on the bird's head. For an instant I thought I was too late, but the snake's fangs had no effect; in fact they seemed to break on the bird's invulnerable neck. Then he shook his head, and the snake was thrown off. 'Peep!' he said, reproving the reptile, and the snake hastily departed, its bruised mouth hurting. Then the bird nodded his head to me, agreeing to the deal, and flew up to my shoulder and perched there, and has been there ever since." She glanced across at the ugly bird and smiled. "I mean with me, not necessarily on my shoulder."

The bird flew quickly to her shoulder and chirped agreement. It would have been cute, had they both not been so hideous.

"Then I oriented on the racing animal, and found a rabbit caught in a briar patch. He had evidently thought it was similar to the ones he normally used to escape predators, but this was a magic one masquerading as innocuous, actually a predator itself. The plant would hold him with its vines and thorns and slowly feed on him, and he was doomed. But I reached in, unscratched, and touched him, and he became invulnerable and able to break out on his own. I made my offer, including the ability to assume any rabbit form, and if he made the effort, any other mammal form, and he was impressed, and accepted it." She glanced at the ugly rabbit, who hopped up and onto her lap. She stroked him. It was clear that they got along well enough.

"Finally, I oriented on the crawling animal, and came to a lake where fishermen were casting a net. But my business was not with the fishermen; my sense of direction led me to the water, and I entered it and dived below, discovering that I could now get along without breathing if I needed to. Truly, as an Oma I was impressive! I came up on a big green turtle who was caught in the fishing net, on the verge of drowning. I poked a finger through the net to touch him, and felt the power surging to him. Then he changed to a small turtle and scrambled through the net. But he remained close to drowning, so I took him in my hand and stroked to the surface, holding him up in the air so he could breathe. Then I made my case to him. For one thing, he would no longer be subject to drowning, now that he knew it wasn't necessary. He would be immune to harm, able to convert instantly to the form of any other turtle, or maybe reptile, practically immortal, and of human intelligence, like the bird and rabbit he would work with. He could leave at any time, but then would revert to his natural state, becoming mortal and stupid. He considered, and decided to join me. We have been together ever since."

The ugly turtle come up to join her, and she laid a hand on his shell. They, too, were friends.

"Now our consciences won't allow us to do further harm," Incident concluded. "But it is getting harder to cope. The longer we go without doing our jobs, the worse it gets. We can't hold out much longer."

"What happens to you?"

She frowned. "It's like having to urinate. You need to do it to live, but you can pick and choose to an extent. You can hold it for a while. You can find a private place to do it. You can drink less water or juice so you can go longer. But eventually you simply have to do it or burst. Well, having tumors to place has some leeway. It can take time to locate suitable prospects. But every day there are new tumors, and if you don't keep up, the need to properly handle them gets increasingly pressing until it is painful. I haven't placed a tumor in a week, and I don't think I can go another day. I have seven tumors to dispose of before the discomfort eases."

"How do you get them?"

"The Demon Oma distributes them. They appear in a special box I have. This box." She held up a small ornate closed container. She popped the lid open, and showed the tiny seed inside. "This is a medium one for Rabbit to handle. But he's already backlogged, so I left it in the box for now. Tomorrow there will be another. We never see the Demon Oma himself, just his handiwork."

"Do you have specific folk to give them to, or is that your choice?"

"It's our choice, to a degree. My sense directs me to a suitable prospect, but I don't have to use that one. But it can be awful finding a different one."

"Are these prospects deserving of this fate?"

"No! Most of them are innocent folk. Not good or bad, just average. They don't deserve to suffer horribly and die. We've been searching out bad people to give the tumors to, but the average person is a mixture of qualities so that it's just sort of a mishmash. There's a little poem I heard once that illustrates it. 'There's so much good in the worst of us / And bad in the best of us / It ill behooves the most of us / To talk about the rest of us.' Only we're not here to talk about it, but to select a few for what can be an awful fate. We hate it! But we have to do it. We have to—" She broke off, plainly on the verge of tears.

"You have to pee," he said. "But what happens if you hold it until you burst?"

"The seeds fly out randomly and infect the closest folk, who may be downright *good* people. We can't do that."

"If you quit the job, what happens? Apart from losing your magical powers?"

"We can't quit when we're backlogged. We're locked in." She smiled wanly. "Like having a muscle spasm when you want to pee. You just can't do it. When we are caught up, then we could quit. Then a new Incident and new animals would be selected, and the job would continue. No one would benefit, except maybe the new crew with its immortality and all, while we fade and die in the mortal manner, and finally go to Hell for eternity anyway." She was clearly near tears. He wanted to comfort her, but had no idea how, and probably she didn't want it from an ugly killer golem like him anyway.

"And somehow the Good Magician thought that putting us together would solve our problems," he said. "Instead of compounding them."

"Somehow," she agreed, and the three animals nodded. They didn't speak, but they understood, and had been following the conversation. They were in the same sinking boat.

"Maybe he has a weird sense of humor."

"Maybe. I understand that all he does is grump, so it's hard to tell. Anyway, we looked for the worst people to give the seeds to, but there's a limit of one to a person and we're running out of them."

"I never thought about it before," Goar said. "But I suppose it is true that something has to deliver the tumors people get. Now I know."

Incident shook her head. "It's a huge business. We handle just the incidental tumors, the ones that are discovered only by accident. Most others make themselves known when they make their hosts sicken. That is often too late."

"Incidental. Your name is Incident. Is that a coincidence?"

"Not at all. As a Sylph I was Elle. Incident is my business name, which I share with the others in this business."

"The folk you give them to—are they all Xanthians?"

"Oh no. They are mostly Mundanes, because there are a whole lot more of them, and they lack magic defensive wards and healing elixirs and such."

"But you are here in Xanth. How do you get to the Mundanes?"

She smiled. It did not help her appearance. "That is part of what the animals do. They can travel between realms when they need to. Mundania pretty much parallels Xanth. So we orient on a given Mundane from here, then one of my associates takes the tumor and tunnels through to deposit the seed. The victim never even knows. Maybe years later he will accidentally discover it, and by then it may be also be too late." She sighed. "The Mundanes mostly think it is just chance. They don't even believe in magic. That shown how deadly dull they are."

"Why not just give them to folk who are about to die of something else, so they have no real effect?"

"That's way too easy! One of the requirements is that a seed must grow and mature into a tumor that eventually kills its host. Otherwise it doesn't count. In fact, sometimes we get rejections, when the host body simply won't accept the seed, because that host won't live long enough for the tumor to prosper. The seeds are able to sense the potential."

"That's ugly."

"And so are we. But we're stuck with it. It is depressing." It was indeed. Then Goar got an idea. "Is there any way that a tumor seed could be a benefit to a person, instead of a liability?"

"A benefit? I don't see how."

"Maybe if someone were dying of something else, like a witch's curse or an inflamed brain, not only painful but making him crazy, but he stood to endure years of it before he inevitably died. The right tumor might take him out much faster, sparing him pain. It would be a mercy."

"I never thought of that! I wouldn't mind placing some seeds for that." She glanced at the animals, and they nodded. "Let's go find some positive placements!"

"What, now?"

"What better time? I don't want to burst."

He thought of the urine analogy, winced at the thought of flying pee, and kept his mouth shut.

They set off on a mercy tumor delivery. Now he saw Incident and the animals in action. She closed her eyes, turned slowly around, and oriented roughly north. "The first prospect is some distance away," she announced. "We'd better fly."

"Fly? I understand that Mundanes have big noisy flying machines, but we don't. Unless you have a levitation spell—"

"We have better than that. Remember how I needed to recruit one flying, one racing, and one crawling animal?"

"Yes, but Bird can't—"

"He can change form to become any kind of bird, and more if he has to."

"Yes, but that won't help the rest of us."

She glanced at the bird. "Do your thing, birdie."

The small bird spread his wings, flew out to the nearest open space in the forest, then changed. To a roc.

Goar gaped. The hugest of all birds! Large enough to carry a Mundane elephant in each talon. He hadn't thought of that.

They trotted out to rejoin the big bird. The roc spread his wings out on the ground so that they could mount them like feathery hills and settle down on his downy back. "But is it safe?" Goar asked. "We could readily fall off. Any little gust could dump us."

"He will be careful," Incident said. "And of course we'll hold on. Grab a flight feather." She demonstrated by taking hold of a massive feather. "Don't let go while we're aloft."

"I won't," he agreed fervently, taking hold of a second huge feather.

Rabbit wrapped all four limbs around a third feather, and Turtle locked his powerful jaws on a fourth. None of them would be dislodged.

"Ready, Bird!" Incident called.

The monstrous wings drew in, lifted off the ground, then pumped down and spread again. The whole body shuddered with the effort. A second heave, and a third. Then the body lifted up with the huge feet supporting it on the ground. They ran along the land; Goar could feel the echoes of their pounding proceeding like tsunami waves through the flesh of the body and down the back to the gargantuan tail. He couldn't see any of it directly, but the vibrations were like secondary eyes that enabled him to picture it.

The head came up as the wings thrust down again. The body lifted.

They were airborne! He felt the eddy currents as they angled up to clear the trees at the edge of the clearing. Then it was nothing but open sky.

The ascent continued. How high were they going? Then at last they leveled off. Now they were traveling rather than taking off.

"Now we can look," Incident said. "Flight will be steady until the landing." She smiled again. "As a dragon would put it, the smoking light is on."

Goar opened his eyes and sat up. Indeed, there was no harsh wind tearing at him. Incident was already upright, though she kept firm hold on the feather with one hand. The two animals had anchored themselves similarly.

Goar looked around and down. Beyond the curve of the roc's back he saw the colorful landscape of Xanth. There were fields and forests, mountains and lakes, thickets and thinnets, and here and there, inset like gems, villages. Rivers coursed around the hills, seeking out the more comfortable valleys.

"Cloud alert," Incident said.

He looked ahead. They were flying right toward a small cloud that was floating at the same elevation. They plunged into it, and fog surrounded them. The vapor seemed to slow the big bird slightly but not dangerously. In two and a half moments they were out the other side.

Goar looked back. The cloud, disturbed, looked dark, and little jags of lightning radiated from its surface. But they were already out of its reach.

So it formed into a big male bottom in the shape of the moon and flashed them. A female pantied bottom would have been interesting, but this one was insulting, and the insult reached out and smote them so hard that the roc suffered a buffet as if struck by an errant gust of wind. They all had to hang on as Bird struggled to regain his course.

"I'd like to give that nasty cloud a tumor," Goar muttered.

A small fleet of dragons came into sight, evidently looking for some fun, but the roc eyed them warningly and they sheared off. It was a mighty big bird.

Then they angled downward. It was time for the landing.

In due course they glided into a glade and landed with only a minimal jolt. The passengers dismounted, and Bird became sparrow sized and perched on Incident's shoulder.

"That was impressive, Bird," Goar said.

"Chirp."

"This way," Incident said, and led them to a weedy forest pond. The weeds formed the letter C.

"That's C Weed," Goar said. "What's it doing so far from the sea?"

"Just marking the spot, as it happens," Incident said. "The Mundane with the chronically inflamed brain that keeps him in misery is in a hospital cell at this spot in Mundania. Rabbit will tunnel through to make the delivery."

Indeed, Rabbit was already digging a hole beside the pond, that would evidently slant down to intercept the Mundane location.

"Those must be some rabbit holes," Goar said.

"It is just part of his magic. He delivers the medium fast seeds himself, and makes holes for Bird and Turtle for the others."

"They have different speeds?"

"Oh, yes. Bird delivers the fastest ones, that will take out a person before anything can be done to stop it. Rabbit delivers the medium ones, that can be stopped if folk discover them in time and act immediately. Turtle delivers the slow ones that probably won't act before something else does. But they will get there if given time."

"I am impressed, again. I'd like to see a delivery."

Incident shook her head, making her dirty brown locks bang unattractively. "The hole is too small for you, and you wouldn't want to be seen there anyway."

"Maybe if he took my cam."

"Your what?"

"My web camera." He produced it. "The webbing clings to clothing or whatever, and the lens takes the pictures."

Incident shrugged. "We can ask him. But we need to key him in. When he appears, you say 'Where is the Updoc?'"

"Does this make sense?"

"Just trust me. Do it."

What could he lose? This whole business seemed to be getting nowhere anyway. "Very well."

"Okay with you, Rabbit?" Incident called.

Rabbit emerged from the hole and hopped to her with a questioning look. She in turn glanced at Goar.

"Where's the Updoc?" Goar asked. Following the script.

Rabbit transformed into a large comic-style hare standing on his hind feet and eyed Goar. "What's Updoc?"

"This is Beetle Bunny," Incident said. "His comic version. He can talk, but he seldom has anything serious to say."

Oh. Now Goar was beginning to make some sense of this. Incident had caused the rabbit to transform into a variant who could respond in human language. "I have a magic web cam I would like you to take with you when you make your delivery. It will let us see your action. Are you amenable to carrying it?"

Beetle Bunny looked at Incident. She nodded affirmatively. Now it was Rabbit's turn to trust her. He turned back to Goar. "Sure, doc."

Goar extended the cam. "Put it anywhere on your body where it won't get in your way. Then ignore it. But remember, we will be seeing your scene. You have no privacy."

Beetle took the cam and put it on his chest. Incident gave him the tumor seed. Then he transformed back to Rabbit. Then he dived into the hole.

A picture formed in the air above the hole. It showed the tunnel ahead. "This is a holo image," Goar explained. "When it seemed that I had failed to kill the two I had been sent after, Larry and Squid, my masters dictated that I wear the cam and do the deed again, so they could be sure that I really did it this time. Now my masters are gone, but perhaps the cam will still be useful."

"I have not seen the like," Incident said.

"It is Mundane-style holo technology, not much seen in Xanth. You can think of it as a kind of magic mirror."

"That's easier," she agreed.

Meanwhile the scene was changing. The tunnel opened into a square room where a Mundane man lay groaning on a bed, obviously in terrible pain, but no one was ministering to him. A paw reached out and set the seed on his shoulder, where it quickly dug in. That was Rabbit, out of sight because he was behind the cam.

The view spun about and entered a hole in the wall. Rabbit was returning to Xanth, having completed his mission. Soon he emerged from the hole, and the holo image faded out.

There really had not been much to see, but Goar's curiosity was satisfied. He had seen how a lethal tumor reached its victim. It wasn't nice, but it was efficient. Incident and the three animals were as much killers as Goar, just more subtle about it. They wanted out as much as he did.

The other deliveries were similar. They used up the backlog of seeds, until only one was left. Incident focused, and faced a new direction. "Uh-oh."

"There is a problem?"

"Yes. There is a suitable prospect there, but that is the direction of the sub-realm of the Goddess Isis. She is not one to mess with."

"You are not invulnerable to her?"

"Oh, we Oma are, physically. But she is, among other things, the Goddess of Sex, and her teasing can be quite embarrassing, particularly since we are ugly."

"How does that make a difference?"

"When a pretty person is ensorceled into performing a sexual act in public, it can be interesting and even gratifying to bystanders, who may envy the participants. But the same act performed by an ugly person could make her a laughingstock."

"You would be the person?"

"Yes. We have met before, and Isis doesn't like me because of my business. She can't hurt me physically, but if she catches me in her domain, she might cause me to do something that I may never live down. Like seducing one of my animals."

"Would it help if I remonstrated with her, with my blades out? She might reconsider if I sliced off one of her arms."

Incident considered. "Maybe the threat of that would set her back, even though the damage would not be permanent for a Goddess. I might accomplish my mission while you occupied her attention."

"Maybe that is why the Good Magician put us together. To facilitate your business. But there is a problem: I don't want to do more evil."

"And neither do I. But this particular one is a masked blessing."

"True. So I will help you. I will try to distract the goddess so you can accomplish it."

"Thank you. But I recommend caution. She can be devious."

"Caution," he agreed. But he wondered how devious Isis could be in the face of whirling blades. They were not very subtle things.

"Now let's go see the Goddess. Bird, take us southeast," Incident said. "You know where Isis hangs out."

The roc reappeared, and soon they were on their way.

Chapter 5

TIAMAT

They landed beside a kind of translucent curtain that extended from the ground to the sky. "The Goddess Isis is physically confined in her own environment," Incident explained. "Because she does not necessarily accept the existing order of Xanth. She can visit the rest of it spiritually by borrowing an amenable host for a while, and sometimes she does."

"Why would a regular girl accept a foreign spirit running her life, even just for a few hours?"

"If she is plain, the Goddess can make her sexy enough to seduce any man, and even some women. There are those willing to make that deal." She smiled sadly. "If I saw a man I just had to have for an hour, I'd make it. I miss being beautiful."

Goar considered that from the male perspective. If he could become temporarily handsome and sexy by hosting a foreign spirit, there might be occasions when that would appeal. "I appreciate your point."

"Actually, you might intrigue her," Incident said. "You have an unusual history. Also, some beautiful women are fascinated by ugly men."

"Any Goddess who wants to be fascinated by me is welcome."

"However—"

"I know. Caution."

They pushed through the curtain and were in the realm of Isis. It was much like the rest of Xanth. Somehow he had expected more.

There was a swirl ahead of them, and a phenomenally lovely woman appeared. She wore a low-cut, high-hemmed dress with a very tight bodice that threatened to pop her ample breasts up and out like pumpkin seeds, and her dark tresses curled around her shoulders like living things.

"Incident!" she exclaimed. "You must have excellent reason to show your ugly face here."

"I have a routine call to make, Goddess," Incident replied evenly. "And I thought you might like to meet my friend Goar Golem."

Isis oriented on Goar with disconcerting intensity. "You are an interesting one. Complete with several of the Good Magician's socks that Sofia has sorted. She must have liked you." She returned her gaze to Incident. "Very well, Oma filly, proceed about your business and begone before I finish with the golem."

They had a deal just like that? Incident sent Goar one more Caution look, then she and the animals walked away, intent on their mission. He had been passed off to the Goddess.

"I saw that look," Isis said. "But you have no need to be cautious with me, Goar. If I wanted to seduce you, I would do so." Her features intensified as her dress shrank, becoming so sexy he was in danger of freaking out. Yes, she could seduce him! If she wanted to.

She faded back to her original aspect, still quite sexy but not overwhelmingly so. She clearly could fine-tune the level of appeal. He was a little sorry she was not interested in proving her point. Just the passing glimpse of her supercharged self had put an urgent notion into his mind, as she surely knew. She was teasing him.

"Whatever," he agreed uncertainly. So what *did* she want of him?

"A day or so back I heard from an anonymous acquaintance who advised me that I might find a certain golem interesting. I would have dismissed that out of hand, but he slipped me several small artifacts that I found most intriguing. It is hard to buy the favor of a Goddess, as we are largely immune to bribes, but these items were quite amusing, and I shared them with a friend. So now I am obliged to follow through. You are evidently that golem."

"I know nothing of this," Goar said uneasily.

"Indeed. You are ignorant. That is part of the appeal."

Why was she giving him this attention? He didn't trust it or her. But he was supposed to distract her while Incident completed her business here. "What do you want of me?"

"I have a visitor," she answered as if reading his mind, which she might indeed be doing. "I want her to feel welcome, and you just might fill the slot." There was something about her tone that would have made him blush, had he been capable of it. "Her name is Tiamat, and she is a Goddess like me." She pronounced it TYA-mat. "I hail from ancient Egypt, while she is from Akkad, next door to the north, as it were. We've known each other a while, ten thousand years or so, and have parallel interests. She is the mother of the early gods as well as of the monsters, including especially the dragons. But the old order changes, and new deities have come to rule the day." She sighed. "I remember when Yahweh was just an idea in a primitive wandering tribe's fancy. Who would have thought he would ever rise so high? Anyway, Tiamat needs a new home, and this might be the place, if it suits her taste. I would like to have her resumed company. But of course she needs the right male. Would you like to meet her?"

"I am no god!" Goar protested.

"All she needs is someone to play with for a while. She will surely be gentle."

As if gentleness had ever applied to him. How long did Incident need to place that seed? Isis had mentioned playing; she was clearly playing with him, verbally, so far. "For a while," he agreed. "But I am not much for playing games with anyone. I am not the type." An understatement.

"Excellent." There was no transition, but suddenly he found himself walking along a path through a rocky plain toward a distant castle. That must be where the Goddess Tiamat dwelt during her visit.

His foot scuffed a fist-sized stone. The thing cracked open and a creature scrambled out. It quickly expanded to chicken size, flexing its wings and tail. It was a baby dragon!

Then it oriented on Goar and shot out a line of fire that toasted his face-plate. He reacted automatically. He ripped off his gloves and revved up his saws. "Ease off, reptile. Don't make me hurt you." When the dragon did not retreat, instead inhaling for another shot, he sliced off its tail, then its legs, then its head. The pieces fell to the ground, quivering before they expired.

But the incident had evidently shaken up other stones, which it seemed were not rocks but eggs. Dragonlets of all types and sizes were bursting out of their shells and orienting on him.

Had he taken a wrong turn? It was Tiamat he was looking for, not a passel of dragons. Yet this was where he found himself, evidently guided by Isis. Had she sent him into mischief instead of an interview? Or had she made a mistake? Regardless, this was where he was, and he would have to make the best of it.

The little dragons advanced on him menacingly. They surrounded him, so there was no escape, had that been his preference.

"Begone, dragonlets," he warned. "I am no safe target for attack. I will destroy any who attempt it."

But the little monsters were heedless. They closed the remaining gap and tackled his legs with fire and teeth.

So be it. Goar lifted his saws and waded into them. Heads and tails and legs and segments of torso flew everywhere, and blood spattered the landscape. In under ten moments he had slaughtered them all.

But this turned out to be only the beginning. He was evidently in the dragon nesting area, where the eggs could slowly mature in the warm sunlight. Now the grown dragons were arriving, and they seemed distinctly unpleased by what had happened to their offspring. They charged.

"Beware, dragons," he called. "I have no inherent quarrel with you. I am merely traveling to yon castle. Let me be and I will let you be."

They showed no sign of letting him be. They swarmed at him.

He sighed. Some folk had no appreciation for restraint, taking it as cowardice. He revved up his saws.

First came an airborne fire breather. It fired a searing blast at Goar that heated his armor and scorched the ground behind him. He leaped up as it passed close overhead after strafing him, and sliced it across the belly. It chugged on, leaking fuel, until it crashed some distance beyond and exploded in a ball of fire.

Then a ground-borne steamer was before him, hissing out a superheated jet that coated his armor in boiling water. He leaped directly at its snout, evidently surprising it, and lopped off the end of its nose. It tried to stifle the escaping steam, but that only resulted in the pressure building up and blowing its head apart. Two down.

Then came a smoker, with cloyingly thick smoke that formed a cloud he could not see through. But he whirled his saws where he judged it should be, and when the dragon tried to bite him, its tongue and teeth sprayed out, soon followed by the rest of its head. Now it was only a quivering mound of smoked flesh.

The next was an ice dragon, its freezing breath coating him with ice. But he was still hot from the prior dragons, and the ice melted. He kneed it with his knee spike, puncturing its neck, then sawed the creature's head in half lengthwise, and it collapsed into a mound of frozen meat.

Finally, he faced a gas dragon. A hideous stench surrounded him, reminiscent of rotten eggs soaked in flatulence in a ripening decay pit, tended by an ill skunk with plenty of spoiling vomit. Fortunately, his breathing mechanism featured assorted filters and toxic gas nullifiers. He angled his spinning saws to blow the surrounding air upward and away until he could see clearly enough to chop the beast's head into thin slices that would quickly decay into fertilizer. Then he moved on to find a deep river. He plunged in and washed himself off, seeing the remaining gas bubbling as it reacted with the water. Several fish approached. "I wouldn't," he said, but they took bites of it anyway and quickly flopped belly up, sickened to death.

At last, more or less clean, he emerged to resume his trek toward the castle. No more dragons attacked him. It seemed he had made his point.

He revved up his treads and accelerated, covering the ground rapidly. Soon he was at the castle gate. He did not bother to put the socks back on his head or arms or legs; if the Goddess Tiamat was paying any attention at all, she now knew his nature.

"Open up!" he called at the gate. "Or I'll saw my way in."

"No need to do that, warrior," a dulcet voice said as the gate opened. Another dragon came into sight, this one inside the castle. He wasn't certain what kind it was, as he saw no fire, smoke, steam, or ice, and the smell was of perfume rather than sick sewage. It had shining golden scales on its body, and thick black hair on its horned head. It was unlike any other dragon he had seen, and rather comely in a serpentine way.

"I came to see Tiamat," he said. "The Goddess Isis sent me."

"I am she." The dragon slowly transformed into a transcendently lovely human woman with the same black tresses and small iridescent horns on her head.

Goar gaped. "You surprise me," he said after most of a moment.

"I am the mother of dragons. Those were my eggs you disturbed."

This was bad. "I didn't know. Isis told me you were the mother of dragons, but I didn't make the connection. I tried to warn them off, but they would not be dissuaded. I apologize."

"Be not concerned. They attacked you. You defended yourself. That is to be respected."

"But if they are your children—"

She lifted a delicate hand to stay him. "Children can be vicious, mine more than most. This was an ad hoc examination to see how you handled yourself, to verify my friend Isis's judgment. It is clear that you do not fear physical attacks."

"I do not," Goar agreed. He was still keeping caution in mind, knowing that goddesses were far less like ordinary women than they might choose to appear. What did she really want of him?

"Come walk with me, warrior." She reached out as if to take his hand.

But of course his hand was a circular saw. He quickly put the socks back on his head, arms, and legs, so that he had a hand to take and feet to walk with. Then he accepted her hand. "As you wish, Goddess."

She smiled. "Nicely done, Goar. Call me Tiamat."

"Tiamat," he agreed.

The castle faded out, and they were on a path through a forest of giant trees. Tiamat squeezed his newly formed hand evocatively. "Do you have any children?"

"None. I am not sure this golem body is capable of siring children."

"It is capable, when appropriately evoked."

"And in any event, I have not had a girlfriend." He shrugged awkwardly. "Not that any woman would be interested in me in that manner." Not that he needed to tell her that; it was obvious.

"Incident Oma is interested. But her appearance is a turnoff."

She knew about Incident? "True, and so is mine."

"Here is a hint: try chips of reverse wood."

Could that actually work? "They don't necessarily reverse things in the manner anticipated."

"True. But if you get a collection of chips you may be able to select from different varieties, to obtain the effect desired. You can each appear appealing, at least for long enough."

This was distinctly intriguing. "I will ask her if she wishes to try that."

"She surely will. Being an Oma is a lonely business. You are the first male she has encountered since she lost her Sylph status who might be remotely interested."

The Caution flag was waving in his mind. "Why are you directing our dialogue in this direction?"

She smiled, and it enhanced her beauty so that even the horns were esthetic. "Because you interest me, and I may wish to help you."

"Why should I interest you? You are a lovely goddess. I am an ugly golem."

"True again. But Goddesses get lonely too."

He noted how her Goddess was capitalized, while his goddess could take or leave the capital. "You can ensorcel any man you choose. You don't need to mess with a patchwork golem like me."

"True yet again. I could enchant you too, but it wouldn't be the same."

This was suspicious, but also wickedly intriguing. "The same as what?"

"The same as genuine passion. I prefer to seduce my males voluntarily. I would rather have you do it because you understand the situation and truly want to do it."

"Do what?" But of course he knew *what*. He just didn't understand *why*. The Caution flag was practically rigid in the wind.

"But of course you've never done it," she said wisely. "Even when you were physically human."

"Never," he agreed. He had been young, then transformed. She could evidently read his mind, and that was more unsettling than a charging dragon.

"Nice analogy," she murmured. "I proffer you this deal: dialogue with me, hear my history, and in return I will teach you the beastly mechanics. Then you will need have no more fear of erotic passion than of a charging dragon."

"Beastly mechanics? I thought those were the creatures who work repairing Mundane vehicles."

"Not precisely. They are the physical portion of a highly emotional interaction." She squeezed his hand again. "Men are expected to be proficient in them, so that women don't have to sacrifice any more of their delightful innocence than strictly necessary. Of course Goddesses are adept at simulating innocence."

This was confusing. "At what?"

"Faking it."

Oh. “We can talk,” he agreed uncertainly. He had seen her transform from dragon to human, so there was no question that she was a powerful magical creature, but her seeming interest in him was disarming.

Meanwhile the forest path had led them to a glade with a lovely pool. There were two wooden deck chairs angling partly toward each other and partly toward the sparkling water. They took seats.

Goar discovered that he was now wearing swimming trunks, his torso and limbs otherwise bare but still human. This was more of her sorcery, of course. A goddess was not limited to a single magic talent; she could do almost anything she chose, and illusion was relatively easy.

Now he noticed that Tiamat’s dress had become a two-piece swimsuit featuring a scant halter and a very short skirt. His eyes were first attracted to the former, where they were channeled into a softly flexing cleavage. Then to the latter, where they coursed across the firm flesh of her lifted leg to the compelling shadow under the garment. It was as if she had his attention on a leash and was leading it hither and yon. Hither was fascinating and yon was seductively compelling. Or was it yoni?

“It isn’t easy being an ancient Goddess,” she said. “When I started, there were few established protocols. I had to define many parameters for myself.”

He opened his mouth to express his confusion about the unfamiliar words, but she responded before the words made it past his teeth.

“Protocols: the customs for dealing with particular things. Parameters: special boundaries. I am saying there were not many rules, so I had to make them up as I went along.”

That was still not entirely clear. He was about to ask for a further clarification, but she shifted her legs slightly and his gaze and his attention were compelled to their dark juncture. This time his question never made it out of his throat. She had thrown him into a controlled half freak. She was expert at distraction.

“It goes back to Creation,” she said. “There was neither land nor gods nor men. There were only two elements, called Apsu and Tiamat. Apsu was the male spirit of fresh water and of the void. Tiamat was the female spirit of salt-water and primeval chaos. She was the first dragon, a monstrous creature with a scaly serpentine body, stout legs, and horns on her head, and her awesome image has haunted mankind ever since.” She smiled again, compellingly. "I am of course the personification of that spirit, hardly an ordinary girl. I am merely an aspect. Not that it matters."

"Not that it matters," he agreed, basking in that aspect. The Caution flag was fading. He knew her for what she was, and liked her.

"But Apsu commanded the potable, that is, drinkable, water, especially the two great rivers that flowed south defining the first civilization, merge and surge into the sea. There, where the fresh liquid thrust into the salt cavity, was generated our offspring: the first gods of the primordial, that is, early, universe. The first monsters. The first dragons. The new world was forming.

"But all was not well. Children can be unruly at best, and little monsters at worst. These were young gods, with fantastic powers, and they thought they could do whatever they wanted, and nobody had the right to tell them no. They did not heed their parents' cautions; indeed the very notion of discipline was foreign to them. When Apsu tried to restrain them, they sassed him back. He complained to me how their ways were loathsome to him; that he could get no relief from their mischief by day or night. Finally, he had had enough. 'I am sorry I ever sired these wretches. I will destroy them, so that quiet can be restored.' I pleaded with him for our children's lives, but he was adamant, and I could not blame him, for they were bad seed."

Goar remembered his own childhood. Indeed, there were such things as bad children: he had been one of them. Had his own parents had a similar dialogue?

Then he was seeing and hearing it, there in the scene.

"Please, dear, they're just children," Tiamat pleaded. "They don't know any better. But when they mature, they'll improve."

"They won't improve," Goar answered grimly. "They've had too many chances already, and spurned them."

"But how can you hurt your own children?"

"It has to be done. I will destroy them. Then we can try again, for better offspring."

She could not refute that prospect. She watched him go, tears in her eyes.

But one of the young gods had been listening at the window. He spread the word. When Goar came to the children's house and bared his sword, they leaped from the surrounding bushes and charged him in a mass.

They threw a net over him so he could not move freely, then bound him up tightly with ropes. He was helpless.

The brats consulted. Then they came to a decision. They took turns hacking at him with his own sword, cutting him into thin slices, until at last he expired. Then they roasted the slices and had a feast. They were the new lords of the universe!

But they had not reckoned on his ghost. Unseen, it slipped away and flew to Tiamat. "My dear," he whispered, for that was as much sound as he could make without a body. "They killed me. I am done for. You must avenge me." Then he faded out.

Goar came out of it with a shock. The brats had killed him!

Then he went back into the history, listening to Tiamat's narration. As a faded ghost he could no longer manifest or speak, but he could watch.

Tiamat was beside herself with grief. Then she rallied, determined to avenge Apsu's death. She knew better than to approach the children's house. Instead she spawned another brood, a veritable army of ferocious monsters: giant serpents, roaring dragons, demon lions, scorpion men, and centaurs.

But the child gods had spies, and were well aware of their mother's plan. They plotted their own strategy for the inevitable battle. They decided that single combat would be best, publicly performed, so that both sides would accept the verdict. But whom could they marshal to stand up to their ferocious mother alone? They decided on the eldest and biggest and strongest: Marduk. He had the best chance.

But Marduk was reluctant. He knew how deadly Tiamat was, and was not at all sure he could defeat her in fair combat. So he stalled. He told the others that he would do it only if, upon his victory, he would be recognized as king of the universe. While they were considering that, he set about gathering the most deadly weapons he could find. He did not settle on just one; he got a bow and arrows, the points tipped with deadly poison. A powerful club with barbed spikes. An invisible fishing net like the one that had snared Apsu. A poisonous plant whose very nearness could stun anyone who had not first taken the antidote, as he had. And a concealed lightning bolt that could fry anyone it touched, once invoked.

Then he set out on a storm chariot, escorted by the four winds. He was, after all a god; he deserved a suitable retinue.

Meanwhile Tiamat, obsessed by her grief over the death of her consort Apsu, had not taken proper precautions. The watching ghost saw this, and wanted to warn her of the danger, but could not.

Marduk met Tiamat on an open plain. They exchanged routine insults. "You thankless brat!" she said. "How sharper than a servant's tooth is the scorn of a thankless son."

"You overbearing she-dog!" he retorted. "You deserve nothing but further scorn."

Then, the protocol satisfied, they fought. Marduk was better armed, but Tiamat was more experienced, and it was even. Until he managed to brush her with the poison plant, making her reel. Then he unlimbered the lightning bolt and fried her with it. His trick weapons had made the difference, and she was dead.

Actually, she wasn't completely dead, because as a goddess she was immortal, but her physical presence was now banned from Akkad. She would have to find a new locale, where she had not died, and where the people might accept her and believe in her. Meanwhile Marduk went on to be the King of the Universe as it existed then. Opinions differed on how good he was or was not, but the ill-gotten power was his.

"And thus I came at last to this Land of Xanth," Tiamat concluded. "It has been a long search."

Goar emerged from the setting of her history. "You were ill-treated," he said. "Your children should never have rebelled, simply because you and Apsu wanted to enforce some discipline."

"I am glad you understand," she said. "Now I shall repay you for your courtesy in giving me a fair hearing, by showing you how to be a great lover."

"I am interested," he agreed. Indeed, experiencing her history had warmed him to her nature. He liked her, and wanted to be closer to her. He knew she was thousands of years old, but as a Goddess she was ageless, and exceedingly shapely.

"First you must compliment your lover," she murmured. "You must tell her how beautiful she is, and how much you value her."

"You are the most beauteous woman I have seen," he said, and it was no lie, because he had not seen many and had gotten only a brief glimpse of the Goddess Isis.

"I am indeed," she agreed, kissing him on the cheek. "Continue."

"I really value you, and—" But he had run out of things she had told him to tell her.

"Perhaps we should cut to the chase," she murmured in his ear. Wearing the headsock he had regular ears. The sock no longer showed, but the ears remained. "You wish to see more of me."

"I wish to see more of you," he echoed. That was actually an understatement.

Her swimsuit diminished to a string halter and g-string, uncovering her matchless torso. "Of course." She kissed his ear, and sweet music sounded.

He gazed at her exposed body, on the verge of freaking out. He wanted to wrap his arms around it and draw it in even closer to his own body. He wanted to put his head against the valley of her frontal cleavage and kiss the twin soft mounds.

"You may do so," she murmured. "After you kiss my lips, so as to pretend that my face is my primary appeal."

He obeyed, setting his rough metallic lips against her soft dainty ones. He felt as if he were floating into the sky.

After a timeless instant she drew back a bit. "Now if you want to explore my bare bosom . . ."

But then the Caution flag made a last desperate effort. "Why should a Goddess ever want to mess with a passing golem?" he demanded. "You are everything while I am nothing." He knew he was understating the case, but could not find the proper terms.

"You now know my history," she replied without evasion. "I desire a manly consort who can't be killed by rebellious ungrateful children, and who will be true to me forever after once he chooses me."

"I can't guarantee that. I don't know my future."

"But I do, at least in this limited respect. If you choose me, you will be loyal. Meanwhile, I mean to give you every chance with Incident that I can, so that if it doesn't work out with her, you will know that I was not the cause of any mischief between the two of you."

"You want me to court Incident?" he asked incredulously.

"Yes. Because she is your fated partner, and not even a Goddess can change that. It is in the Master Script. But if the unlikely happens, like untimely death or a rogue amnesia cloud, and you do not make it with her, and have no other prospects, come to me as a last resort."

"A last resort? Why?"

"Because then you will know you have no other alternative, and will stay with me forever. It is that ultimate loyalty I crave. I am tired of betrayals."

"How can you be sure I won't attack you in a fit of whatever? I am a killer golem. You know how dangerous I am."

"I do know. But I know also that you have a conscience. You won't attack a person without cause."

That was true, now. "Still—"

"And you have no desire for power or notoriety. You just want to clear your guilt for your prior killings. I can help you with that, given time. You will certainly do for a paramour."

She had him pretty well defined. Still, there was a doubt. "But what of, of—" he hesitated, then used a word he had only heard, but could not begin to know the meaning of. "Love?"

"Love is not integral to my agenda. It dawns, flowers, and fades in the mortal realm. A long-term relationship is best forged without it."

He realized that she was eminently practical. Permanent loyalty probably was safer than passing love. And, as last resorts went, she was not bad at all. The Caution flag gave up the ghost and faded out entirely. "I will go to see about Incident."

She bit his ear, not painfully but playfully, sending a thrill through his head. "Not yet, golem. You are not yet ready."

"But you told me to—"

"To court her," she agreed. "But you must do so competently. I mean to see that if you lose her, it won't be because you are a poor lover."

What did he know about loving? Next to nothing.

"Precisely," she agreed. "Now to those beastly mechanics. The object of this exercise for the male is to insert Tab A into Slot B, as it were."

"A and B?" he asked, befuddled.

The rest of their scant clothing evaporated. She stood revealed in her remarkable splendor. She approached him. "This is A" she said, touching it briefly. "This is B." She poked her finger into herself.

Oh. Where they each urinated.

"Not exactly. The body can have more than one use for a particular part."

Still he did not see the point. "Is there a reason for this odd action?"

"It is the female's object to cause the male to want to perform this act, which is integral to procreation. That is, making babies. Perhaps it is time for the first demonstration."

"I don't see why," he began.

Then her body shifted not so much in outline but in atmosphere. It had been stunningly shapely before; abruptly became so compelling that his thoughts disappeared and he found himself clasping her and jamming Tab A into Slot B, she cooperating with finesse. Suddenly, there was more pleasure than he had ever known or even imagined before, followed immediately by a volcanic eruption and potent surge of burning lava.

"Oh my," he panted as the last of the lava completed its urgent journey.

"Indeed," she agreed. "That delivery should generate several fine monsters, fire breathers all. But you need have no concern about the details that follow. Now we shall try it another way."

Their brief interaction had left him pleasantly exhausted. "But I thought it was finished. Nothing could match it today."

She kissed him. He floated again.

"You forget that a Goddess can make a man perpetually potent. Now there are numerous positions and frameworks for the merging of Tab and Slot, and I will guide you through a fair sampling."

His fatigue vanished. He discovered that he was as eager as he had been before the first connection. In little more than half a moment he was holding her and erupting again. Then, restored, again. And again. Each time was remarkably different in detail, yet similar in pleasure. She was indeed a Goddess.

"Be sure to make mental notes," she murmured. "You never can tell when a particular variant is best. You want always to impress her with your competence."

His competence? This was all wonderfully new to him.

"And kiss her and compliment her between times," she said. "So she will think there are other things about her that you value. That it's not just her body."

Other things? What else could there possibly be to value beyond Tab and Slot?

Tiamat laughed. "Fake it."

Oh yes. She had explained about that. While she was faking innocence, he had to fake interest in things other than her hot bare body. "You have lovely eyes."

"Oh, I do? I never knew. Thank you so much for informing me." Then she kissed him and led him into another round.

Just so.

At last, she called a halt. "I believe you have the idea, Goar. You have done well. When the time comes, do this with Incident, starting with the most sincere compliments, and she will be yours. You can have endless pleasure, and she may like it somewhat too."

"Somewhat?"

"Women have different and sometimes inexplicable motives. The rule is that the man desires the woman, while the woman desires the desire of the man."

But first Incident had to become desirable. There was the catch. He really needed to find that reverse wood.

"She has a talent for locating the things she needs. Persuade her to orient on reverse wood. That should do it."

Goar was impressed. "Goddess, may I pay you an honest compliment?"

She frowned prettily. "Must you? You know that my only sincerity has been the need to educate you in the essential erotic forms, so that you will have your best chance at a normal relationship before you have to settle for the abnormal one I offer you as the last resort. Sincerity on your part could spoil the effect."

"I will risk it. Goddess, you are the best faker I can imagine. Even when you tell me the depressing truth, you remain so appealing that I think I would rather have that fakery than the real thing from any ordinary woman."

She gazed at him a good four fifths of a moment. Then a tear formed in her left eye. "Thank you, Goar. I don't believe I have ever been gifted with a more sincere compliment. Just for that I will give you something even more valuable than my advice." She pressed something onto his front plate.

"What is it? I don't see it."

"It is a chaos bomb. My friend Isis gave it to me. It's a charming toy. It will be invisible and inert until you need it. Then use your mind to hurl it forward."

"I don't understand."

"You don't need to, dear. Just remember when the time comes. Who knows, you might save the universe, or at least your hide."

"I still don't—"

But she cut him off with a kiss. There was a dizzy interlude.

He found himself walking away from the castle, garbed as he had been when he came here. Dragons were all around him, but none of them bothered him. They knew that he was, at present, one of them in a way that counted. Perhaps also the father of the next generation of monsters.

Then it occurred to him that the tear, too, might have been faked. But there was the slim chance that he had actually touched her ageless heart in a tiny way.

There is that chance, her thought agreed.

He had to smile. The Goddess was teasing him. But he liked it. Maybe she did too. Certainly, he had a new respect for Goddesses.

Thank you.

He looked ahead. There was Incident, ugly as ever, but now he saw an aura about her that showed the shape she could become if things worked out in the long term. Not as lovely as the Goddess, but quite good enough for him. "Ah, there you are!" she called. "Did you enjoy your visit with Tiamat?"

What could he tell her? The truth was hardly adequate, but it would have to do. "Yes."

"I placed the last seed," she said. "Thank you for providing me the time."

"You are welcome."

The Goddess Isis appeared. "Tiamat tells me you had a good interview, Goar. She likes you. She is seriously considering remaining here in Xanth. That means I will have compatible company. Thank you."

“She is a skilled interviewer,” Goar said. It was a huge understatement.

Isis laughed knowingly. “She is that,” she agreed. Naturally, she knew the nature of their dialogue, and wasn’t telling. Goddesses didn’t.

Chapter 6

WINGS

As soon as they were clear of the Goddess demesnes, or region, as Tiamat would have clarified it, Incident had questions. "What happened with Tiamat?"

This could be awkward. "Are you sure you want to know?"

"No! I fear I won't like it, and I'm jealous. Why does the Goddess like you? You distracted her for hours. That had to be more than just hello, how are you, I am fine, farewell. Goddesses are notorious."

Goar considered. "You are jealous? The Good Magician put us together, perhaps thinking that we could become a couple, but we agree that our ugliness prevents us from interesting each other in that manner. So we are not a couple, are we? What is there to be jealous about?"

"Oh, bleep, you caught me. We are not a couple, but we might become one later, if somehow we managed to become less ugly. So I am free to dream it just might maybe possibly theoretically someday happen. I'd like to have a boyfriend, or at least know it might perhaps incredibly come about someday. Girls are foolishly romantic, and I'm still a girl inside where it doesn't show. But if a Goddess fascinates you, that dream would be gone. So yes, I am jealous, even though I'm the one who set you up to make a distraction so we could place the last seed. Isis said Tiamat liked you. That couldn't be because she thought your face-plate was cute. Did you give her reason to like you?"

He was going to have to tell her, and hope it didn't blow their theoretical future relationship out of the water. "Can we talk? Maybe do more? Maybe even kiss?"

She looked at him doubtfully, maybe thinking he was joking. "Now?"

"Yes."

She glanced at the animals. "Take a break, friends. We might decide to kiss."

Bird, Rabbit, and Turtle shared a glance. They evidently appreciated humor when it came their way. Then they walked off to inspect an uninteresting clump of broken-down casual-trees.

Now alone with her, Goar nerved himself and tackled a dialogue that he feared would be more difficult than a swarm of attacking dragons. "Tiamat said that fantasy tradition means that when two people are put together as we were, it means that in time they will become a couple. She said I should court you, and—"

"Court me!"

He plowed on. "She told me how. And that if it didn't work out, I should consider her as the partner of last resort."

"The Goddess!"

"Yes. She told me how to approach you, by complimenting you. That is not hard to do, because I can see already that you have skill and dedication in your job. You even—" He broke off, fearing that he had the wrong words.

"I am listening," she said.

Was that good or bad? He would just have to play it through and hope for the best. "You even have dreams that I appreciate, and maybe share. You are a good person, caught in an ugly job. I know how that is."

"You think that saying that will make me want to kiss you?"

Was it going wrong? "I had hoped."

"Then kiss me."

She was agreeing? Best not to question it. He stepped up to her, took her in his arms, brought his socked face to her, closed his eyes, and kissed her in the manner he had so recently been taught: firmly, verging on passionately, as if he really enjoyed it. As if she were precious to him.

It wasn't exhilarating in the manner of Tiamat's kisses, but neither was it disgusting. It was almost halfway pleasant.

"You did it," she breathed. "You actually kissed me."

"I did."

"Competently."

"Thank you."

"The Goddess taught you how."

"Yes."

"What else did she teach you?"

Danger was looming again. "She said we should get reverse wood, of the right kind, to make us pretty to each other."

"I mean, in the line of courting."

He was afraid of that. "How to make love. The beastly mechanics."

She considered, smiling faintly. "I will find some reverse wood."

Now it was his turn to be taken aback. "Now?"

"Yes." She closed her eyes, turned around, and pointed. "There's some close by, that way."

They walked to it, and found several fragments, hardly more than sawdust. "She said there are different varieties, so the reversal might not be of a convenient type."

"I know about reverse wood. This is the right type. There's not enough to affect more than our upper torsos, and it will expire soon, but it should enable us to judge the prospective case."

They each took a fragment. Then they came together for another kiss. Her face, as he approached her, was beautiful, with large blue eyes and full lips. Her auburn hair was lustrous. He hoped his face was similarly handsome. Her upper body was no longer bent out of shape, but upright and steady, with a firm bosom, a pleasure to hold.

They kissed. This time it was more than adequate. In fact, it was quite enjoyable.

After a nice interlude they broke the kiss and looked at each other. "That worked," he said. "Maybe we can find more reverse wood, enough to cover our whole bodies."

"No. This was only a tryout, to verify the potential. It is definitely there. We must wait for the real thing before going farther." She brushed off her chip and returned to ugly.

Bleep. But he had been warned about this too. He had to evince interest in other things than her immediate body, if he wanted to get further access to that body. That was the paradox of the gender. "You are sensible." He brushed off his own chip.

She laughed, and it was pleasant. "I know your real interest. Every woman does, because it's the same for every man. But we have other things to do first." They resumed their walk.

Still, it was good progress.

Incident felt something. The little box appeared in her hand. She lifted the lid and glanced inside. "This one's for Turtle. At least it won't kill anyone soon." Then she put two fingers to her mouth and whistled. The three animals came back to rejoin them.

"For Turtle," Incident announced. She pointed. "That way. No hurry, but it would be best to get it placed before the next one arrives." She was back in business mode.

They walked that way—and soon came to a wandering crevasse. "Far side," Incident said. Turtle made a shell-shrug of frustration. Goar appreciated why. It would take half a moment short of forever to trudge all the way around that crack.

"Too bad the rest of us can't fly," Goar said.

"Actually, the other animals can," Incident said. "Rabbit can become any other mammal, including a bat, but it requires a lot of focus. Turtle can become any other reptile, such as a pterodactyl, but again it is tiresome, hardly worth it for a routine delivery. So we'll let Bird transform and carry us across."

"It would be easier if you and I could fly," Goar said. "Then we could carry Rabbit or Turtle across, in their small forms, no extra focus required. Too bad that's not possible."

Incident considered. "Now that notion may be worth playing with, as was the reverse wood. Let me orient." She closed her eyes and turned around in place. "That direction."

She had a way for them to fly?

But the way was also across the chasm.

"Okay, a two-purpose flight," she decided. "Deliver seed, fetch wings."

Bird became Roc, and the group crossed the chasm and continued on to the indicated site. It was in a village, so they landed, disembarked, Bird went small, and they waited in the woods while Turtle hauled shell to one of the huts and went inside.

"Maybe three-purpose," Incident said. "I know where there is a significant supply of reverse wood."

Goar took her gnarled hand and kissed it.

"Well, there's no sense in playing too hard to get," she said. "Not if I have a promising relationship on the line. Men have been known to wander when the chase becomes too difficult. An occasional night should be okay. Can't let the Goddess have all the fun."

He drew on her hand, bringing her closer. He kissed her mouth. It was fun despite their mutual ugliness. There was so much hope there!

"Maybe frequent nights," she concluded.

In due course Turtle returned. Soon they were airborne again. They cruised to a distant village, where the destination was an outlying old house. It was open, but wreathed in cobwebs; no one had lived there for some time. No villagers were in the vicinity.

They went inside, and Incident oriented on a concealed closet. Goar angled one saw and cut through the corroded bar that locked it closed. Inside, hanging on twin hooks, were two feathery backpacks. No wings.

"They're here," Incident said, lifting one pack down. She put it on her bare back and tightened the straps around her shoulders and waist. The pack was evidently meant to fit quite securely.

She walked outside and stood in the clearing. She focused.

Giant wings erupted from the pack. Two socks on strings dropped down, together with a feather cap. She put the two on her feet, and they became feather flippers. She put the cap on her head and it became a plumed crest. She was very like a bird, except that she lacked a tail.

Goar fetched the second pack. He put it on over his clothing, but nothing happened. Then he stripped, so that the pack touched flesh, and it responded. He, too, became a pseudo bird. But his arms had not converted to wings: the wings were anchored on his back and seemed to have separate muscles and nerves connecting them. He now had six limbs, including them, and he was sensing all of them. Incident was the same. As incidental spells went, this was a sophisticated one.

Welcome, user.

What?

Incident saw his started expression. "I got that too," she called. "The wings want to be used. When they lost their prior users, they were desolate. Now they are happy again."

It was true. Goar felt the joy of the wings. They seemed not to belong to anyone, but to be available for those in need. They had been borrowed by their prior users, and now were free for the two of them.

"Next stage," Incident said. She flapped her arm-wings, and lurched into the air off-balance, tumbling back to the ground. "Caw!" she screeched in avian irritation.

She recovered her footing and tried again, this time managing to hover awkwardly just above the ground, flapping furiously. Goar followed suit, every bit as clumsy as she, but he managed to stay slightly aloft without tumbling.

"Up, up, and away!" Incident cried, fluttering faster. She managed to lift half a modicum higher.

Goar followed, doing no better.

"Flying high into the sky," she said, striving to her utmost. She rose unsteadily to about waist height.

Goar had no better luck.

Bird shifted to eagle size and took his place before them. He launched into the air, moving his wings in elegant circles rather than straight up and down, so as to provide forward thrust as well as upward lift. In fact, the forward motion helped provide lift.

They imitated him, and began to navigate the air more efficiently. The wings were performing; the people merely had to learn how to use them properly. Their flipper feet helped steer them, in lieu of their missing tails. It was somewhat like swimming with water wings, a compromise in the different medium of air.

Soon they were at treetop height, increasingly competent, turning wide circles and gliding in rising air currents. Then, tired, they sank down to land to make bumpy but happy landings.

They came together and hugged.

They had their wings.

Now Goar saw his shed clothing on the ground. That wouldn't do; he might have to fly somewhere away from his starting point. He checked the straps, and discovered that the wide belt contained a pouch. He tried fitting his trousers into it, and not only did they fit, the belt did not bulge. It was one of those larger inside than outside devices, so useful when needed.

Incident was watching. "If I ever get pretty, I will need clothing, so as not to freak out passing men. It is good to know I can carry it with me."

Goar thought of what he hoped was the right response. "You could use some clothing now."

"I don't need it now. No one will get any ideas while I'm ugly."

He just looked at her.

"Though I suppose when I get the reverse wood . . ."

He continued to look.

She was incredulous. "You mean *now*?"

"An idea," he agreed. "Maybe not as much of one as when you're pretty, but you're still a bare girl to me. It's a distraction."

She glanced down at herself, and blushed from her face to her waist. Then she came to him and kissed him avidly. "I know you don't mean it, but I appreciate the implication that I'm interesting even in my hideous shape. I'll harvest some clothing."

He had scored with an oblique compliment. The Goddesses' advice was proving itself again. He didn't have to be sincere, and he didn't have to fool her; the mere effort sufficed. She was flattered that he even *wanted* to get an idea about her. But it had not been an entire fake; he had seen enough of her when they used the reverse wood bits to have a notion of her original sylph self, and that was indeed conducive.

They still wore the packs, which were now just that. The wings required a mental effort to invoke. That was good, because it meant the wings could always be available without being constantly used. However, Goar needed to remove his pack, don his shirt and trousers, and put the pack back on. It would not enable him to fly this way, but would be ready on short notice.

Incident closed her eyes and oriented. "A clothing tree clump, that way," she said, pointing.

They walked that way. Bird perched on Incident's shoulder, and she carried tiny Turtle in her hand, while Rabbit raced ahead. "Why do you care what I think?" Goar asked her. "You know that with reverse wood you should be able to nab any man you want. I'm not only ugly, I'm a killer."

"Why did the Goddess care?" she returned.

"I can kill young dragons, or other monsters. She has had a bad experience with her dragon children, so she wants to be sure that any man she takes up with can handle himself in that respect. She doesn't care about appearance."

"I'm invulnerable as long as I do my job. But now, with a conscience, I'll have to stop doing it. Then a dragon could chomp me. I don't think it would happen if you were with me. You don't depend on outside magic to maintain your toughness."

"It would not happen," he agreed.

"A handsome regular man could not defend me the way you could." She took a breath, though in her present state it did nothing for her torso. "But you—you know me in my ugliness, and we can't be sure I'll ever be pretty again. Why don't you go protect some prettier girl?"

"I am a killer. You knew that when we met. But still you saw me as a prospect. What pretty girl would?"

"The Good Magician sent you to me. There has to be a reason. The more I get to know of you, the clearer that reason becomes. You understand about ugliness and guilt. Few others do."

"Because I am ugly and guilty."

"Exactly. We understand each other."

He nodded. "We do." Then: "Incident—"

"Yes, I will kiss you."

They paused in their walk and she did. It was pleasant, nudging into more than pleasant.

"We have no business falling in love," he said.

"Love is for pretty people," she agreed.

They kissed again. Definitely more than pleasant.

If Bird and Turtle were getting impatient with this nonsense, they were too polite to object.

They resumed their walk, hand in hand. In a scant due course, they came to the grove of clothing trees. Incident donned a bra and panty, and he felt their magnetism though he did not freak out. There did have to be a reasonably fleshly basis for them to have full effect. Over this foundation she tried on a red dress. "What do you think?"

"It is lovely, and it enhances you." Indeed her crookedness was largely masked by the bright color, making her look more feminine.

"But men are no judge of dresses." She set it aside and tried a blue one. "This?"

"It is lovelier and it enhances you more." Now she looked almost attractive, as if the sun were shining on her.

"Still not quite right." She set it aside.

She tried a green dress. "This?"

"You are radiant as nature." *Almost* attractive? Goar had not realized before to what extent clothing made the woman.

"Maybe." She set it aside and quested for another. "I remember a tale about a merwoman who made legs instead of a tail and donned a particular color." In barely two instants she found a plaid dress. "There it is." She donned it. "This?"

Goar couldn't help himself. He stepped in, took hold of her, and enfolded her for another kiss.

"Yes, this is the one," she decided, satisfied. "I will save it for the right occasion." She removed the dress and put in her backpack. Then she donned the green dress. Its low back allowed her to wear it without removing the pack.

Then she sprouted wings and sailed up into the air, passing over his head. Surprised, he looked up. There was her spreading dress, and . . .

"Wake," she said, snapping her fingers by his ear. He was sitting on the ground, evidently having lost his balance.

"What happened?"

"You freaked out."

"But all I did was look up as you flew over me."

"And saw my panties under the dress. You didn't even punctuate your look."

It had to be true. The skirt of her dress had flared out to show her legs and . . .

He managed to cancel that memory before it could take him out again, though it did delete the punctuation. It wasn't that the vision was unpleasant, far from it, but he could not afford to freak out randomly. "I will try to be more careful in the future."

"You do that," she said. But she did not seem annoyed. Now he realized that she had done it on purpose, testing out the new clothing. She had verified its potency.

It seemed she had known what she was doing from the start, just as Tiamat had. It seemed to be an inherent female trait.

She added the red and blue dresses to the pack, plus a pair of dainty slippers. "I don't want to have to go shopping again," she explained, then smiled. "Much."

They were done here.

Just in time. Incident heard something, and produced the seed collection box. There was a new seed in it. "This one's for Turtle," she said. "It's not urgent; his never are. But we'd better get on it before the next one comes."

"We can perhaps fly there," Goar suggested.

There was a crack of thunder. A mean-looking cloud was boiling up over the horizon. "Oopsy!" she exclaimed. "We don't want to fly in that!"

But it was already too late to find cover. The storm had sneaked up on them and caught them by surprise. Storms liked to do that when they had the chance.

Goar was uncertain what to do. He himself was immune to weather, but what of Incident? She might be invulnerable to personal attack, but the weather was something else. She could get unpleasantly (for her) soaked. And what about the animals?

She glanced at him. "You're new to this. Let me handle it."

"As you wish." What did she have in mind?

She cast briefly about, then selected a broad mound in an open field. "This shouldn't flood. It will do." She ran to the spot, then put Turtle down on the top of the mound. "Give us a minute to get clear, then go giant," she told him.

Incident, Rabbit, Bird, and Goar stood back. Then Turtle expanded rapidly from tiny to large, and on to giant. His shell was now treetop height. It was as if a big new building had suddenly been built there. Goar was amazed.

Meanwhile the storm was rushing in, already buffeting them with its outlying winds. Incident's hair blew wildly in a manner Goar discovered he liked.

They ran to Giant Turtle. His head, legs, and tail had disappeared inside his shell, so that it looked as if it was an empty dome. They ran inside just as the first rain sheeted down.

"He's here, just withdrawn." She caught his hand in the dark and made it point. There was a giant pair of eyes, visible only by their faint glow. "He is giving us room."

Goar looked outside, where the deluge was complete. This was saving them all a thorough soaking. "Thank you, Turtle," he said for them all.

The eyes blinked acknowledgment.

Goar wondered what other surprises the animals had in store. Bird could become a roc, Rabbit could tunnel through to Mundania, and Turtle could become a giant. They had a lot going for them. As long as they continued doing their jobs.

"No one can see us," Incident said.

That was obvious. They were in almost pitch-black dark, riding out the storm.

Then he caught on. She was giving him a hint.

"You mean I can safely do this, and no one will know?" he asked, taking her hand, which was right by his hand, perhaps by no coincidence.

"No one," she agreed. "No one who might object."

"Or this?" he took her in his arms.

"No," she agreed, her no meaning yes, please.

"Or this?" He kissed her.

She kissed him back. After a moment she gently reproved him. "I can't answer you when you do that."

"What about this?" He took a handful farther down. It felt better than it looked, his hands not being as experienced as his eyes. Ugliness, like beauty, was largely in the eye of the beholder, and there were times when sight was a liability.

"It's a good thing I can't see what you're doing, or I might have to slap you."

"A good thing," he agreed. This promised to be fun.

By the time the storm passed, that promise had been fulfilled. He had never felt better, as it were. Incident had done some feeling herself, taking advantage of her anonymity to perform some unladylike but very female explorations. Not that he would ever tell.

Somewhat disheveled, they emerged to find a washed-out landscape. Gullies had been carved by the rushing waters, and there were piles of brush caught around snags. But no water had reached up to their elevation; Incident had seen to that. Turtle shrank back to tiny size.

"We'd better get on with the delivery," Incident said. "I think your target is that way." She pointed so that Turtle could see. "Some distance."

Bird became roc, and they made a short, for a roc, flight, landing before an ancient run-down mausoleum. Some bygone noble or even king must be entombed here, now long forgotten.

“But your seeds are not for dead folk, are they?” Goar asked.

“There must be a live person in the vicinity,” Incident said. “Maybe a groundskeeper.”

The indication was that the prospect was inside the tomb somewhere. “Maybe we should wait outside,” Goar said. “So as not to spook the target.”

“Maybe we can think of something to do while we wait,” Incident agreed.

They gazed at the entry, which was not closed. All was quiet.

Turtle assumed a small tortoise form and walked in, moving at a good pace for his configuration.

Bird and Rabbit settled down for naps.

Incident sprouted her wings. “Catch me if you can,” she teased as she angled up into the sky, her dress flaring as before so as to flash her legs. “I’m orienting on a small cache of reverse wood. There seems to be a fair amount of it in the vicinity.”

There had to be, because her legs definitely looked full and esthetically curved and sexy, instead of gnarled. Goar undressed, grew his own wings and followed.

She hovered in air, facing him, her bosom full and firm. “You look shapely!” he said.

“Thank you. Let’s see if we can kiss without colliding.”

“No, really. You’re pretty.”

She paused. “You’re serious? Because it’s all right if you’re not: the pretend game is fun.”

“Look at me. Am I handsome?”

She looked. “You know, you are. There must be reverse wood sawdust in the air.” Then she hovered closer, and they came carefully together for a kiss, only their lips touching. The darkness kisses and feels had been nice, but this was exhilarating despite being somewhat bumpy.

He put his arms around her as they hovered. That was nice too.

Then she reconsidered. “This is too easy. That could be mischief.”

“Why?”

“Easy things can be traps. Tangle trees make easy paths to their trunks for unwary animals to follow. Carnivorous plants make lovely flowers and sweet perfume.”

“Men make insincere compliments to women,” he said with a smile.

She laughed. "Precisely. A girl who is not careful can get carelessly used." She made a mock frown. "Assuming she doesn't *want* to be used."

Goar realized that he was no longer falling in love. He was already there.

Then Incident sobered. "Maybe there's no problem. But I'm suspicious. We'd better go back and check how Turtle is doing. He should be done by now."

Part of what he liked about her was her sensible caution. "We'll check."

They flew back to the mausoleum. Bird and Rabbit woke and came to attention. There was no sign of Turtle.

"Turtle should be back," Incident said to them. But he plainly wasn't.

Now Goar's own suspicion was kindled. A standard ploy in competition was to separate the members of an opposition group and deal with them separately. Had Turtle been separated? Yet he had demonstrated the ability to become huge, and probably could take care of himself in other ways. "Do you maintain mental connection with them on missions? If only by orienting on them the way you do on people and things?"

"There's always a background connection. I focus on it when I need to locate one. I am starting to get a connection to you, too. But Turtle seems to have faded out."

"Is that suspicious?"

"Yes."

"Is he dead?" Goar asked grimly.

"No. I got no bad jolt. Anyway, no ordinary thing could have killed him, because of the invulnerability. This has to be different."

"Then we should go in after him."

"Yes. We'll follow his trail."

"He left a trail?"

"It's part of my ability. I can make his tracks glow, so we all can see them."

"You keep surprising me. I'm impressed."

She gave him a serious look. "I like you, Goar. Ever since I learned you got touched by the same conscience cloud we did. So I am happy to impress you in what ways I can, beauty not being available to me."

"Similar here." It made him feel good just to agree with her.

"We will track him down. That's part of what I do: organizing missions, and untangling complications. We have to keep the unit together."

They entered the mausoleum. There were the turtle tracks, leading in the direction Goar had seen Turtle go. They went around a monument, to a stairway down into darkness. The tracks led down, as Turtle had evidently tipped over the edge of a step and dropped, perhaps by accident, before changing to large enough to handle them without falling. The size of the footprints confirmed that. At the base he resumed smaller size and plodded on; the tracks glowed brightly enough to light some of the surrounding passage.

Then something attacked. It was a fearsome glowing wraith with huge staring eyes, hair rising straight up off its head, and arms ending in talons. Fear smote them as it flew in for the kill. Its glow illuminated the whole murky chamber.

It came right up to them, then swerved off, screaming. *Goo awaay!*

Incident screamed and fell back, almost falling. Rabbit and Bird looked scared.

But Goar paused, assessing. Something wasn't right. Why was the spook making such a show? If it wanted to keep visitors out, why not simply keep the door closed? And when they discovered it had no solidity, why would they fear it?

Then the wraith struck at Goar, and its blow was solid. Goar wasn't hurt, of course. He grabbed the offending arm, lacking his saws because he was wearing the socks. He hurled the thing back against the wall.

Where it fell to the floor crying. Literally. It was in tears.

Goar turned to Incident, but she was no longer there. In her place was a lovely princess, obvious because of her sparkling crown and golden robe. *I will destroy you!* She hissed viciously.

Yet again, it *was* Incident. He recognized her face, except that it was now the one the reverse wood had shown, surpassingly lovely. Except for the expression, which was wild and cruel.

And there beside her were a phenomenally handsome rabbit and a bird of paradise, both staring at him and making sounds of total antipathy. That wasn't right, because though he had not known them long, he had gotten along well enough with them, and they both knew that he was becoming Incident's boyfriend. They were not his enemies. So why the hostility, coupled with their completely changed appearances? It simply did not make sense. Had they blundered into the Gulf of insanity?

Then it came to him: the animals were reversed. As with reverse wood, whose sawdust seemed to be in the local air. So was Incident. And so, surely, was he. And so was their dialogue. None of them hated the others, but here it was made to seem like hate.

"Incident," he said. "Listen to me!"

"You utter cad!" she screeched. "I'll claw out your eyes!"

Reversals. He had to get around them.

He tackled her and bore her back against the wall. He kissed her. He knew he risked getting bitten, but it was the only way he could think of to get through to her in a hurry.

She fought him, her jaw tensing as if to bite. Then she relaxed and kissed him back. "Goar! What's happening?"

"Reverse wood dust! In the air! Making us seem opposite."

"Reverse wood! Of course. That's why you're so handsome."

"But it is also reversing our seeming actions. You seemed to be reviling me."

"No! You were cursing me!"

"I think I have a way around it. When we are in direct contact, we are unchanged, but when we're apart the illusion governs. We are not altered, we only seem to be."

"Yes. You are no longer betraying me. But we can't stay in physical contact all the time." She smiled fleetingly. "Even though we might like to be."

Especially-looking the way they did now. But he could not afford to let that prospect distract him. "When we separate in a moment, say the exact opposite of what you mean, and I will too. The reversal should change it to what we mean, because it's not smart in itself. We'll still look different, but we can ignore that. We must tell Bird and Rabbit to do the same."

Her eyes widened with understanding. "That must be what happened to Turtle! He got caught in horrible reversals. And the wraith—"

"Must be the man he took the seed to, not hostile at all, but terrified of us."

"Yes!" she agreed. "I think you have figured it out."

"We'll still look different, but we can ignore that."

She smiled. "If I catch him, I'll kiss him. That should get his attention."

"But you won't be stunningly lovely when you actually touch him."

"Oops. I'll just hold his hand and tell him."

"Meanwhile I will try to rescue Turtle. I will follow his tracks."

They separated. Her beauty returned, as did her furious expression. "You. Are. A. Good man," she said carefully, speaking in reversals.

"Curse you, too, wretch," he replied, frowning.

She grimaced, then caught herself and smiled. "Rabbit, dear, come to me." She caught herself. "Oops. I mean, Rabbit, you vicious monster! Go away."

Rabbit, confused, stayed still. He looked like a handsome zombie bunny. Incident reached out and touched him. Goar knew she was explaining, using her contact telepathy. Then she did the same with Bird, who seemed to be a perfect raven. Neither animal had changed much, hunkering down during the confusion, but the reversal was still having its way with them. "Nevermore," quoth the Raven after a moment.

That startled Goar, because Bird didn't talk other than in chirps or trills. He must have made a peep of understanding, and that translated to the odd negation.

Meanwhile Goar oriented on the glowing turtle tracks, which now looked like nasty little monster prints. He followed them, ignoring all else. In little more than three and a half moments he reached their end, beside an ornate coffin. A scintillating tortoise was there, with a horrified expression.

"I'm not Goar, you revolting creature. Do not let me touch you." He reached slowly toward the image.

Turtle held still, surely confused that this confusingly handsome image was asking for physical contact. He had remained still because like the others he had not known what to do in this completely confusing situation.

Goar touched the shell. Now he saw Turtle as he was, and knew that Turtle saw Goar as he was. "It's illusion," he explained, knowing that Turtle understood his words. "Things are reversed. We need to get out of here, to get out of the field. Let me lift you and carry you."

Turtle nodded. He shrank to miniature size. Goar picked him up and started back. That kept them in physical contact, which was best. Had

Turtle not wanted it, he could have changed to giant size and crushed Goar against a wall.

The wraith appeared. "The. Woman. Touched. Me," he said, in halting reversals. He forced the caricature of a neutral expression. "She. Explained. I. Am. The. Caretaker. New. On. The. Job."

"I'll never understand!" Goar snapped. "I hate meeting you, oaf!"

The man made a somewhat shaky smile, reversed from a frown. "Thank. You."

Did you deliver the seed? Goar asked Turtle mentally.

Yes. It might kill him in 200 years.

Good enough. No real harm done.

They emerged and walked some distance away from the mausoleum with the caretaker, getting clear of the reversals. "They told me the tomb was haunted, and that's why they had trouble getting caretakers for it," the man said, evidently glad of understanding company. "But I don't believe in haunts, so it seemed like the perfect job for me." He smiled, then grimaced, remembering that he no longer needed to reverse his expressions. He meant that he had been fooled, before.

"Now you can seek another job," Incident said.

"No, I will stick with this one, now that I understand it. It is perfect job security. No one will take it from me."

"That does make sense," Goar agreed.

"Time to move on," Incident said as the caretaker returned to his duties.

Goar glanced at Turtle, whom he still held. They had gotten to know each other mentally, because it seemed that the animals, like Incident, all had contact telepathy. "Too bad you and Rabbit can't fly. Then we all could frolic together in the sky, now that Incident and I have wings." Then he paused. "I wonder."

"You are getting an idea," Incident said warningly. "I know the signals."

He was indeed. "You told me the animals can assume any variant of their natural forms, and sometimes more."

"Yes. We discussed this before. We really don't know their limits."

"Can we discuss it again? How they aren't limited to variations of their original forms? How they can do variants on their more fundamental natures? How maybe Turtle could be any reptile, and Rabbit any mammal."

"Maybe," she agreed reluctantly. "But they'd still be ugly, in real life."

So that was the actual issue: appearance. She was sensitive to it in a way the animals were not. He plowed on. "How there are forms of mammals that can fly, like flying squirrels. Or bats."

Incident was grimly silent, but Rabbit perked up.

"And reptiles that can fly, like ancient pterodactyls."

Turtle perked up.

"If they practiced those flying forms, zeroing them in so they could do those particular ones without much extra effort, maybe then we could all fly together, no one ultimately dependent on anyone else for transport. There might be times when that would be convenient."

Incident shared a four-way look with the three animals or maybe five or six ways considering the cross currents. She might have stifled this dialogue before, but this time they overruled her. "It would be more convenient," she agreed. "Let's try it."

They worked on it, and before long Rabbit manifested as a large bat and Turtle as a medium pterodactyl. They could do it, once they thought of it and made the effort. They did not need clumsy practice flights; once they had the forms, the forms knew the ability.

Then Goar and Incident sprouted their wings, and all five of them flew up, up, into the sky, reveling in their togetherness in this new manner. They swooped and circled, and dived, raced each other, and landed refreshed.

What especially pleased Goar was that now he was relating to the animals as readily as he did to Incident. They had become a team of five, thanks in significant part to their wings.

Chapter 7

MATRIX

They relaxed that day and night, with Goar enjoying his acceptance by the team. The three animals had decided that he was all right, maybe because they appreciated the way he had thought of them all flying, and of course Incident liked his kisses. For the first time in his largely negative life, Goar was accepted by a worthy group. That thrilled him in a way he had not experienced before. Yes, they were all ugly, but they were ugly together. He realized that he valued that acceptance as much as he might value becoming handsome.

They harvested some pies for breakfast. There was a woman trying to pull off an edible gourd, but it wouldn't come loose. Goar walked across to her. "Permit me," he said. He unsheathed a saw and quickly sawed through the tough vine so that the gourd fell free. Then he put the sock back on.

"Thank you," she said. "This is the only variety I haven't eaten before, because I couldn't get them loose."

"Welcome." He turned away.

"Wait! I must repay the favor."

"No need. I have a dark past, and I am trying to do what bits of good I can now, in an effort to make up for my prior evil."

"Even so, I think I owe you one. I am Jill."

"I am Goar Golem. I am glad to have helped."

"My talent is to tell the obscure truth. This is not in the sense of honesty, but in the sense of revealing what folk may not know, like the near future or hidden motives, or obscure facts."

"I want only to do the right thing."

"Let me touch you."

He shrugged and extended his socked hand. She touched it. "Oh my!"

"You are feeling my evil?"

"No. I am feeling your near future. You are about to encounter a phenomenal challenge upon which thousands of lives depend, if you can only figure out how to handle it. I can't tell you how; that is complicated beyond my talent. But I can say that it will affect you profoundly for the better, if you rise to the occasion. Be ready."

Could this relate to his association with Incident and the Companions? He would surely find out. "Thank you, Jill."

Now she was the one who turned away. "You're welcome, Goar." She walked off, carrying her gourd.

"That was interesting," Incident said. "I believe it is a portent. Something is developing."

"Something big," he agreed.

There was a faint bong. "That's the grapevine," Incident said, going to a vine hanging from an acorn tree. She put a grape to her ear. "Uh-oh."

Goar and the three companions looked at her. Had she received news of a bad load of seeds to deliver?

"We have a call to meet at the junction of JKLMN," she said. "That's not likely to be good news."

"What is this junction?" Goar asked.

"I am one of a number of Oma servers. Each boundary line is designated by a combination of letters, the whole of it defining the local mosaic. My tessellation—"

"Your what?"

"A tessellation is a tile or pattern that fits together without any gaps and can expand outward indefinitely. My particular tile is square, but others are not. They can be any shape as long as they fit together perfectly to form the larger mosaic. What makes it feasible is that the corners of each tile add up to three hundred and sixty degrees, defining the matrix."

Goar struggled to understand, but came up short. "Matrix?"

"A pattern of invisible tiles across the landscape," she clarified. "So that the whole land is covered, and every seed is delivered appropriately."

"Oh, you have territories."

"Yes, so there is no confusion about who delivers what to whom. Anyway, the local matrix extends from AA to AZ. Mine is AL, so I am Incident AL Oma. My neighbors for this junction are AJ, AK, AL (me), AM and AN. At the key juncture they all meet." She took a stick and drew lines in the dirt, marked by the letters. "Incident AJ Oma, Incident AK Oma, and so on."

"Thus JKLMN," he said. "You and your neighbors. I had no idea that your business was so well organized."

"The entire universe is better organized than most folk realize. It's like a giant clockwork with everything in its proper place. The underlying order just doesn't show on the surface."

"It doesn't," he agreed.

She looked at her wrist where a little dial showed. "Oops, I'm spending too much time trying to explain what doesn't much matter to you anyway. It's not smart to be late. Good thing we learned to fly."

They organized and took off together. Of course Bird could have become roc and taken them as readily, but this was more satisfying. Bird was now a hawk.

"Maybe I can make the lines show, if only to you," Incident said as they flew side by side, the three companions above, below, and behind them. "Like the turtle tracks." She focused, then reached out to touch his hand.

The lines appeared, duly marked. They were in AL, coming up on AK. Then he saw the juncture, with five tiles touching cornerwise. Incident's and one other were square corners; the other three were the points of triangles. It all added up to the full circle, 360 degrees, he knew. They glided to a joint landing just inside the AL territory.

And there were the four other teams, marked, at least to Goar's sight, with their designations, just as Incident and the companions were labeled AL. Five ugly humans and fifteen ugly animals. But there was something different about the others; they lacked something. What was it?

"They lack consciences," Incident murmured. "They didn't have the ill luck to blunder into a conscience cloud."

"Ill luck? That's what brought us together."

"Yes, but it vastly complicated our existence."

He could not argue with that. But at this point he wasn't sure he would trade that complication for freedom from his conscience, if it meant he could no longer associate with her. Maybe he just wasn't thinking straight.

AK approached. He was as repulsive as a male as she was as a female. "Hello, AL! You look changed."

"I am ugly as ever," Incident said. "It must be my new conscience."

"You got a conscience? Whatever for? It will mess up your performance something awful."

"It does," she agreed. "It was an accident. Now I'm stuck with it, as are my companions."

Now the companions eyed each other. AK's animals were a giant insect, a flying fish, and a small carnisaur. The AL companions retained their hawk, bat, and pterodactyl forms. It was as if they preferred anonymity. Goar was beginning to see why.

Then AJ approached. "And who are you, robust golem?" she inquired flirtatiously. She was grotesque, but that was no liability in this gathering. Her animals were all female: a small fiery dragon, a griffin, and a harpy. Reptile, mammal, and bird?

"Keep clear of him!" Incident AL snapped.

"Or what, snippet?" AJ asked nastily, and her animals hissed. "Will it make you cry real girlish tears if he gets into it with a real female?"

Meanwhile the other female, AN, was coming up. This was getting awkward, but Goar didn't know how to get out of it. They had yet to learn the reason for this unusual rendezvous.

"Hey, foulface, we hear you got a conscience," AN called.

"Stay out of it, ANnie," Incident said.

"Why should I? No sense in letting AJane have all the fun." She turned to Goar. "In fact, I hear you got into it with a Goddess. Really reamed her channel, nine times."

"What?" Incident asked, surprised. Goar had tried to be discreet, a concept evidently foreign to these witches.

ANnie turned briefly to her. "You didn't know, ALma?"

That was her nickname among these folk? It did make sense, since all of them technically were Incidents. But to him she was THE Incident.

Incident recovered some of her poise. "I didn't know Goddesses blabbed secrets."

"They don't," ANnie said. "But watching reptiles do." She glanced at her trio, consisting of a hovering ugly fairy, a centaur, and a serpent. "Garter snakes can get almost into the action, and they share hot gossip with their friends."

Goar had heard of garter snakes. They could be useful to hold up the stockings of young women, and thus indeed be close to the action. Had Tiamat worn garters? He didn't remember, having been distracted by other aspects of their encounter. Maybe she had, as she certainly had legs.

ANnie returned to him. "Have you tried making it with a woman without a conscience? We're really bad girls. We'll do things that would freak out a conscience-bound doll, but the men seem to like it."

Incident was silent. That was a bad sign. He was actually quite intrigued by the bad girl implication, but knew he was verging on a dangerous social mire. "I'll remain with ALma." He stepped back.

"You'll never know what you're missing, Golem," ANnie said.

That was surely true, to his regret. But he held firm. "I will settle for ignorance."

"If we were pretty, it would be a different story," AJane said.

Goar suspected she was right. Then he caught half a glimpse of Incident's face, and knew that she was pleased with him. That counted hugely.

There was the sound of a gong. "Meeting is called to order," AMos said. "We have a problem."

All the Omas and their animals paid immediate attention.

"We have received news that in Mundania, near this site, there is about to be a massive killing. Because it will be in our joint territories, it is our business. As you know, we service both Xanthian and Mundanian folk, but most of our business is Mundane because they are so overpopulated. A crisis there affects us much more than a similar crisis here. They have something called a New Clear Bomb that will wipe out several hundred thousand people. Most of them will be safely dead, and most survivors will be obviously sickened, but it is the peripheral ones that concern us. There may be half a million cancer seeds to deliver, to keep up with what they term radiation poisoning." AMos shook his head. "They think cancers just pop up on their own, more or less randomly; they don't know about us and the way we fill the Oma orders. They don't appreciate the work we do. But this will swamp us. We can't possibly keep up with such a massive case load, yet we will be blamed and punished for our failure to deliver. So the question is, what can we do?"

There was an ugly (of course) silence. Then Incident AL spoke. "My companion Goar is not of our number, and has a different perspective. He has come up with helpful ideas before. Maybe we should ask him."

All the Incidents and their animal associates oriented on Goar. He was suddenly on the spot, and ill prepared for it. "I, uh—"

"This may offer an avenue," AMos agreed. "What might we do, that is not apparent to those of us who think in an extremely similar mode? Speak to us, outsider."

Was he taunting Goar, to make him look ignorant? These were not nice folk. They cared only about their own hides, not anyone else's.

Well, what about the obvious? "Maybe you can stop it from happening."

"And how may we accomplish that?" AMos was almost purring as he set up the outsider for his supreme embarrassment.

Goar plowed on. "Go there, find out who will set off the Bomb, and stop him."

"Would that not be risky?"

"Well, yes, but the risk to a few should be more than counterbalanced by the good to be accomplished."

AMos glanced around. "Any volunteers?"

The silence became downright hideous.

"Isn't that funny," AMos said with a cruel smile. "None of us wish to risk harm to our own hides to benefit anyone else. Not that we are in the business of benefiting anyone."

Because they had no conscience. But there was a job that needed desperately to be done. "I will do it," Goar said.

"Because you have a conscience," AMos said with evil satisfaction.

That was when Goar realized how he had been set up. AMos knew that folk with consciences could do what conscienceless folk would not.

AMos nodded. "Yet you lack our ability to cross into Mundania to do such a thing."

Goar looked at Incident. She sighed and nodded. "Yes, we will assist you."

Because she and the animals all had consciences too. They could not get him into a job to benefit them without helping him accomplish it.

The trap was complete.

"We appreciate the way you have volunteered," AMos said cynically. Oh, he was pleased to have maneuvered them so cleverly! But they were stuck with it. "We will now leave you to your work, unhampered by our presence."

"Thank you," Incident said through her crooked teeth. "We appreciate it."

"We'll do our best," Goar said. The irony was that they really would try their best, though the others would gain a huge benefit they did not deserve. The home team had no choice.

The others retreated into their several territories, the two other females pausing to grin maliciously at Incident. Then they glanced slantwise at Goar, the looks practically reeking of filthy implication. "Maybe some other time, potent golem," ANnie murmured, making a gesture as of flipping up her imaginary skirt and flashing her nonexistent panties.

"For sure, Goddess touched," AJane agreed, making as if to remove mock garters from supposedly full-fleshed thighs.

Even the other animals snickered, especially the snakes. Goar wasn't sure how a snake managed a snicker, but they did.

What utter phonies! Fortunately he did not find them at all appealing. Though a dusty corner of his mind was ready to explore further, if he ever let it. Worse, he suspected that the wretched females could somehow peer into that corner.

But that made him wonder. Incident was no less ugly than the others, yet he now found her appealing. Why the difference?

"The irony is that if I had known what was to happen here," Incident said glumly, "I still would have had to come. We can't let so many people suffer and die, even if they are only Mundanes. They're not bad folk, just different."

"Conscience considers character," he agreed.

And there it was. She had a conscience, as did he. That was a common bond between them. They were obliged to consider more than the convenience of the moment. That distinguished them from all the others they had encountered. That also made their physical appearance less important; without character it counted less heavily. He could love Incident regardless of her appearance. In fact—

"You're getting an idea again," she said.

She had caught him. “I am. Maybe when this is over—”

“Maybe,” she agreed. “You know, we were so sure it was impossible for ugly folk to love and be loved. I am not so sure anymore.”

“It was too shallow a definition. Maybe beauty facilitates love, but when you think of it, if that were the whole of it, wouldn’t that mean that if a young pretty couple fell in love and married, that it would break up the moment they lost their youth and beauty?”

“That’s what happens in Mundania. Half their marriages founder when they lose their looks.”

“The other half must have a better basis, so it lasts.”

She nodded. “Maybe it is better to fall in love ugly. Then the loss of looks can’t end it.”

“I think that is what we are doing.”

“It must be,” she agreed. “But right now, we need to plan our approach. We’re going to have to go to Mundania and interact physically with the people there, and this is bound to be a challenge. All I know of Mundanes is what I have picked up watching my associates track them down for the placements, and from hearsay. Actually being there physically, well, it scares me. I’m afraid I’ll mess up our mission.”

Goar appreciated how she felt. He had never been to Mundania himself, and knew he was likely to foul up. “We will have to observe first, so we can learn exactly what is destined to happen, and when and where. Then maybe we can steal the Bomb and dump it in the sea.”

She shook her head. “We can’t. Literally. We can go to Mundania, but we won’t be entirely real there. It’s the same for the animals; they deliver their seeds in a sort of semi-solid state, and once emplaced they develop and become real.”

“Then how can we stop the Bomb?”

“We shall have to act thorough the Mundanes who are already involved with it. We can manifest to them as sort of ghosts if we concentrate and if they are halfway open-minded. Try to persuade them not to detonate it.”

“Will they listen?”

“Maybe. We have to hope so.”

“But Mundanes are notorious for not listening well.”

“Yes. I think the lack of magic in their environment affects them and makes them stupid.”

"This is already more of a challenge than I thought."

"That's why AMos was satisfied to stick us with it. If it was easy to do, he'd have done it himself and taken the credit." She glanced at him with forlorn hope. "As we know, your mind works differently from ours. Can you come up with an original approach? One that might actually work?"

Goar pondered. "I think we'll have to reconnoiter first, as you suggested. Maybe the animals can scout out the terrain in advance. Then we can organize to use what we learn, halfway effectively, with luck. Work out arguments that are more likely to persuade them." This did not seem likely to him, but what else was there? Who would take ghosts seriously, if not terrified of them?

"We can but try," she agreed.

She called the three animals together and explained the situation. "So if you can go there, and bring us back a report," she concluded, "Then we can decide on a course of action."

"Take my camera," Goar told Rabbit. "Bring back any good pictures." Then, belatedly, he remembered the note that Wira had given him, saying it was important. Suddenly he understood its relevance. He brought out the note. "Check out the folk with these names that the Good Magician gave me: Hack. Gloria. Moxie. Xylia."

They looked at Incident. "They have to be relevant. The Good Magician always knows," she said. "Bird, you check the first two, Hack and Gloria. Turtle the last one, Xylia. Rabbit, the third one, Moxie. You all know how to orient on a given name. Think of it as for delivering seeds, only in this case just observe. My sense tells me that they are indeed important."

The three companions set off for Mundania. Being ghostly was an advantage when merely observing. For one thing, they could not be caught and confined.

"They have the night to learn what they can, there," Incident said. "We'll have the night to ourselves, here."

"In that case—" The idea loomed huge.

She saw it forming. Maybe its growing size made it more visible. "No. We need to rehearse our speeches for different scenarios. If we do manage to pull this off successfully, then we should improve our looks, and I promise I will give you a night that will make you forget about Goddesses."

That seemed like a good exchange.

They looked for a good place in the vicinity to spend the night, but there did not seem to be any suitable shelters or caves. Then Incident perked up. "There's a boxer close by."

"A martial artist? That's not what we need."

"No, not fist fighting."

"A kind of Mundane dog? We don't need that either. We want shelter."

"You'll see." She set off to intercept the boxer. Goar followed, hoping she would start making sense soon.

They came upon a nondescript creature sniffing around trees as if looking for something. There was a trail of small boxes in its wake, as if it were shedding them. "Hey, you!" Incident called, advancing on it.

The thing turned to face her. It stood on its hind feet and raised its front paws as if measuring her for a meal. Goar stepped in close to her, drawing a sock off a saw, just in case. "Do your thing," she told the creature.

Then wooden panels formed around them. They were boxed in!

"Take it easy, Goar," Incident said. "This is what we want. The boxer has boxed us. This box is all bark and no bite. It will do for the night."

Oh.

Goar used his exposed saw to saw open a small hole for a window. "It's weird when you do that," Incident said. "Changing your feet to treads. I'm not complaining, just observing."

"The Good Magician's wife, Sofia, set me up with the socks. They're her specialty."

"Sofia Socksorter," she agreed. "I've heard of her. They say the Good Magician's socks piled up so awfully and stunk so bad that he had to marry her to get them in order. I guess she did the job."

"It seems to be a full-time position."

Then his right ankle tingled. "That reminds me. She gave me an anklet so the folk I killed can track me. She said if I ever needed help, I could use it to summon them. I never thought of it until now. Maybe it's time."

"Time?"

"First we need to know who explodes the Bomb," Goar said. "Then we can orient on him."

"But how can we find the one person in millions of Mundanes?" Incident asked, frustrated. "It will take forever to search him out."

"That's just it. A charm I can use to invoke help when I really need it. I thought I never would, but now I think I do."

"To find the Bomber," she agreed.

Goar touched the invisible anklet and thought, PLEASE.

The box shelter doubled its dimensions. Then three new people appeared. All women. "It's about time you signaled, Goar," the brown-haired young woman said. She glanced at the Oma. "Hello, Incident. I'm Squid. This is my beloved companion Laurelai." She indicated the lovely woman with the blue/black tresses. "We are the two that Goar murdered a day or so ago, when she was in her male aspect."

"You!" Incident exclaimed. "But then why would you—"

"And this is my protector, Fornax. She is more than she appears to be."

Incident looked at the third new person, a regal older woman with rich gray hair and matching eyes. "The only Fornax I know of—"

"Yes, I am a personification of that one."

"But you're a—"

"I am Squid's friend. That suffices."

"Uh, yes." Incident was plainly awed.

So that was the one who had banished the Dwarf Demons who had controlled him. Goar had not known her identity, only that she was powerful.

Fornax turned to Goar. "Precisely. I am the one who will help you perform your mission."

"I do not understand why. You know what I did."

"My motives are devious. But my friends must remain in this frame until they are able to forgive you your transgression. Only by accomplishing this present mission, among others, can you achieve sufficient grace to merit that forgiveness. Therefore, I will provide that minimal assistance you require, in the interest of enabling my friends to return home." She paused just long enough for him to assimilate that, then resumed. "Do you comprehend the framework of alternate realities?"

"No." Because he had never heard of them.

"This world you know is only one of an infinite spread of similar realities. This is true for Xanth and for Mundania. The adjacent ones are almost but not quite identical. But the more boundaries we cross, the more they differ, in physical detail and in time. I will take you and Incident to that frame which is just far enough ahead of the present one so that you can witness the Bomber in action." She smiled somewhat grimly. "The mischief he accomplishes is somewhat greater than yours, in that he kills approximately a hundred thousand Mundanes and injures myriads more. So he is in that sense a greater criminal than you, yet also a victim of manipulation, as you were. Then you will know him, and will be able to orient on him in your present frame, so as to prevent him from accomplishing this evil."

"You wish me to kill him? I now have a problem with that."

"I know you do. So your challenge will be to find a way to stop him without killing him or anyone else."

Goar was relieved. "I will try."

"Now I will take you and Incident to that nexus, while my friends relax in your comfortable house box. Are you ready?"

"I am ready," Goar said.

"I guess I have to be ready too," Incident said. "Though I fear I am dreaming."

Goar took her hand. "It is what we need."

"Now, the two you take my hands instead," Fornax said.

They did, one on either side of her.

Then the weirdness began. The box vanished so that they were in the glade. The scene darkened, then lightened. Night had passed and dawn come in seconds rather than hours. The day passed and night resumed, faster yet. Soon (as it were) the days and nights were flickering so rapidly that they became a blur.

The disconnect somehow triggered a thought. "Why were the other Incidents so eager to mess with me? They had to know I'm not worth it."

"You're a new face," Incident replied. "Our line of work is incredibly isolating. We are all desperate for social contact we know we can't achieve. No ordinary person will touch any of us. But you have shown that you will. They aren't fooling about wanting to do things with you that no conscience will allow. Give them the slightest chance and they'll prove it."

"And yes, it is normal to be halfway tempted," Fornax said, surprising him. Of course she could read his mind! "But Incident AL will do those things too, in due course."

Incident did not respond, but she blushed a deep purple. Her mind had been read also.

Then the flickering slowed, and finally halted. They were in daylight in the glade.

Fornax released their hands. "This is approximately two days in the future, as experienced in your frame. That is the amount of time you will have to accomplish your task. That should be sufficient."

"Assuming we know what we're doing," Incident said.

"Assuming," Fornax agreed.

They walked on either side of Fornax as she followed some path only she could detect. There were just trees and small fields.

They halted at a nondescript place in the forest. "Now we will cross into Mundania. Take my hands."

They took her hands again. The forest faded and they stood on what appeared to be a Mundane city street. People were walking along it, ignoring the three of them. "They are not aware of us," Fornax explained.

That was just as well, because they were not garbed in the manner of Mundanes. Goar and Incident were bare, and Fornax looked like a queen, hardly a trio to pass unnoticed.

"From here you can orient," Fornax said to Incident. "Focus on the suicidal intent."

Incident did. "That way." She pointed at a several-story-high building.

They entered it, and went to a wall with several doors. Now Incident pointed up. "He is above us."

"Select a door."

"A door? But we need to find a stairway."

Fornax smiled. "No, this is faster." She indicated the wall.

Bemused, they walked beside the wall.

One door opened as they approached. Beyond it was a cubical chamber. "This is what is called an elevator. It will take us to an upper floor."

Amazed, Goar and Incident stepped into the chamber. Fornax touched a lighted button. "Tell us where to stop," she said.

Then the chamber rose, causing Goar and Incident to jump in surprise. It was elevating them!

They passed a level labeled TWO and went on up. Then THREE. Then as they came to FOUR Incident pointed. "This one."

Fornax touched a button and the elevator stopped at FOUR. The door slid open. They stepped out.

"This way," Incident said.

They walked down a hall and stopped at another door. Incident tried to turn the door handle, but it resisted.

"There is insufficient time remaining," Fornax said.

Goar unsheathed a saw and sliced a hole in the wooden door panel. In a moment—Mundania did not have proper fractions of moments, so clumsily rounded them off—the defeated door opened and they entered.

There was a young man seated at a table. There was a kind of mirror on it, and a panel with letters of the alphabet marked on its little squares.

The man looked up as they approached. "Who the hell are you?" It seemed that Mundania also lacked sanitary bleeps. It was a really backward land.

"Are you the Bomber?" Incident asked. "Hack?"

"You're too late, she-dog!" The man's agile fingers danced over the letters on the panel.

"Too late," Fornax agreed grimly. "We have only ten seconds to vacate. Take my hands."

They grabbed her hands and the flickering of frame travel started. As they watched, there was a dim flash where they must have been.

"That was the Bomb," Fornax said. "Too bad for all those people."

"But it was only a mirror and square letters," Incident protested.

"A computer screen and a keyboard. He must be a hacker. Hence his name."

"A what?"

"A person who finesses computer codes to make illicit things occur. In this case it seems a nuclear detonation. He must have used his ability to locate and intercept the secret code."

"But why would he do that?" Incident asked. "It looked as though the explosion took him out too."

"It did. He committed suicide."

"And he took a hundred thousand others with him," Goar said.

"And will do so two days hence in our frame," Incident said, putting it together. "If we don't stop him."

"But why?" Goar asked. "He looked young and healthy."

"That you must divine," Fornax said.

"A woman," Incident said wisely. "They make men do crazy things."

"Now you know your challenge," Fornax said as the flickering stopped and they arrived back in the box.

"Now we know," Goar agreed.

They practiced scenarios, but they really didn't have enough to go on, and soon fell asleep, she leaning comfortably against a wall, he with his head on her lap. Neither was dissatisfied.

In the morning he sawed a door in the box and they emerged. There was a stream nearby for washing, and pie plants around. If this was what domestic life was like, Goar was for it.

The three companions arrived back. They had a huge report to make. So Bird transformed into an expressive parrot and started talking. The essence was that a young Mundane man named Hack was very good with the Mundane magic called computers, and had devised a way to sneak into a military complex and do something awful there. Bird did not know what, but it reeked of importance.

"He can set off the Bomb from his computer," Incident said. "That is what we have to stop."

"Rabbit found Moxie," Bird continued. "She's a prisoner in a cell, due for lifetime imprisonment or worse. Turtle found Xylia. She's a country girl, very pretty and shy, in town seeking a better life and not making much progress because she's not very good at socializing with people."

"I see how Hack relates," Goar said. "He sets off the Bomb."

"And it is a fair bet that it is because of Gloria," Incident said, figuring out the relevance of the last name on the list. "She must be about to dump him, making him suicidal. But I don't see how a prisoner or a country girl relate."

"We will make them relate," Goar said, the idea flashing loudly. "We can introduce Hack to Xylia before Gloria dumps him. Then he won't mind so much, and won't set off the Bomb."

"But Xylia is too shy to just go and take him away from Gloria," Incident said. "She may be pretty enough, but she'll never have the initiative or nerve."

"Moxie has both," Bird said. "But she's not pretty or free."

"And why would he want to date a criminal?" Goar asked, suddenly relating to that aspect.

Incident eyed him. "Maybe if she reformed?"

"They will never let her out of prison," Bird said. "She can reform all she wants, but it won't do her any good at this stage. She spent all her life ruining it. It is way too late for her now."

"Yet if somehow she could reform and get out and get pretty," Incident said musingly as she continued to look at Goar, "he might like her. There's so much good in the worst of us."

"Moxie's reformed personality in Xylia's body," Goar said. "Too bad we can't merge them."

"Maybe we can," Incident said thoughtfully. "Just as my associates have rather special powers when they truly try, so I may have some myself. Sometimes when I tune in on a prospect, I almost think I could step into that body myself, if it is female. Or at least enable someone else to."

Goar and the three animals gazed at her. Was this possible?

"Who is willing to experiment?" Incident asked. "To see if I can do it."

"I am," Goar said.

"So am I," Bird said. "Temporarily, anyway."

"Then let's try it, only for a minute or so. Goar, take Bird in your hand."

Goar extended his hand, and Bird flew up to perch on it.

Incident came to them both. She put one hand on Goar's arm where it was bare above the sock, and the other hand on one of Bird's legs. "But as with the Mundane magic of psychiatry, you have to really, really want to change. Try to will yourselves into each other's bodies."

"This is weird," Bird said. "But I will try."

"So will I," Goar said. He focused, trying to will himself into the small avian body.

Then he felt Incident's will taking hold. It caught hold of his soul and drew it gently out and into the parrot.

And there he was. He opened his beak. "I'm here!" he said in wonder. "Me, Goar."

"And I am here in the golem," Bird's voice came from the other body.

"Now let's go home," Goar said from the bird beak.

"You bet," Bird said from the man mouth.

"I am . . . letting . . . you go," Incident said.

The two snapped back to their own bodies as if on stretched elastic.

Then they gazed at each other in amazed wonder. “It worked!” Incident exclaimed.

It worked.

Now they had a plan. Assuming *it* worked.

Chapter 8

SALVATION

The animals had obligingly scouted out a secluded public park for them to cross into, so they would not attract undue notice. They would be in ghostly form there, but ghosts did have some visibility if credulous Mundanes were paying attention, and that was best avoided.

They walked to the site. Then Rabbit got large, and rapidly dug out a rabbit hole big enough for human beings or man-shaped golems to climb through. They were on their way.

In little more than a moment and a half they were in the Mundane park. "Now we should be solid to each other," Incident said. "But insubstantial to Mundane things." She tested by passing a hand through the low branch of a tree, and Goar did the same. He saw his hand and he saw the branch, but the two did not see each other, as it were. They truly were ghosts. "Still, we need to be careful, so as not to spook anyone. We don't want to be noticed at all." She turned to the animals. "Bird, take us to Hack."

Incident picked up Rabbit, who was now a little bunny, and Goar picked up Turtle, who was small enough to fit in a pocket. Bird flitted ahead of them as a dusky sparrow, who tended to be dark to the point of invisibility in the manner of that kind; they had to watch closely to track him. They left the park and came to a busy highway. Bird changed to the parrot form. "Watch out for the traffic," he said. "The cars, as they call them, charge through heedlessly. They won't actually hurt us if they hit us, but it may look funny and draw attention when they pass through us like ghosts."

"Think invisible," Incident said. "Or at least unnoticed."

"Our mental attitude does make a difference," Bird agreed. "We spooked several Mundanes overnight before we got it straight. We're not used to staying around; normally we sneak in, plant our seeds, and sneak out quickly."

"Got it," Goar agreed.

Bird changed back to dusky. They waited until there was a pause in the traffic, then hurried across the road. No one seemed to notice them. Success!

There were sidewalks on either side of each road. Some of them had people walking on them. They selected one that was empty and walked along it, thinking invisible.

Goar was nervous. They could not open a door themselves; how were they going to enter a building? He trusted the animals to have a way.

They came to a larger building where people were fairly constantly going in or coming out. Goar recognized it: it was the same building Fornax had taken them to. Bird led them to the rear, where there was nobody. He made a gesture with a wing indicating "Follow me," and flitted through the closed back door.

Oh. Of course. Go *through* the door. He realized that he had known the answer all along, such as when his hand passed through the branch. What else did he need to remember that he knew?

They had been more solid when Fornax took them here, in the other frame. But of course her rules were different. They had actually used the elevators.

Incident took his hand. "We can do this," she murmured.

They stepped through the door together. There was some slight resistance, like passing through a mesh curtain, and then they were through. The floor inside seemed to support their feet; maybe their attitude that floors were supposed to be solid enough for that made it so.

Incident drew him in and kissed his cheek. She was delightfully solid to him. "I'm relieved," she whispered. "I haven't done this before."

"You can kiss me anytime."

She spanked him on his rear plate. "I mean ghosting in Mundania."

Of course. "I prefer kissing." And more.

"Keep that Idea out of my face," she snapped without real force. "Or wherever. This is serious business."

They followed Bird up several flights of steps. "The locals all use the elevators," he said. "They avoid exercise whenever they can. So the stairs are pretty safe."

They came to the room and quietly phased though the door. Hack was there, pacing the floor. "Oh, Gloria!" he said to empty air. "You're so beautiful! I love you. Will you marry me?"

They stood against a wall, trying to imitate its color. They were here just to spy out the terrain, to get to know him better.

"No, that's no good," Hack said, shaking his unruly shack of blond hair. "There needs to be more art to it. "Gloria, let's take a nice walk. I have something I want to say to you."

He was practicing his proposal. He was really serious about Gloria.

"Damn, damn, damn!" Hack swore. "I can play beautiful music on the Internet. I can make programs dance to my whim. There's no one in the world who can do it better than I can. I even broke the most secret code controlling the New Clear Bomb the military hides from the people. I'm a genius; there's nothing I can't do online. But I can't figure out how to ask my girlfriend a simple question. So I'm an idiot offline. Damn, damn, damn!"

Goar had half a notion how that was. Until he met the glorious Goddess, he had never approached a woman romantically. She had truly educated him, so now he knew what it was all about. But even so, it was tricky getting it on with ugly Incident. because he cared about her. He could saw enemies into chunks, but handling Incident was more challenging. Hack had a problem.

The man continued his frustrating rehearsals. "We have a date for this afternoon," he said. "That's when I need to do it. Gloria, may I ask you a personal question? No, that's not right either. Damn, damn, damn!"

They quietly departed. Now they knew that the two would be meeting in the afternoon. That was when Hack would try to ask her to marry him, fumble it, and she would dump him like week-old garbage. So that then he would do what he did best, and set off the Bomb.

"Well, we confirmed our diagnosis," Incident said when they were back on the street. "So we either need to talk Gloria into marrying him, or find him another girlfriend in a hurry."

Now Bird led them to a different building. In due course they were in Gloria's apartment.

Gloria was a beautiful young woman with hair the color of passion. She was in bed, nude.

In the late morning?

Then Goar saw that she was not alone. There was a man under the sheet beside her, handsome and evidently potent. “That was great, Glo,” he said. “Give me about ten minutes to recharge so I can do you again.”

“Five minutes, Buck,” she said firmly. “Then you have to get out of here so I can clean up to be ready for my date with Hack.”

“Why are you messing with that creep, anyway?”

“Well, I had this credit card balance I had to pay off pronto, and I didn’t have the money, so I went to Hack.”

“He has money?”

“No. Not exactly. But he can do neat tricks with online accounts. So I turned on the charm.”

“You’re good at that,” Buck agreed.

“And just like that my debt was gone, and I had a positive balance. No way to trace the change, either. It was permanent. It was like magic.”

“Ah. Maybe you can get him to pay off my card too.”

“No. In three hours I dump him, because his usefulness to me is done.”

“You’re pretty cynical.”

“Look who’s talking! You cheat card sharks for a living.”

Buck changed the subject. “What else did he do for you?”

“There’s this lady dog at work who had the nerve to call me a name. So I had Hack anonymously mess up her bank account so bad that it’ll take her years to clean up her credit rating. I had to flirt up a storm to get him to do it, but he did it.”

“And now he’s in love with you.”

“Yes. So it’s time to get rid of him, before he demands more of me than I care to give.”

“What is that ‘more’?”

She laughed. “Anything. He’s a nerd. Soon he’ll want more than kissing.”

“*I* want more than kissing.”

“You’re a bad boy, Buck. That’s what I like about you.”

And she was a bad girl. Goar exchanged a glance with Incident. They had heard enough.

Back on the street, Goar squeezed Incident’s hand. “I hope that’s not the way you regard me.”

"Not," she agreed. "She led him on to get him to do the dirt she wanted, and now she's dumping him. What gets me is that she's way dirtier than I am, but she's beautiful physically."

"It isn't fair," he agreed.

"It's the deal with Oma. I knew it when I signed. I get a good life and some pretty good power, but it makes me ugly. Now if I quit, I'll still be ugly."

"But you'll get less ugly if we save those Mundane lives."

"That's a consolation." She glanced at him. "If this makes me less ugly, or even plain, or even pretty, and I quit, will you stay with me?"

"Yes."

"That's much of what I need to know. But I'm doing it because it is the right thing to do."

"To save all those people who don't deserve to die because of one man's unusual mode of suicide."

"Yes. Even if they are just Mundanes."

"May I kiss you?"

She looked again at him, surprised. "That turns you on?"

"I have done so much evil that I prefer to associate with someone who doesn't much like evil. Maybe we can escape evil together."

"You must mean it, because it sure isn't my looks that turn you on."

He kissed her. Each time it was better. Unless she dumped him, he was not destined for the Goddess.

Then it was back to business. "Rabbit, take us to Moxie," Incident said.

Rabbit changed into his talking form, Updoc. "The prison is out of town. To get there fast we can take the light rail."

"Whatever."

Rabbit led them to a station. Soon a small train came and paused to pick up passengers. They got on, too, unnoticed, which was just as well as they didn't have tickets. This was another slightly weird experience, riding a Mundane vehicle. In very little time they got off at the prison complex.

"We can ghost on inside, Doc," Rabbit said. "But think inconspicuous."

"Right."

They followed Rabbit into the complex, thinking unnoticeable, passing through walls when necessary to avoid guards and office personnel. In due course they reached the cell of Moxie. She was a tough-looking, unpretty, but fairly fit woman with reddish brown hair and blue eyes that didn't match. She was running in place, going nowhere, but sweaty from the effort.

"We need to get her attention," Incident said. "Let's see if I can manifest."

Goar was vaguely amused that they had been trying to hide from people, and now the challenge was to meet one. "Maybe you can connect with her mentally."

Incident stood directly before the woman. She closed her eyes, focusing.

Moxie stopped running, startled. "What?"

"I am Incident," Incident said, speaking aloud to better focus her thoughts. "Can you see me?"

Moxie looked, surprised but unafraid. "Yeah. Ugly little thing, aren't you? What are you anyway, a haunt?"

"I am a visitor who is, well, immaterial here. I am not really a ghost. I need to talk with you."

"Then talk, sister."

It was working! Incident had contacted Moxie's mind, making it possible for the woman to see her. Others might call it illusion, but it was what was required.

"We need a woman with plenty of know-how, experience, and nerve."

"I'm the one, sis. But I can't help you. They'll never let me out of the can."

"There may be a way for you to get out. To be free, and beautiful, and be the girlfriend of a smart but unstable man. To guide him to accomplish better things."

"Honey for that I'd kill. I have before. But you know, I've had enough of the bad girl life. So no. It's a dream, but I want to reform, if only in my mind."

She wanted to reform! This was a good sign.

"No killing," Incident said. "We know about killing. We don't like it."

"You keep saying we. You and who else?"

Incident paused. "You really want to know?"

"Sure, I really want to know! If I'm to be imagining things, like being pretty and having a man to micromanage, I want to understand them."

"I am Incident. I am an Oma. To you, a supernatural creature. I deliver cancer to innocent people. I want to stop, but there are constraints. My friend is Goar Golem." She glanced at him. "Come and stand by me. Focus on showing yourself."

Goar obliged. "Hello," he said.

"I see you! I hear you!" Moxie exclaimed. "You're not only ugly, you're weird!"

"I am," Goar agreed. "My body was assembled from spare parts. That's what a golem is. My soul is human, salvaged to animate this body. I was designed to be a killer."

"Yeah? How?"

Goar pulled off his socks from head, arms, and legs. "These are circular saws that cut up wood, flesh, bone, anything. I was sent to kill a couple that was just about to marry. I slaughtered them, and for that I am sorry."

"Then why did you do it? The time to be sorry is *before*, not after. Don't I know it!"

"I know it now," Goar agreed. "I blundered into a conscience cloud, and got a conscience, and that made me sorry."

"This gets wilder and wilder. But assuming I believe it, which I don't, what has that to do with me?"

"A great many lives will be lost tomorrow, unless we stop the New Clear Bomb from being detonated. With your help, we think we can stop it."

"A nuclear bomb," Moxie said thoughtfully. "Just when I thought you'd passed the limit, you take it another leap into nonsense."

"We can make you believe," Incident said. "If you agree to do what we ask."

"How?"

"We will bring Xylia here. She is pretty and innocent. We think she lacks the courage to do what we require, but with your help she can do it. We want to put you into her body with her, not to rule it but to share, and to provide her what she needs. To win over a key man and stop him from setting off the Bomb."

Moxie laughed. "If she needs nerve and savvy, sure. Give me a pretty body, and freedom outside, and I'll have that man eating out of my—" She changed her mind as Incident flinched. "Hand."

"We will bring her here," Incident said. "Within the hour, if we can."

"Look, honey, dreams are fun. But she'll be outside this cell and I'll be inside it. Ne'er the twain will meet."

"No. I will transfer your soul to her body. Your body here will lapse, while you live on with her."

"Have it your way. I don't believe any of it. But what do I have to lose? You come, do your thing, and I'll still be here in hell until I die. But at least it'll be fun pretending."

"We shall return," Incident said.

"You do that, sis."

They moved on out of the cell, and out of the prison. "There's not much time to spare," Incident said. "I believe this experience has taught me how to become more persuasive for the next interview."

"Turtle, take us to Xylia," Goar said once they were outside. "Can you direct us, or can you lead us?" He put Turtle down on the ground before him.

Turtle transformed into a man-sized turtle standing on his hind legs. "I will guide you mentally." He reverted to small size. Goar picked him up and put him back in the pocket.

"That's his mutant ninja form," Incident said. "The form that can talk."

So all three animals had talking forms, when they chose to activate them, just as they had flying forms. That was good to know.

Take the train back to the city. That was Turtle talking mentally. For that, he didn't need to assume a special physical form.

They boarded the train and soon were back in the metropolis. Turtle then directed them to the park. The one they had arrived at. The girl was walking there, alone. She was indeed rather pretty, with curly blond hair and a slender figure. She seemed to be deep in thought.

Incident approached her, using the same technique she had employed with Moxie. Xylia stopped, surprised, rubbing her eyes.

"I am not a ghost or a spook," Incident said carefully, and Goar felt her improved mental persuasiveness. She was sending belief as well as language. "I am a visitor who is not completely material. Please, I must talk with you. There is an urgent matter to discuss."

"Am I hallucinating?" Xylia asked, perhaps rhetorically.

"Not exactly. I am not a figment of your imagination, but your imagination can enhance me if you focus. Please, it is extremely important."

The girl focused. "You are a gremlin?"

"I am an ugly woman, but do not judge me by that. There is a great crisis, and you can help us defuse it if you choose to."

"If this is a form of mental dialogue, okay, let's have it. How can I help you when I can't even help myself? I am looking for a job so I can afford an apartment and make something of myself. But I can't find a job I would care to take, and my time is running out. If I don't find something tomorrow, I will have to give up and go home."

"We can help you," Incident said. "But it's a very special situation you may not want to get into."

"Try me. I'm desperate. I'm trying to figure out what to do, when there doesn't seem to be anything *to* do."

"Let's get off the path so we can talk privately," Incident said. "I will tell you what we need and what we offer, and you can decide."

Xylia shrugged. "It isn't as if I have anything better to do at the moment." She walked to a nearby mulberry tree and stood beside its trunk. "What is it?"

"A smart young man is soon to be dumped by the woman he loves," Incident said. "We want you to intercept him and win his heart so that he won't commit suicide tomorrow."

Xylia laughed ruefully. "In what, one hour? I'm too shy to bring myself even to say hello to a strange man, let alone interest him romantically, let alone do it quickly. My tongue gets tied, and I'd be lucky if I didn't wet my pants."

"Yes. But suppose you had a female companion with a lot of experience and nerve, who could take over for the introduction, and any other time you needed her help? It would be like standing beside her and watching her do it, only it would be your body doing it."

"Like remote control? I don't know."

Incident explained further, and gradually Xylia came to understand the nature of the deal. "But can you guarantee that she couldn't just abscond with my body, and I'd be buried somewhere, helpless? I wouldn't want that."

"It is your body. You have ultimate control. You could force her out if you had to, by mental rejection, though that would be unkind."

"And the reason to do this is why?"

"To prevent a New Clear, I mean nuclear, bomb from being detonated tomorrow and killing everyone."

Xylia whistled. "That's a pretty good reason!"

"Yes."

Finally, Xylia agreed. "It's crazy, but if it offers a way for me to make good, and for *her* to make good, and to save all those lives, I am willing to try it. It isn't as if I have other good options." Which was similar to what Moxie had said.

Then they were on their way to the prison. Xylia took the train, and Incident and Goar stood invisibly beside her. When Incident took her hand, she was able to communicate mentally to a degree, mainly reassurance.

This time they had to make a formal visit, since Xylia was a physical person. She went to the front desk, with Incident prompting her, and said she needed to visit the prisoner Moxie.

"She never gets visitors," the desk man protested.

"Yes. All the more reason for me to see her."

She got through, and soon stood outside the cell. This wing of the facility didn't have fancy telephonic protocols; she just was there with a guard keeping an eye on her to prevent contraband from being brought in.

Moxie came to the bars. "I'll be damned," she murmured. "You *are* pretty."

"Incident and Goar brought me here," Xylia said. "To be your host, so we can distract Hack and save the city. I—I am willing to try it if you are."

"If what she says is true, my mind will join yours, and give you advice, and take over when you need me to," Moxie said. "I do know how to handle men, and this one sounds okay. But to win his love in an hour we'll have to seduce him. Are you game for that?"

"No," Xylia said, blushing. "I have no sexual experience. But if you can handle it for me . . ."

"I can. So you're a virgin."

The blush continued. "Yes."

"He'll like that. Men do. I'm not virginal, but he won't know of my mind, only of your body. Just make sure you're the one who answers when he speaks to you."

"I won't know what to say."

"I'll prompt you. It's like a play with a prompter. You're the actress who makes the gestures and speaks the lines."

"A prompter," Xylia agreed, relieved.

"Now take hands," Incident said to them both. "And I will clasp them both. Do not resist; just allow me to exercise my power."

"The proof of the pudding," Moxie said. "If you can do it, I'll become a believer."

"Me too," Xylia agreed.

They clasped hands through the bars, and Incident put her hands around that clasp. There was a pause as all three focused.

Then they let go. Moxie sank to the floor, unconscious. The guard rushed up. "What did you do to her?"

"Nothing, sir," Moxie said via Xylia's voice. "We clasped hands in friendship. Then she fainted."

That was the truth. Lacking her soul, Moxie's body was now just a body, alive but in a coma. It would recover when its soul returned to it, if ever.

"Get out of here!" he snapped. Then he buzzed for a medic.

They got out of there. But in a moment, he reconsidered. "Stay! You're a Person of Interest."

"Uh-oh," Moxie muttered. "It'll take days to clean that up."

"We don't have days," Incident protested. "We have only hours, and not many of them."

Another guard entered the chamber. "Hold that woman!" the first guard said. "She did something to the prisoner."

The second guard looked at Xylia as if he would really like to hold her. She quailed, until Moxie took over. "Easy, big boy. I'm just an innocent visitor."

"They were touching through the bars," the first guard said. "Then this one collapsed. She may be dead. Maybe fast-acting poison, to silence a witness. At the very least, the visitor is a material witness."

The second guard reached out to take Xylia by the arm. She shrank away, but he pursued her. "Come here, doll. You and me got business together."

"Goar!" Incident cried.

Goar efficiently stripped his arm socks and revved up his deadly saws.

"Unhand that woman, varlet!" he shouted, focusing so that his sentiment could be heard.

"What's this?" the guard demanded, intent on Xylia's décolletage, which was loosening in her struggle to escape his grip.

"I warned you," Goar said, and sliced into the man's shoulder.

The ghostly cut did not affect the living body. But the pain did. "Ow-oooo!" the guard screamed exactly like a man being cut apart alive. He let go of Xylia and staggered away.

"Get out of here," Incident said, leading the way. Xylia hastily followed.

"Nice trick, Goar," Moxie said, glancing back as they left the chamber. Then they were gone. "But I can handle the next one myself."

"After them!" the first guard cried, dashing to the desk where he pressed a button. Immediately, a strident alarm sounded.

Goar lurched after the women. Guards were appearing from every cranny and maybe even a nook or two, thronging the corridor. Another grabbed hold of Xylia.

Goar paused. She thought she could handle it herself? Maybe he should let her try.

The woman gave the guard a direct stare from point-blank range. "Unhand me, varlet," she said, copying Goar's language. "Or else."

"Or else what, girl?" he demanded.

"Or else I will rip off my own clothing and tell your supervisor you tried to rape me. Want to bet which one of us he'll believe?"

"You wouldn't dare!"

She used her free hand to catch her blouse and rip it asunder, exposing her bra. When he didn't release her, being too busy staring, she hooked a finger under the bra strap and pulled the cup off her right breast. "Do I have to scratch myself there too, to make the point?"

He had had enough. He could indeed be framed for an attack. He let go and backed off.

Goar nodded to himself. That was Moxie's nerve showing as clearly as her anatomy.

She drew the bra cup back on, and covered it with the blouse, which had not actually torn. She had made her point.

Now the animals got into the act. Bird became a huge ugly vulture.

Rabbit became a snarling tiger. Turtle became a monstrous crocodile. As the guards became aware of them, they became increasingly visible. There was nothing like beginning belief to confirm their presence.

"What the hell?" one man asked disbelievingly. But his disbelief was clearly not complete.

The tiger charged him. He drew his taser and fired at it, to no effect. That scared him worse.

But there were peripheral efforts. A squad of guards were closing in on Xylia, heedless of the animal distractions.

Goar got to work. He sliced into the ones ahead, carving an alley for Xylia to scramble through.

"Go, man, go!" Moxie said, not at all upset by the imagined slaughter. "I like your style."

Goar was oddly buoyed by her support. He didn't much care for her as a person, but it was nice that she understood the usefulness of mayhem.

They plowed on, with Goar brutally intercepting anyone who got in Xylia's way. Xylia herself seemed somewhat freaked, but of course she was a nice girl.

They reached the front desk. "Hey, where are you going?" the desk man demanded. "You have to sign out."

"Officer, there's something going on back there," Moxie said. "Maybe a prisoner riot. I don't know what it is, but it's headed this way." She looked back fearfully.

He followed her gaze. Bird appeared as a ghostly raven. "Nevermore!" he croaked.

And while the desk man's jaw dropped, Xylia walked out unchallenged.

Before long they were outside the prison, then on the train to the city. Goar put the socks back on.

"Now you believe, both of you," Incident said.

"Now we believe," Xylia said. "We are talking, in my body. We're as different as night and day, but we like each other, we think."

"We do," Moxie agreed. "Niceness has its points."

"So does toughness," Xylia said.

"We are opposites, attracting."

"Yes. You have the qualities I lack, like experience and steel hard nerve."

"And you have ones I lack, like innocence and youth."

"Apart, we are partial. Together, we are whole."

"We are complete. I don't ever want to leave you."

"And I don't ever want to lose you."

Goar nodded. So it was working out. He was glad.

"Ooo!" Xylia exclaimed. "So that's how you seduce a man! It's not nearly as fearsome as I thought."

"Not when you know what you're doing," Moxie agreed.

"Now we must reach Hack before Gloria does," Incident said.

They headed out, but the dialogue continued. "I used to sing this song to myself," Xylia said. "It goes 'I wish I were a fascinating bitch, instead of an innocent child.' You're that bitch."

"I sure am," Moxie agreed proudly.

They went to Hack's apartment. He looked up from his keyboard, surprised. "Who are you?"

"Take it, Moxie," Incident said tersely. "Bird says we have barely forty-five minutes."

No one needed to ask for what. Xylia needed to nail him before Gloria arrived.

Xylia's body took a deep breath, which made her moderate but well-crafted bosom show to best advantage against her general slenderness. That was something the real Xylia would never have done before a real live man. "I am Xylia. A friend told me what a great guy you are, and I just had to come see for myself. You do look halfway handsome."

Hack was interested, as any man should be. "I'm a nerd."

"My friend said you know more about computers and the internet than any man alive," Xylia continued. That was surely Moxie, extrapolating from what they had told her. "She said you can make beautiful music in cyberspace. She said you're a genius." She smiled, and it was a truly effective expression. "I like smart fellows."

"Really?" Hack was plainly intrigued.

Even Goar was impressed. She was playing Hack like a violin, right from the start. The way the Goddess had played Goar. There was genius, all right, but it wasn't all the man's.

"Really," she said. She sat on a chair opposite him and crossed her nice legs so that her firm thighs showed up to the Arctic Circle. She leaned forward so that her neckline showed inside to the Antarctic Circle. "I could just sit here and watch you all day, knowing that even the tiniest of the little motions of your fingers can be moving unseen worlds. It's just so utterly impressive." She made a little stretch of her upper body that caused her supposedly hidden flesh to ripple like waves on a secret sea. "It simply does things to me. It makes me want to—" She broke off. "But I'm boring you."

"It makes you want to what?" Hack asked somewhat breathlessly.

"To—to get closer to you." She took another evocative breath. "To touch your greatness. To do things with you."

Goar, despite his awareness that this little act was not meant for him, was getting interested. What a combination of body and inference!

"What things?"

She gazed at him and blushed. It was intense, extending from her face on down into her revealed cleavage. Goar realized that Moxie must have turned the body over to Xylia, who was horribly embarrassed by the implication. Moxie could never have forced a blush as impressive as the real thing.

"With me?" Hack asked disbelievingly.

"With no one else," she breathed. "You're just such a wonder, I can't help myself. I've never done it before, but with you it just seems so right. Be gentle with me, please."

How close could she get without spelling it out? The blush might reach all the way to her waist now.

Hack opened his mouth. She quickly got smoothly to her feet and came to close it briefly with hers. This would be Moxie back in control. "Is there a bed?" she whispered.

"It's unmade." Obviously, Hack was at a loss for words.

"All the better."

They disappeared into the bedroom. "It's a pleasure to see a professional performance," Incident remarked.

"While they're out of sight—" Goar said urgently.

"There's that idea again," she chided him playfully. "Is that all you ever think of?"

"Just about. Especially after watching that scene."

She shook her head. "Not yet. Not while I'm ugly."

He sighed. Was she simply teasing him? Did she ever intend to deliver?

"No, I'm not," she said, reading his mind. "And yes, I will. In due course."

There was a delighted squeal from the bedroom. "Oh, she's good," Incident said. "But is she good enough?"

"We'll know when Gloria gets here."

There were more sounds from the bedroom. "They're doing it again," Incident said, surprised.

"So soon? Does she have a potency spell?"

"Just Moxie's skill with a young body."

He could not let it drop. "Are you sure we can't—?"

"Not at all sure." She listened, perhaps with her sensing more than her ears. "There's number two."

Goar got an idea for another approach. "If they do it a third time, will you—"

She sighed. "That turns me on too. Very well, if they make it a third time."

Victory! Maybe.

Soon Incident shook her head. "I didn't think it was possible. They made it a third time. So . . ."

Goar enfolded her.

Then Hack and Xylia emerged from the bedroom, happily disheveled. "Something else we have to tell you," Moxie said. "Your girlfriend, Gloria—she's been cynically using you for internet favors. But now she's ready to move on. She's going to dump you."

"Gloria? I don't believe it."

"Use your talent. Bypass the passwords, sneak into her most private account, on Mug Shot. She's bragging how she bamboozles you."

Hack's fingers played over the keyboard. In moments he had verified it. "Damn. I trusted her. I've been a fool!"

"Not anymore, lover," Moxie said fondly.

There was a peremptory knock on the door. "Oh no!" Incident said. "The she canine is here."

Just in time to deny Goar his reward. If only she could have waited five more minutes!

Hack stood up, tucking in his shirt, as Xylia retreated to the bedroom. "Did I hear a knock?"

There was another knock.

"I did." He walked to the door and opened it. "Gloria," he said as if surprised.

"Indeed," she agreed, entering the room. "I believe you wanted to speak to me about something important?"

"I was going to ask you to marry me. But—"

"But you feared I would turn you down. Well, you were right. I am tired of you and your geekish ways and I am officially dumping you as of this moment, you loser."

"But—"

"But me no buts. I am through with you." She whirled in place and walked back out, slamming the door behind her.

"But I changed my mind," he finished to her absence. "Because I have found someone I like better."

Xylia emerged from the bedroom, looking fresh and clean. It was amazing how well she had primped in such a brief time. "Who was that, dear?"

"Nobody who matters." He took her in his arms. "You are the only one who matters to me now."

She kissed him. "I love hearing you say that. I will never leave you."

Incident whistled. "Only forty-five minutes! Not only did she win him, she made him proof against the false hussy. What a demonstration!"

Moxie looked at her. "I heard that."

Hack looked too. "Is that the ghost you told me about, dear?"

Goar was shocked. She had told him?

"Yes, we told him," Xylia said. "He deserves to know the truth, so there will be no deception between us, ever. How we are two, and together we will take care of him as long as we three shall live."

"After I take care of that small remaining nuisance," Hack said. He sat down at his computer. "There will be no investigation at the prison. I will pie the record so that Xylia's name is purged. The officials will never know she even visited."

"And they will think that the prison guards got high on opioids and had a mass hallucination about invading animals and a golem with circular saw hands," Moxie said. "And that I got some of it and it put me into a coma."

"You got it," he said, squeezing her bottom.

"Hey, you didn't do me," Xylia said. "Share and share alike, remember?"

"Sorry." He pinched Xylia's bottom. How that girl had changed!

"So which of us was the best lay?" Moxie asked mischievously.

"Which was which?" he asked as his eyes tracked the computer screen.

"I was the first," Xylia said. "The virgin, remember?"

"And I was the second," Moxie said. "The pro."

Incident caught Goar's eye. So that was how they had cranked him up again so rapidly. They had taken turns seducing him. A new woman in the same body.

"The third was the best," Hack decided.

"That was both of us together," they said together. Then all three laughed.

"I think our job here is done," Goar said.

"It is," Moxie answered him. "But thank you. You gave me back my life."

"Thank you," Xylia said too. "You gave me a new life."

"As long as you three are satisfied," Incident said. "We had an external reason."

"And there will be no nuclear explosion," Hack agreed. "Because I have a much better life. I will get a high-paying legitimate job and buy nice things for my girlfriends. I thank you also."

"You're certainly welcome," Incident said. "Now we must depart."

"Will you come to the wedding?" Xylia asked.

"If we can," Incident said. "But do you really want ugly ghosts attending?"

"Just stand in the back and be quiet," Moxie said. They all laughed.

"And your animals too," Xylia added.

The three animals gazed beseechingly at Incident. They wanted to attend. It would certainly be different from delivering poisonous seeds. "Oh, all right; we'll try," she agreed.

They went to the big rabbit hole in the park and returned to Xanth. It was a job well done.

Except for one thing. "I thought this would turn us beautiful, or at least less ugly," Incident said. "Isn't it a good deed, saving all those lives?"

But they were unchanged. "Well, it was worth doing regardless," Goar said.

"Bleep."

He tried to make her smile. "Use language like that again, and I'll kiss you."

She turned her face away, declining to play the game. "I so wanted to kiss you pretty, and do the rest. To walk in beauty like the night. This wounds me." Now her tears flowed.

Goar hugged her, but it was small compensation. He was disappointed too. So were the animals. But it wasn't as if they had had a firm deal in that respect. They had simply assumed.

They returned to the box, foraged for a supper, and retired for the night. Goar didn't even try to implement his idea; she plainly wasn't ready for it, and neither was he, really. They slept chastely side by side.

In the morning they washed, ate, and went to the five-way nexus to make their report. The other teams were there. "How did it go?" AMos inquired. He wasn't being snide; he cared, at least about how much work was ahead.

"We did it," Incident said. "We turned off the nuclear blast."

"The what?"

"The New Clear Bomb," she said carefully. "So there should not be the overload of deliveries."

"That is wonderful news." He paused, looked at her. "You seem unchanged."

"I foolishly thought—"

Then something odd happened. They all looked about, startled.

AMos saw it first. "You're beautiful!"

"What?" Incident looked at Goar.

"You are," he said. "Suddenly, you're not just improved, you are scintillating."

"So are you," she said in wonder.

"You both are," AMos said. "So are your Companions."

They went to the nearest puddle and gazed at their reflections. They were so attractive they seemed to glow. All five of them.

"And the rest of us are somewhat improved," AMos said.

"You contributed to a lesser extent," Goar said. "So you received a lesser compensation."

"So it seems," AMos agreed. "That's worth something."

"But why now?" Incident asked. "It was yesterday we did it."

Then Goar caught on. "But history wasn't actually changed until today. When the Bomb didn't go off. That's when it counted."

"That's when it counted," Incident echoed.

"Bleep," ALma muttered. "We'll never seduce the golem now. Not with her looking like that, conscience or not."

"Bleep," AJane echoed. "And he's so intensely handsome now."

"Sorry about that," Incident said insincerely. "But the rest of you are no longer ugly, merely plain. You can probably seduce some regular folk if you catch them in bad light." She took a spectacular breath. "Well, we'll be on our way." She was plainly trying to stifle her smugness, but wisps of it were leaking out around the edges. Goar could hardly blame her.

They left the intersection, heading farther into their own territory.

"You know, you can retire now, Incident," Goar said. "With your outstanding beauty, you should be able to get any other position you want."

She brightened. "That's right. No more dire deliveries." She glanced at the animals. "Same for you, friends. You can lock in your looks, maybe get nice girlfriends, form families." Then she looked at Goar. "But what about you?"

"I can't retire until I win the forgiveness of the folk I killed."

"Which is weird, considering they are alive."

"Those are visitors from another frame, who took the place of the ones I slaughtered. It is really their forgiveness I seek."

"So you will continue hanging around, trying to do more good deeds."

"Yes. Saving all those Mundanes doesn't count, for this."

"Yet now you are handsome. So there must be some relevance."

"I think I was rewarded, as you were, for my good deed. But I still have to earn my absolution."

She considered briefly. "Then I don't think I can retire yet. Not until you, too, are saved."

"Oh, you don't have to make that sacrifice. My fate is not your concern."

She turned on him almost fiercely. "But it *is* my concern, because you are my concern. I owe you a fabulous night."

"I'd rather have you *want* to be with me, not sacrificing yourself."

"I do want to be with you, and not just because you are handsome now. You helped me win my salvation; now let me help you win yours. I'll stay until then, at least."

He was moved almost to tears. "Oh, Incident!"

She looked at the animals. "How about you? You can take your freedom now; you don't have stay with me."

The three circulated a glance. Then Bird became the parrot. "We'll stay with you. And him. Until he, too, is free."

Now there was a tear in her eye. "Oh, companions!"

The four clustered together, hugging in their fashions. Then they moved across to Goar and hugged him similarly. "Oh, all of you," he said, and his tears flowed. He had not realized until this moment how much their support meant to him.

"Now that the mushy stuff is done," Incident said, "it is time for that night I promised you, Goar. You're the protagonist, so you are being watched, and I don't care to be the cynosure for this particular encounter. But I think they don't watch between chapters of your story. So let's make that break here." She leaned closer and kissed him. It made him float inside.

"Let's make that break," he agreed.

Chapter 9

PRINCESS

It was a beautiful morning. They emerged from the Box to clean up in the nearest pond. The beautiful animals were still reveling in their new appearance. Goar understood that feeling, as he shared it. "You were right," he said to Incident. "I doubt I will ever return to the Goddess."

"She clearly taught you how to be a perfect lover," Incident said. "I had nothing to teach you there."

"I just wanted to please you."

"You did. I lost count of the times." Then she paused. "Oh, darn! Another seed just arrived. A bad one."

"It can surely wait till we've eaten."

"Yes. I just want to wash, eat, and sleep."

"But you just had the night."

She looked at him. "How long did you let me sleep?"

Oh. Hardly any time. "I apologize. You were just so wonderful I couldn't leave you alone."

She laughed. "And neither could I leave you alone. It was a mutual fault."

"Maybe we can slow down hereafter."

"Maybe. Do we really want to?"

He had to laugh. "Got me there. As long as you know I wanted you even before you turned beautiful." Then he became aware of something. "I feel you."

"As you did all night. I'm lucky I don't have bruises on my torso."

He smiled. Teasing each other was fun. "No, I mean your mind. You're unsnagging your toe from a vine under the water and there's a fish kissing your knee."

"So I am. So there is. I'm not surprised. It seems I gave you everything I had, including some of my mind. Physical closeness is not the ultimate; mental is."

"Yes. I feel wonderful. I feel the companions too. I know what each is doing, when I orient."

"That's part of it. It is one of the talents I got with becoming an Oma. Now it seems you have it too, at least to a degree, from our association."

"Unless I am just imagining it."

"You can readily verify it. Go away from me, physically, and I will do something you couldn't guess, like sucking on my own big toe while braiding my eyelashes, unless the connection is real. Same for the companions. Who knows, maybe you will start delivering seeds."

"I will. I mean the separation, not the seeds." He was really intrigued by this new development. He waded out of the water, shook himself dry, and went to the empty box. He lay down and closed his eyes, picturing her in his mind.

The picture came clearer as he concentrated. Incident was splashing water on her body, then dipping her luxurious hair and wringing it out. She kept her eyes closed because their washing had stirred up some mud.

"Well, now." It was an unfamiliar male voice. Someone else had happened upon this pond. "What a lovely nymph! You're for me, for sure."

"Not interested," she said, eyes still closed.

"Well, I am." He forged into the water to grab her.

"No!" She struggled, but he drew her into him relentlessly for a demanding kiss and feel. Goar felt and resented both,

"Take that!" she exclaimed angrily, hitting him with the seed box. But it didn't deter him. She was invulnerable, but not super strong.

This was actually happening! Goar leaped up, ripping the socks off his arms. He revved up his saws and charged out of the box.

But Bird was already there, in roc form, swooping down to catch the man with a single talon hooked into the collar. He hefted the man up and hurled him across the pond, where he landed in a crumple. He scrambled up and staggered into the forest, surely never to be seen in these parts again. That was still better for him than Goar's arrival would have been.

Rabbit was bounding toward the pond, and Turtle in giant tortoise mode was pounding toward it similarly. Of course the animals were tuned in! Bird had simply been the fastest. No one was going to molest this damsel and survive intact.

By the time they got there, Incident had cleared the water from her eyes. "Thanks, fellows," she said. "I'm okay. We can all relax."

"He saw you bare, and he just grabbed," Goar said, outraged.

She nodded. "Men have seen me before, but I forgot I'm no longer ugly. Now they don't turn away in disgust."

"Maybe you should not go nude anymore. I know it's your natural mode, but things have changed."

She eyed him appraisingly. "Same to you, golem. Any normal woman who sees your luster is likely to have a similar urge, though she may be slightly less candid about her interest."

"We both need to wear clothing now," he agreed.

She cocked her head prettily. "Rabbit says there's a clothing grove not far afield. We'll go there immediately."

They went there. In three moments apiece, she was appealingly outfitted in blouse, skirt, bra and panties, with matching slippers, and a sheer veil, and he was in shirt and trousers with conservative black shoes.

Then she paused. "Oops, I think I did something I shouldn't have."

"You look perfect to me."

"I mean back in the pond. I was so mad about the attack that I gave him the seed."

Goar realized what she was saying. "Now he has hidden cancer!"

"Yes. But he wasn't supposed to be a target. That was an abuse of my office."

"Serves him right."

"No. As long as I do this job, I have to do it right. I can't go giving people cancer just because I don't like them."

Now he appreciated her point. "We have consciences. We have to try to do what is right."

"Yes." They headed for the pie plants.

There was a woman with a head of hair like a breaking ocean wave. She looked at Goar, and was so surprised that she dropped her newly harvested pie. "You're him!"

"I'm who?" Goar asked, somewhat inanely.

"The protagonist! I used a Token, but it didn't seem to work, and I thought it was a bad one. But you were on the way."

Goar was nonplussed. "I think you have mistaken me for someone else. I'm just looking for a pie."

"No, it flashed your picture. You're the one! The viewpoint character for this story."

Goar glanced at Incident. "Does this make sense?"

"Well, you *are* the protagonist. That carries a certain responsibility. So maybe you should find out what she wants."

He seemed to be stuck for it, whatever it was. "Hello. I am Goar Golem, no particular talent, just passing through. What can I do for you?"

"Hello, Goar. I am Sue Nami. Never mind my talent."

"I have heard of you," Incident said. "You can make giant waves."

"Not always when I want to," Sue agreed. "They can do horrible damage. That's why I am now staying far from the sea, so there can be no accidents. But it's my daughter Min I'm concerned about. She is cursed to get blamed for things that really aren't her fault. Now she's in a picklement and I'm trying to get her out of it. So I used a Token, and it showed me you, Goar Golem. You must help her!"

"But I have no expertise in solving other people's problems," he protested.

"The Token says you do. Please, I beg of you."

He looked at Incident again, and again she was not much help. "You did okay in Mundania. Maybe that's what put you on the map for this, as a problem solver."

Again, he seemed to be stuck for it. "Tell me the problem."

"She is Min Tu Bi. She has the attribute of seeing negative space. Like two candlesticks that define faces when you look at the negative space between them. Maybe you could call it the talent of parallax perception, seeing the truth however much it has been distorted."

Goar twisted his mind to orient on that, and began to see it. "She sees what others don't."

"Yes, exactly. Well, some mischievous demon noticed that, and co-opted her into a contest of talents that seem like curses."

"A demon?" Incident asked. "They don't usually bother messing with humans."

"This one did. A sexy female, Mentor, Mentra, something like that. She tended to mix up her words."

"Metria!" Incident said. "I know of her."

"Who is Metria?" Goar asked.

"Never mind. She's sheer mischief."

A small cloud of smoke formed beside them. It extended arms, legs, and a head, and shaped into a marvelously provocative torso with a largely translucent dress trying desperately to cover its assets. "Did I hear my nomenclature?"

"Your what?"

"Terminology, personality, identity, recognition, individuality—"

"Your name!" Incident snapped.

"Whatever," Metria agreed crossly.

"That's her," Sue said. "Because of her, my daughter is caught in this pointless contest." She glared at the demoness. "Will you let her go now?"

"Absotively not. It is time for the showdown."

"The only way to get rid of her is to satisfy her, or bore her into leaving," Incident muttered.

Metria eyed Goar. "Maybe you could satisfy me, handsome." Her dress illuminated in three places, two above and one below, calling attention to her burgeoning assets. Goar felt his eyeballs heating, even though he didn't actually have eyeballs.

"Oh no you don't!" Incident snapped.

"What's this about a contest?" Goar asked, desperate to head off mischief.

"I thought you'd never ask," Metria said, and he realized that he'd been played. "You are the protagonist, so you must be the judge of which of the three talents most perfectly fits the definition of gift/curse. That is, it's hard to tell which it is. You may use the Tokens to summon the contestants."

"Tokens?" he asked blankly. Sue had mentioned that.

The demoness produced what looked like a coin. "This. It is a Token appearance. It will show the subject, and summon it for an hour before letting it revert to its starting place. Take it and say the words 'Contestant One.'" She handed it to him.

Goar sighed inwardly. What was there to do but play it through and be done with it? "Contestant One."

A face appeared on the Token. She appeared to be an ordinary girl. "Hello?"

"Invoke!" Metria said.

Then the girl stood before them. "Oh!" she exclaimed, surprised.

"Min!" Sue said. "I tried to get you out of it. You're in a talent contest."

"Mother!" The two hugged.

"Summon the second contestant," Metria said, handing Goar another Token.

What could he do? "Contestant Two."

The face of a young man appeared. "Yes?"

"Invoke," Metria said, and the man appeared before them.

"What is this?" he asked, astonished.

Goar stepped in. "You have been magically summoned for a talent contest. Who are you and what is your talent?"

The question seemed to steady the man, maybe because it gave him something else to orient on. "I am called Combo, because my talent is recombination. That is, combining any two magical items to make a third. Such as a suck-seed and a cess-pit making a success. Fall into a cess pool and emerge smelling like a rose. But the stronger the magic the less reliable the result, so I try not to use it. Once I tried to merge a pit and a pendulum, and almost got someone killed."

"So it's as much a curse as a gift," Goar said.

"Exactly."

"Here is the third Token," Metria said, handing it to him.

"Contestant Three," Goar said with resignation.

A young woman's face appeared in the coin. "Hello?"

"Invoke!" Metria said, and the woman was standing before him.

The girl eyed him. "Well, aren't you the handsome one. Maybe this time I fell through a good crack."

"You have been summoned for a talent contest," Goar said, steeling himself against her prettiness. After all, Incident was watching. So was Combo. "Please state your name and talent."

"I am Crystal, and my curse is falling through cracks."

"Do your job, Judge," Metria said.

"But I am not competent to judge anybody's talent," he protested.

"You're the protagonist. It's your job."

He looked again at Incident. "Do it," she muttered grimly.

Again, it seemed he had no choice. "I am Goar Golem, and it seems I have been co-opted to judge your talents, incompetent as I am," he said. "The one that is most confusing about being a curse or a blessing will win." He glanced a Metria. "Is there an award?"

"Of course there's a prime."

"Prize," Incident said before the demoness could go into her routine.

Metria waved a hand and a small mirror appeared in it. "This Reverse Glass. It reflects things reversed."

"All mirrors do that," Incident snapped.

"Not like this. See." She held the mirror so that it reflected Rabbit, who was quietly watching the proceeding.

Goar could not make head nor cotton tail of it. "What is this?"

"It's a tibbar."

"Oh, rabbit spelled backward," Incident said.

"Hey, that might be fun," Min said. "It sort of complements my talent."

"Mine too," Crystal said. "I couldn't fall through a kcarc."

"Me too," Combo said. "I might merge it with something else and make something really phenomenal."

It seemed the prize was satisfactory.

"Min, please demonstrate your talent,' Goar said.

"There's no need to proceed further," Min said. "The winner has already been decided."

"I haven't decided," Goar protested.

"Not consciously. But subconsciously you have. I can see it in the mental spaces. It is Crystal's talent of falling through the cracks."

"But the other two shouldn't approve of that!"

"Yes they do. Combo likes Crystal's look, and wants to date her. She's glad to have someone to catch her if she falls in another crack, and maybe find a way to merge her talent with his for romantic magic. And I'm happy for them. In fact I expect to attend their wedding."

Combo and Crystal looked at each other. A small heart formed between them. It was happening already.

Goar threw up his hands. "Then so be it. Crystal's talent wins."

"Oh!" Crystal exclaimed, jumping up and down. "I won!" A crack formed beneath her, but Combo reached out to catch her and draw her safely into himself. They kissed.

"I posilutly love it when things come together," Metria said, and faded out.

"So be it," Incident echoed. She glanced meaningfully at Goar, and his knees turned mushy.

They took their pies back to the box. "Let's eat and sleep," Goar told Incident. "I promise to let you repose in peace."

She eyed him mischievously. "Can you keep that promise?"

He was doubtful. "Maybe if I find another box to sleep in."

"No. I like being warm and close and irresistible. That's part of the problem."

"Maybe if I have a distraction?"

A bulb flashed prettily over her head as she tasted her blueberry pie. "I have it. You can practice sensing the companions."

"I'd get bored. Then I'd become aware of your exquisite body beside mine."

"Not if they're doing something really interesting. Like rescuing fair damsels in distress."

"There couldn't be any as fair as you."

"Stop it," she snapped appreciatively. "Let me focus." She took a bite of pie, closed her lovely eyes, and turned slowly around as she chewed. "There. A genuine damsel in distress. But she's too far away for Rabbit or Turtle. So it has to be Bird."

"Bird," he agreed agreeably.

"The thing is, you will have no responsibility. No contest judging."

"No sexy demonesses," he agreed.

She banged him lightly on the shoulder in reproof. "That too. You're just along for the ride. So you can relax."

Bird flew to them, in mini mode, responding to the signal. He landed on her shoulder.

"Bird, there's a damsel in distress, but I need more rest. Can you handle it alone?"

Bird sent a feeling of uncertainty. Incident was normally the brains of their team.

"Suppose Goar follows you, mentally? He's learning to do it now, but he needs practice, and I need to keep my tasty torso to myself for a while." The companions, of course, were well aware of their night's activity. "He can advise you if you have a problem: just tune in."

Bird glanced at Goar, and nodded. He could always alert Incident if Goar proved to be inadequate.

"Good enough. Here's the azimuth." She made a mental signal. "About half an hour as the roc flies."

Bird jumped off her shoulder, spread his wings, ascended, and became the roc. He headed into the brightening sky.

Goar and Incident finished their pies and retired into the box. They removed their new clothing so it wouldn't get mussed, kissed, lay down side by side, and Goar focused on Bird. He saw the patchwork geography of the Land of Xanth passing below, a bird's eye view, with now and then a stray cloud obscuring a section. It was interesting. The bird's eye did not pick up the same details as Goar's own eye had when they rode the roc. But it did pick up shades Goar's eyes did not. It was a fair exchange.

"Well, I didn't expect you to be that distracted that fast," Incident complained. "Not that I want your full attention on me right now, either."

Goar compromised in the manner the Goddess had taught him in her spot course *Managing Women 101*. He put a hand on her plush bottom, squeezed appreciatively, and continued watching. Secondhand flying, like firsthand bottom squeezing, was an exhilarating experience. "Good enough for the nonce?"

"It is," she agreed, satisfied. He was paying her attention without threatening to make more of it than she wanted at an inconvenient time.

Bird zeroed in on the distressed maiden. He tuned in on her mind, picking up on her situation. She was locked in an isolated tower, able to see the landscape in all directions, but had no human company. At least she could see the birds up here.

Bird took the form of a dusky sparrow and landed on her sill. "Oh, I love your little cloud of dusk!" she exclaimed, spying him immediately. "It's so cute!"

She wore a neat little gold crown. She was a princess!

Bird was taken aback. *What now?* he asked Goar mentally.

So much for having no involvement. This was *Managing Women 102.* Goar thought fast. *Assume a form that can talk her language and engage her in conversation. Make sure to be really interested in whatever she has to say, no matter how dull.*

Bird hopped off the sill and became a junior bird man, essentially a man with wings, so he could talk with her. "I am not really a sparrow," he said somewhat awkwardly.

She took stock, surprised by not affrighted. "You're a shape changer!"

"To a degree. I am a bird who can assume any bird form. In this case, a bird man."

"I love birds!"

"Then we should get along. Why are you being held captive here?"

"I am Princess Birdie, my nickname. I am of the Shee, known in Mundania as the Sidhe, a species of Light Elves. We look mostly human, but we're not."

"You do look human," he agreed, hardly needing to fake his interest. If she had wings, being a bird maiden, she would have been quite attractive.

"There are many roughly humanoid species, the Shee among them. I suspect we have a common ancestor somewhere in the dim reaches of the forgotten past. Does it matter to you?"

"No, since I am a bird."

"I love all manner of birds, though my father the King complains they eat the crops outside and poop on the rugs inside. But I just can't give them up. So finally he had me confined here, to keep me out of mischief."

Be really interested, Goar reminded him.

"Just for liking birds? I find that really interesting."

She grimaced cutely. "That, and my refusal to settle, marry, and have broods of children who will keep me too busy to be concerned any more about birds."

Follow up on that.

"You don't want to marry and have a family?"

"I didn't say that. I just don't want to marry some dull lunk of a prince whose only idea of a bird is a baked turkey or a chained hunting falcon. The man I marry must love birds as I do. So it is a contest of wills between the King and me. I'm not being tortured, just confined until I come to my senses, his way."

Express sympathy.

"That's cruel."

She nodded, appreciating the sympathy. "He sees it as practical. My father loves me, I know he does, but he just can't tolerate the thought of a woman, any woman, having a mind of her own. My mother doesn't." She contemplated him. "But what brings a remarkable creature like you here? I'm sure you have a most interesting story to tell."

Tell her your mission.

"I came here to rescue a damsel in distress. I didn't know she'd be a lovely princess."

She gazed at him. "You think I'm lovely?"

He had misspoken. Princesses were by definition lovely. Actually, by bird standards she was nothing special, physically. She had floating blue hair, blue eyes, and a trim body, but as birds went these were fairly standard attributes.

Belay that! Tell her yes, she's lovely.

But I'm not sure that is true.

The lessons of the Goddess Tiamat were increasingly relevant. *Truth has little to do with it. A woman needs to be constantly complimented. You can't establish a relationship otherwise. Do it.*

"Yes, you are lovely."

She melted around the edges. "Really?"

Really!

"Really."

"Oh, you're just saying that."

Bird opened his mouth to agree, but Goar tackled that thought before it got fairly out of its crevice. *What else can I say, in the face of such charm?*

"What else can I say, in the face of such charm?"

The melting continued deeper into her body. "You have a way with words."

It was time to change the subject. *Ask her more about what will make her father relent.*

"Your father the King—is there any other way you can placate him?"

Birdie shrugged in a way that Bird would not have found interesting before he assumed the bird man form. "Placating him is easy. Either I marry a prince he chooses, or I find one of my own. But it's sort of difficult as long as I am cooped up in this isolated tower. When he left me here, he made a joke, I think he said maybe a bird would come to rescue me."

"He didn't know about me," Bird said. "I will take you out of this tower and set you on the ground, free."

"That wouldn't do it. He'd just lock me up again. It isn't as if I could just wander the countryside. I'm a princess."

"I'm sorry. I am not much familiar with the ways of kings and princesses. I wish there were some other way I could help."

She considered, contemplating him. "Maybe there is. Why don't *you* marry me?"

Bird was amazed and dismayed. "Me? I'm a bird!"

"I love birds," she repeated.

Uh-oh. Goar felt Bird's desperation. He had come on a rescue mission, not a marriage mission. *But you're not a prince or king.*

"I am not a prince or king."

Her gaze became canny. "You can assume the form of any bird, you say?"

"Yes. And some in between forms, like this bird man. But I'm not royal in any of them. So I don't qualify."

"How about a king bird?"

Bird became a kingbird.

"I could marry a king bird. That's technically a kind of king, isn't it? My father did not specify the species, so he'd be stuck with it. A king's word is a king's law, even if he misspeaks."

Bird changed back to the bird man form. "But I came only to rescue you, not to marry you."

But she had found an avenue, and intended to pursue it with diligence. He should have realized before that she was not one to be readily balked. She came to him and took him in her arms. She was marvelously soft. She kissed him. Suddenly, she appealed to him in a way he had not experienced before. "Are you sure?"

Goar recognized the way a woman managed a man. He had learned a lot from the Goddess, but he was an amateur compared to a real woman. Bird was probably lost.

Bird was coming to a similar conclusion. The irony was that he no longer really wanted to resist her. "But why would you even want to, to—"

“Did I mention that I love birds? I’m sure you are a very birdly bird, and I am eager to explore all your avian forms in intimate detail. But you can surely also be a very manly man, and I mean to explore that too.”

“I—I—”

“Exactly.” She kissed him again, and pressed herself against him.

Goar recognized that ploy too. She was seducing him, and after that, he would be silly putty in her hands, a creature of her will. Goar knew the route.

“You seem disturbed,” Incident said, lying beside him.

“She’s seducing him!”

“Oh? I need to know more about this.”

He quickly filled her in. “Now she’s getting out of her robe, and—” he concluded.

“I believe I have the idea. Let’s leave them to it.”

“But—”

“She’s a princess. He could do a lot worse than that.”

“But—”

“And she could do worse than Bird. He has good qualities.”

“But—”

“You talk too much.”

“But—”

“Stop saying it and do it.” She caught his hand and set it on her butt.

Oh. A pun. But and Butt. But a most interesting one.

She kissed him, and in most of a moment their situation echoed that in the distant tower.

The two couples were finished about the same time. Goar tuned in on Bird and Birdie as they and Incident slept a while, then got up, got clean, and went outside.

“Now that that’s settled,” Birdie said, soon waking. “Let’s go meet your folks. I’m sure they are interesting too.”

“But what about the King?”

“He will soon enough discover the empty tower. Let’s let him stew for a while. In due course I will return and present you to him as my betrothed, the Bird who rescued me, and he will know that I have won this round. He will accept you perforce.”

Bird was overwhelmed by the pyramiding implications. “I don’t know.”

She squeezed his hand. "You have an objection?"

He was lost and knew it. He could never oppose her will; she had seen to that. "No."

She smiled. "That's good." She knew her victory was complete. "Now let's get out of here. You can assume big bird form?"

"Yes."

"Go outside the window, cling to a bar, and get big enough to carry me. I'll climb out and on. Then we will gloriously fly. Free as birds, by no coincidence."

He obeyed, and soon she was riding his roc form. "Oh my! This is just so wonderful! I always wanted to fly like a bird, and now I'm doing it. What marvelous scenery!"

"Squawk!" he agreed.

But it was a long flight, and she soon became restive. "Now tell me all about you and your friends."

"Squawk?"

"Oh, that's right, I forget. You can't talk human in that form. But I can fix that. Just let me invoke my bird talk translation spell. There. Now talk."

"Squawk."

"And you said, and I quote, 'All right I will.'"

He was amazed. That was exactly what he had said.

"Now I will ask questions, and you will answer, and by the time we get there I will know all about you and your friends."

She was correct. By the time they reached the box in the glade, she had an excellent idea of all of them, as well as Goar's need to gain the forgiveness of Squid and Larry. But there was just one problem.

"When you retire as a deliverer of cancer seeds, you will lose your special powers?"

"Squawk."

"Mice!" she swore villainously. As a princess she was unable to say bleep. "I suppose we will simply have to select a form for you to stay in, and retire to a bird sanctuary I will arrange. I will still love you, but it won't be as exciting."

"Squawk!"

Her ears reddened and set fantasy fire to her earrings. She couldn't speak bad bleeps, but she understood them. "My sentiment exactly."

They coasted to a landing in the glade. Birdie quickly remade her mussed hairdo and tightened her loose robe. She even got her maidenly halter firmly aligned so that it looked as if it had never been disturbed.

Goar, Incident, Rabbit, and Turtle stood beside the box. They had of course known the two were coming. "Greetings to you all," Birdie said. "I am Princess Birdie, the damsel in distress so gallantly rescued by Bird. He has told me what wonderful companions you are." She smiled. "Just call me Birdie; I am presently off duty."

"Hello, Birdie," Incident said.

"Hello, Incident." Birdie glanced at the sky. "I suppose I had better go settle with my father now, so as to be out of your way. But I will marry Bird in due course, regardless."

It seemed to make sense. There was a royal aura of command about even her passing whims. Soon they were all aboard the roc, chatting as he winged swiftly for the King's palace.

Two hours later the turrets of the Royal Castle hove into view. Bird circled it once, making sure they were seen, then spiraled down to the frontal turf. They slid down to the grass.

A volley of arrows flew at them. Goar hastily enfolded the Princess, protecting her, because while the five of them were invulnerable, she wasn't.

"They must think it's an invasion," Incident said. "They don't realize it's the princess."

"Father!" Birdie called. "It's me!" She waved a royal gem-encrusted hankie.

The King stood at the central turret, gazing down. He saw her. He pointed. "Destroy them!"

"Father!" Birdie repeated desperately. But she was answered only by another volley of arrows.

It seemed that the King was not in a forgiving mood.

"This is outrageous!" Incident said. "He's trying to kill his own daughter!"

"He's pretty stubborn," Birdie agreed. "So am I. I suppose he'd rather see me dead than getting away with rebellion, even in so slight a manner as marriage." She seemed sad rather than frightened.

Turtle had had enough. He expanded to mountainous size and tramped toward the castle. He crossed the moat as if it were merely a ditch, and forged into the castle, shoving the wall down before his phenomenal mass. He plowed a furrow through the center of the castle and emerged from the far side, leaving a trail of ruin.

The archers, distracted by Turtle's bulldozing, were no longer loosing their arrows. But there seemed little point in staying.

Turtle looped around and returned to them. He turned small. "Let's depart," Incident said grimly.

They boarded the roc and took off. In less than a moment the ruined castle was far behind, with its population running around aimlessly like ants.

"I think you won't be returning soon," Incident told Birdie.

"I won't," the girl agreed. "I suppose I am no longer a princess. I am dead in my father's eyes." She wiped away a tear. "He's a good man, really he is, but he hates to be balked."

"That does not seem to be the best quality in a ruler," Incident said.

"He was more amenable when younger. I have seen him hardening inside. But he won't listen to advice." Birdie took a breath. "Well, I simply have to make the best of it. I do want to thank all of you for your support. Bird, of course, for rescuing me from the tower."

Bird waggled his wingtips slightly, showing that he heard her.

"And you, Turtle, for standing up for me," she continued. She reached out and picked up the tiny turtle. "Thank you." She kissed the top of his shell.

It was evidently a potent kiss. The whole shell blushed pink before fading back to green.

"And you, Rabbit, for enabling your group to visit Mundania and save all those people from the Bomb." She took hold of him, brought him close, and kissed the top of his head. His fur turned briefly pink. "Which in turn converted all of you from ugly to beautiful, physically."

Goar was increasingly impressed. The Princess had evidently taken the trouble not only to learn about all of them, but to assimilate the information.

"And you, Goar, for protecting me from the arrows, which would have harmed me if you had not interceded." She kissed him on the side of his face-plate, and he felt it heating with color as he reacted the same way the others had. Her kisses were indeed magical.

"And especially you, Incident, for rescuing the others from their fates and making it possible for me to get to know all of you."

Goar was surprised again. Birdie had just suffered the trauma of being rejected by her father, indeed, almost getting killed by his order, yet here she was focusing politely on each of them.

"You don't need to kiss me," Incident said.

"Oh, but I do. Among the Shee, a kiss denotes friendship, and I want to be your friend." Birdie drew Incident in and kissed her firmly on the mouth.

And Incident blushed, smitten silent.

"And now I think I should be on my way," Birdie continued sadly. "Bird will not want to marry me now that I am a commoner, nor will the rest of you wish to associate with me. I hope you remember me kindly. Just set me down anywhere convenient, and I will no longer interfere with your activity. I apologize for wasting so much of your time."

What? Goar felt Bird stiffen in flight, and so did the others.

Incident was the first to recover. "There may be a misunderstanding. Our interest in you was as a distressed maiden, not as a princess. You remain distressed. We will continue to help you until such time as you no longer need it." She paused, picking up something else. "And Bird still would like to marry you. You made an impression on him as a woman rather than as a princess."

Now Birdie froze. "You know that I no longer have any power, yet you are still supporting me?"

"Yes."

Tears appeared in Birdie's eyes. Apparently, she had never before encountered folk who did not want something from her.

Then she recovered. "But you have a job to do. My presence would only hinder your performance. It would not be mannerly to continue to interfere when I can no longer offer any recompense."

Evidently, Birdie had missed one detail. "We do not like the work we have been doing," Incident said. "We expect to retire from it as soon as we can expediently do so, now that we are beautiful."

Birdie seemed genuinely curious. "Why are you delaying?"

"Goar has a situation. We want to see that resolved before we lose our powers."

"A situation?"

"In his prior employment he murdered two people," Incident explained. "It was not his choosing; he was under orders. Now he has a conscience, as do we all, and wishes to make up for his earlier transgressions. That will be accomplished only when those he murdered forgive him for that ill deed."

"Yes, Bird told me about that, and how he will lose his powers when he retires. I was not concerned, because I expected to make up for that by making him my princess consort. But if they are dead—"

"Their selves from a parallel frame are here on a mission of their own. We seem to be somehow involved in it. They are the ones who will forgive. We do not know what he can possibly do to alleviate that guilt, but we understand that his association with us will enable it, so we are holding on."

"Though you know you will lose your powers when you do retire."

"Yes. The powers are nice, but not when we have to kill people."

Birdie shook her head. "My father would have no scruples about such a choice. He sees killing as part of the price of power."

"And you don't?"

"I don't," Birdie agreed. "I could order war if I had to, but there would have to be compelling reason for killing anyone or anything. Any other course is an abuse of power. There has to be a better way."

"A better way," Incident agreed. "So I will keep killing only until Goar is forgiven."

"Because you love him," Birdie said wisely.

"That too."

"Have you asked them how he can earn their forgiveness?"

"No."

"Why not?"

"It wasn't our place."

Birdie smiled. "I no longer have power, but my training remains. Perhaps I can advise you on a course that may facilitate your progress."

This was interesting. "How?" Goar asked.

"Negotiate. This is how honorable kingdoms settle their differences. It can be effective in lesser cases too."

"We have no skill at that."

"But I do. Perhaps I could talk with them."

Incident exchanged a glance with Goar, then broadened it to include Rabbit and Turtle. They nodded. What was there to lose?

"And I know Bird agrees," Birdie said, patting a giant feather. "I understand you have a way to get in touch?"

"Yes. But I don't know that this would be appropriate for that."

"Try it anyway."

Was this proper? Yet if it proved to be an avenue for a better outcome, maybe it was worth the risk. Goar touched his anklet. *PLEASE,* he thought.

Fornax appeared, riding with them on the roc's back. She looked like an ordinary woman, surely by choice. "Yes?"

"This is ex-Princess Birdie," Goar said. Then, to Birdie "And this is—"

"A friend with connections," Fornax said. "State your case." She evidently preferred to remain anonymous.

"These nice folk rescued me from a difficult situation," Birdie said, evidently accustomed to dealing with intermediaries. "I wish to do them a return favor. Goar needs to obtain the forgiveness of Squid and Larry, for killing them in this frame, but he has no idea how to accomplish that. He may better earn that forgiveness if he is informed exactly what is expected of him."

Nicely stated. Birdie did have expertise in dialogue.

Fornax frowned. "That is indeterminate. They will know it when they see it."

What kind of answer was that? But Goar had the sense to keep his mouth shut.

Birdie nodded as if this made sense to her. "Some situations are like that. There can be parameters. However, there is a related complication."

Fornax was expressionless. Goar suspected she was reading Birdie's mind. "Yes?"

"At such time as Goar earns their forgiveness, his friends who are helping him will be free to retire, as they do not like their present business. But when they do, they will lose their remarkable special powers, such as invulnerability, shape changing, and human intellect. Perhaps this is my misunderstanding, but this seems almost like punishment of his friends for helping him. He might try harder if he knew that no such punishment of them would occur."

Goar whistled inwardly. That was not a connection he had made, but it did make a certain sense. He did not want to hurt the only folk who had ever befriended him.

Fornax gazed at Birdie for a full third of a moment. Then she closed her eyes as if focusing on something privately. Then she nodded to herself. "They will retain their powers."

"Are you sure? There are surely protocols."

Goar had to intervene. The Shee did not know she was talking with a phenomenally powerful Demoness. "She is sure."

"Then I thank you," Birdie said.

"We may meet again," Fornax said, and vanished.

"I'm sorry I was unable to learn your better course," Birdie said.

"But you saved our powers!" Incident said.

"That was merely a confirmation, helpful to know, but not remarkable."

Goar wasn't sure of that. He had seen some of the power of Fornax.

"Perhaps," Incident said, and let the subject drop. She had seen some of it too.

Fornax returned. "I almost forgot. Birdie, things have happened in your kingdom during your absence. Folk were annoyed by the crisis your father the King precipitated, resulting in considerable damage to the castle. There has been a coup, and the King has been bloodlessly deposed and confined to quarters. He understands that he will be allowed to live out his remaining life in peace and comfort only if he makes no attempt to recover power. Now they need a new ruler. You are popular; you are the only royal personage who ever defied the King and made it stick. They trust your judgment and philosophy. They wish to invite you to return so that they may proffer you the crown. If this interests you, I suggest that you return promptly, before they look elsewhere."

Birdie's mouth hung open in astonishment. She had expected never to return to her kingdom, and suddenly things had reversed. If she did not return, and they chose another person, that person might see fit to kill the King as a matter of prudence. That was not the kind of thing she wanted.

"She will do that," Incident said. "Thank you."

Fornax made one of her quarter smiles and disappeared again.

Now Goar was sure: the Demoness had interceded to reward Birdie for her effort to help Goar and the animals, without hurting her family. She had known how. The unwritten text was that the King would fall in line, or else. He, like Birdie, understood the parameters of power.

Now, belatedly, Goar thought of something else. Tiamat had given him a chaos bomb, which might someday prove to be useful. That would be true for the others too. If only he had thought to ask Fornax about that while she was present!

Good thought, Fornax answered him mentally. *Each creature is hereby given three chaos bombs. You may inform them how to use them.*

But he had no idea how to use them!

Yes, you do. And suddenly he did.

Now all he needed was some quiet time to explain this to them.

The roc changed course and winged rapidly back toward the Shee kingdom. The six of them would have a rather different reception this time.

Birdie tapped the feather meaningfully. "Mind you, our betrothal stands," she said firmly. "All birds in the Shee Kingdom are going to be very well treated hereafter." She emulated one of Fornax's quarter smiles. "Maybe I will put my father in charge of the Royal aviary. Not that you will be there; you will be constantly with me." She bent down to kiss the feather.

Bird gently waggled his wings, amused and quite satisfied.

Chapter 10

RUBY

In due course, duly feted, they left the Princess to her job of reorganizing the kingdom. She would be busy for a month or so, and did not need the distraction of a fiancé at the moment. Once things were in order, Bird could return to make her his bride.

They parked on a quaint secluded island in a lovely little lake in a quiet friendly forest and considered what next. "It occurs to me," Incident said, "That now that we all are beautiful, and know we will retain our powers upon retirement, we should orient on that retirement. What is to stop us from quitting now, and continuing to help Goar try to win his forgiveness?"

Goar had an answer for that. "Something else is going on, something we don't know about. Something big. Otherwise there would not be a Demoness lurking. Your retirement may provoke a settlement we are not prepared for."

"Fornax," Incident agreed. "We should indeed be wary." She shrugged, her body making the motion remarkably appealing. "Apart from whatever else, I like her."

"She did a singular favor for Birdie, giving her back her kingdom."

"And for the rest of us. I doubt that our powers were permanent before she intervened."

Goar smiled, something he could do now without horrifying others. He still wore the head-sock, but it covered completely handsome features instead of ugly ones. Which he realized was curious, since he was not an Oma. Maybe that was the Demoness's doing too. "If the rest of you are willing to wait until I am forgiven, if I am forgiven, I shall be glad to have your continuing help."

Incident glanced at the three lustrous companions. They nodded. They would hold off on retirement.

Now Goar remembered his last brief dialogue with Fornax. "There is something else."

Incident turned her lovely gaze on him. "Oh?"

"I was in touch mentally with Fornax. I mentioned the chaos bomb the Goddess gave me."

The four looked at him with surprise. This was new to them. "It is invisible and unfeelable, but with me. When mentally detonated, it will generate a region of chaos about six paces outward, lasting about an hour. Things will go crazy."

He saw that they didn't understand. He needed a specific example. "Suppose you, Rabbit, got surrounded by goblins intent on making you into rabbit stew. You could escape them by doing a Harvey and turning invisible, or by suddenly growing too large for them to handle. But suppose you didn't want to attract attention? You could set off a chaos bomb, and they would abruptly lose all organization and dissolve into bedlam, going every which way for an hour. Only you would be unaffected. You could simply walk away from them unnoticed, because the chaos would remain centered on you. They would not even realize that you were the source. So you could escape without attention and continue with your mission unmolested."

"That does sound useful," Incident said, as Rabbit was back in silent form.

"Or if rogue men caught you, Incident, and tried to molest you," Goar continued. "A chaos bomb would break that up immediately, and you would be long gone by the time they recovered their wits."

"Extremely useful," she agreed, evidently remembering the man who had tried at the pond. "I'm sure your chaos bomb will help you when you need it. But the rest of us will have to make do on our own."

"No. That's what Fornax told me. Each of you now has three chaos bombs. You don't want to waste them by using them frivolously, but they are there when you need them."

She eyed him again. "You got these for us?"

"I mentioned it to Fornax."

"The Demoness must be quite taken with you, Goar."

"I doubt it. I don't know what purpose she has in mind for me, but I do know she associates with the young woman I killed, so surely has no love for me."

"And means to facilitate your progress, as I would help a creature I needed to fetch me something." She made half a pause. "That does not reassure me."

"Nor me," he agreed, glad he had been able to explain the matter. He relaxed.

But Incident was not finished. "I have a boyfriend. Bird has a girlfriend. That leaves Rabbit and Turtle. Why don't we prepare for retirement by getting them similarly settled? I'm sure they would appreciate girlfriends too."

Surprised, Rabbit and Turtle nodded.

"Very well. I shall orient on more distressed maidens. Maybe start with a rabbit girl."

Rabbit looked uncertain. "What's Updoc?" Incident asked him.

He became Beetle Bunny. "I don't know anything about girls."

"Nonsense. I'm a girl."

"You're an Oma. Our friend, not girlfriend."

"He has a point," Goar said. "None of us know how to handle girls."

Incident eyed him with implication. "You seem to be doing a competent job of it, especially at night."

"The Goddess Tiamat tutored me. I'm just following her instructions. Otherwise I'd be completely lost. That was true even before you turned beautiful."

She frowned prettily. "You mean I've been making love to the Goddess?"

That stalled him. "I—"

She relented. "Just teasing, Golem. You never hid that aspect from me. But you did learn well from her."

"Thank you." That seemed to be the only safe response.

Incident focused on Rabbit again. "Why don't you invite Goar along, mentally, when you go on your rescue mission? He did well enough for Bird."

Rabbit looked at Bird, who nodded. "All right. If he wants to help."

"I do," Goar said. "You folk have been helping me, and I want to help you back. I don't claim to be an expert on girls, apart from the material the Goddess gave me, but another perspective might indeed help. I can ask Incident and relay her advice to you if necessary."

"So I can stay safely out of your crude male minds, and not get mine dirty," Incident said. "When you see a girl, do you boys ever think of anything other than sex?"

"There is something other than sex?" Goar asked, mystified. Then they all laughed.

Incident closed her eyes and turned around.

"What *now*?" Beetle Bunny asked, alarmed.

"When else? I just got a glimmer, so I am orienting on it."

Beetle shifted back into normal rabbit format, not chancing any more dialogue with her.

"There," she said, pointing a direction. "A lady rabbit just got into trouble." Then she frowned. "But it's pretty far distant. Too far to catch her in time."

"In time for what?" Goar asked.

Incident focused again. "There's some sort of limit. I can't fathom exactly what it is, but there's a danger if she waits too long. You need to get over there soon." She opened her eyes. "We'll take you close enough."

Bird became the roc and they scrambled aboard. Soon enough they came to a mountain range. They landed in the nearest clearing, out of sight of what Incident was orienting on, and Rabbit bounded away toward it. It was obviously no tower.

Goar tuned in and looked with Rabbit's eyes as he arrived at a bush-shrouded cave. But there was something distinctly odd about it. *What is it?* he thought.

That's no cave, Rabbit thought. *That's a rabbit hole! Very old and very large. It must have been a giant ancient rabbit.*

"A giant old rabbit hole," Goar relayed verbally to the others. After the experience with Princess Birdie, they were all interested in this one.

"This is intriguing," Incident said. "Giant rabbits don't grow naturally. There must be magic involved. Be careful."

Caution, Goar relayed to Rabbit.

They cautiously entered the hole. It was dark, but Rabbit had eyes for rabbit holes and could make out enough detail. It plunged deep into the mountain.

Then there came a light. The walls were faintly glowing. As they progressed the glow brightened, until it was almost as good as overcast daylight. "Light down deep," Goar relayed.

"Beware," Incident said.

Caution, again, Goar relayed.

The cave opened out into a larger cavern. In the center was a figure of a woman with long rabbit ears. She was sitting on the floor, hunched over, sobbing. This was surely the damsel in distress.

Where is the rabbit? Rabbit asked, confused.

Goar described her to Incident. "A crossbreed," she concluded. "Maybe a human and a rabbit met at a love spring, and she was the result."

That made sense. *A rabbit/human crossbreed,* Goar told Rabbit. *Talk to her.*

Rabbit thought *Updoc* and became Beetle Bunny. "Hello," he said.

The woman's head snapped up, but her eyes were tightly closed. "Don't you dare touch me!" she cried. "I'll bite!"

She's not really looking at you, Goar thought to Rabbit. *She's terrified. Tell her you're a rabbit.*

"I'm a rabbit," Rabbit said. "Look at me."

Slowly she forced her eyes open and turned her head to look at him. "You're a rabbit!"

Tell her who you are. That you came to rescue her.

"I am Beetle Bunny. I came to rescue you."

She began to think about maybe possibly believing. "You're not a cruel mirage?"

"Not," Beetle said.

She gulped and made a decision. "Let—let me touch you. To see if you're real."

Rabbit walked slowly forward and extended one hand. She touched it fleetingly with one finger. Her eyes became two shades less dull. "You're real!"

"Yes."

He needed more prompting. *Explain how you learned of her. How you came here. How you want only to help her.*

"I—I have a friend who sensed your distress. She sent me to rescue you. So I came into the rabbit hole to find you. I want only to help you."

She burst into more tears.

Rabbit was baffled. So was Goar. He quickly updated Incident.

"Those are tears of relief, not grief," Incident explained. "This is how a stressed woman can react. Tell him to put his arms around her. To repeat 'there, there,' until she calms."

Goar relayed that information and advice, meaningless as it seemed.

Rabbit sat down beside the girl, put his arm around her, and murmured "There, there."

Her sobs diminished. The magic was working, amazingly.

"Ask her about herself," Incident said. "How she came to be here."

Rabbit did that, and she started talking. "My name is Ruby Rabbit. My parents ran afoul of a love spring without realizing, and sent a mixed message to the stork, and I was delivered. Mom was the human: she mostly raised me."

"That's interesting," Rabbit said, duly prompted.

"I grew up lonely, because I didn't fit well either into the human or the rabbit side of my ancestry. I was way too big and smart for the rabbits, and my ears and bunny tail turned off the humans."

Prompted again, Rabbit reassured her. "I think your ears and tail are lovely. And I like a smart girl."

Ruby melted. "So I was constantly looking for something better than the neither here nor there life I had. I heard there was a cave with a footlocker that contained a magic mushroom that could make a person large or small, depending on the side of it nibbled, the weight in proportion to the size. If I could use that, I could become a bunny-sized rabbit instead of a giant. I can't change my mass, you see; I am the same weight regardless which form I choose. So I'm a small human or a huge rabbit. Then I could hide my intelligence and merge with the other rabbits. So I was determined to find that mushroom. I got a map that led me to this cave, and I ventured inside, and saw the footlocker."

"You did? I see no locker."

She smiled wanly. "Yes. That's the problem. There was a locker, right here, anchored to the floor by a chain. It was transparent and I could see the magic mushroom inside. It was even labeled MAGIC MUSHROOM, and I could smell its earthy aroma through the screen at the top. I tried to open the locker, but it resisted my effort. I needed the key to its lock." She took a deep breath. Since she was in human form, and wore no clothing, this made her front suddenly more interesting to his vaguely human form. "Whereupon it suddenly changed and became this manacle on my front leg." She lifted her left arm to show off the chained bracelet on her delicate wrist. "Too late I realized that it wasn't exactly a footlocker as in a container, it was a footlocker as in a manacle. I was chained to the floor. I tried to pull free, but it's too tight. I tried to pull the chain from the floor, but it's too strong. I need the key to unlock it."

"The key," Rabbit echoed.

"And the key is right there. I can see it, on its hook on the wall." She gestured, and Rabbit saw the hanging key. "It's the cruelest tease, because I can't get to the key."

"Maybe I can—" Rabbit started.

"Caution!" Incident said so that both Goar and Rabbit heard her. "It could be a trap."

"I could get it for you," Rabbit resumed after most of a moment. "But I am afraid it might be another trap. Maybe that's why it is right there in plain sight. To catch your rescuer. Then they'll have two rabbits instead of only one."

"Oh my," Ruby said. "That just might be."

"I wonder why they set this trap?" Rabbit asked.

"Oh, I know that. All rabbit's feet are lucky. Good lucky and bad lucky. They want our feet to help their friends and jinx their enemies."

"And eight feet are worth more than four feet," he agreed, seeing it. "They may have more than two friends and enemies." Then, mentally: *Could I use a chaos bomb for this?*

Goar and Incident held a quick consultation, and concluded that chaos would not get Ruby free of the manacle. *Not at this point.*

Then there was a small commotion. A white rabbit hopped rapidly by, holding a watch. "I'm late! I'm late!" he lamented as he passed by without seeming to notice them. In hardly an instant over a moment he was gone, having passed from the entrance passage to the exit passage deeper in the mountain.

Beetle and Ruby exchanged a glance. "This is weird," she said.

"Late for what?" Beetle asked.

"Maybe for the two-rabbit stew," Ruby said cynically. "After they salvage the feet. No sense in letting the rest of us go to waste."

"Why didn't they take that white rabbit?"

She smiled ruefully. "He was evidently late. I got here first."

"I think we need to get out of here before anyone else comes." Beetle pondered half a moment. "I think I have a plan. When I touch that key, it will probably set off an alarm or something, so we'll need to act swiftly. I will assume a large size so I can take the key and use it without having to cross the chamber. The moment you are free, and the foot-lock reverts to the foot-locker, open it and grab the magic mushroom."

"That is what I came for," she agreed.

"But since I fear this is also a trap for me, my action will spring it. So I will fool them by becoming a shape they won't recognize. While they are trying to figure it out, you hop on out of here as fast as you can."

"But that would leave you in trouble," she protested.

"I am, among other things invulnerable. I'm sure I can handle the trap, and I am curious about exactly what it is. So don't worry about me: just get out of here with the mushroom."

"If you say so," she said uncertainly.

He expanded to Giant Rabbit size, his ears brushing the ceiling. He reached out and picked the key off his hook, then put it to the lock on her wrist. Sure enough, it not only clicked open, it converted to the locker. He returned the key to its hook and shrank back to bunny size.

And sure enough, someone came. It looked like another rabbit. Rather it was a grim-looking hare. "Haa! Caught you!" he cried, charging at Rabbit.

But Rabbit had already become a Welsh rabbit, a dish of melted cheese over toast.

"What's this?!" the Hare demanded, with mixed punctuation. "Am I mad?"

"Yes, you are mad," Ruby called. "I recognize you: you're the March Hare, crazy mad. That must be why they didn't take *your* foot."

It occurred to Goar that Ruby was a pretty spunky female. Surely, a good match for Rabbit, once they rescued her.

Rabbit wanted to tell her to shut up and get safely out while the Hare was distracted, but he was unable to speak in this form.

However, Goar managed to hurl a thought at her. *Get out now!*

"Oh. Of course." She moved toward the exit. The wrong one. The distraction had confused her too.

Rabbit formed into Beetle Bunny. "What's Updoc?" he asked the Hare.

"This is crazy," the Hare said, observing the change from cheese to bunny. "I love it!" Probably because he was crazy himself.

Beetle launched after Ruby. "The other way!" he cried. But she was already through the exit and into the next passage. He had to follow her.

"Did the lock not work?" the Hare asked plaintively behind them. "There were supposed to be two rabbits caught here. The Queen will be most annoyed. Oh, this is utterly insane! I love it!"

Ruby clutched Rabbit's hand as she ran. "I hate to agree with him, but this is indeed strange."

The commotion behind them continued. There was no longer much of an escape in that direction. There was no help for it. They had to move on into the mountain.

They turned a corner. There was an amazing sight.

The cave seemed to have vanished. They faced a weird panorama. There were oddly colored trees, curious meadows, strange streams, and downright weird paths. There was a sun in the sky, but it looked more like a painting than a ball of fire. It was as if a child had fashioned an imaginary landscape without much concern for realism.

Ahead was a fancy castle. "Maybe that's where they use the rabbit's feet," Beetle said. "I think we had better avoid it, and find another way out."

"Yes. I don't trust anything about this place."

Most paths led directly toward the castle, but they spied one that sneaked away to the side. "It must go somewhere else," Beetle said.

"Anywhere else seems promising," Ruby agreed.

They followed it to a kind of garden where several shaped objects rested. Beetle picked one up. Around its edge it said TUIT.

"I recognize that," Incident said. "One of our Mundane clients had one. It's a Round Tuit. It helps you get a job done when you invoke it."

"I wish it were edible," Ruby said. "All this nervousness has made me hungry."

"Maybe one of these," Beetle said, spying another. He picked it up and read its print. "This is a Square Meal." He took a bite. "Yes, it is edible."

"Oh, goody!" Ruby picked up another and bit into it. "Yes, very tasty."

They came to a patch of little disks growing on stems. Beetle picked one and nibbled it. "Mint," he said appreciatively. "Suddenly, I understand things I never did before."

"That's an Enlighten Mint," Ruby said. "I have heard of them. When you eat one, it affects you." She checked and selected one. "This one is an Accomplish Mint: feel as if I could do marvelous things."

Beetle tried another. "I want to tell the whole Land of Xanth about my accomplishments!"

"So that's an advertise Mint," she said as she picked another. Then she spat it out. "I just got an Excra Mint. Ugh!"

"Let's move on," he said.

The path descended to a bog. There lurking in the muck were several toothy green creatures. "Oh no," Incident said. "Those are gators. Stay away from them."

But Ruby had already ventured too close, trying to follow the path down a narrow section fronted by plants that resembled small buildings. Suddenly a gator scrambled out before her, its jaws gaping wickedly.

"That's an Alley Gator!" Beetle said, jumping forward to intercept it as Ruby retreated.

Another Gator climbed onto the path. "We have to look into this," it said.

"And an Investi Gator," Goar said, knowing it by its attitude.

A third Gator got onto the path behind Beetle, orienting on Ruby. She screamed and fled. "EE—" But she didn't finish her scream.

"And an All E Gator," Incident said. "That eats all the E's so girls can't properly eeeek! when chased."

Beetle shook his head. "I can handle puns as well as the next rabbit. But these are dangerous."

The two rabbits bounded along a new path. Then rocks popped out of the ground, tripping them so that they both fell flat on their whiskers.

"Pop Rocks," Incident said. "Easy to avoid when you're paying attention."

The two picked themselves up and brushed off the dirt.

A new figure loomed before them: a royally garbed queen with hearts decorating her robe. "Caught you!" she screamed. "My minions saw you skulking around my gardens, you marauders!" Behind her appeared a number of uniformed henchmen.

"We weren't skulking," Ruby protested. "We were just trying to get away from the gators."

"You were raiding my gardens!" the Queen screeched. She turned to the henchmen. "Off with their feet!"

The henchmen converged on the two rabbits. Goar knew that they couldn't hurt Beetle, but Ruby was another matter. *Now use a chaos bomb!* he thought to Beetle.

Beetle did. Suddenly, the scene went wild. The henchmen ran every which way, splashing into the muck and trampling the gardens while the Queen looked on with royal dismay.

Carry Ruby out, he thought, realizing than unless she were in physical contact with Beetle, she could be part of the chaos.

Beetle picked her up and charged through the melee, untouched, because no one was paying any further attention to the rabbits except the irate Queen, who was beyond the range of the bomb. But her words had no further effect.

Then Goar got a nasty idea. *Get close to the Queen*, he thought.

Beetle was too distracted to argue. He bounded to stand next to the Queen. Now she was part of the chaos. The henchmen charged by her and into her, knocking her over. Her crown rolled into the muck and her legs kicked high, flinging her royal slippers into the air. Actually, her exposed legs were fairly shapely. So were her royal bloomers with the imprinted hearts. Goar had to look away, lest he freak out.

"Off with their feet!" the Queen screeched again as she struggled to get back to her own feet. But the chaos caused two henchmen to grab *her* feet.

"Lovely," Incident remarked. Goar was pretty sure she did not mean the Queen's feet, but her situation.

Now the Queen was truly angry. "Off with *everyone's* feet!"

Then the scene faded. Beetle found himself standing with Ruby in his arms, outside the gardens and the cave, facing a bird, a turtle, and a very pretty woman.

"We're out!" he exclaimed. "How did that happen?"

It took them a good three moments and half a dozen instants to figure it out. "The Magic Mushroom!" Incident said. "When Ruby sniffed it, it put her into a dream, a hallucination. Everything thereafter was her imagination, and then Rabbit's imagination when he joined her. *That's* the real danger in that cave."

So it was. They settled down and discussed it. Only the mushroom, in its locker, was real; just about everything else was illusion. Deadly illusion, because now they were able to peek into the cave and see the assorted bones and skeletons around the edges. The faint fumes had masked those ugly hints. Those who sniffed the mushroom got caught up in the dream world and eventually starved to death. First Ruby, then Beetle, then Goar and Incident, because they had locked into Beetle's mind and perception. They could have been doomed if they had not come out of it.

Now Incident addressed Bird and Turtle. "How did you do it?"

It turned out that the two, slowly coming to understand the trap that had sprung on Rabbit, then on Goar and Incident, had consulted, then acted. They knew that the mischief was inside the cave. They had guided Goar and Incident, unresisting, toward the cave, and left them standing there. Then Bird had assumed sufficient size, anchored his claws firmly in the ground, and flapped his wings as if flying. They blew up an increasing wind. He oriented on the cave and directed that wind directly into it, so that whatever fumes were in it were forced back and on out the other side. Then Turtle had assumed an intermediate size, about man height, held his breath, and scrambled into the cave. He had found the two rabbits standing together in delirium, unresponsive to his presence, with Ruby still chained to the floor. He noticed that all of the decaying bodies piled around the edges of the cave, and the skeletons, were missing all their feet.

Then he had changed to Ninja Turtle form, gotten the key, unlocked the lock, thus freeing Ruby as the manacle reverted to footlocker form. He used his shell to slowly push them out of the cave. They were unconscious of his action, but the nudging got them hopping in the right direction, which was directly into the wind of Bird's ground flying. He continued herding them until they emerged from the cave. Only then did he take a breath. Either the fumes had blown the fumes clear, or his failure to breathe them had protected his awareness, or both, but the combination got the job done. It was not the most sophisticated operation, but it had worked.

"It worked," Incident agreed. "You didn't have me to do your thinking for you, but you had enough wit of your own to figure out enough of it. I'm proud of you." She hugged each of them in turn.

Then she turned to the two rabbits. "Hello, Ruby. Goar and I were tuned into Beetle, helping guide him. We got too well attuned, so that we didn't think to return to our own awareness, assuming we could. Let me introduce us all." She did so, with a brief summary of their business as a team. "So when I located a damsel in distress, Rabbit headed in to help you, and instead of immediately rescuing you, he got himself and us tangled in the dreams. This is a warning for the future: we shall need to put safeguards in place so we don't get caught that way again." She took one of those now fabulous breaths. "Now it is your decision to make, Ruby. Do you prefer to return to your home on your own, leaving us to our own devices, or to remain with Rabbit in whatever form he chooses? I know he would like to have you stay, but you have no obligation."

"I would like to stay," Ruby said without hesitation. "I would have been doomed if the group of you had not come to rescue me. But I don't know whether Rabbit would really be interested in a further relationship, as I have none of the special powers he has and might be a drag on him. Besides which, I'm a crossbreed."

Incident glanced at Rabbit. "Do you have anything against crossbreeds, Beetle?"

Beetle Bunny gazed at Ruby, who was in her humanoid form. "She's beautiful, ears and all." But his gaze wasn't on her ears. She was of course completely unclothed.

Incident smiled. "As you can see, that's most of what matters to a male; actual content is, if I may use the term, incidental. You will do, in that respect. As for the special powers, perhaps we can arrange some for you."

"For me? I don't see how."

"Next question: you came for the magic mushroom. In your hallucination you took it with you, but actually it remains in its locker, chained to the floor, bait for folk like you who have lucky legs to offer. We can, if you wish, fetch it for you, and put it in an airtight container so it can't affect you unless you want it to. It might be useful on occasion."

Ruby shuddered. "Leave it in the cave. I don't want to meet the Queen of Hearts again." She glanced at her feet and winced.

Incident nodded. "That is probably sensible. We now know its nature, and where it is, if we should ever decide that we need it. It will surely keep well in the cave. I mention it only because it might enable you to change sizes, a valuable special power."

"A special power," Ruby breathed, causing Beetle's eyes to glaze. Female nude breathing was of course a constant magnet for male attention. "To become small like a regular rabbit, or big like a human person, mass in proportion. I'd like that; it would greatly facilitate my interactions with others. But the risk is horrible."

Now Goar spoke, wrenching his own gaze away so that he could orient on something intellectual. "You were thrown into hallucinations by its aroma, and Incident and I were carried along with you and Beetle. But I suspect that was a side effect. I think that mushroom really does enable folk to change size, depending on which side of it they nibble; it is known historically. However, it was left in the cave along with the decaying dead bodies and skeletons. The collectors wanted only the feet, and simply piled the remains along the sides, of no further use. That rotten environment may have polluted the odor of the mushroom, corrupting its magic and causing it to generate unkind visions. In its pure state it may be inoffensive. We should find out." In his mind he was thinking of the way the Good Magician's old socks, contaminated with his magic, had assumed other properties, enabling Goar to have serviceable face and hands and feet. The underlying force of magic could be adapted, for good or ill.

Incident nodded. "There is also the matter of those collectors who are killing rabbits for their feet. It may be that they consider other feet useful too, like bird, turtle, golem, or human." Bird and Turtle winced along with Goar. "It doesn't seem right to let them continue that ill pursuit. We should remove it so they can no longer prey on innocent folk."

Ruby whistled. "You make a devastating case! I hate the way I was trapped and set up for mutilation and death. I have another idea: Why not take the mushroom and substitute one of those cute chaos bombs Beetle has? I assume he didn't really use it before: that was all in our imagination. But he has real ones, right?"

Now Incident whistled. "I like the way your mind works, Ruby. Why not, indeed!" She glanced at Goar. "Is this feasible?"

Goar yanked his memory away from the effect of the bomb in the vision, when the Queen of Hearts had fallen on her back with her legs in the air, and explored his memory of what Fornax had thought to him about the bombs. He knew that she had not made them; someone else she knew had done that. Yes, they could be passed along from person to person, as the Goddess Tiamat had done with him. Yes, they could be left quiescent until disturbed. It could be done. "Yes."

"Then I think it is Beetle's turn," Incident said to the Bunny. "What you need to do is hold your breath, which you can do when you try because you can't be suffocated, go into the cave, get the key, unlock the locker, and swap out a chaos bomb for the mushroom in the locker. Then scamper out before you decide to take a breath. The mushroom will make a nice gift for Ruby."

Beetle didn't answer. His eyes remained glazed. "I see we are going to have to harvest a shirt for you, Ruby." Incident glanced at Bird.

Bird took off, and was back in two and a half moments with a nice freshly picked T-shirt. Incident took it from his beak and put it on Ruby, who was evidently pondering the uses she might make of the mushroom.

Beetle came back to life. "I'll do it," he said. He hopped into the cave.

"You are making an impression on him," Incident told Ruby. "And on Goar. You had better carry that shirt with you when you change forms, so you can use it when in your humanoid form."

"I will," Ruby agreed. Apparently, she had been unaware of her effect on the males when in this form. She was still somewhat innocent.

In a hop, skip, and a jump Beetle was back. He took a breath. "Here it is," he said, presenting the mushroom to Ruby.

"Why thank you, Beetle," she said as if surprised. Goar recognized the art of being feminine, constantly making males feel special. It seemed that all females practiced it. Then she nibbled tentatively on one side of the mushroom.

And abruptly grew to giantess size, fifty feet tall, standing directly over them. Goar and Beetle looked up, startled.

Goar woke to Incident's impatiently snapping fingers. He had freaked out. So had Beetle. Even Bird and Turtle seemed somewhat awed. That was odd, because Ruby wasn't even wearing panties. He had gotten a very good look and was quite sure of that. So how could panty magic work without them?

"There may be things we males are destined never to understand," Beetle murmured, having been similarly snapped out of it.

"And shorts," Incident told Bird wryly. "Assorted sizes." He took off again.

"It works!" Ruby boomed from far above. She was talking about the mushroom. This time Goar was careful not to look up.

"We suspected that," Incident said.

Ruby tried the other side of the mushroom. Suddenly, she was imp size. Goar saw that the mushroom changed size with her. That was nice of it.

"Smaller bites," Incident recommended.

Ruby tried again, and this time made it to normal human size. "Oh, this is wonderful! I'm not hallucinating at all, unless I only imagined I was changing sizes."

"The imagination was all theirs," Incident said, shooting a reproving glance across the boys' bows.

Bird returned with panties and shorts, and Ruby quickly donned them. Goar and the others had the sense this time to look away until she was properly covered.

"I think we are done here," Incident said. "Ruby, if you assume small enough size, you can perch on one of Beetle's ears and whisper sweet nothings if you are so minded."

"Oh yes," Ruby agreed. She nibbled a tiny fragment of mushroom and became normal rabbit size. She jumped up onto his shoulder. She nibbled again, becoming cricket size, then hopped up onto and into his right ear. She became smaller yet.

Beetle paused as if listening. Then that ear blushed, fur and all. He turned rabbit.

Goar was sure Ruby's whisper was very sweet, but probably not exactly nothing.

Chapter 11

TERZA

They relaxed for the rest of the day, getting to know Ruby Rabbit, and she them. The more the others learned of her, the better they liked her; she was human in many important ways, thanks to her mother, but she thought of herself as a rabbit, which made her ideal for Rabbit. She was perfectly happy to find a good briar patch and browse with him, or to nibble berries or fruits. She wanted to have a large family, in due course. That clearly interested Rabbit increasingly. But she could also converse human style with Incident and Goar.

At night, alone together in a crude shelter, Incident addressed Goar. "You had no business freaking out when you looked up under Ruby's skirt."

"She wasn't wearing a skirt," he protested.

"Exactly. Any skirts you want to peek under hereafter had better be mine." She was becoming quite possessive. He liked that.

"I'll try," he promised.

"See that you do. And when you saw the Queen of Hearts's bare legs—"

"She was imaginary!"

"Exactly," she repeated. "I can provide you all the imagination you need in that respect." Then she set about doing exactly that. It was a good night.

Next morning, having delivered a seed to a deserving person, they settled down for another brief conference. "We have one to go," Incident said. "I am extending my antennae for a lady turtle in distress. In fact I have been listening since we got Rabbit settled. Now I think I am getting a glimmer. But the signals seem mixed; she's certainly in distress, but I'm not quite sure she really is a turtle."

Bird became Bird Man. "Princess Birdie is very like a human, being a Shee, and I am quite satisfied with her."

"Ruby is a crossbreed, and I am satisfied with her," Beetle said. He twitched an ear. "She says I'd better be."

"So how do you feel about it, Turtle?" she asked. "Does she have to be full turtle?"

He became the ninja, since in that form he could talk. "Not if she's anything like you."

Incident, caught by surprise, managed a third of a blush. "Thank you, I think. Let me tune in more specifically." She focused.

It made perfect sense to Goar. Incident had rescued Turtle from likely death, and arranged for him to have phenomenal powers and an excellent life. She associated with him daily on an equal basis. She was the only human woman he had known. She would be the model of his aspirations. A turtle girl like her would be ideal.

Incident faced a new direction. "That way. Toward the sea. Some distance. But there is something distinctly odd. I can't quite figure it out."

"If she needs rescuing, we'd better save her," Goar said. "Turtle doesn't have to take her as a girlfriend if she's not right."

Turtle nodded and returned to straight turtle form, where he was more comfortable.

They piled on to the roc, which impressed Ruby, who assumed human form for the ride. "You folk travel in style," she said.

Somewhere between soon and timely they reached the seashore, where a girl was selling seashells. But she was not the one. They passed her and landed on a rocky promontory. "That way," Incident said, pointing not at the sea but at the stony ground.

"Underground?" Goar asked, perplexed.

"Not exactly. There's—there's an inlet."

Bird assumed seagull form and flew along the shoreline. "There's a cave," he reported when he returned.

"That's where," Incident said. "But there's a mystery. I am not entirely easy about this."

"But there is a damsel in distress," Goar said.

"Yes. Still . . ."

"She's not a distressed lady dragon looking for a meal?"

"Oh no. Nothing like that. But I don't know what she *is* like."

"So it is time for Turtle to check her out. He's invulnerable, so there's no danger to him."

"Unless there's a magic mushroom in a spoiled environment," Bird Man said.

"Let's take no chances," Incident said. "You track him, Goar, and I'll track you. If you start hallucinating, I will send you a mental jolt."

"And I will immediately disengage," Goar agreed. "So we can decide on the next step. We should be proof against mushrooms."

Thus armed, they seemed to be ready. "Go get her, Turtle," Incident said.

Turtle plunged into the water and stroked strongly down beneath the surface. He might be a bit slow on land, but he was a powerful swimmer.

Goar tuned in on Turtle's mind and perception. It was like swimming himself, only far more proficiently than he could ever manage. Not only did he see the graceful seaweeds and passing fish, he heard and smelled them. The chill water was like a caress across his whole body. What a lovely environment!

He came to a vertical wall near the shore, where the depth from the surface went suddenly from a few feet to a few hundred feet. He swam along it, following the increasingly clear signal. She was not far ahead.

He found a hole big enough for a big green turtle and swam into it. It descended deep, then turned back up, and exited in an air cave.

There was a human woman standing beside the water, looking at him. She was bare and shapely, but that didn't bother him. "Who are you?" she asked, her tune between curiosity and concern.

He became the ninja and climbed out of the water to join her. That put him closer to her, and made him a step closer to human. Now her nudity bothered him, albeit in a pleasant way. "I am Turtle. Who are you?"

"I am Terza."

"You're human."

"Yes."

"I am looking for a turtle."

"I am the only person here, apart from you."

"I came to rescue a distressed lady turtle."

She smiled, to a degree. "I am at any rate a distressed lady. I am trapped in this cave and I can't escape. I think there is a way out, in fact with your arrival I am sure of it, because you must have found an avenue, but I can't swim well enough to use it. I am desperate."

Turtle turned his attention inward. *What do I do now? This is the wrong place.*

Goar answered. *Incident says this is the right place, and that is the right maiden.*

But she's HUMAN.

Maybe that was what was odd about her.

Ask her about her situation, Goar suggested.

"How did you come to be caught here, if you can't swim well enough to come here the way I did?"

"I really don't know. I have searched for some other exit, but there does not seem to be any."

"You don't know? Think back: Exactly how did you arrive?"

She teared up. "I don't *know*."

"How can you not know?" he asked, frustrated. "You must have been outside, and then you got inside. How?"

Now her tears flowed in earnest. "I can't remember."

"But it must have been only hours ago."

"I have amnesia."

"How do you know that?"

"Because the cards told me."

This was confusing. "What cards?"

She went to the cave wall in back and picked up a pile of shiny cards. "These ones."

Turtle couldn't read, but Goar could. He looked at the top card through Turtle's eyes. PERSON. YOU HAVE MEMORY LOSS. IT IS CALLED AMNESIA. YOU CAN'T REMEMBER RECENT THINGS. THAT IS WHY YOU ARE CONFUSED. SEE NEXT CARD FOR GUIDANCE.

That set Goar back. Inanimate cards knew what Terza's problem was? He did not quite trust this.

Ninja looked at the next card. YOUR MEMORY EXTENDS BACK ONLY A FEW HOURS. IT ALL FADES OVERNIGHT. THESE CARDS ARE HERE TO REMIND YOU SO YOU WILL BE LESS CONFUSED.

Goar checked again with Incident. *Can this be true? She is a patient needing cards to handle her amnesia?*

Incident mentally shook her head. *I don't trust this.*

Talk with her, Goar advised. *Ask relevant questions.*

"Do you have any idea who made these cards?" Turtle asked her.

"I think maybe I made them myself, to shore up my memory, knowing that I would need the reminders."

It was possible, as he saw a pile of blank cards and a pen. Still, it was curious. "Why would you come here and put yourself through this?"

"Now I remember. The cards tell me that I am a person with talent, but need to eliminate some bad training. It is easier to forget all of it and start over, than to correct it detail by detail. I will be a more effective person once I accomplish this."

"I don't trust this," Turtle said, echoing Incident.

"Neither do I," Terza said, surprisingly. "I don't like being without my memory."

Why does she so readily accept you? Goar asked. *Shouldn't she be at least apprehensive about a shape-changing male?*

"You don't know me," Turtle said. "Why do you so readily accept me?"

"I'm lonely," Terza answered with surprising candor. "Maybe I know you, but can't remember."

"We have not met before. Aren't you at least suspicious of my motives? You are an esthetic young woman."

She glanced down at herself. "I suppose I am. But you're a green turtle. You shouldn't have any designs on me."

Ha, Incident thought. *All males have designs on all females, especially the young pretty ones. Species hardly matters.*

"All males have designs on all females," Turtle said, before realizing that he had automatically spoken the received thought. He paused, embarrassed.

"That's weird," Terza said. "That was a female thought."

"Yes. That was Incident." Then he paused again. "You read my mind!"

She nodded, surprised. "I suppose I did. I see now that that is why I trusted you. I read your mind and knew you wished me no harm."

"You're telepathic!"

"I suppose I am. I didn't realize."

"Don't the cards tell you?"

"They don't. Unless I read that card too long ago, and forgot it."

"Forgot what?"

She stared at him with dawning alarm. "Oh no! Now *you're* forgetting things. Because of the ambiance of this cave."

Goar! Incident! Help!

Goar scrambled to oblige. *There must be gas or magic in that cave that affects anyone within it, so she needs the cards. But you have us. We're not there, so are not affected. We can be your memory cards.*

What did I forget?

That this is an amnesia cave, Goar thought.

Oh yes. Now I remember.

"Now you remember," Terza agreed, reading his mind. "But who are your mental friends?"

Complete candor was best at this point. "I am part of a group of people and animals who are trying to do the right things. At the moment we are trying to rescue a damsel in distress, having tuned in on that. Only we thought she was a turtle."

She laughed. "A turtle! Whatever gave you that idea?"

"Well, your mind seemed turtlish. I guess I just wanted to rescue a lady turtle, so that—" He paused again. Why did he keep embarrassing himself?

"So that you might have a grateful girlfriend," Terza finished. "What a disappointment!"

This was still going wrong. "I didn't mean to insult you. I do want to rescue you. I just got confused."

"I was teasing, Turtle." She considered half a moment. "Let me talk to your friend. The female one. She's human, isn't she?"

"Close enough. She's a sylph."

"Close enough," she agreed.

Turtle oriented on Incident. *Would you talk to her?*

I will try. Take her hand firmly so that you have physical contact. That will facilitate my mental contact.

Turtle looked at Terza. "May I take your hand?"

She smiled. "I heard, I think. Yes." She put her hand in his.

Terza, Incident thought forcefully. Goar, the silent partner here, could feel the connection strengthening.

Incident, Terza agreed.

What he told you is true. I am able to tune in on things when I focus. I tried to orient on a lady turtle in distress. And—oh my!

What's wrong?

Terza. You are *a turtle.*

Terza laughed mentally. Oh, I don't think so. Turtle here can tell you that I look and feel completely human. He has seen enough of me to know. Her mental gaze echoed her physical one, noting her human breasts not at all concealed by her curling green hair and the absence of any shell. All the way down to her dainty human feet.

Terza, I am exploring your mind. It is like Turtle's mind. You're the same species.

It's a human *mind.*

I have found a hidden memory. One too embedded to be caught by the amnesia. Look inward, Terza. To when you were young, a recent hatchling. When you barely escaped a hungry bird as you scrambled over the sand toward the water. You have feared birds ever since.

Not anymore. I am way too big for any bird short of a roc. Even a roc couldn't catch me deep in the water. Even if it pursued me, I can hold my breath longer than any bird. Then Terza paused, her eyes widening. *Now I remember.* I am *a turtle!*

That's why I oriented on you. Only there was something amiss. Now I know it was that you thought you were human.

Terza opened her eyes to gaze at Turtle in wonder. "I thought I was human," she echoed. Then her green shell formed around her and her features became turtilian as she sank to the sand, letting go of his hand. She was indeed a big green turtle.

Turtle was amazed but gratified. She was just as pretty as a turtle as she had been as a human. "But turtles can't read cards," he protested.

"When I thought I was human, I adopted human ways," she said. She wasn't actually speaking, because her turtle mouth was not designed for it; she was sending him her thoughts, which he interpreted as vocal speech. "So I was able to read because I thought I could."

And she thought she was human because the cards told her she was, Incident thought.

"We were right not to trust the cards," Turtle said. "Those are generic cards, that could apply to any person."

"Maybe that made me suspicious," Terza said. "But I couldn't get enough of a focus to follow up mentally. I believed I was human, and dismissed contrary indications."

"You seem pretty smart for a turtle," Turtle said.

"So do you."

"I am smart because it comes with the package of powers. I wasn't smart enough to avoid a fisherman's net before Incident rescued me."

Terza considered. "I am a lot smarter than the average turtle, but I am not sure why. I don't have any package of powers like yours. I am just an ordinary sea turtle."

Because she is telepathic, Incident thought. *She draws on the mind of the one she is with.*

On my enhanced mind, Turtle agreed, seeing it.

On your enhanced mind, Terza agreed.

But before I got here, he thought, *she was reading the cards.*

"I was reading the cards," Terza agreed. "But I see now it was telepathic. I simply reached out to the nearest mind capable of reading, and borrowed its power. I didn't know that that was what I was doing, but I see it now."

That cave is set up that way for a reason, Goar put in. *It has to be a trap. You need to get her out of there before it springs.*

"Good point," Terza said. It was clear that she was not just a telepath, she was a powerful one.

"Now you know you can swim and hold your breath," Turtle said. He realized as he spoke that that was another of his enhanced powers: he could speak in the human manner despite having a turtle mouth. Magic was marvelous. "Follow me out of here."

"Gladly!"

He shifted to regular green turtle mode and splashed into the water, and she splashed after him. He took a breath, held it, then dived deep into the tunnel. She did the same, picking up the technique from his mind. She was a turtle, but the remnant of her indoctrination as human remained, fogging the details.

They emerged from the hole and swam up though the sea to the shore. They found a landing spot and scrambled onto the ground, then on up to where the others waited for them.

Then came the introductions, which Incident neatly performed. "Hello, friend! I am Incident, and this is Goar Golem, Bird, Rabbit, and his friend Ruby." Ruby jumped out of Rabbit's ear and became human size. "Folks, this is Terza Turtle, with whom we have been in mental contact. She is telepathic." Goar noticed that Terza froze momentarily when Bird was introduced, though he was in small sparrow form. Yes, she did not like birds.

She returned to Terza. "We shall soon all get to know each other better. But I think before we do, we need to understand your situation better, Terza, in case we need to take precautions to protect you against whoever is trying to capture you. It wouldn't be much of a rescue if we lost you as soon as we found you. Why were you in that cave, and why did they try to make you think you were human?"

"I don't know," Terza said. "I'm just an ordinary girl, I mean turtle. I'm really not special."

Incident laughed. "Except for your telepathy. I'm a little bit telepathic, in that I can sense my friends from a distance and tune in on others with qualities I focus on. But you have an enormous mental power, compared to mine. It is so strong that when you thought you were human, so did we. We even saw you as a human girl. I don't think we need to guess; they are after your telepathy. The question is why."

"I still don't know."

"How did you get to that cave?" Goar asked.

Terza considered. "It is starting to come back. I was ranging about, appreciating the minds of any creatures in the vicinity, when I received a powerful signal. It was like a mating smell that summons males from all over to a female of their species in heat; I have felt their urges many times. But this was not for that: rather it was the promise of personal fulfillment, the realization of my full potential, whatever it might be. To become my ultimate. I think now in retrospect that this promise was false, like a mating smell from the wrong species. But I did not know it then. I simply was drawn in. I had to go to it. So I did, swimming to the tunnel and to the cave, then exploring it. Then I started forgetting."

"The ambiance," Incident agreed. "I have heard of such caves. They are isolated, so that the air does not circulate, and fumes from the rocks collect, and anyone caught in them starts to forget. The effect is temporary if she departs promptly, but if she remains even a few days it becomes permanent, and she loses her personal history. She can die there, because she forgets how to get out, or even that she wants to get out."

"I forgot," Terza agreed. "I thought I was human, and could not swim out. But it was new enough so that I still knew I *wanted* to get out. I just didn't know how."

"That was your distress call that I picked up," Incident said. "Since you were a turtle, we sent Turtle in to rescue you."

"And rescue me he did," Terza said, sending a warm mental appreciation to him. Goar felt Turtle's pleased reaction.

"But I don't think they wanted you to die," Incident said. "They wanted to convert you to their cause."

"It was the cards that informed you that you were human?" Goar asked.

"Yes. I believed them, because I could not remember otherwise."

"Why would they want to make a turtle think she was human?" Goar asked the others.

"That is the question," Incident said. "This seems to be a trap for telepaths. Did they want only human telepaths, so you were an error?"

"I doubt it," Goar said. "If all they wanted was humans, why put the lure in a cave that was far more accessible to a turtle?"

"That suggests they wanted telepathic turtles," Incident said thoughtfully. "That they wanted to think they were human? This grow curiouser."

"There are kingdoms in the sea," Turtle said. "Some are ambitious. When I was alone, I steered clear of them, but I knew of them. I heard of one that even had aspirations to extend its domain to some of the land. But land creatures are a different kettle. It would be tricky unless they were very careful."

"Now it begins to fall into place," Incident said. "They may need telepaths who can survive in water and on land."

"If they had a seeming human to negotiate terms of surrender," Goar said. "Who seemed to be one of them. Who could read the minds of the opposition, so that no surprises could occur."

"I think we have enough of a notion," Incident said. She turned again to Terza. "You can see mentally that Turtle would very much like to have you stay with him, but he is committed for now to our group. So to have him, you will also have to suffer the presence of the rest of us. You are free to depart if you prefer."

"No! Turtle saved me, and you others enabled him to do it. I want to be with him and you. I like your minds."

"Even Bird?"

The lady turtle froze for half a moment. "I know he does not wish me any ill. My aversion is a gut thing. I know better, but that may take a while to overcome."

"Your telepathy," Incident said. "Mine is token, mainly orienting on something I need without knowing its mind beyond that, but yours is thorough. You are aware of the thoughts of all of us."

"Yes, now that I realize its nature. I can see what you see, hear what you hear, feel what you touch, when I focus on you. But mainly I know your conscious thoughts. Isolated as I was in the cave, with no companions, I had no way to understand what I could do. But I think it is short range. It helps to be able to see a person, so I can orient on his mind." She made a mental smile. "I have read Turtle's mind, and I like it. Even as a human I liked his reaction to me."

"That was mainly appreciation of your nude human form," Turtle said. "But I prefer your turtle form."

"Exactly. It seemed I crafted that human form to be appealing to a human male. But you like my natural one." She sent another appreciation at him. Goar was no turtle, but it made even him warm to her.

Rabbit had a question. "How could you not know you were telepathic before you were lured to the cave? You must have been among others."

"Not so many. Sea turtles are a fairly solitary lot. I think it developed when I matured and wanted to find a male. Then I started reaching out mentally—and got the call to the cave."

"They were looking for a telepath," Incident said. "That's when they discovered you."

"That must have been," Terza agreed. "Then once I was there, I started to forget, and so was trapped."

"Once your amnesia was complete, they would have sent one of their kind to contact you," Incident said. "You would have believed you had always been one of them."

Terza shuddered in her shell. "That horrifies me. I am glad that you were the ones to contact me first."

"We should not remain here," Goar said. "They may soon realize that she is gone, and come after her."

Incident nodded. "Ruby Rabbit has a mushroom that enables a person to become instantly small or large. You could nibble on it and become small enough to ride in my pocket, along with Turtle."

"That would be nice."

Ruby produced the mushroom, and soon Terza and Turtle were pocket size.

"Let's get out of here." Incident glanced at Terza in her breast pocket. "Normally, we carry the flightless members of our group on the back of Bird when he becomes a roc. I will ride on him, and so will the others. Can you handle that?"

"Close to you and Turtle, I should," Terza agreed. Her voice sounded the same, because it was carried telepathically, as before.

"Actually, you and I can fly on our own now," Goar reminded her. "We have the wings."

"That's right! I forgot."

"I feel something," Terza said, looking about. "Something is coming."

The others looked. Flights of dragons appeared in the sky, converging on their position.

"Uh-oh," Incident said. "We may have dallied too long."

"I think the sea kingdom is not ready to give me up," Terza said. "They must want to put me back in that cave and wipe away all my memories, so I can be schooled to do their bidding without resistance. Now I find it in their limited minds. They have no regard for the rest of you, but they mean to capture me. You can't escape that many dragons, even in roc size. Maybe you should let them have me, to save yourselves."

Goar appreciated Terza's willingness to sacrifice herself. She was a nice person. But she did not know of the powers of this group.

"Bleep on that," Incident snapped. "You are now a member of our group, Tez. We will not sacrifice you."

"I will handle them," Goar said. His background as a killer was serving him well, now. He knew how to organize for a battle. "Give me a bite of that mushroom."

Ruby produced the mushroom, and aimed the enlargement size at him. He ripped off his assorted socks and bit.

Then he was fifty feet tall, standing over the others. "Stay low," he boomed. The others hunkered down between his huge metallic feet.

The dragons came at him from all directions. They were water shooters; he realized that sea dragons would not exhale fire or smoke. Still, they were formidable, with copious teeth.

"WARNING, DRAGONS!" Goar boomed. "I am an invulnerable warrior. Any who tangle with me will be destroyed. I do not want to kill you but will if I have to. Go away in peace. It is the smart thing to do."

But these were not smart dragons. They ignored the warning and charged in. Too bad for them.

Goar windmilled with his arms, revving up his circular saws. The dragons fired jets of cold water at him. The water splashed off him harmlessly.

Undismayed, the dragons came in with their jaws gaping. Goar let them have a few bites, showing them that they could not even dent him. "You can't hurt me. Give up this foolish attack. This is your last warning." He felt he owed them that much. His conscience disapproved of unnecessary slaughter.

When they still did not back off, he sliced into all within range. Pieces of them flew out. "Now you see the consequence of attacking me! Leave off! Depart!"

They still did not quit, so neither did he. His conscience was at rest, not suffering fools gladly. Before long all that was left of them was meat and bone fragments littered across the landscape.

Goar looked down, and discovered that the ground was soaked in blood. Bird had assumed roc form and spread his wing over the others to protect them from the red rain. Now that the action was over, Bird drew back his wing, shifted to seagull size, and flew to the sea, where he dived into the water to cleanse himself.

Goar realized that he, too, was clothed in blood. So he tramped to the sea and plunged in. The water around him turned pink, then cleared as the currents flowed past. Then, clean, Goar emerged. But he was stuck in the huge size.

Incident, now winged, flew up to him. He saw the two tiny turtles in one breast pocket, and two bantam bunnies in the other pocket. "Have some mushroom," she called, flinging something like a grain of sand at him.

He opened his mouth and caught it, and swallowed. He shrank back to his normal size.

The others joined him, returning to their own regular sizes. That mushroom was proving to be really useful. Bird, now in hummingbird form, came to perch on Terza's shell. Goar glanced at that with surprise.

"After that business with the blood," Terza explained, "I knew Bird was my friend. He saved me from an ugly wetting."

That, and telepathy to read his mind, had evidently been enough. Girls did not much like getting dirty.

It had, nevertheless, become ugly. "I'm sorry it came to this," Goar said.

"You did what you had to do," Incident said. "You warned them several times. They wanted to kill the rest of us and carry Terza back to the cave."

"But now I am safe," Terza said. "Thanks to you, Goar."

Goar was uneasy about being thanked for shedding blood, so he changed the subject. "We should move on before they try something else."

"We should," Incident agreed.

Then something else occurred to him. "Terza is a telepath. But so are you, Incident. You enabled me to tune in on Bird, then Rabbit, and finally Turtle."

"That's different," Incident said. "The animals and I were granted special powers, to enable us to deliver the seeds. We have special rapport as a team and know each other well. We know how to relate. So I can tune in on them mentally, to help guide them on missions. I can see through their eyes in order to appreciate specific situations accurately, but only because they welcome me. It is a limited form of telepathy; I can't do it with other people or creatures. Even with my friends here I can't project my image; I can only pick up their impressions. Terza, in contrast, is a true telepath; she can read the minds of strangers, and appear to them as she chooses. Her power is far more comprehensive."

"But I am not telepathic at all," he protested. "Yet you enabled me to enter their minds."

"Not originally. Only when we fell in love. That's special. Then I was able to share my awareness with you, with their acquiescence. They love you, too, in their fashion. That closeness makes it possible."

Goar was silent, appreciating the significance of that. For the first time in his life he had true friends, folk who accepted him as he was, his ugly past and all. He never wanted to give them up.

Incident took his hand. "Nor we you."

A snout poked out of the nearby water. *Pause*. It was a mental message.

They all oriented on it. It was a small sea dragon. "Uh-oh," Incident repeated.

Peace. I come to parlay.

"She's from the sea kingdom!" Terza exclaimed with dread.

Goar aimed a circular saw at the snout. "I don't want to have to kill any more dragons," he said grimly. "Leave off."

The dragon became a lovely nude human nymph standing in the shallow surf. "Is this enough left off?" she inquired coyly.

"Listen, slut," Incident snapped. "He's taken. Besides, he knows you're not a real girl."

The nymph shook her lustrous blue waves of hair. They could never have moved like that if they had been real locks of wet hair. "I come to talk, not to fight or seduce. I am assuming a form that facilitates that, so we can dialogue. I am Doris Dragon, from the Sea Kingdom."

Terza became another bare girl, with green hair. "I am not going back."

Goar realized that it was telepathy that caused the transformations. They were both able to project the images and sounds they wished, to all who were here to see and hear. It was more apparent than real, but effective. Extremely effective; he had to squint to avoid glazing of eyeballs.

"At least listen to our case," Doris said. "That's only fair, isn't it?"

"You tried to trick her into believing she was human," Incident said. "Then you sent dragons to kill us and take her back. When the other devices didn't work, you are trying another tack. What's fair about that?"

Doris ignored her and focused on Terza. "It is true we tried deception, then violence. But there is more to our mission than that. We believe that when you properly understand the situation, you will want to join us."

"Chubby chance," Incident muttered.

"I don't want to join you," Terza said. "Speak your piece and leave me alone."

"Our kingdom is expanding. We need qualified personnel to forward our aims. We can offer very nice positions for the right folk. In fact, these offices can seem much like princesses, with all manner of privileges. The best quarters, the best foods, servants for every purpose. We are in special need of competent telepaths."

"Why not do it yourself?" Terza asked. "You are a competent telepath."

"I am indeed," Doris agreed. "But I am the only one of the necessary mental caliber who can handle both sea and land. You are another. We need more to be truly effective. That is why we want you. We could work together. We could be friends. We are of different species, but the camaraderie of telepathy extends well beyond the limitations of species."

Goar froze mentally. This had to be a compelling argument. He felt Terza being swayed. Here was another telepath on her level, the only one she had encountered. That association of minds was beyond anything their own group could offer.

Terza considered. Then she glanced at Turtle. Goar felt her attraction to him. The sea kingdom could not offer any creature with his powers or niceness. She glanced around at the others, including Bird. She understood all their powers and their minds. She felt their friendship for each other and wanted to be a part of it. Goar understood that perfectly.

She decided. "No."

Doris didn't argue. "If you should ever change your mind, just think my name and I will come to you." She reverted to dragon appearance and disappeared under the water.

Goar relaxed. So did the others. But he wondered why the dragon girl had yielded so readily. He did not trust that.

"Yet it was a compelling offer," Incident said.

"It was," Terza agreed. "But I realized that however sincere Doris might be—and she *was* sincere—I could not trust her, because she is not the ruler. She is merely a pampered functionary, a small cog in a much larger machine. Her superiors can overrule her at any time. That is not the kind of position I desire, however lucrative it might otherwise be. I prefer to have my freedom."

"And here I thought it was because you liked me," Ninja Turtle said with mock turtle dismay.

She laughed as she kissed him on the shell. "That too."

"Let's get out of here," Goar said. "Get far away from the sea, in a hurry."

"Before we encounter their next ploy," Incident agreed, understanding his concern. There was no telling what else the sea kingdom might be up to.

They quickly gathered and piled onto the roc bird, Terza included, after a nip of Ruby's mushroom. Bird took off and winged inland at high velocity. Only when the sea was well out of sight did Goar began to feel at ease.

Chapter 12

GOBLIN

"I do not trust this," Incident said as they flew inland. "Doris Dragon yielded too readily. We need to discover why, lest it cost us dearly."

"I agree," Goar said. "To send a flight of kamikaze dragons after us, then give up without a struggle does not make much sense. They have to be up to something."

"There was no guile in Doris's mind," Terza said. "She wanted to be my friend. She's lonely as the only border-creature telepath."

"Then why did she quit so readily?" Goar asked.

Terza explored the parameters of her memory of the other telepath's mind. There were nuances in the shadows. "She was directed to." Then she nodded to herself, mentally. "I am not suspicious of her, but I turned down her offer largely because I could not trust those beyond her. Her superiors. They might not tell her their real intentions, knowing that another telepath could read them."

"I think we need the input of a ruler, someone who thinks the way they do," Incident said. "Perhaps a princess. Or queen."

Bird's thought came. "I know a queen."

"Exactly. Set course for her kingdom. We're going to visit your fiancée."

They all felt Bird's wash of pleasure. He wanted to be with Birdie. She might be human, or close to it, but he loved her and she seemed to love him. He reset his flight vectors and headed for the Shee kingdom.

In hardly more than soon they were there. There were avian sentinels now who quickly recognized the roc and guided him down to a landing in a lovely garden within the main castle courtyard. They dismounted and Bird reverted to sparrow size.

Queen Birdie came forth to greet them, with her royal retinue. "Take a break," she murmured, and the retinue retreated to obscurity. Then she lifted one hand, and Bird flew to perch on it. "Good to see you again, beloved," she said, and kissed him on the beak.

Then she faced the others. She stepped forward to hug Incident. "I see you have added a couple in the interim."

"Ruby Rabbit," Incident said. "Rabbit rescued her."

"I know exactly how that is," Birdie said, hugging Ruby as she assumed her human form, complete with shorts and halter.

"And Terza Turtle," Incident said. "Turtle rescued her."

Birdie approached her as she manifested as human, then paused. "You are wary of me."

"I have been leery of birds," Terza said. "It's a childhood thing. I'm getting over it."

"There's something else."

"I am telepathic."

"Ah. Then read my mind. I love birds, but that doesn't mean I hate turtles."

Terza nodded. "True. In fact you really like Turtle."

"Ever since he bulldozed the castle in support of me. I think that could have been the turning point when our people rejected my father and turned to me. Any friend of Turtle's is a friend of mine."

"I see that." The two apparent women hugged.

Birdie signaled a servant. "Fetch this woman a suitable gown," she said. "Prepare a feast for me and seven guests. We shall be in the aviary."

The servant faded back, to reappear promptly with a lovely green gown. Terza's human aspect donned it and looked quite fetching.

"Now I will introduce you to my birds," Birdie told Terza. "So that you will know that all of them wish you well."

"I know it already."

"But the forms must be observed." Birdie led her to the aviary. "Birds, this is my friend Terza Turtle. You know what that means."

They did. There was a cascade of cheeping, led by a turtle dove. Any friend of the Queen's was a friend of theirs. Goar could see that it was all right. If any of Terza's concern about birds remained, it was rapidly evaporating. The Queen knew how to make a guest feel at ease.

"And you boys," Birdie said. "I like you too." She hugged Beetle Bunny, then Ninja Turtle. "In fact, I'd rather be in your company than among royalty anytime, and not just because you're part of the group that rescued me, and friends of my beloved." She tilted her head to press her cheek against Bird, who now perched on her shoulder in love bird form. "You're good company."

They nodded. So was she.

Birdie led them to a pavilion in the middle of the aviary. "I wish privacy," she said to the hawks perched around it. They nodded.

"They will make sure that no creature spies on us," Birdie said to the group. "I know you did not come here out of turn just to be social. There has to be something important afoot, something that you, even with your remarkable powers, do not feel competent to handle. Now it is my turn to listen."

So Birdie had masked their visit as purely social while she got them into a securely private place. She had a queen's touch for intrigue.

Incident spoke. "Thank you, Birdie. It is in part social, because I wanted you to meet the newer members of our group. But it is also business. Terza was being recruited for telepathic work on behalf of a sea kingdom that is ambitious to expand onto land. They sent a flight of dragons after us. Goar gave them fair warning, then chopped them to bits."

Birdie flashed a smile at Goar. "I can imagine."

"Then they sent Doris Dragon, a telepath. She assumed human nymph form and tried to talk Terza into joining them voluntarily, and we know it was tempting, because there are not many full semi-aquatic telepaths around. There is no camaraderie like that of mind to mind. They must long to associate with their own kind, regardless of species. But Terza declined, not fully trusting this. Doris said okay, and departed."

"Just like that? That's odd. It was obviously not okay with them."

"Exactly. We are suspicious that the sea kingdom should try so hard to recruit her, then give up so readily. But we are not conversant with the politics of empire. We thought you might have a better notion what we should expect."

"I do," Birdie said. "They tried the hard touch, and when that was ineffective, they tried the soft touch. You may be sure they will now try something else." She signaled a pigeon and whispered in its ear. It flew away.

"Something else," Incident agreed. "That unknown is what we fear. But what?"

"Oh, there are options. They might try to abduct someone Terza values, such as Turtle, and threaten to torture him to death if she does not relent. This is Empire SOP, Standard Operating Procedure, independent of ethics or morals. Or they could set a trap to eliminate all of you, so that you can neither offer further resistance nor warn others of their effort. You may be sure they know exactly where you are at all times."

"How so?" Terza asked. "I did not know where we were going, so she could not have read it in my mind."

"Nor did she need to. She was surely there to mark you. This, too, is SOP."

"Mark me?"

"I am not a telepath, but I have read the SOP manuals. There are techniques to mark bodies or minds so that they can be tracked thereafter. Animals can be branded. Minds can be imprinted with code thoughts the markers know to look for."

"Doris had nothing like that on her mind," Terza protested.

"She was probably innocent. She did not realize the significance of acquainting you with her, so that your awareness of the nice lady dragon telepath would remain in your mind, there for any other competent telepath to spot when he knew what to look for. Once she had accomplished that, there was no need for her to remain, and she was told to depart. She, too, can surely be tracked. They probably did not expect her to persuade you; that was not the point. Marking you was."

"Oh my," Terza breathed in mortification. "I am new at this, and evidently innocent."

"But you are learning. At least you were suspicious, as was Incident, who has more experience with evil."

"I do," Incident agreed. "My name may sound like Innocent, but I am not, after years of sending largely random innocent folk to death. But this is new to me."

Birdie smiled. "You have not read the manual. It is not widely circulated, for obvious reasons. I did not really assimilate it until I became Queen and knew I would have to rule. Then I did my homework. I don't like much of what is in it, but ignorance in this respect is hardly bliss. It was from that

that I learned my father's strategy: attempt to persuade, and when that fails, eliminate. He applied it to me. That almost killed me." She smiled again, less kindly. "At least that incident, if you will excuse the expression, showed me who my real friends were. I did not need telepathy for that."

"Nor do you now," Terza said. "We are your friends." She was not merely being polite: she knew their minds.

"Yes, and I am your friend. I hope when your business is done and you can truly retire, the group of you, that you will come to spend your remaining lives with me, so that we can all be together." She looked at Terza. "In fact, we could use a competent telepath. I promise you that this would not be for ill purpose."

"I appreciate that," Terza said. She of course could verify that, too, in Birdie's mind.

Goar was struck by the power of his own feeling. He wanted to accept the Queen's offer. There could not be a better retirement, with his friends, in a compatible environment, along with Incident.

The pigeon returned with a note. Birdie took it and quickly scanned it. "I asked our researcher to ascertain to the extent feasible what the Sea Kingdom might be planning. We kingdoms keep a close eye on each other, lest relations not always be as amicable as they are today. We have comprehensive files."

Incident perked up. "Did you find anything?"

"Yes. The Sea Kingdom has forged a secret alliance with the Godforsaken Goblin clan. They plan to commence a conquest of Xanth on two fronts, sea and land, working together. They are working to neutralize other kingdoms, using threats, bribery, and telepaths. They are almost ready to strike." She looked up at them. "Do you know, I have been so busy reorganizing my minor Shee kingdom that I had not thought to check on this sort of thing before. As it happens, we are right between the Godforsaken Goblin Horde and the sea. We would be among the first to be overrun, for we have hardly a wisp of the power of either of those kingdoms. This is sobering."

"I am glad we checked with you," Incident said, shuddering. "Is there something you can do to stop it?"

"I don't know, apart from fleeing to the mountains and hoping for the best."

"Maybe I can help you as well as us," Incident said. "I will focus on a person who may be a key figure."

"You know such a person?"

"No. But my talent orients on situations as well as people. If such a person exists, I may be able to find him. Just as I found you, as a distressed maiden."

"This is amazing."

"She is amazing," Terza said.

"This may take a while, as I am not certain exactly whom I seek."

"I have errands to see to," Birdie said. "I will return shortly. Meanwhile the rest of you feel free to explore the garden. We have some amusing things here." She walked away, her guards falling in behind her. Goar realized that she was being polite; they were taking valuable time.

"Yes, but she does value our company," Terza murmured. "As Queen she must compromise efficiently, balancing preference with duty. She is quite a woman."

"Do explore," Incident said. "I am safe here."

"You are," Terza agreed.

Incident closed her eyes, concentrating.

The others looked at Goar: one bird, two rabbits, two turtles. He realized that with Incident unavailable at the moment, they regarded him as the leader. That was not a role he had ever expected for himself, but it was easy enough to do. "Let's explore," he said, and looked around.

He spied a clump of growing bottles. Some were fat while others were slim. "What are those?"

"I can read minds, but these are mindless," Terza said. She was a turtle, but used her telepathy to generate a human voice. The voice of the turtle.

Ruby assumed her human form, quickly putting on the panties, bra, shorts, and shirt she stored in her purse. Where she stored the purse Goar didn't know. He saw the Queen's guards standing at a medium distance, keeping their eyes on things; their disappointment was evident as the bare girl torso got unbared. "Those bottles contain liquid. It is surely edible, not toxic, since it is being cultivated. I will drink one and discover its nature." She plucked a fat bottle, popped its cork, and tipped it to her mouth. She took a swallow.

They waited for her reaction, but it didn't come. She just stood there, perhaps savoring it. For some time.

Terza assumed human form, clothed. Goar realized that since her appearance was a projection, she could make it whatever she wanted, nude or not. Maybe she had merely emulated the gown Birdie had gotten for her to wear. "Ruby?"

There was no reaction.

Then Terza faced the others. "Her mind is there, but she is thinking very slowly. This is curious."

Goar stepped forward and took the bottle from Ruby's hand. He peered more closely at it. On its side was printed two words: SLOW GIN.

"Oh, that's misspelled," Terza said. "It should be sloe gin, a liqueur." Then she paused. "Or maybe not. This is Xanth: it's a pun. Drink it and it makes you slow."

Goar picked on of the thin bottles. It said FAST GIN. "Give her this."

Tersa took it and tipped it to Ruby's still-open mouth. A few drops fell onto her tongue.

The effect was fast, unsurprisingly. First her tongue accelerated, then the rest of her. "Delicious," she said.

"But I think not for casual consumption," Terza said. "However, it might be expedient to save a few of these bottles, in case we should encounter thirsty monsters." She went on to explain what had happened.

Goar spied a third kind of fruit in the patch. This was not a bottle, but a miniature machine of some kind, surrounded by puffs of fluff.

"A cotton gin," Ruby said, laughing.

Now the others got into it. Turtle found a plant with spinning seeds. He snapped up one, but immediately spat it out. "His mouth aches," Terza said. "It's spin-ache."

Then they spied a patch of melons, only not of the ordinary garden variety kind. They were melon-shaped and cohesive, but some resembled balls of water, while others looked like balls of earth, or air, or even fire. "I have seen these before," Ruby said. "They are elemelons, after the elements."

"But aren't there five elements?" Terza asked. "What about the Void?"

"There may be a fifth type here, but since nothing comes out of the void, not even light, we can't see it. But I wouldn't care to put my foot into that patch."

Goar thought about putting a foot into a void melon, and saw her point.

They came to a small pond where there were several white ducks.

"Wanna see my talent?" a child asked. She was sitting beside the pond. "I'm a garden brat; my dad's a gardener. I'm Sara."

Why not? It was unlikely to be a dangerous one, here in the safe garden. "Sure," Goar said.

The girl gestured toward the ducks. They swam together and formed a straight line. "Getting my ducks in a row."

"That is very nice, Sara," Terza said. She had of course read in the girl's mind her desire for recognition.

"Nah. My sister has a better one. She's got the Heaven Scent. She can smell if anyone's good or bad." She looked across the pond. "There she is now. Hey, sis—are these people okay?"

The other girl walked around the pond to join them. She lifted her pert nose and sniffed. "They're all good, except the golem," she reported. "And he's not as bad as he was." She gawked at Goar, evidently intrigued by his non-goodness.

Queen Birdie returned. "Scat, kids. We have ponderous adult business."

"Ooo, ugh," the two girls said together, and ran off. The ducks broke their formation and resumed foraging around the pond.

Incident opened her eyes. "I have her," she said.

The Queen had returned just in time for that. Goar suspected it was not coincidence. Maybe Incident had started stirring, as she completed her mental search, and a watcher had sent immediate word to the Queen.

"The banquet will be ready in half an hour," Birdie said. "We should have time for our serious business before then."

They gathered around her in the pavilion. What was this serious business?

"It's a goblin girl," Incident said. "She has some sort of problem, and is hiding. She doesn't seem to have any special magic talent: goblins often don't. But my sensing suggests she is critical to our mission. That somehow she can stop the war of conquest. I don't think she knows how, or even that there is a war about to start."

"She surely is relevant," Birdie said. "You must go to her and recruit her for the effort. However." She paused significantly.

“Oh my,” Terza said appreciatively.

“Let me phrase this positively,” the Queen continued. “I would like to have more time to get to know you ladies, and enjoy your company.” She glanced at Ruby and Terza. “We have things in common apart from our boyfriends. We were all distressed maidens, rescued by the bold companions. I would like to have you as friends.”

“But you’re a queen,” Ruby protested. “You can have any company you want, replete with knowledge and manners none of us can match. Why bother with a nondescript animal crossbreed like me? Regular folk might associate, but not royals.”

“My children will be animal crossbreeds,” Birdie said, glancing at Bird. “Some of my courtiers might privately disapprove, but you never would.”

“Never,” Ruby agreed. “Still—”

“I am, as you reminded me, a queen. Never in my life did I encounter anyone who was not obsequiously flattering, while privately detesting my privileges. Until I met you folk. You don’t care about my royalty. You don’t want anything from me.”

“Except your advice,” Incident said.

“That doesn’t count. You came to me as an equal. You accepted me when I lost my position. You defended me when my father tried to kill me, and it wasn’t because you wanted anything from me. Except maybe my friendship.”

“True,” Terza said, reading their minds.

“I can’t have true friends among the royals or the peons. Only fake friends. But in this respect the motives of you here are clean. You can be true friends.”

“We can be your friends,” Incident agreed. “Once our job is done.”

“Yes. Meanwhile, Ruby and Terza can stay here with me. You don’t need them on your goblin mission, and I would enjoy their company.”

“Actually, a rabbit who could masquerade as human might be useful on occasion,” Incident said. “And a telepath of any species could be invaluable.”

“Indeed. And of course the choice is theirs to make. But there is one other factor.”

Now it comes, Goar thought. He saw that Terza agreed.

“Factor?” Incident asked.

"The telepath is being tracked. If you take her on this mission, the agents of the sea kingdom, and perhaps also their goblin allies, will know what you are up to."

Incident's jaw dropped. "That's true! I never thought of that."

"You haven't read the Empire SOP manual," Birdie said, smiling.

Incident shook her head, amazed. "And we thought *we* were rescuing *you*, originally."

Birdie looked at the turtles. "The tracking, as I understand it, is not the same as mind reading. They are not in your mind, Terza. They are out of range for that. They don't know what you are thinking, seeing, hearing, or feeling. Only your location, the way Incident zeroes in on the distant location of her targets. They may assume that you remain with the group. So if you stay here they should think that all of you are here, taking a break in a pleasant environment. That would be understandable. You are three and a half couples overdue for some convenient time together."

"Oh, if only!" Incident said fervently. "I am so tired of business."

"You others may also want to depart from here inconspicuously," Birdie said. "Just in case they have other spies watching. Perhaps on foot, while the distraction of the banquet continues. When you are well away from here, you can resume flying."

Incident nodded. "I hate to make you miss the banquet, boys, but she is making uncomfortable sense."

Bird Man appeared. "That's my girl," he said proudly.

Birdie sent him a sultry glance. "I believe I can spare fifteen minutes before you go. I know a private place." She surely did, this being her garden.

Bird Man ran to her and they hugged. Then they headed for the place.

Ruby turned to Rabbit. "Let's find another place. I think I saw a nice briar patch." They disappeared into the garden.

"Under the pond," Terza told Turtle. "We can hold our breaths as long as we need, and the fish won't care." They splashed in and submerged.

That left Goar and Incident. "Right here," she said, and pulled a cord that dropped a comprehensive curtain around the outer wall of the pavilion. "She gave us the hint and arranged to give us time alone together. I like Birdie better every hour."

"So do I," he agreed, enfolding her.

They were delightfully done well within fifteen minutes.

When the group got back together, pleasantly refreshed, Goar thought of a detail. "We should take the mushroom along, just in case."

"Indeed," Incident said.

Ruby handed it to her.

All of them made it to the banquet on schedule. They had eager bites of the delicacies. Goar was seated between Incident and the Queen.

Then he felt Birdie's hand take his hand under the table. "Do not react," she murmured, and he quickly masked his startled expression. "Just listen." She was looking straight ahead, not at him.

Goar used his free hand to continue feeding himself. What was she up to? She knew he had no romantic interest in her, and he was pretty sure she would not deceive Incident without reason.

"SOP amendment," Birdie murmured. "Always have a hidden ploy to guard against betrayal, just in case. Goblin males are not to be trusted. The King will know if Incident knows, so you must handle this detail." She pressed something into his hand. "There are instructions with it. Eat them after reading. Tell no one until it is done." She withdrew her hand, leaving him with a small object. She ignored him completely thereafter. They both continued eating.

Then the key five of them left their places, while Ruby, Terza, the Queen, and the several servitors pretended not to notice. They were on their way, untracked.

Rabbit sniffed out an unobserved route out of the castle. Turtle grew large and carried them across the moat. They made their way through an adjacent forest. Then when they were a fair distance from the castle, Bird became roc and they boarded and hung on. He taxied to a clear area, spread his wings, and took off.

Incident guided him in a widening circle to be sure no one who happened to see him would know exactly where he was going. Only when they were amid a cloud did he orient on the correct direction, and he stayed in clouds as much as possible.

Now, in flight, Goar had a chance to look at what he held. It was a tiny silver locket. He pressed the side and it popped open. Inside was a transparent capsule and a folded piece of paper. He closed the locket with the capsule inside, and unfolded the paper. He read it, nodded, then put it in his mouth, chewed it up, and swallowed it. He knew what to do. It did make sense.

The signal got stronger as they approached the Godforsaken Goblin mound. The girl was definitely in the vicinity, which confirmed her relevance. But she wasn't in the mound itself. In fact, the signal led them to an adjacent troll village. That was odd.

They landed in a secluded spot. Then Bird became sparrow-sized and got into Incident's right breast pocket. Turtle turned miniature and she put him in her left breast pocket. Rabbit remained normal size and scouted the way ahead so that she could follow without mischief in the intensifying darkness. He could see almost as well with his nose, ears, and whiskers as with his eyes, and she could track his mind well enough to be safely guided. They were an efficient team. Goar followed her, ready to defend her at need.

They came to a trench, which, by the odor, was used for refuse. There beside it in the wan moonlight was a goblin male. No, it was an exceedingly ugly female, digging a hole in the ground. This was the one. The surprise was her appearance. Goblin males were normally ugly and foul spirited, while the females were lovely and nice. What could have happened to her?

Incident approached to a moderate distance from the goblin, while Goar stayed back out of sight. "Hello," she said, not loudly. She was human-sized, twice the height of the goblin girl, but different species were used to the sizes.

The girl looked up. "Who are you? This spot is taken. Bury your garbage somewhere else."

So that was what she was doing. A strictly low menial chore. Now Goar saw that there was a brimming bucket beside her.

"My name is Incident. I'm a sylph. I need to talk with you."

"Never heard of you. Now let me work, because the troll will bash me if I'm late getting done."

"You work for a troll? Goblins hate trolls!"

"That's why I'm the only one they can get to do this chore. The lowest of the low."

"But why? If you have to do this dirty work, why not do it for your own kind?"

The girl stood up straight in the moonlight, gnarled and hideous. "Get a good look at me. I'm the ugliest goblin girl in the tribe. No goblin wants me to do even the most menial work for them, for fear of superstitious contamination. No male will touch me in even the slightest lechery. I'm a pariah. The trolls don't care; their women are as ugly as their men. So I get work where I can find it, saving the women from having to slop the slops. They don't care if I stink. Are you satisfied? Then go away."

But Incident was not to be put off so readily. "Until recently I was even uglier than you. I know how it is."

"You? You're beautiful!"

"Yes, now. But for much of my life I was grotesque. Then recently it changed. It's a long story and not relevant to you, except to show that I understand."

"Well, unless you can make me beautiful, I'm not interested." The girl bent to her spade.

"Rabbit," Incident murmured.

Rabbit hopped from her pocket, expanding to normal size.

"Dig a good hole for her."

Rabbit got down and did what rabbits could do so well. In hardly more than a moment he dug a good deep hole.

"Bury your garbage," Incident said. "That gives us time to talk."

Amazed, the girl dumped the bucket into the hole. Rabbit then quickly covered it up and tamped the earth down firm by jumping on it several times. The job was done in only a fraction of the time it would have taken ordinarily.

"I told you my name," Incident said. "Now please tell me yours."

At this point the goblin was more inclined to talk. "My name is Gusta. Gusta Goblin. It means majestic or sacred. Laugh if you want to; everyone else does."

"I am not laughing. Gusta, my talent is to sense people I need to work with. There is a lot of trouble coming, and I need your help to avert it. My talent tells me that."

"Your talent plus a milkweed pod could make you a decent drink. Everyone knows our tribe is marshaling for war."

"The tribe may know it, but not those outside it. Swarming goblins are generally bad news for others."

"What's your point?"

"You're female. That suggests that, inside, you are a nice person."

"That, and a pod, could make *me* a drink."

"I can't make a promise, but it occurs to me that your appearance may relate to your importance for my purpose."

"Only if your purpose is to scare innocent children."

"It is to avert the coming war. Somehow you connect."

"Maybe as a scarecrow to serve as a mascot as the army advances."

Goar was impressed by Incident's patience in the face of such negativity.

"You are bitter," Incident said. "So was I, when I was ugly. But in some manner, you are instrumental in preventing that fateful march. Have you any notion how?"

"None. As far as I know, I'm completely useless. To myself and anyone else."

Incident cast a glance of muted exasperation at Goar. It was clear she wasn't getting anywhere despite her patience. So he stepped in. "Hello, Gusta. I am Goar Golem." He smiled, knowing that the head-sock made his face look normal, and that his new handsomeness shone through, having an effect on any females in range.

Gusta melted. She surely knew better, but a handsome smile on a man was like an evocative torso on a woman, forcing a positive response. "Hello, Goar."

"We are trying to benefit you and ourselves, but we don't yet know how, only that there is a way. We simply need to discover the key. We need your help."

She melted further. "I want to help."

He reached out and took her hand in his sock-gloved hand. He felt her shiver at his touch. Incident's beauty had had little effect on a female, but he was male. "I know you do. Let's explore this together."

"Together," she echoed blissfully. An experienced woman would have been affected less, but no male had ever treated Gusta with such civility.

What next? He was not an experienced interviewer, but he had her attention. Maybe the others could help. "We are a party of five. Three of us are animals. You have met Rabbit. Here is Turtle. He can change his size." He gestured to Turtle.

Turtle cooperated by becoming a size larger, a terrapin. Then larger yet, two feet high. Then still larger, as tall as the goblin girl was. Then down to a tiny painted turtle.

Goar picked him up and handed him to the goblin. "As you can see, he is talented but friendly. He is cute now, but when there was a storm, he became so large that the rest of us were able to take shelter under his shell. He is nice to be with."

"Ooo," she gushed girlishly.

"And there is Bird," Goar said. "He can change sizes too. Right now he is very small." He extended his hand, and Bird fluttered up to perch on a finger. His plumage was especially pretty. Then he hopped to Gusta's finger. She was clearly thrilled.

"I think you would enjoy their company," Goar said. "And we might take you with us, if we knew how you relate to our need."

"I wish I could help," she said, now eager to be cooperative. "But the only unusual thing about me is my appearance, and that's awful."

He did not try to argue with that. "Your name intrigues me, apart from its meaning. Does it have a history?"

Fascinated by the two animals in her hands, and wowed by Goar's handsome attention, Gusta seemed hardly conscious of her words. "There is a connected story. I was of a royal goblin family, until they cast me out. I was delivered in the royal suite the same time as King Gustave was, because my mother was one of his mother's privileged handmaids. Of course, when they saw how ugly I was, they sent me to the boondocks and pretended I didn't exist. But at least I am the exact same age as the king." She managed a blush. "Oh, I'm gushing! I'm sorry."

"Not at all," he said generously. Actually, he was enjoying having such an effect on her. His current appearance was like a sword, wielded emotionally. "It's an interesting coincidence, having such similar names and being the same age."

"Yes. The same stork could have brought us. Oh, if only I had been beautiful, I could have been his companion, and maybe in time his mistress. Maybe even more." She shed a tear. "But that's a ludicrous fantasy."

"I wonder," Incident said. "I read of a case once where two people, a boy and a girl, got the wrong names. It took them forever to find each other so they could exchange them and be the way they were supposed to be."

Gusta shook her head. "We got the right names. That's not my problem."

"I am getting a glimmer," Incident said. "Could it have been your *appearances* that got mixed up?"

The goblin laughed. "Well, I do look a lot like a male."

"And what does the king look like?"

"Why, I don't know. I never saw him. I hear he's pretty secretive."

But Incident was on to something. "Suppose he looked like a female? What would he do?"

"Oh, he'd hide, the way I do. No king could afford to be woman-faced."

"You said he is secretive."

"Yes." Then Gusta saw her point. "He's hiding!"

There was a tramping sound, and a figure appeared in the gloom. "Goblin! What's taking so long?"

Gusta quailed. "Oh, I got to talking, and now I'm late. I'm in trouble."

"I think not," Incident said firmly. "Come with us."

"But I can't be any use to you. You don't need your garbage buried."

"We need you," Incident said, taking her hand. "Goar, remonstrate with the troll. Tell him that Gusta has found a better position."

"Goblin," the troll said, advancing. "I'm going to whip your lazy butt so hard it'll come out of your ugly mouth."

Goar took the two animals from Gusta, set Turtle down on the ground and flicked Bird into the air. He took a step toward the troll.

"Don't hurt him," Incident warned him as she led Gusta away. "Just let him know she's through with him."

Goar faced the troll, who was an ugly creature taller than he was. "I am Goar Golem. Gusta Goblin has found other employment. She bids you a polite parting."

"Har har har! Get out of my way, Golem, before I smash your head down through your ankle."

Goar did not get out of his way. "Perhaps you did not hear me, sir. I said the goblin girl is departing your employment."

The troll smashed a massive fist down on Goar's head. It bounced. "Ow!"

"Is that your name?" Goar inquired pleasantly. "Ow Troll? It is not very alliterative."

"Why you smirking robot! Take that!" He smashed his other fist into

Goar's face. It also bounced. "Ow!" Now both his fists were badly bruised, while Goar was unaffected.

"I trust we will not need to have this dialogue again," Goar said, and turned his back on the troll.

Just in time to receive a violent kick in the butt. And a third "Ow!"

Goar walked away as the troll limped back the way he had come. He rejoined the others. "I did not hurt him," he reported. "He hurt himself."

"I saw that," Gusta said. "I hope I don't have to find work with him again. He'll remember."

"If our business does not work out," Incident said, "we will find some other compatible situation for you, Gusta. But I think we have found the key. It has to have been an inadvertent exchange of appearances, wrought by a stork confused by the similarity of names."

Gusta began to have faint hope. "But if that's true, how can it be fixed?"

"I have a certain power of facilitating an exchange," Incident said. "I am hoping that it can work for appearances."

"Hoping," the goblin echoed prayerfully.

"Now let me orient on the King. I assume he is here with the tribe."

"I think so," Gusta said. "But he's so secretive it's hard to be sure."

They paused so Incident could orient. She closed her eyes.

"She is zeroing in on the King, just as she zeroed in on you before," Goar explained. "To find out exactly where he is."

"I wish I had a talent like that! I'd zero in on the perfect employer. One who wouldn't beat me for being late with the slop."

She still thought in terms of getting a menial job.

Incident opened her eyes. "That way. I get the feeling he is alone right now; if we can get there quickly enough, we can catch him."

"They've got guards everywhere," Gusta said. "You can't get through just by walking. They'd club you and rape you, and if you didn't scream hard enough, they'd get nasty."

Incident smiled. "You forget that Goar is with me."

The girl tittered. She was becoming downright relaxed.

Incident looked around. "Rabbit, scout out a safe, fast route."

Rabbit bounded into the brush.

"Now we need to get you better clothing," Incident told the goblin. "You stink, no offense intended."

"I should. I handle the stinkiest slops. The ones even troll women balk at."

She evidently sacrificed pride to expediency. Goar admired that.

"See to it, Bird," Incident said. "Turtle, is there a suitable pool within range?"

Turtle sniffed the air, then scrambled in a new direction. They followed closely. Soon they stood at the edge of a small clear pond.

"In you go," Incident told the goblin. "Um, strip first. We'll throw away your clothes, and get you new ones."

"I will depart for the nonce," Goar said.

Gusta laughed. "Don't bother, handsome. I'm too ugly to give you any ideas at all. But I'd love it if you did get any." She ripped off her soiled dress, then splashed into the water.

"Hair too," Incident said.

The girl dunked her head and strained her hair through the water. That much was nice enough: it was only her fleshly features that were ugly.

She emerged clean but still ugly. Incident had harvested a towel, and Gusta toweled herself dry. Goar saw that she was a fully developed girl, but she was right; she excited no untoward interest in him. An ordinary female goblin would have; they were small but perfectly shaped.

Bird returned with underclothing, dress, and slippers, all in the goblin's small size. Gusta donned them. Now she looked repulsive in fine clothing. In fact the clothing was evidently designed for a shapely figure, and her body pushed it out in all the wrong places.

Rabbit returned. He became Beetle Bunny and reported. "No feasible path through the defensive cordon. But there's a gap by a crevice they don't watch. If we fly over that, we can make it through."

"Good enough. Let's fly from here, low enough to avoid scouts watching the sky."

Bird became the roc, to Gusta's amazement, and they piled on.

It was a very short flight, and they were safely past the goblin guardline. They landed behind the central hill. It was night, but some activity remained; there were muted lights moving in and out of the myriad entrance holes.

"The King's royal chamber should be in the very center," Gusta whispered. "With guards and servants everywhere. You can't just walk in."

"Indeed not," Incident agreed. "I hadn't thought of this." She looked at Goar.

Goar thought fast. "We have the mushroom. We can make ourselves very small and sneak in unobserved."

"Yes. This time we can ride Rabbit, in his smallest size. He is good at rapidly navigating tunnels."

Rabbit nipped the mushroom and became mouse-sized. The rest of them tasted it and became flea-sized. "Please, I'm frightened," Gusta piped. "Everything is so *large*."

"Take her hand," Incident told him. "This is new to her."

Goar took the tiny goblin's hand and led her to what now seemed like an elephantine rabbit. He lifted her up, and Incident caught her hands and drew her in. Then Goar climbed up, took firm hold of Gusta with one arm and a strand of rabbit hair with the opposite hand, and settled in. But the goblin was still nervous, so he folded her in close to his chest. She loved that. It was amazing the difference being handsome made.

"Say nothing, just listen," he murmured in her ear. "I am going to give you a love spell. That will ensure that the King will be completely smitten with you, when the time comes." He brought out the locket, which remained in proportion, and took out the capsule. "Swallow this."

She obeyed. She would have done anything he asked of her. He was halfway bemused, knowing that goblin women preferred their men ugly, yet could be impressed by handsomeness in other species.

"Tell no one. It will start to work when he touches you, and soon will be complete. You need do nothing else."

She nodded. He knew she was glad to have this assurance.

They hung on to the fur of Rabbit's back, and he ran rather than hopped up to the nearest vacant entry hole. He popped in, sniffing out the clear passages while Incident mentally guided him toward the King. They came to an intersection where a pretty goblin maidservant was passing and scooted right under her legs without her noticing. Goar resisted the urge to peek up under her skirt; she surely wore panties and there was no sense in freaking out right now.

"She has gold panties," Gusta said, surprised. "I had some of those when I was royal, but then I changed to goblin black."

Yes, he would have freaked! "Only royals wait on the King."

"Right, it's been so long I forgot."

Then they came to the Royal Suite. The door to it was barred and locked closed. Now what were they to do? Only an authorized servant would have the key, and the door would open to let her in and out. It would be difficult to sneak in then.

"He has to get food and drink," Gusta said. "Often, I hear. Maybe if we hid in a cookie jar?"

"Good idea," Incident said.

Rabbit sniffed out the waiting meal. It was on a tray on a table, and smelled delicious. They scrambled up the side of the cookie jar and hid under the cookies. Rabbit took a bit of mushroom, became flea-sized, and joined them.

They were in luck. In hardly more than two and a half moments a servant came to pick up the tray. They felt the motion as she carried it to the door to the King's suite, unlocked it, stepped through, and locked it again behind her. Oh yes, they were careful. The King truly valued his privacy.

The servant set down the tray, rang a bell, and departed. They heard the door unlocking and re-locking as she left. Only when she was safely gone, did they hear the King emerging from his chamber. He picked up the tray and carried the meal into his room, then locked that door behind him too. He was certainly a glutton for privacy!

They heard him take a glass and pour himself some boot rear or the equivalent. "He's facing away, I think," Incident said. "Out."

They clambered out from under the cookies, up the wall of the jar, and out onto the table. Sure enough, the King was facing away, enjoying his drink. They jumped on down to the floor, which really wasn't as far down as it looked because they were so small. Ants could drop long distances without getting hurt; so could they. Incident held out the mushroom, and each of them took a bite from what they hoped was the correct side.

It was. Suddenly they were normal size again. Incident gestured them back into the shadows, then she took a breath, touched up her hair, and spoke softly. "Your Majesty."

The King jumped, dropping his glass. Fortunately, it was almost empty by this time. "Who?" he demanded, putting a mask over his face.

"I am Incident, a former Sylph. I have urgent business with you."

He whirled around angrily, but paused when he saw her beauty. "How did you get in? I'll have somebody's head for this!"

"I used magic. No one is at fault, and I mean you no harm. Please, I am hoping I can do you a significant favor."

He shook his head. "You are the loveliest creature of any species I ever saw, but I already have a discreet mistress."

"Let me see your face."

"So you can blab my secret appearance to the whole mound? Depart, spy!"

"I was the ugliest wench I ever saw," Incident said evenly. "Then it changed, and now I am as beautiful as I was ugly. So I may understand your case."

He laughed. "You think I am ugly?"

"No. I think you are handsome."

He hesitated as if struck by an unexpected truth. "Why?"

"Because I met a goblin girl who is ugly."

"So?"

"She is Gusta, exactly your age, delivered here the same hour you were, Gustave. I think the stork got confused and got your appearances switched. Sometimes there are similar mixups."

The King paused in thought. "There was a girl baby. They spirited her away and I never saw her. You say she is ugly?"

"The ugliest girl in the mound."

"This intrigues me. But how can I trust you with any personal information?"

"I am partially telepathic, when I try. If you take my hand, you can read my mind. Then you will know."

He sighed. "I doubt I believe you. But what have I to lose?" He stepped forward, reached up, and took her hand.

They stood, hands joined, for a moment so long it almost fissioned into two. Then he let go and stepped back. "I believe you."

Goar knew that Incident did not know about the love spell he had given Gusta. That was just as well. The King had not been able to pick up that detail from her because it wasn't there. She was being honest with him.

Incident smiled. "Then let me try to fix it, for both of you."

The King removed his mask, and stood revealed as the handsomest goblin male extant. "How?"

"I have a certain power of transference, when the other parties agree and desire it. I don't know whether it will work with you, but if it did, it would transform your life and hers. You would be suitably ugly, as you were meant to be; she suitably lovely. It seems worth a try."

"Bleep, this is tempting! Where is this girl?"

Incident glanced back. "Gusta, come here."

The goblin girl stepped hesitantly forward.

The King studied her. "It is true; there has never been an uglier goblin girl."

"True," Gusta agreed sadly.

He faced Incident. "I have touched you and shared your mind. You really do mean well, and have certain powers. I agree that this is worth the try. What is the procedure?"

"Take her hand. I will put my hands on yours. I will try the exchange. Either it will work or it won't."

"And if it doesn't?"

"We will depart and never bruit your secret about."

"Deal!" He grasped Gusta's hand. The girl seemed amazed that he even touched her; he was, after all, the King.

And the love spell was starting.

Incident put her two hands outside theirs, enclosing them. She closed her eyes. "You have to really *want* to change."

"We do," the King and Gusta said almost together.

Goar could see Incident concentrating. And he saw the change occurring. The King grew steadily uglier, while Gusta grew steadily prettier. It was working!

At last, Incident removed her hands. "It is done."

The King looked at Gusta. The girl looked at the King. Both were astonished.

"You're beautiful!" he said.

"You're ugly!"

It was true. The King was no longer handsome of face, but hideous, and his bearing had become stooped and gnarled. The girl's face had become radiant, and her crooked body was now upright and supremely shaped. Now she fit her clothing more than perfectly.

He stepped forward and took hold of her. She yielded gracefully. Then he drew her in and kissed her passionately. "You will be my queen."

Gusta did not even need to accept; his word was goblin law. "I will never tell what went before," she agreed.

Somehow that seemed natural. The love spell was taking hold.

The King turned back to Incident. "You want payment for your service, of course. Gold? Territory? Slaves? Name it."

Incident did not hesitate. "Call off the war of conquest you are planning."

He hesitated. Warfare was dear to a goblin male's heart.

"Please," Gusta pleaded. Her new beauty made her plea marvelously appealing. "I would be so grateful."

That did it. "For you I will do it. I didn't much like the sea folk anyway."

"My business here is done," Incident said. "I will depart."

"But of course you will return to attend the royal wedding," Gustave said. "And say nothing about the nature of our connection."

Incident smiled. "Agreed."

"Then begone." He turned to Gusta. "You and I have urgent business in the bedroom."

"Of course," she agreed, delighted. Oh yes, the love spell was exercising its imperative, affecting both of them.

The two headed for the bedroom. Gusta turned her face their way just long enough to mouth "Thanks!" Then they were gone.

And very soon so were the rest of them. The mission was a success.

Only when they were airborne on the way back to the Shee castle did Incident speak about it. "That was too easy," she said. "I don't trust Gustave. He may revert to war the moment he is safely rid of us."

"No he won't," Goar said.

She eyed him. "How can you know that? Goblin males are notoriously untrustworthy. Their minds are as ugly as their bodies."

"Because I gave her a love spell to use on the King. I got it from Birdie. That's why he was so instantly smitten with her. It wasn't just her beauty."

Incident remained dubious. "He could take her to bed, have his will of her, then banish her to the scullery, summoning her only when his passion rose again. Meanwhile he could wage warfare unabated. It isn't only goblin kings who do that."

"It was not a garden variety love spell," Goar said. "It was a love compulsion spell."

Incident pursed her lips in a soundless whistle. "That's another kettle! He will not ever try to counter her will. He thought he was being smart, but he is truly caught. There will be no war." Then she thought of another aspect. "And you did not tell me, because the King would have known if I had known, when he read my mind. A neat ploy."

"SOP," he agreed, satisfied.

Chapter 13

SMOKE & SMOG

They arrived back at Shee Castle in good order, only to learn of a message. "It is from one Squid," Birdie said. "For Goar. I don't know of her."

"I killed her," Goar said. "I am trying to do good deeds until she forgives me."

The Queen lifted an eyebrow. "I suspect that is a pretty steep challenge."

"Yes. But in the course of it I have had adventures I would not trade, including interacting with you."

She laughed. "I see you are practicing flattery."

"It is a social skill. I am trying to become more social."

"And it is not an exaggeration to say that I owe my present position to your participation."

"Not at all. I may have helped Incident and her companions to begin their quest for good deeds, but they could have done that without me."

"Perhaps. But I was thinking of the Demoness Fornax."

Goar was surprised, because Fornax was supposed to be anonymous. "What do you know of her?"

"We did dialogue briefly, and there was something about the timbre of her voice and the certainty of her manner. I have long since learned to judge people by small hints; it is a necessary capability for royalty. I knew she was far more than she evinced. My ascent to the Queenship seemed fortuitous. I was suspicious about that, so I investigated. I learned that the Demoness Fornax has been subtly helping you. I believe it was her intervention that promoted my ascent."

She had pretty well scoped it. "I killed her friend. I don't know why she is helping me."

"It is a mystery," Birdie agreed. "I suspect that this girl Squid is also more than she may choose to appear. There was a rumor that she was once the most important person in the universe, and still may be. The record indicates that she is truly a nice person."

Truly nice. That was part of the awfulness of it. He had not killed a nasty person, but a nice one. "Yes."

"At any rate, I suspect Fornax is the one who left the message, via Squid. It is that you can gain significant favor by enlisting the smoker dragons in the defense of Xanth."

"Favor with Squid," he said. "Fornax knows I will do anything for that. But is Xanth being attacked?"

"Not yet. But I gather it soon will be. Your group is assigned to enlist the Godforsaken Goblins, the Sea Kingdom, and the Smoker Dragons. The last first."

"Which means that may be the worst challenge," he said grimly. "If we don't accomplish that, there may be no point in approaching the others."

"That would be my guess," she agreed. "I suspect that Gusta Goblin will agree, and that Terza can approach Doris Dragon, pointing out that once aliens conquer Xanth, it won't be long before they cast their covetous gaze on the riches of the sea. But the dragons hardly seem to care about the rest of Xanth. I understand that the smokers are largely separate from the other dragons, and don't necessarily follow where they lead."

"We'll go," Incident said.

"Leave the telepath here, as before? Terza and I are getting along marvelously well, perhaps because she knows my objections to anything almost before I do."

"Yes, I think it should be just our core group," Incident said.

Goar smiled. "I trust you won't be slipping me any more spells this time, Birdie."

"Oh, do you miss our secret touching of hands?"

"No offense, but it's Incident's hand I prefer to touch."

Birdie laughed. "Still, practice your flirtation. You never can be sure when it might be useful."

"Oh?" Incident asked.

"I understand that Smote Smoker, the dragon queen, can be a sultry wench when she tries, and she likes to impress visitors. She's good at smoke signals."

They all laughed. But Goar suspected there was good advice there too. He was gaining proficiency, but there was a world of manners he had yet to master.

Soon they were on their way, with no more fanfare than before. The roc flew to the vicinity of the boundary. Then they landed, and Goar and Incident sprouted their wings. A roc in dragon territory was likely to be considered a threat. Turtle accompanied Goar, while Bird and Rabbit went with Incident. If there was trouble, Turtle could grow giant, while the roc could haul Incident quickly away. But trouble was likely to mean the immediate failure of their mission.

They came to a large dragon snoozing in a clearing. "We can be sure he's not really asleep," Incident murmured. "He's watching us to see what we're up to."

They landed not far from the dragon. "Hallooo!" Goar called.

The dragon opened his eyes. He puffed out a warning column of smoke.

They continued their approach. "We are two ground-bound folk using magic wings," Incident said. "We come to meet the Queen."

The dragon snorted. The smoke formed into a question mark. "I am Incident Oma and this is Goar Golem. It is alliance business, for her ears alone. Please allow us to pass."

The dragon puffed out more smoke. Several balls of it floated up into the sky. In about two moments there was an answer from the distant castle: several more smoke balls. Smoke signals indeed!

The dragon looked, then lay his head back on the ground and closed his eyes. That was his way of letting them pass. Their presence had been announced.

"Thank you," Incident said, and stepped forward to pat the dragon on the snout. The fact that she was allowed to do this was a tribute to her beauty; even dragons appreciated feminine pulchritude. They spread their wings and took off.

Shortly, they arrived at the castle, a thoroughly smoked stone edifice. They landed at the front gate, where a human servitor awaited them. Human servants were a signal of class among dragons, and they were useful for chores requiring digital dexterity. He ushered them into the central court where the Queen Dragon awaited them. She was not large as dragons went, but that was no indication since she was reputed to be a shape changer.

They stood before her and bowed. "Your Majesty," Incident said. "I am—"

The dragon belched out a cloud of smoke. "Yes, yes, I know," a voice said. "You flew here from the Shee Kingdom. State your business."

Goar realized that it was a translation. The Queen had a device to interpret her smoke signals so that her visitors could understand.

"We have received word that—"

There was another blast of smoke. "I will speak with the golem."

Incident did not protest, diplomatically. She withdrew a few steps, letting Goar take it.

"Word that there may be an invasion of Xanth not long from now," Goar continued, from where Incident had been interrupted. "We have come to solicit your alliance to defend against it."

The Queen breathed out more smoke. It clouded around her so that for a moment she entirely disappeared within it. Then it dissipated, leaving her in a new form: nude, sultry, and human. Her tail had disappeared, her snout had retreated into a hardly noticeable chin, and her eyes were smoke-colored. Strategic wisps of smoke imperfectly covered her more intimate portions, and her hair was a trail of smoke extending from her head to her bottom. The trace coverings served more to enhance rather than conceal their neighboring flesh. "Well, now, handsome," she said smokily. "How about a kiss?"

"I hesitate to try to touch a queen," Goar said cautiously.

"Then hold still while I touch you." She glided forward and put her charcoal dark lips to his. She smelled and tasted of burnt hickory, and her touch was remarkably conducive.

Goar stood still, careful not to presume; she was after all, a queen.

"What, you didn't try to grab a feel?" she asked. "Then it will come to you." She nudged her body closer until her frontal wisps stroked his chest plate. "Embrace me. I am quite feelable."

He put his arms around her, carefully impersonal, yet somehow his hands came to rest on her curvy bottom. He wasn't sure how she had managed that, as he had tried to be discreet. She wanted a compliment, of course. "You are nice to hold."

"Now we shall dance while we dialogue." Her arms circled him and guided him so that he moved as she wished. Her bottom remained in his grip as it flexed with her motions, and her body shifted limberly against his. "What's this about an invasion? Who is invading?"

"We don't know," he answered, trying to focus on his words. Her supple torso was somehow stroking his evocatively. She reminded him obscurely of the Goddess Tiamat. She was trying to seduce him, and was doing a fair job of it. He needed to get their official business done quickly, before he forgot whatever it was he had come to say. "Just that it is a force from outside, that will require considerable effort to repel. We need you."

She rubbed lithely against him. "I suspect you do. But we dragons do not participate in the projects of others without reason. What do you offer in return?"

"Uh—" He was at a loss for further words. "What do you desire?"

"Desire," she echoed. "Interesting choice of words. Shall we retire to the bedroom chamber for further elucidation?"

"No!" He spoke before his mind shushed him. Queens were not accustomed to hearing such a word unless they spoke it themselves.

"No?"

He thought fast. He couldn't tell her that he was getting desperate. "I mean I will never be able to remember what to say, if we go there."

She did not challenge that, for it was surely true. "I understand that you had a fair session with the Goddess Tiamat. Did you enjoy her company?"

Tiamat! How did she know about that? Had she read his mind?

"Tiamat is the ultimate mother of all dragons," she explained. "And I am a dragon, as perhaps you noticed. We are pleased to have her visit Xanth."

She was clearly well informed about his background. "Tiamat taught me much. I like her very well."

"Let's see what you learned." She drew him in even closer and kissed him again. He didn't think she was using a love spell on him, but then she hardly needed to. She was clearly well experienced in this art. "The bedroom," she repeated huskily.

Turtle spoke in his mind. *If she seduces you while Incident watches, she won't respect you.*

That jolted him straight. He had forgotten that Turtle was with him, so communication between them was easy. Turtle was right: this wasn't merely a temptation, it was a test. How easy a mark was he?

"I think not," he said. "I came here to negotiate a deal, and I intend to do it, however tempting the distractions may be." There was an art to saying no without insulting her.

Smote paused almost an instant. Then she relaxed and turned him loose. "Then we shall negotiate." She glanced beyond him. "Rejoin us, Incident."

Incident came forward as if there had been no interruption. Goar realized that he had won some respect not just for himself, but for Incident, as obviously he preferred her to the dragon. "Apart from saving Xanth for all its creatures, what else is your interest?" Incident asked. Because dragons, like goblins, did not do things for nothing.

"There is something I want, that possibly you with your special powers might obtain. It may be a challenge, however."

Incident smiled. "We have encountered challenges before."

"Not like this one. I want a Spinosaurus."

Both of them paused, drawing blanks. Then came the voice of the turtle. *An ancient reptile predator. Very large.* Turtle was of course conversant with his reptilian lineage.

"Why would you want a large ancient reptilian predator?" Goar asked.

If the Queen was surprised by his knowledge of the term, she didn't show it. "I want it for a pet."

A pet! It would gobble her up! It's the largest dinosaur carnisaur known.

"That dinosaur would gobble you up," Goar protested. "It's the largest carnisaur known."

"A wild one, yes. But if I raised it from the egg, it would see me as its mother. I alone would be safe from its hunger. Fetch me an egg."

That could be. They do respect their families. However, they died out about a hundred million years ago.

A hundred million years! "We may have a problem," Goar said. "They're extinct."

She nodded. "I believe I mentioned it might be a challenge."

"We would have to travel in time."

Smote eyed Incident. "Is that not feasible? You do have special powers."

Incident considered. "It could be done if I focused."

It could? Goar concealed his surprise.

"Bring me that egg. When it hatches, I will commit to the defense of our territory from alien invasion."

This did not seem like much of a bargain to Goar. Surely, the dragons would defend their territory regardless. Then again, maybe not, as they might simply move, rather than endure the hassle of fighting aliens. Even landbound dragons like these ranged widely and did not value land as such.

"We'll see what we can do," Incident said.

She was willing to do it! Goar held his silence.

"Welcome to stay the night," Smote said to Goar as streamers of smoke curled around her curves. "I have not before encountered a golem as handsome as you. You may share my bed."

That handsomeness was turning out to be a two-edged sword. He could now sway women with it, but it also made him a target. "I stay with Incident."

She shrugged. "Some other time, perhaps."

"Perhaps," he agreed. Always leave a chance. *Managing Women 101*, again.

Smote eyed him appreciatively. "Oh, Mother taught you well!"

They extended their wings and took off. The three companions had never made their presence known.

Actually, it could have been interesting, Turtle thought. *But Terza might not approve.*

Smote had made a solid impression on Goar. She must have made even more of an impression on another reptile. But telepathic Terza would know instantly, and that would be mischief.

They landed outside the dragon territory, and switched to the roc for faster travel back to the Shee domain.

"How can we travel in time?" Goar asked Incident.

"It is one of the lesser exploited powers of the Oma. The Queen evidently knows of it. It is indirect, and of course dangerous if incorrectly used."

"Paradox," he agreed. "Go back and change something that eliminates you in the present, like giving your grandmother a headache on the night she sent the stork signal for your mother."

"Yes. That is frowned upon. However, the dinosaurs were eliminated sixty-five million years ago, so whatever we change before then may have little or no impact on today. That makes long-distance time travel easier in some respects than short distance."

"But how do we do it at all?"

"If Turtle focuses on an ancient relative, or rather if he identifies it in his mind so that I can get a fix, then we can go, just as we do when I orient on a contemporary person."

"Turtle will locate it, and you will orient? But the paradox could still strike, because any ancestor of his could affect his existence."

"We would go, not to interfere with the ancestor, but to orient on the time period. Once there, I would seek a spinosaurus."

Goar shook his head. "This seems complicated to me."

"It must be done precisely."

He thought of something else. "In Mundania there is no magic, or too little to count. What about the distant past?"

"It is my understanding that the time of the dinosaurs was before science and magic separated. So both should work."

"That's a relief!"

"Still, it will be a challenge. We need to be careful."

We need informed help, Turtle thought.

Incident agreed. "We know nothing about this creature. Any large predator is dangerous, but it helps to be informed. We may or may not be able to fetch one of its eggs without antagonizing it."

"Does anyone in Xanth know much about it?" Goar asked.

"I doubt it. When we land, I will orient on a Spino Expert, and we'll see."

In due course they landed by the Shee castle and were admitted. Incident explained the situation to Birdie.

"Oh, I wish I could go and see the ancient creatures!" Birdie exclaimed. "But at the same time, it makes me exceedingly nervous. The paradox and all."

"We will be careful," Incident assured her. Then she oriented on the expert: someone who knew about Spinosaurus, and might be available and willing to help them. A stiff order.

Incident opened her eyes. "There is one," she announced. "But she's Mundane."

Goar and the companions heaved a joint sigh. This was likely mischief.

"We can go and talk to her," Incident said. "But we'll lose our powers in Mundania. I believe we'll still be pretty creatures, but we won't speak her language and we won't be able to change our shapes. We'll be whatever shapes we are when we cross the border."

"So how will we talk with her?" Goar asked.

Incident made a wry face. "I haven't yet figured that out."

"Would telepathy help?" Terza asked.

Incident considered. "It might. If I can zero in on her with my talent, that suggests that telepathy can work in Mundania. You might be able to talk with her."

"Then I'm in. Except that I would hesitate to go there in my natural form. I'm really mostly a sea creature, not handy on land."

"If you take a bite of the mushroom," Goar said, "you could get small and ride in my pocket. Then you could translate for me."

Terza manifested as the green lady and hugged him. He liked that more than he cared to admit, though of course she knew it. He trusted that she had the wit not to tell.

I do.

They worked it out. The roc would carry them all to the closest region, then Goar would cross into Mundania alone except for Terza. They would go see the Mundane woman and hope to bring her back to join the party.

They got on it immediately. Terza bit the mushroom and became pocket size, joining Goar. They boarded the roc. Soon they were winging to the border. They landed and stood at the spot.

It was time. "Suppose she doesn't want to come?" Goar asked worriedly.

"Persuade her," Incident said as she adjusted his suit to make him look more Mundane.

"But what if she's not interested?"

"Use your manly charms. They worked on Smote."

"But you're the only one I want to impress that way."

"This is business. Do what you need to enable us to accomplish our mission. Seduce her if you have to."

"You—you would not be jealous?"

"Of course I'll be jealous! But I'm a realist. I refuse to let my feelings interfere with the larger good. You should not either."

And if she had to seduce a stranger to accomplish the mission, she would, Terza thought. *The mission is not just about the two of you.*

That put a new perspective on it. She was surely correct.

Yes. Being a telepath has educated me a lot recently. I have been harvesting the true thoughts of ordinary human people. I feel as if I have been wading in ambrosia mixed with garbage. I'm glad I'm a turtle.

"I will do what I have to do," he agreed, speaking to Incident.

Incident kissed him. "Just try not to enjoy it too much."

Rabbit dug a hole big enough to let him crawl through. Those rabbit holes were really special.

He passed through into Mundania. Immediately he felt the loss of something intangible. It was his magic. He was no longer invulnerable.

He was also choking on a cloud of corrosive vapor. He reset his lungs to detoxify it, but the fog of it still obscured his vision. He realized that this was smog, the natural environment of Mundania. Who would ever live here voluntarily?

Yet it had not been there so much when they visited Mundania to stop the New Clear explosion. Maybe it came and went, and this just happened to be a bad day locally.

"Are you still there?" he asked aloud.

I am, Terza's thought came. *It seems telepathy is science, not magic. Or maybe both.*

That's a relief.

Incident gave me the location. I will guide you. Just keep walking. She sniffed the air. *What a stench!*

"Smog," he explained. "There must be a local cloud. I believe it comes from the pollution they ceaselessly put into land, sea, and sky."

The Mundanes must like it, to generate so much of it.

He kept walking. In due course, he came to a Mundane town. He followed the course Terza charted for him, and came to an apartment building, then to a door on the second floor. *She is home. Knock on the door.*

He knocked. In exactly a moment, because Mundania did not have fractions of moments, the door opened. A rather plain middle-aged woman stood there. Her dark hair was bound back into a bun and she was a bit overweight, but otherwise average. "Yes?" Terza translated so that he hardly heard the real word, which was gibberish.

"Um, I am Goar, from Xanth. You are Sarah Spinel? We need your help."

She started to close the door. "You say you're Goat, from a fantasy land? I'm not buying anything."

Evidently, the translation wasn't perfect. "Goar. It's important."

"Look, Mister Goar, I am struggling with an important paper, and I have little patience with practical jokes. The smog is suffocating today. I am plainly not in the mood. So kindly be on your way." She pushed harder on the door.

He was getting nowhere. Failure stared him in the face. What was he to do?

Kiss her. She's lonely.

He did it. He leaned quickly forward and kissed her on the mouth.

Sarah was so surprised she fell back, letting go of the door.

Catch her!

He leaped forward and caught her before she fell to the floor.

Kiss her again. It's her secret fantasy, to be swept off her feet by a handsome stranger. You are that.

So he really did have to use his appearance without restraint to forward the mission. So be it. He kissed her again. Sarah kissed him back. It was after all her fantasy.

But she was also a sensible woman. "Enough! I know the difference between fantasy and reality. What is your purpose here? I'm sure it is not to romance me."

Level with her. Name the creature. I think she is ready to listen.

He turned her loose. "It is not. We need help with a Spinosaurus."

"Oh my! You said the magic word."

He was startled, but Terza steered him through it. *It is a figure of speech. She means you have her attention. Continue.*

"We have to fetch the egg of a Spinosaurus. We know nothing about the creature except that it dates from a hundred million years ago. We understand that you are an expert on it, so we need your help."

She was bemused. "You kissed me twice because you want to know more about Spinosauruses?"

"Yes. It is important. If kissing you is the price of your cooperation, I will do it. Whatever you require."

She shook her head. "I fear the smog is getting into my head and making me hallucinate. I am almost tempted to yield to it before I get an intolerable headache."

Go with it, Terza thought. *I will send acceptance to her mind. She's a very intelligent woman, but also imaginative and feeling.*

Goar had to smile. "I am surely less bothersome than a headache."

Sarah yielded. "This is becoming better than a daydream. Kiss me again, then sit down. Tell me more."

He kissed her again. She was not physically attractive in the normal sense, but he found her attention conducive. There was after all more to a woman than appearance, and a lot more to this one. She was desirable in a way that the cynical lady dragon was not.

Then they sat on her small couch. He told her about the Land of Xanth, and the smoker dragon, and her demand for the Spino egg. "So we need to go there and fetch it," he concluded. "But we fear we will mess it up unless we have expert guidance. You can provide that guidance. We will make any deal you wish if you will help us."

"You know this is completely incredible," Sarah said. "So why do I find myself straining to believe you?"

He smiled. "The pollution twisting your mind?"

She laughed. "That must be it. But I suspect there is something else. I have not before indulged in such illusion. I know that a handsome young man like you would not cater to me even for an hour without excellent and cynical reason. I feel intrigued, not threatened."

She feels my presence in her mind.

"It is probably because of Terza."

"Because of whom?"

"Terza. She is a telepathic turtle." He tapped his pocket were Terza was peeking out. "She is translating our thoughts to each other so that we can have this dialogue. Otherwise our speech would be mutual gibberish."

"A telepathic turtle. I trust you will pardon me if I question this additional improbability."

Goar smiled again, knowing she liked it. "This much we can prove. Think something I could never guess."

Sarah paused, concentrating.

That maybe you have polka dot underpants with green stripes.

"Polka dot underpants. Green stripes."

"Oh my!" she repeated. "May I hear from her directly?"

I am Terza, a telepathic turtle, Terza thought to both of them. *We do need your help.*

Sarah shook her head. "Is there any way you can make me believe any of this delirium? That is, that this is not a weird dream I have having?"

"Come with us," Goar said. "See Xanth for yourself. Meet Incident and her three amazing animals. Then you will believe."

"Meet whom?"

"Incident is the woman who arranged this excursion. She has three companions: a bird, a rabbit, and a turtle, all of whom have special powers."

"Isn't Terza one of them?"

No. I am the girlfriend of her Turtle.

Sarah considered. "Even if this is all a dream, I think I would like to meet those folk before it ends."

"You can. We need you for the mission."

"So it is a business arrangement. That I can appreciate. Quid pro quo. And what do you offer in return for my assistance?"

"What do you most desire?"

She smiled. "I am tempted to say I most desire your intimate company. But just in the off chance that this is not a total dream, I will answer my real desire. The Chair. As a woman I face the Glass Ceiling. Only a truly phenomenal published paper will shatter that glass."

She means she wants to become chairman of her department at the university, Terza clarified. *That there is an invisible barrier women face that prevents them from having the success men enjoy. She might write an essay that would get their attention, if only she had the means to do the proper research.*

Goar got an idea. "Suppose you could see a live Spinosaurus yourself, and write about that?"

Sarah laughed. "That would do it. But of course it's impossible."

"Not if you accompany us when we go to fetch the egg."

"And how could I ever do that?"

"By coming with us when we travel through time to a hundred million years ago. That way you will see everything."

"Now it's time travel! Don't you fantasy folk know of paradox?"

"We believe it will not apply to that period, because it would affect only dinosaurs, and none of them exist today."

Sarah considered. "Why settle for partial madness, when complete madness is so close at hand?" she asked herself. "Very well, I will take you up on that. Take me to your friend Incident."

"Immediately," Goar agreed.

"How did you come here?"

"Through a rabbit hole. Then we walked."

"It will be faster to use my car."

"Car?" But he remembered how common they had been during the other Mundane excursion. Traveling boxes.

Then, amazingly, they were riding in her car, a vehicle that rolled forward on four wheels exactly like the others while she steered it with another wheel inside. Soon they came to the rabbit hole.

"I see nothing but more trees," Sarah said.

"Take my hand. We are Xanth natives, so we can cross, and you can cross with us."

She took his hand and they stepped through the rabbit hole and into the other realm. "Oh my!" she said a third time as she saw the changed landscape of Xanth and smelled the air. "The breeze is so fresh!"

"We prefer it that way," Goar said.

"And I understand you directly, without Terza's translation. How is that possible?"

"You are now in the Land of Xanth, where everyone understands the common language. It is part of the magic."

"I believe I am going to like this fantasy land of yours."

Goar smiled. "Most folk do."

Then Incident appeared. "You came!" she exclaimed. Then, picking up on Terza's mental message: "Hello, Sarah Mundane. I am Incident, and these are Bird, Rabbit, and Turtle."

"And I am of course mundane," Sarah agreed wryly, evidently picking up on Incident's beauty. "You are Goar's girlfriend?"

"I am."

"Obviously, he was charming me merely to persuade me to come here."

"Uh," Goar said, embarrassed.

"I told him to do whatever was necessary to persuade you," Incident said. "I knew you would not come just from curiosity."

"You are a realist."

"I am."

"So am I." Sarah turned to Goar. "I suspected you were playing me, but I thought it was pure fantasy. Now I am certain of it. Nevertheless, I appreciate your effort, arduous as it may have been for you."

"Oh, it wasn't," Goar protested. "I mean—" What could he say?

But Sarah was already addressing Incident. "Perform some magic, please." Because she still did not believe, even in her supposed dream.

Incident lifted Bird in her hand. "Do it," she said.

Bird transformed into woodpecker, then a wren, then a seagull. Finally, to the giant roc.

Sarah nodded. "And the rabbit?"

"Updoc," Incident murmured.

Beetle Bunny appeared. "What's Updoc?" he asked.

Sarah laughed. "Like a childhood cartoon! And the turtle?"

Incident set Turtle on the ground. He transformed into a house-sized turtle.

You can see that he has powers I can only envy, Terza thought.

"Very well," Sarah said, still reserving her belief. "Let's see what else you have to show me. But may I request one favor? I would like to have Terza with me, to clarify things as I encounter them, even if I no longer need her for translation."

The turtle was pleased to agree. That meant she would be in the center of the action throughout. So Goar lifted her from his pocket, and Sarah tucked her into her pocket.

"One other thing," Goar said. "The Land of Xanth is largely made up of puns. If that is a problem for you, be warned."

"I love puns, if they are appropriate and not harmful."

Incident smiled. "I think we have time for a short walk around the local landscape. Let's see what offers."

They walked out across the nearest meadow. In the distance were several dog-like creatures. “Are those tame or wild?” Sarah asked. “I like animals, especially ancient ones, but it does make a difference.”

“I believe I recognize those,” Incident said. “They are not tame, but they shouldn’t bother us. Timbre wolves.

“Timber Wolves? They can be dangerous.”

“No. Listen.”

Four of the wolves looked their way. They lifted their noses and howled resonantly.

“I’m not sure,” Sarah said nervously.

“They’re just warming up, now that they have an audience.”

Then the wolves sang. “Down by the old mill stream, where I first met yoooo.”

Sarah’s jaw dropped. “They’re singing!”

“Yes. That is what they do.”

“Yooo were sixteeen . . .” the wolves sang in marvelous four-part harmony.

“Amazing!” Sarah said. “So reverberant!”

“Well, they are timbre wolves.”

“Timbre, not timber. Now I get it. It’s a pun.”

“It’s Xanth,” Goar said.

The wolves finished their rendition. Sarah applauded, clapping her hands. “Encore!”

“Don’t do that!” Incident said, dismayed.

“Why not? They sang so beautifully.”

The wolves went into their encore. “Down by the oold, not the new but the oold, mill streeam, not the river but the streeam . . .”

“That’s why,” Incident said.

“Oh, I see,” Sarah said.

“Where I first, not the second but the first, met yooo, not me but yooo.”

“Let’s move on,” Goar said.

They walked away, but the song followed them. “Yooo were sixteeen, not seventeen but sixteeen,”

They walked faster.

“My village queeen, not king but queeen.”

Finally, it faded in the distance.

Ahead of them was what appeared to be a small bear. It approached a weed tree, which resembled a giant dandelion. The bear touched the trunk, and suddenly the plant was a magnificent acorn tree.

"It changed the tree!" Sarah exclaimed. "Into a better one."

"Yes," Incident agreed. "I recognize it now. It's a koala-t bear."

"A quality bear?" Then Sarah laughed. "Oh, another pun. Kaola-tee. Quality."

"Yes. It changes the quality of something."

They moved on. Sarah paused at a clump of plants. "Are those legal here?"

A girl sat up. Evidently, she had been sleeping in the clump. "Of course they're licit," she said indignantly. "Why should they not be?"

"Where I came from, in many places they discourage the growing or use of this plant."

"Oh. Mundania."

"Yes."

"This is Xanth."

"So I am learning. I apologize for doubting."

"That's all right."

Sarah held out her hand. "Hello. I am Sarah."

"No!" Incident said.

Too late. The girl took the hand and they shook. "I am Mary."

Sarah wobbled unsteadily. "Oh, suddenly I'm dizzy!"

"That's all right," Mary said. "It will pass."

They moved on. "What happened?" Sarah asked unsteadily.

"You touched Mary Wana," Incident said.

"Oh no! Marijuana. In the marijuana clump. I should have guessed."

"Maybe this will help," Incident said, leading her to a small shelter housing several books. She opened a loose-leaf binder. "Touch this."

Sarah touched the exposed page. Something jumped from her hand to it. "Oh! I feel much steadier now. What is that?"

"It's a spell binder. A place to keep your spells."

"But I have no magic, no spells."

"Fortunately, it worked anyway for your spell of dizziness."

"Oh my," Sarah said weakly. "Perhaps I have had enough now of the animated puns of Xanth."

"It does take a while to get used to them," Goar said.

"Now Bird will take us to Shee Castle," Incident said.

They boarded the roc, Sarah silent as she absorbed Terza's mental explanation. Bird spread his wings and took off.

Her unbelief is reluctantly fading, Terza reported privately to Goar and Incident. *The puns may have helped.*

They arrived at the castle and introduced Sarah to the Princess Birdie and Ruby Rabbit. They gave her a tour of the garden. Then Incident settled down with her and went into detail on their planned excursion to the distant past to fetch the egg. Goar knew that Terza was happily assisting.

"Either I am having the most remarkable dream, or you really do have a way to fetch a Spinosaurus egg," Sarah said. "I am ready to follow it through to the end." She took a breath. "Now there are things you need to know about the Spinosaurus and the period it lived in. This is no minor creature you will encounter; in fact, it is probably the largest carnivorous dinosaur we know of, with the jaws of a crocodile, front claws like a bear, hind feet of a mud dweller, and a sail like that of the Permian Dimetrodon. I know of nothing else like it in the paleontological record. And there are other dangers. You will have to proceed extremely carefully."

"My companions are invulnerable," Incident said. "They will protect us."

"Perhaps. But they can do so better if they understand the challenges they are likely to face."

By the time Sarah had clarified the nature of the Cretaceous Period they were satisfied that it was indeed a high challenging environment, and were glad to have her along. That meant, however, that they would have to be prepared to protect her, because she was far from invulnerable. But she was also invaluable.

Chapter 14

SPINOSAURUS

They decided to use only the core group again, apart from Sarah and Terza. They delivered a few more seeds, got a good night's rest, and set out in the morning.

This was not exactly physical. The seven of them gathered in a guarded private room with a crystal ceiling that showed the sky above. Turtle grew to giant size, and the others went into his shell next to his head as if seeking shelter from rain. In that seeming cave they settled down, nestling together, Goar, Incident, Bird, Rabbit, Sarah, and Terza. They would not move physically until they got there. They had to be in contact so that all of them were affected together and none could be lost. If they merely held hands, they could let go when distracted and lose contact, so this guaranteed that they would always be in contact with Turtle.

"I am amazed again, but Terza is reassuring me," Sarah remarked. It seemed the two were becoming friends.

"We must not only be in contact," Incident said, "we must remain in a fixed place, geographically. I had it explained to me once, but it's complicated and I can't say I understand the theory, but I know that if we travel in time, we must not move anywhere physically, and if we travel physically, we must not go anywhere in time. One of them must always be fixed."

"Oh, I understand that," Sarah said. "You see, the planets are constantly moving physically, orbiting their stars, and their stars are orbiting the center of the galaxy, and the galaxies are pursuing courses of their own. So were you simply to jump, say, a year into the past, you would find yourself in deep space, because that is where our planet was a year ago. Even if you time traveled only a second, it would still be disastrous, because you would intercept a tree or something."

"That's exactly what I did not understand," Incident said. "And still don't. So why aren't we stuck in deep space now?"

"Because we are anchored to this spot on this planet," Sara answered. "In effect it carries us along with it, so that we are traveling physically, but in lockstep with the planet. That spares us deep space. It is as if we are clinging to the saddle as the mock horse spins around the merry-go-round. We seem to be in one place, but we are actually doing a complicated spatial dance."

"Now I am *really* confused."

Sarah smiled. "Fortunately, your guideline is good. Stay in one place or one time, not traveling in both at once."

Goar listened, appreciating the confirmation that they were doing the right thing. Don't do both time and space together.

Turtle focused on his ancestral line. Incident tuned into his mind, tracking the temporal locale. Goar, Bird, Rabbit, and Terza tuned in on her, and Terza shared with Sarah. Incident was seeing out through Turtle's eyes, perceiving the sky beyond the transparent ceiling with its passing clouds and the sun above. She focused on Turtle's ancestry.

At first there seemed to be little if any change. But it was indeed happening, because Goar saw the sun start to move slowly backward in the sky. He remembered the way they had traveled across the frames of reality when Fornax took them. That had accelerated, becoming a blur.

The same happened here. The sun sped up, dropping below the horizon. Darkness came, the night before dawn of that day. Then came the glow of the prior dusk, and the brightness of yesterday. The sun continued backwards, accelerating, coming to dawn and on into day again. Faster and faster, until the flashes of day and darknesses of night were like blinks of the eyes. Then they became a gray of blinks too fast to distinguish. They were going backwards at light-speed, as it were.

"Oh my," Sarah murmured. "Even for a dream, this is remarkable."

Goar had no idea how fast they went thereafter, or maybe therebefore, but suspected it was years per minute, then years per second, then centuries per second, then millennia. The mere concept was dizzying.

Then it slowed, and stopped. They were there.

"Now we can go abroad," Incident said. "We don't have to stay in physical contact. Not until we are ready to make the return trip."

"Yes," Sarah said. "But when we return, we must do so at this exact place, to be sure we won't intercept that tree at the other end."

Goar was satisfied to take their words for it. They trooped out, and Turtle became miniature and Goar put him in his pocket. They were in the remote past.

"However," Incident said as she marked the spot exactly with a pointed stick poked into the ground, "Sarah and Terza should stay close to Goar and Turtle, who can protect them when there is need."

"Terza agrees," Sarah said, moving close.

It was certainly a change. The air was hot and steamy and smelled strange. It sustained them, but in a slightly suffocating way. Goar saw no familiar oak or pine trees, few flowers, and no grass. Instead there was unfamiliar foliage, giant ferns, and some palmetto. He saw a browsing creature that did not look like a horse or cow, but more like a giant lizard. But of course this was the age of reptiles, a hundred million years ago.

"Anatosaurus," Sarah said, observing his gaze. "One of the so-called duck-bills. They forage most efficiently in the shoreline sludge."

Oh.

"And those flowers are magnolia, one of the few to survive virtually unchanged to the present time."

Incident closed her eyes and oriented. "This way," she said, pointing.

But the way was soon mucky. Goar took Turtle out and he grew large again, and they clambered onto the top of his shell and rode as he plowed ahead. Bird stayed small and with Incident, not trusting this strange habitat, and of course Terza remained with Sarah.

Goar suspected that he would regret asking, but he was curious so asked anyway. "Why are you so interested in this particular creature? I understand that there are many dinosaurs with remarkable properties. Was there a reason you fixed on this one?"

"Oh yes. It started partly by elimination. There were a number of students in my class looking for particular creatures that would make the best study prospects. I wanted to find one that nobody else was interested in. Spinosaurus is a mix of features that don't seem to make a lot of sense. That turned off others, but intrigued me slightly. Then one feature caught my attention. It has powerful claws like those of a bear, a foot and a half long, that could be used to hook fish out of streams. But

Spinosaurus really didn't seem to be a stream browser; it was more of a marsh dweller, as indicated by its hind duck feet. Also, further study indicated that Spinosaurus couldn't actually see its claws. That makes no sense for swiping fish out of water: for that you need a good sight of your prey. It was that mystery that finally hooked my attention; I couldn't turn loose of it. What use were claws that it couldn't see? It would be like a fat man trying to tie his shoelaces when he couldn't see his shoes. It might be done, but it wouldn't be very efficient. There had to be some other reason. I finally concluded that they were used for digging clams out of the muck; you can't see anything in it anyway, but if you could strain through it you could catch anything solid that was hiding there. I also suspect that they could be used while fighting another Spinosaurus, one male against another for the affection of a female, or maybe for self-defense when something gets in close. Those claws could gut its exposed belly. But I don't know. At any rate, by that time I was hooked by the claws, you might say. I wish I could observe a Spinosaurus going about its business for a few days and see those claws in action. Then I would finally know."

Goar's cautionary thought had been correct: this was more than he really wanted to know. Still it made him wonder: Why *did* Spinosaurus have those gargantuan claws?

Before long, following Incident's directive, they came to their target: a giant reptile snoozing in the sun, in the shallow margin of the sea. Its lower body was sunk in the muck, its upper body featuring a kind of fleshy sail reflecting the light. This was Spinosaurus!

"What a beauty!" Sarah whispered. "The sail is marvelously adapted for temperature regulation. At dawn it is angled to absorb the most sunlight, quickly warming the creature up so it can forage and hunt efficiently while other creatures are still torpid. But with activity in the heat of day, it is angled to minimize the sunlight and maximize the effect of the wind, so as to cool the body most efficiently and prevent heatstroke. So in the morning it catches the slothful prey, and at noon it catches those who can't flee it without keeling over from heatstroke. Got you coming and going." She paused, admiring the beast. "In between it can rest, saving its energy for the hunt."

She certainly had figured the rest of it out.

Goar remembered something. "Reptiles are cold-blooded. They rest a lot."

"Not cold so much as matching the environment. But it is true that they don't need to expend energy constantly heating their bodies. We mammals are using energy even when resting or sleeping, which means we need to eat several times as much to keep up. You won't catch a reptile wasting energy while waiting." She eyed Spino. "Note the formidable claws on the front feet, capable of holding or even tearing apart fresh prey. Yet the hind legs have webbed feet suitable for maneuvering in water or mud. This is a shoreline creature, not really at home in either pure water or land, but ideal for the edge zone between them."

"Now we just need to get one of its eggs," Incident murmured. "And be on our way before it wakes." She focused again. "And there's a clutch of them right here." She pointed.

"I'll get it," Goar said. He waded into the muck where she indicated and bent to reach down with his hands. He found an object about the size of an ostrich egg, just under the surface and hauled it up.

Mother Spino vaulted into action. It seemed she had not really been asleep, but biding her time, watching them. Maybe letting them get close enough to catch. Or maybe simply guarding her eggs. Supposedly, dumb or inattentive animals, he had learned, were not necessarily either. It was hard to outsmart a creature in its own habitat.

"Get back well behind me," Goar told Sarah tersely. He was knee deep in the marsh, unable to move rapidly, but he could still block the reptile off with his body, even while holding the egg.

Instead Sarah splashed forward to stand ahead of him as Spino loomed, its sail rising twice as high as Goar despite the creature's legs being in the water. The head was as big as Goar, bristling with its alligator teeth.

"Oh, you big beautiful creature!" Sarah exclaimed in rapture. "Perhaps the most fearsome predator ever! I have admired you from afar all my life, and now here you are in person! I could just hug you!"

Goar saw Incident standing appalled. What phenomenal folly! Was Sarah utterly crazy? Or was this her way to commit suicide?

The giant head swung down to within a yard of Sarah. Spino eyed her, taken aback. *What kind of prey is this?* Terza translated its thought. *It must be mad!*

Then Spino backed off. It did not want to catch that madness, as it might if it ate infected prey. Sarah's folly had saved her, ironically.

"Get back before it changes its mind," Incident called desperately.

Sarah recovered some common sense. She backed away, out of the muck. She was safe for the moment.

But Goar wasn't. He held Spino's precious egg. Sane or mad as he might be, she would not let him get away with that. The head swung toward him, jaws gaping.

Goar held the egg firmly in his arms and stood his ground, mushy as it might be. "Terza!" he called. "Transmit my thought: Spino, if you try to chomp me, you will destroy your own child!"

The head paused. The thought had been relayed. Goar had a hostage.

That did not mean Spino had given up. She closed her mouth and nudged him hard enough to knock him off his feet. She was trying to dislodge the egg!

He splashed into the water, but held on to the egg. He scrambled back to his feet. "Yeah, bite me!" he taunted. "You can't hurt me without hurting your egg." Actually, she couldn't hurt him regardless, but there was very little way to make her understand that.

Then Spino moved to the side, and forward, and around. She was cutting him off from the shore. He could not wade or swim around her as long as he held the egg.

Incident started toward him, but Spino cut her off. All she could do was get herself chomped. She might be proof against that, but it wouldn't help him get the egg to land. They were at a standoff for the moment.

"This is eerie," Sarah said. "It is as if Spino knows we have to take the egg to our exact spot of arrival. So she's preventing us from doing that."

My fault, maybe, Terza thought. *When I relayed Goar's thought to Spino, about holding the egg hostage, I must have included some of the background along with it. So now she knows about the spot. She may not understand why, but she knows what.*

"Just as I know the need without understanding about the whirling planets," Incident said. "We never thought telepathy could be dangerous."

"We need to distract her," Goar said. "Is there a form you could assume, Turtle, that is native to this setting, that would do it?"

If I knew what, Turtle thought.

"Pteranodon," Sarah said. "The early flying reptile. I can provide the specs, and Terza can relay them to Turtle."

Now it was Sarah who closed her eyes, concentrating. Then Turtle scrambled to land and shifted into flying reptile form, not the same as the pterodactyl he had practiced before, but larger, with a long trailing crest on his head. He had some trouble taking off, but finally found a lifting wind and slowly gained altitude. He was not huge, maybe thirty pounds, but his leathery wingspan was about twenty feet from tip to tip. Sarah had thought the specs, as she put it, and Terza had sent them on to Turtle, and they had a magnificent flying creature.

Pteranodon looped about and came at Spino's head. Spino snapped at him, annoyed, but missed. Goar was alarmed until he remembered that Turtle was invulnerable in any form; he could not be crunched.

Pteran looped about again and came back, and Spino snapped again with her formidable crocodile teeth. Goar started wading to shore, but Spino moved to block him. She was not distracted enough to forget her main purpose. That forced his grudging respect; this creature was no dummy.

Pteran tried harder, actually smacking into the back of Spino's head. She whipped it around, trying to bash him into the water where he would be relatively helpless, but did not stop blocking Goar.

It wasn't working. "Maybe another form," Goar called.

"Allosaurus," Sarah said. "The most formidable land predator of this time."

Terza relayed the specs, and Pteranodon glided to a landing on the shore and transformed into a monster some thirty-five feet long and fifteen feet tall: Allosauras. That was not quite as big as Spino, but in a similar league.

Allo roared a challenge. Spino's head whipped about, and she looked tempted, but remained in the water between Goar and the shore. Goar received Sarah's relayed thought that Allo was more mobile on land, while Spino was better in the marsh. Neither was quite willing to venture into the other's terrain and be at a disadvantage that could get it killed. It was a stalemate.

Then Sarah focused again, and Allo became another Spinosaurus, a male one as big as the female. He waded into the muck, at no disadvantage there. The female stood her ground, not at all intimidated.

But they did not fight. Goar got the relayed whiff of the female, a potent invitation to mate. Except that she was out of season. That meant that while he would not fight with her, neither would he mate with her. A male who attacked a female out of season was unlikely to find her receptive when later she was in season. That balked him. It was another standoff.

So Turtle took it to another level. He shifted back to his natural form, and expanded to giant turtle size, beyond anything known here, but of course he was not limited to here. He could become so big that he could carry the world on his back. He did not go that far, but did grow big enough to dwarf Allo. He barged toward Spino, shoving her aside.

But she managed to remain between Goar and the shore. When he tried again to go there, she intercepted him. Turtle could block her from the shore, but could not stop her from blocking Goar.

It was Rabbit's turn. There were no rabbits in this period, but magic was another matter. He became Beetle Bunny. "What's Updoc?" he asked Spino.

Spino gaped her jaws and snapped him up, trying to crunch him in half. But two things happened. First, he didn't crunch, being invulnerable. Second, he let out a blast of gas that put her into a choking fit. She spat him out and dunked her head in the water, trying to clear the stench.

That was a ploy Goar hadn't thought of. He hurried toward the shore.

But Spino still was aware of him, and her stolen egg. Still hacking, she intercepted him again.

Then he got an idea. *Turtle,* he thought. *Join me, then carry me out to sea. Spino can't swim well.*

Turtle barged past Spino, shoving her aside. Goar grabbed his tail with one hand as he passed. Then Turtle stroked out into the sea, so strongly that he left a wake. Goar hung on.

Spino tried to follow, but she was a shallows creature, not a deep-sea swimmer. She was soon left behind.

But could they make it back to shore without Spino intercepting them again? Goar doubted it. The Spinosaurus would be patrolling the shore, alert for them.

But maybe they didn't need to encounter her. *Bird!* he thought.

A seagull flew toward him. *Here.*

Find an island, Goar told him. *We'll go there. Then you can land and take us aboard the roc, and take us back to our departure place.*

The gull flew higher in the sky, searching.

Terza, Goar thought.

Here.

We are going out to sea. But Bird will bring us back to the departure place. Tell Incident and Sarah and Rabbit to meet us there.

Will do.

The gull returned. *Found an island.* He gave the location to Turtle, who changed course to head for it.

Soon they were there. There was a broad rocky beach suitable for a takeoff field. The gull landed and become the roc as Turtle clambered out onto the beach. He came to Goar, became the ninja, grabbed Goar's pocket, and went to tiny size, clambering into the pocket. Then Goar mounted the roc's back, carrying the egg. He took firm hold with one hand. *Ready.*

The roc taxied, then took off over the sea. He ascended into the sky, flying toward the rendezvous.

On our way, Terza reported.

They flew over the land. Then there was another complication. There was no suitable landing place in that vicinity. *Land where you can*, Goar thought. *We'll foot it across to the site.*

They landed in good order. Then Goar forged toward the site.

Only to encounter yet another complication. *Spino is headed our way.*

She had a general notion where the site was. Could they reach it before she did? She was not fast on land, but surely fast enough, considering her size.

I will distract her, Rabbit thought.

The roc landed. Goar dismounted, and Bird became small and perched on his shoulder. He tucked the little Turtle back into his breast pocket. They forged toward the site.

Terza tuned in. *We're on the way, Incident, Sarah, and me*, she reported. *Rabbit is trying to lead Spino astray, but she knows where the site is and is determinedly driving for it. It will be close. Hurry.*

Hurrying, Goar agreed. *Turtle, Bird, me, and the egg.*

Goar hurried, but could not risk tripping and falling. A fall would not hurt him, but might break the egg, which was the point of all this.

As they neared the site, he heard a crashing. It was the dinosaur plowing through the brush. Goar hurried faster.

As he came in sight of the site, he saw Incident and Sarah arriving from the opposite direction. Then Spino burst into the site. Rabbit was trying to distract her, dancing in front of her nose, but she was ignoring him, intent on the target. She was going to get there first.

Rabbit became full man size. He stopped, stood on his hind feet, and spread his paws as if making a magical gesture.

Then Spino stopped completely. She seemed to be frozen in place.

He's Harvey, the magic rabbit, Terza thought, picking up the information from Rabbit's mind. *He has just frozen time for everyone except us.*

They rushed to the site. Goar set Turtle down on it, and stood back as Turtle expanded to house size. They all piled in, except Rabbit. *Ready*, Terza thought.

Rabbit returned to small size and hopped to and into Turtle. But Spino came back to life the moment Harvey was gone and pursued. She was about to barrel into Turtle, knocking them off the site.

The day flickered. Incident had started the return trip. Just barely in time, as it were. They were on their way home with the egg.

There was a sound, a kind of knocking. It wasn't Turtle, and it couldn't be the realm outside. They looked at each other.

Terza was the first to realize. "It's the egg! All this disturbance must have jogged the embryo alert. The chick is waking. Pipping—breaking out of the shell."

Oh no! "We're not equipped to handle a dinosaur hatchling," Incident said.

"It should be a pretty tough creature," Sarah said. "We know almost nothing about the care spinosaurus took of the hatchlings. I would have thought none at all, but Spino's attitude suggests otherwise. She kept the eggs underwater, to maintain the temperature, and must have been ready to move them onto land when they hatched. Reptiles don't nurse their young in the manner of mammals, but they can protect them and guide them to suitable prey."

"And we would be regarded as prey," Incident said.

"More likely minnows, or maybe a fresh carcass their mother provides. But I agree: we are not equipped. However, it may take several hours for it to hack its way out of the egg, and it may start by eating the shell, such as it is. There should be good nourishment there."

"Let's hope."

Their journey continued, but so did the pipping. The shell was not hard in the manner of a chicken egg, but more like leather. It would be a job to chew through it. Goar realized that that was part of the point: to make the chick learn to use its teeth, to bite and tear efficiently, an ability it would need the moment it emerged.

The flickering became the blur of rapid time travel. They were moving at a phenomenal temporal rate. But was it fast enough to get them back and to the smoke dragon castle before the mean little dinosaur emerged?

"Maybe Harvey Rabbit could freeze time to halt its hatching until we get there," Goar suggested.

Incident considered momentarily. "No. That's too likely to freeze our time travel, too, and we can't afford that."

Get frozen somewhere between their Now and a hundred million years ago? Indeed, that was not to be risked.

They made it back to the chamber in Shee Castle, and emerged from Turtle's shell.

Goar brought out the egg. But the pipping was proceeding more rapidly. "It's about to hatch," he said, alarmed. Indeed, a hole was forming and widening.

"Give it to me," Sarah said, taking the egg from him as the small reptilian head popped out of the hole. "I love this species." She kissed the damp top of the head.

"Uh-oh," Incident murmured.

Sarah glanced at her as she cuddled the emerging reptile, heedless of the gel surrounding it. "There's another problem?"

"Imprinting."

Goar recognized the term. Baby ducklings fixed on the first adult they saw, which was supposed to be the mother duck. But if they saw something else, they thought it was their mother, and diligently followed it. Were dinosaurs the same?

"Oops! I didn't think of that," Sarah said. "We don't want it fixing on me as its mother! But maybe its eyes won't open for a few days."

The little head turned to fix on her, orienting on the sound. An eye popped open.

"Hello, Mother Sarah," Incident said ruefully.

"Actually, we don't know," Sarah said. "Let's get it to Smote Dragon soon." Terza had updated her on that aspect. "It may be all right. For one thing, she'll have something to feed it, and food will be a primary inducement."

"Let's hope so."

Queen Birdie arrived on the scene, having been alert for their return. "Oh, what a cute hatchling!" she cooed. "I'm so glad he's safe."

"Actually we don't know the gender yet," Sarah said.

"You may not, but I do. I have sexed chicks for years. This one's male."

She probably did know. Sarah's love for dinosaurs was probably matched by Birdie's love for birds, and the two species had points in common.

"We have to get him immediately to the Dragon Queen," Incident said tersely.

"Of course. I am mainly glad that you are back from the fearsome past." Birdie caught little Bird in her hand and kissed his head much the way Sarah had kissed little Spino. "By all means finish your mission in good order."

They wasted no time. Goar, Sarah, Terza, and Incident went outside with Bird, and as soon as there was room, he shifted to roc mode and they took off. Sarah held little Spino as he chewed industriously on the remains of the shell.

On the way, Terza briefed Sarah about the nature of dragons, her thoughts open to the rest of them. *Like dinosaurs, but hotter and smarter.*

Stay with me when we encounter dragons.

I will.

Soon they were there. Two smoker dragons rose from the ground and fell in on either side of the roc as an honor guard, not attacking; they had been expecting him.

They landed beside the castle as Queen Smote emerged and flew to join them. She landed and assumed the sultry smoke queen form. "Did you get it?" her translator asked as they dismounted.

Goar helped Sarah get safely to the ground, because she was encumbered by the increasingly active little reptile she held. Now was definitely not the time for a misstep or fall.

"We got him," Incident agreed. "But there may be a complication."

"What complication?"

"It involves Sarah Mundane, here, who helped us succeed."

Smote was tense. "So?"

Sarah stepped forward and extended Spino. Smote reached eagerly to take him.

Spino squealed in protest and turned back to Sarah.

"That complication," Incident said. "He hatched prematurely and saw Sarah. He may have imprinted on her."

"Well, he's mine!" Smote said, exhaling a roiling cloud of smoke. "She can't have him. I'd say the same even if she wasn't a Mundane."

The two dragon guards aimed their snouts at Sarah. This was about to get ugly. Goar wasn't sure he could protect Sarah from blasts of fiery smoke coming from two directions.

Incident glanced at Goar with a Do Something demand.

"No problem," Goar said, his mouth operating faster than his mind. "Hire Sarah as a nanny. As Spino grows, he will lose his early need for a nursemaid and be glad to go with the one who feeds him. The one who is closer to his kind. You won't have time to be with him continuously, Queen Smote; you have other details to attend to, such as running the smoke dragon kingdom. You need a bit of help at the outset."

The Queen eyed him, and for half a moment he feared she would scream "Off with his feet!" or worse. Then she spoke. "I don't know whether it is sheer genius or sheer luck, but you are actually making sense, golem. I will do that." She glanced at Sarah. "Come this way."

Sarah didn't argue. She was aware how tricky the situation was. She followed the Queen, carrying Spino. Goar and Incident followed her, with Terza remaining in Sarah's pocket and Turtle joining Goar.

I helped her decide, Terza thought.

The telepath was proving to be amazingly useful.

Thank you.

They entered the castle. In the central court was a steamy jungle obviously crafted with a dinosaur in mind. At the edge of the muck was the smoked carcass of some small animal.

Sarah set Spino down beside the dead meat. He scrambled forward to take a bite of it as Sarah and Smote stood close by.

"You know about dinosaurs?" Smote asked.

"Yes. It is my specialty. I am doing a research paper on Spinosaurus."

"This will not interfere with your care of Spino?"

"Not at all. I want to know everything about him, and this is ideal. It is what I have always wanted: to learn what this dinosaur is really like, alive." She gazed fondly on the little reptile as he tore another ragged piece off the carcass and gulped it down.

"But when he grows, you will return alone to Mundania?"

"Yes. I have business there, and it is my home. But I think I would like to visit Spino on occasion."

The Queen turned to a dragon servitor. "Prepare a human-style chamber for Sarah, adjacent to this park. See that she has human-style food and clothing, and anything else she may require. She will have freedom of the castle, and she will come to no harm here."

The servitor departed without any questions. The Queen had spoken.

No dragon will hurt you, or allow you to be hurt, Terza thought. *You will be the Queen's companion. This is about as safe as anyone in Xanth could be.*

Spino soon got enough in his belly to be satisfied. It would take time to digest it, as it had not been chewed up in the manner a lesser creature might have done. He turned around, and Sarah reached down to pick him up. "You need a nap now," she murmured, laying him against her shoulder for a burp. She was plainly in heaven.

Smote nodded, satisfied that her acquisition was in good hands.

Incident caught Goar's eye. It was working out.

"PS," Smote said to Incident, "We will secure our portion of the border, when that invasion comes." She was satisfied that they had honored their part of the deal.

"We need to go," Incident said. "But focus on me when you need to go home, Sarah, and I will come with Rabbit to take you back through to Mundania."

"I will," Sarah said as Spino went to sleep in her embrace.

Goar realized that for her this was as good as a baby. She would get her research paper done, and would love every moment of it. When she went home to Mundania, to publish her paper, she would know that Spino had an excellent home among the dragons. What could be better than that?

I will return with you, Terza thought to Incident. *Sarah will be fine here, with Smote's protection.*

"Yes I will," Sarah said. "Though I am sorry to lose your company."

Goar suspected that Terza also wanted to stay with Turtle. The two had not been together long enough for the romance to become jaded, and there was no certainty about the future.

They went back outside, boarded the roc, and were on their way. Maybe now they could relax for a day or three. But Goar hardly trusted that; his future with Incident was as clouded as that of the animals. He loved her, but his destiny was weird. For one thing, he still had no idea how to win the forgiveness of the cuttlefish woman Squid. The one he had killed.

About that, Terza thought. *My long-range telepathy is not sharp, but I do pick up that Squid is about to ask a favor of you. That could be a positive indication.*

A favor of *him*? For *her*? That was so nonsensical as to be unbelievable.

"I am receiving it too," Incident said. "And remember, her friend Fornax has helped us. There must be something going on."

Goar didn't know whether even to hope. Were the situation reversed, he would find it almost impossibly difficult to forgive the person who killed him.

Almost.

Chapter 15

BEM

They arrived back at Shee Castle in good order, half expecting to learn about the mysterious favor request. Instead there was something else.

Queen Birdie came out to greet Bird, as she always did. She had royal power now, and constant business to attend to, but she had committed to Bird and honored the protocol in that respect too.

Then she turned to Incident. "The invasion has started."

Just like that. There would be no time off for recuperation.

The Queen's minions had connected with their counterparts of other kingdoms, and a cooperative organization of defense was already being activated. Queen Gusta Goblin had already acknowledged; it seemed King Gustave would get to go to war after all, just not the same one as before. Terza would contact Doris Dragon of the kingdom of the sea. It seemed that the invader was the kingdom of the BEMS, the Bug-Eyed Monsters. They had been a perennial threat to fantasy conventions and the like, but now were striking far more authoritatively. They were swarming in on all fronts, battling males, carrying off females, frightening babies, and being a nuisance in general. Their numbers were numberless, and they hardly seemed to mind getting killed; their dead were rapidly replaced by the BEMS charging behind them.

"We have a message from King Ivy of the humans," Birdie said. "They are covering their territory, but there is an uncharted border that no one is in a position to defend at the moment. The BEMs could pour through there and get around the other lines of defense. They ask if we know of anyone who can help immediately." Her mouth quirked. "The humans can be difficult, but they do have their points, and the BEMs seem to have a special taste for their more shapely young women. We prefer to maintain amicable relations when that is feasible. Can we help?"

"That has to be us," Incident said. "There is significant good to be done. Tell Ivy yes."

"Forthwith." The Queen gave Bird another peck and departed. But then she turned back. "I almost forgot: when taking inventory, I discovered a powerful old spell in the arsenal. The instructions have been lost. We don't know exactly how to use it, and it may be dangerous to invoke when uninformed. I gather some of the King's men tried and got nowhere. But maybe it could help you."

"What is it?" Incident asked.

"It's a five-minute forward flash spell. Invoke it and you can see what will happen in the next five minutes at a given site. Then, with that knowledge, you can change your strategy. The problem is, your enemy can see it, too, because you have to be together at the starting point. So he can change his strategy to match your change, and you have no advantage. Unless there is some wrinkle we haven't figured out."

Goar considered. "Alternate five-minute futures. If the two I killed had had that, they well might have avoided being slain. They would have been better off, and me too, maybe."

"You think you could use it?" Incident asked.

"I think I'd like to try. I might even give it to Squid, if that earned her forgiveness. I don't know."

"We'll take it," Incident told Birdie.

"I will have it delivered to you."

They went to the courtyard. Bird returned to roc format. This time Ruby Rabbit and Terza Turtle joined them; the odds were that they could contribute to the effort.

A servant hurried up bearing a box. He handed it to Incident, and hurried away. Then the six piled on, and the roc took off, guided by Incident's tuning on the vulnerable sector.

Incident opened the box as they flew. Inside was a simple copper bracelet. "Anyone ever see one of these before?"

"Maybe," Ruby said. "I did research on magic artifacts when looking for the magic mushroom, and saw reference to lamps, bottles, rings, and bracelets. The general rule seems to be to rub their surface to invoke them, and rub it again to halt the action. But there was a caution: if you invoke a genie, it may be hard to put him back in the bottle if you don't like him."

"This is just a glimpse of the five-minute future. No genie."

"It's still a good caution," Goar said. "Don't start what you may not be able to finish."

Terza manifested as her human illusion. "If this BEM invasion is as bad as reported, simply bashing them as Goar can do may not suffice. A brief glimpse of the future could make a huge difference. I think we should experiment, cautiously, and see if we can use it effectively. It might help us devise a winning strategy."

"You always did make sense," Incident said.

"We turtles try to be well grounded when not completely at sea."

"I will invoke it as we fly," Incident decided as she put the bracelet on her left wrist. "But I want to be sure it is working. Since all we plan to do is sit here, let's set something up. I see a small loose feather." She reached out and plucked it. "In three minutes I will let it go, to be lost forever in the wind. But if it is just a vision, I should have the feather back when the vision ends. Does that make sense as a proof?"

They considered, and concluded that it did.

"Starting now," Incident said, and rubbed the band.

Nothing happened. But of course it wasn't supposed to. That was what made it tricky to verify. That started a chain of thought. What might vanquish nothing?

"One minute has passed," Ruby said. She, as a relative of a late-running white rabbit, had a good sense of time.

Nothing changed. Incident still held the feather. Goar's thought continued. Was there a way to make something out of nothing?

"Two minutes."

Incident waved the feather. "Any second thoughts before I let it go? It is a pretty one."

Time seemed to slow as the third minute approached. And Goar got an idea. There might indeed be a way to make something of nothing.

"Three minutes," Ruby said at last.

"Going, going, gone," Incident said. She let go of the feather. It zipped behind them, carried by the wind, and was soon lost to sight.

They waited another minute. Goar's thought resumed. Could his idea actually work? But of course it was irrelevant to the present situation.

"I'm going to see if I can turn it off before the full five minutes," Incident said. She rubbed the band.

Nothing seemed to happen. Except that now the feather was back in her hand.

A look circled around the group until it, too, was caught by the wind and blown away. The trial seemed to have been a success.

"But don't let go of it this time," Goar said. The others nodded agreement.

They counted off the minutes again. Incident did not let go of the feather.

"That seems to be the proof," Goar said. "She changed her future."

"So it works, maybe," Incident said. "But can we use it to fight the BEMs?"

Goar shrugged. "Now that we know it works, maybe something will occur. We just have to be alert."

"I wonder," Terza said. "If that was just a several minutes long vision of one future that turned out not to be real, what were we doing then? Were we actually living it, or just seeing how it might happen? I am not completely easy with this."

Neither was Goar. Had the release of the feather actually occurred, or just been imagined? The roc had been flying during that time; had they snapped back to the prior time? He had not been aware of a jolt. But if they had just imagined it, suppose Incident had released the feather the second time? Would that have changed their future? He couldn't quite get his mind set on one thing or the other.

"My guess is that the first run-through showed that there was no bad consequence of tossing the feather," Incident said thoughtfully. "If it had flown in someone's face and poked a hole in an eye, we would have known not to risk it. It didn't really happen; it was just a view of what *could* happen."

"And how will that help us defeat the BEMs?" Terza asked.

No one had an answer.

Incident turned to Goar. "You were thinking, during the test, and not of me."

"It was just a chain of thought. I was trying to figure out how to stop nothing."

"What is there to stop, if there is nothing?"

He shrugged. "It was just an idea. Pointless, I suppose. Sometimes my mind takes irrelevant excursions."

She took his hand. "Sometimes you intrigue me."

As they approached the region, they saw the vast array of the BEM army. It covered the ground like a thick fleece, slowly moving forward. Ahead of it were five places where the terrain would funnel them into particular paths. One was straight and level: another was a pass over a high mountain; a third was across a dismal bog; a fourth was highly curvaceous as it twisted around the slopes of hills and ponds; the fifth was through a thick jungle.

"I recognize that jungle," Incident said. "I have heard of it. It's haunted. All kinds of nasty spooks are there, but I understand that anyone who ignores them and stays on the path can get through all right. So it won't stop them by itself."

"What will stop them?" Terza asked.

Incident smiled. "I could stop them by flashing my panties on the path."

"Assuming they are vulnerable to panty flashes. They're alien blobs."

"They have to be vulnerable. They carry off screaming human damsels."

Terza nodded. "True. Maybe we should figure out ways that we can stop them on the other paths."

They consulted, and worked out strategies for each of the paths.

Goar peered at the army. "Hey, the rug has stopped moving."

Terza closed her eyes and focused. "I am picking up the mind of their chief, who has just come into my range. It's late, they have to make camp and park for the night. No sense in blundering though unknown hazards in the dark. Tomorrow morning they'll resume their march."

"So they're not just a horde," Goar said. "They're a disciplined force."

"Yes, in their fashion," Terza said.

"That's the worst kind of opponent."

"And only seven of us to stop them on five paths," Incident said. "We had *better* have a good strategy."

Goar got an idea so bright that the light bulb flashed over his head. "Let's talk to their chief. Maybe we can talk him out of it. Get him to go home."

"A BEM? Lotsa luck on that."

"Using the five-minute future. That's my idea."

The others were doubtful, but were open-minded, and soon Goar convinced them it was worth giving it a try. Except for one detail: they would need to show the BEM boss the five-minute futures today, when the action would most likely occur tomorrow. That was a lot more future than the spell provided.

"But maybe if both parties agreed, they wouldn't have to be physically or temporally there," Goar argued. "The spell is just a might-be anyway, not a fact. So if we set it up theoretically, maybe it will still work."

They considered it from this side and that, and concluded that it just might work. They would set up on that assumption, and if it failed, they would not have lost much.

They glided down to a landing in front of the BEM encampment. Goar and Incident, carrying the hidden Rabbit, Ruby, and Turtle, waved a white flag of parlay. If the BEMs didn't honor it, well, they could defend themselves and depart. The roc took off again, carrying Terza.

Two BEM soldiers approached them. They looked like blobs with arms and legs, no heads, with faces on the front. They did indeed have bug eyes on the ends of antennae. They actually had four arms, holding a sword, a club, and the other two merely gauntleted for grabbing screaming damsels.

"We come to parlay," Incident said. "Take us to your leader." In Xanth the language was universal, but Terza augmented it with a mental sending of truce.

The two soldiers turned about and led them to the camp. Soon they were at the designated headquarters.

"Well, hello, handsome man and pretty girl," their leader said, eyeballing Incident lecherously. His sword and club were strapped to the back of his bulbous body so that all four hands were free. "I am Bezoar BEMking. What do you want to talk about, before we overrun your premises?"

"You are invading Xanth, bees bumpkin," Incident said. "In the past you have largely confined your efforts to Mundanian fan conventions. BEMs and Femmes. Why the change?"

"We decided that it is time for Xanth. It is ripe for the harvest. You have many beautiful girls here." He eyeballed her again, and her clothing began to melt away.

"Stop visually undressing me!" she snapped, slapping at her dress with her hands. Bezoar winced as the slaps affected his eyes. "What's the big appeal of human type females anyway? They're not even close to your species."

He twitched his four large hands as if squeezing something soft but firm, high and low. "Because they are delicious, from their screams to their painted toes, and most of what's between is well worth groping."

"*Most* of?" Incident asked, annoyed. "What's not to like?"

"Their smart mouths, for one thing."

"You mean their brains?" she demanded.

"What use are brains to a femme? They don't need brains to scream cutely, and they certainly don't substitute for bonnie boobs or pert posteriors."

Incident swelled up in all the right places as if about to explode. Goar had to intercede. "He's teasing you. Trying to rattle you and ruin your bargaining ability."

"Bleep!" Bezor swore. "Who asked *you*, golem?"

But it was enough to jolt Incident back to reality. "Why don't you chase your own females? I'm sure some of them are very BEMinine."

"Half the thrill is in the chase. BEMmies don't scream well, don't run well, and don't have panties. There's no challenge." He shrugged gelatinously. "You, in contrast—"

"I, in contrast, am a complete woman. Not at all your type."

Suddenly Bezoar leaped forward, catching Incident before she could move. Now his hands had real groping power. One caught an arm, one held a leg, one bobbed for her bosom, and one massaged her bottom under her skirt while his meaty mouth slobbered her lips.

"Eeeeeek!!!" she screamed involuntarily, putting six E's and three exclamation points into it. "Get your filthy paws off my pristine parts!" He couldn't hurt her body, but her pride had been powdered. Which was perhaps his point.

"Sorry," the BEM said insincerely. He moved his paws to her thighs, squeezing them similarly. "Is that better?"

She punched him in his bulging belly, making him let go with a satisfying "Oooooof!!!" whose O and exclamation count matched her scream. "Still, it was a first-rate feel. You really do have peerless parts."

Goar was stepping in, about to deliver a feel of another kind, but Bezoar backed off just in time. It was after all mainly a tease.

"What is that I felt on your back, wench?" the BEM demanded.

"You felt up my back too? I didn't know you had five hands."

"When I was catching your arm. What are you wearing?"

"Why the bleep should I tell you, you lech?"

The King chuckled. "Just curious. I want to get you all the way nude."

Incident seemed mentally to count to ten. Then she answered. "It's my wing pack. I can fly when I have a mind to."

The BEM seemed really interested. "I have heard of those flight packs. I didn't know any still existed. I understand they have some very special properties."

"Not that it's any business of yours," Goar said gruffly.

The King shrugged. "We'll see."

Meanwhile Incident had chased down and recovered her wits. "Let me show you what you are in for, brute."

"I see it already," the BEM said, staring at her exposed backside below the wing pack. "Absolutely lovely and firm. You scream very well too."

She yanked her hung-up skirt down and put her blouse back together. "We have a telepath who can make things appear, if we care to see them."

"Thanks, but I already got a pretty good look." He eyed her skirt as if hoping for another glimpse beneath it.

He was still baiting her, but now that she knew it, she was largely immune. "This region is largely impassable," she said unevenly. "There are only five paths leading into Xanth proper. Let's examine them in order."

"We'll use them all tomorrow," Bezoar said confidently.

"Our telepath is now on Path One," Incident continued levelly. "I will imagine that path. For this purpose, it doesn't have to be perfectly accurate; this is a thought experiment."

"I am thinking, ready to experiment," the BEM said, staring at her outfit so that it started to turn transparent. This time she didn't slap it: Goar realized that maybe she wanted the King to be slightly distracted. The material made it only to partial translucency; she was not yielding a full glimpse.

The path appeared in the space between them, straight and level, broad enough for soldiers to travel four abreast, going directly ahead with no diversions. The landscape on either side was fraught with poisonous ivy, oak, and other dodgy brush, not safe to touch. "Picture your army advancing along it, and our telepath will animate it from your mind for us here as a vision, and observe what happens."

Goar was silent. It was his idea; would it actually work? Suddenly, he was horribly uncertain.

"Gladly," Bezoar said. In only a tenth of a moment the BEM vanguard appeared, four columns marching boldly forward. The scene was set.

Then Incident herself appeared, only a few paces ahead of the army. She was scantily clad in this scene, her blouse scarcely constraining her burgeoning bosom, her short skirt barely covering her bonnie bottom. The marching BEMs' eyes bugged, of course; this is what they had come for. They eagerly charged, putting away their weapons, the better to grope four places at once, high and low.

Goar was intrigued to see the real Incident still standing beside the imaginary one. There were two of them, but the image was more alluring, deliberately.

Then the pictured Incident turned around, bent over, and hoisted up her skirt, flashing them with her wickedly pink panty.

Goar quickly averted his direct gaze. He knew how potent her posterior had become since she turned pretty.

The four leading BEMs freaked out instantly, freezing in place, their bug-eyes turning pure pink. The ones behind them continued their charge, pushing down the leaders and trampling them underfoot. Only to spy the exposed panty, and freeze similarly. In a tenth of a moment they too were pushed down and overrun by the ones behind. Then the third row caught the view, and fell. In hardly more than a full moment, the path was piled so high with freaked-out bodies that the ones behind were unable to progress. This route was effectively blocked.

"So you see," Incident said. "You can try it for real tomorrow if you want to, but you are not going to get by me. What do you say to that?"

There was no answer. Goar glanced at the King.

He had freaked out, too, his eyeballs pink.

Incident snapped her fingers, and the King snapped out of it. "You freaked out, just from the view of my imagined panty," Incident said. "Do you think your raiders will do any better on that path tomorrow?"

Bezoar sighed. "You were only playing with me, weren't you," he said. "You never let me have enough of a glimpse or feel to freak, and I thought I was immune. You saved it for the morrow."

"Two can play the game of tease," she agreed. "I will wear that briefer outfit tomorrow. Try it for real then, if you insist."

He shook his face. "Let's see the next path."

Incident focused on the scene. "Path Two," she announced.

This one went straight up and over a mountain. The base of the mountain dropped down into a gulf so deep it was lost in darkness: it was doubtful that any creature who dropped into that would ever manage to climb back out. The path was carved into the steep slope of the mountain; there was no other way to pass it. At the tiny level spot at the peak was perched a boulder, and on that giant stone sat Bird, in the form of the roc.

The BEM army appeared, marching four abreast again, their columns solidly behind their leaders. They got halfway up the mountain. Then the roc spread his wings, lifted up a bit, and tugged the boulder forward. It rolled down the path, at first slowly, but soon gathering speed. It smashed into the BEMs, not even pausing, and rolled on. All that was left was green goo, the color of BEM blood.

More BEMs came, but when they stepped on the path their feet got stuck in the goo and they were unable to make progress. In any event, the roc flew down into the gulf and emerged shortly later clutching another boulder, which he set on the mountain top. The BEMs massed before the goo, unable to progress.

The scene faded: the five minutes were up. But the point had been made. There was no easy passage here.

Bezoar BEM no longer looked quite so confident. But he remained game. "Let's see the next one." He glanced again at Incident's body. "Unless you'd like to take a brief break for another look and feel, T and A, just to maintain the interest?"

"Not at the moment, thank you all the same." She was giving him T for T: Tit for Tat, without actually showing either T. A nice T for tease.

The new scene appeared. This path was four-folk wide, like the others, curving gently across a dismal swamp. The tips of toothy snouts were visible in the marshier sections of the bog: allegories, allegations, loan sharks, and the like, all watching for likely prey. Anyone who fell into that murky water would soon be corrupted or consumed.

The BEMs arrived, confidently marching along the path. Then a lone figure approached from the opposite direction: Goar himself. So now there were two of him, the real one and the vision one. But they differed significantly. The real Goar was wearing the magic socks that made his head seem to have a real face, and his feet seem to more or less normal, and his arms had hands with four fingers and a thumb apiece. The vision Goar was naked, black metallic torso, a blank face-plate on the front of the bald dome of his head, with spiked knees, caterpillar treads for feet, and circular saws for hands. He looked absolutely deadly, and that was no illusion.

A single figure to stop four, backed by hundreds more behind? The BEMs laughed and charged on.

Goar treaded up to meet them, starting with their right flank. His saws sang as they revved up to top velocity. They cut into the first BEM, sending its arms flying, still holding their sword, club, and gauntlets. Then they sliced off its legs. Then its face. Then the rest of its body. Nothing was left but scattered green chunks. The whole operation took barely three quarters of a moment.

Then, with hardly the thought of a pause, he was cutting apart the next BEM, sending parts flying. And the third. Then the fourth.

The next four advanced, only to be dismembered similarly. And the foursome after that. The scattered parts piled up, until there was a fair mound. The overlap that fell into the bog did not accumulate; it was quickly snapped up by the muck predators, who were having a royal feast. Goar wondered what BEM flesh tasted like; marshmallow?

Finally, the advance stopped, as the BEMs realized that there was no good future in advancing. They could not invade Xanth via this route.

The scene faded, its time expired. "Satisfied?" Incident inquired.

"Not while your body remains in my reach," the King replied. "Oh, you mean that the path is impassable? So it would seem. Let's check the next."

"Path Number Four," she announced, and it appeared. A highly curvaceous one winding through a forest. There did not seem to be any threatening creatures in the vicinity. Just a lone rabbit in the center, nibbling on a blade of grass. That was Ruby in her rabbit form.

"Where's the threat, titbit?" Bezoar asked, perplexed.

"Watch and learn, bumpkin."

The four BEM columns marched forward, not at all deterred by the bunny. Then, in a seemingly leisurely manner, the rabbit started digging a rabbit hole. It looked to be big enough only for the rabbit; a BEM would hardly fit, even if it wanted to. Not that it mattered: it made sense that the bunny wanted to escape the grimly marching army. Indeed, as the vanguard reached the hole, the rabbit jumped in and disappeared. The hole was evidently deeper than it looked.

The BEMs charged on past the hole, intent on getting through the forest and on into Xanth proper where the delectable femmes were hiding. There would soon be screams galore!

But somehow they did not make it past the rabbit hole. Instead they fell in, all four of them. It was evidently wider than it looked. They disappeared into the ground.

Goar smiled privately. In this future vision Rabbit had dug a much bigger hole, and covered it over with a thin network of branches and leaves. Then Ruby had led them into the trap.

The next four BEMs arrived immediately thereafter, pushed forward by the ones behind them. And fell in similarly. It didn't matter that the hole was now visible: they were on the move and couldn't readily halt. They were followed by the third rank, and the fourth. In fact it became a continuous flow of BEMs coursing into the hole. No fuss, no muss, just a stream of them diving into the ground, never to appear again.

At last, the end of the column arrived, and disappeared into the rabbit hole. Then the rabbit reappeared, emerging from it alone. She dug quickly around the edges, filling it in. There was now no hole, merely the curving path through the forest. She settled down to nibble on some more blades of grass beside the route.

Where was Rabbit? He would be digging another big hole farther along, just in case some BEMs happened to get past Ruby. No need to show them that in this vision, however.

The scene faded out. Time had expired.

"Satisfied?" Incident asked again.

The King stared. "What happened?"

"Rabbit dug a rabbit hole. It leads to a subterranean realm ruled by the Queen of Hearts. Rabbits are popular there. BEMs are not. Her favorite command is 'Off with their feet!' I fear your troops will not fare well there. Maybe you should send some more to rescue them." She smiled, hinting that there just might possibly be an element of humor there.

King Bezoar was not much amused. "The next path, please, tart."

"As you please, cretin. Herewith the fifth and final path."

The path appeared. It was through a kind of wasteland, but did not look very challenging. On it sat Turtle, in moderately small size.

"What's the catch?"

"This is a haunted wasteland, where assorted spooks reside. Will-o-wisps, zombies, ghosts and the like."

"Those exist elsewhere in Xanth," the King said. "They mostly leave you alone if you leave them alone."

"Ah, but these are different," Incident said with a certain relish. "They were banished here by the other spooks because they are bad ones. They *don't* leave innocent strangers alone; they go after them. The zombies like to eat their brains. The ghosts like to haunt them until they go insane. The wisps lead them into ugly traps where they will perish in slow pain; it seems the wisps like to hear them howl, the longer the better. They are not nice spooks. The only limit is that they are not allowed to touch anyone who stays on the marked path. So they assume seductive forms to tempt travelers *off* the path, where they become fair game. Very few make it safely through to the other side of the wasteland."

"But if they know the danger, and know to stay on the path, they should be all right."

"Ah, but how disciplined are your troops? Watch the temptations."

The BEMs appeared, marching four abreast as usual. They were met on either side of the marked path by a slew of seductive sirens, leaning forward to beckon them close. The BEMs immediately broke ranks to charge off the path and grab them with all four hands.

Only to have the gorgeous girls morph into horrible zombies who wasted no time biting off their limbs, looking for their heads.

That, however, had the effect of restoring some discipline to the army.

The following BEMs, observing the fate of the first ones, decided to stay safely on the path. They resumed their forward march.

Then the small turtle ahead grew larger. And larger. And larger yet, until it filled the path from side to side. The BEMs could not get around it without stepping off the path, where the sirens and zombies were lurking. They tried to climb over, but Turtle simply shook his shell and they fell off to the sides where they were promptly gobbled up. They tried to shove him off the path, but he was simply too heavy. They were stuck.

The vision ended, time up. But the point had been made. Turtle was not to be passed.

"Satisfied, dope?" Incident asked politely as her blouse coincidentally (it seemed) fell slightly open.

Enraged or tempted beyond reason—with BEMs it could be tricky to distinguish the two—Bezoar leaped at Incident, all four hands orienting on her body for good gropes above and below. But this time she was ready for him; in fact Goar suspected she had deliberately provoked him. She whirled and hoisted her hem, flashing him with her deadly pink. He froze in place, so freaked out that he didn't even fall, but remained like a statue in midair, his fourfold grope incomplete.

"Time for us to move on," Incident told Goar.

They walked away. The other BEMs did not try to stop them: they had freaked out too. It might be a while before others came on the scene and thought to snap their fingers.

The roc glided in with Terza, and they boarded and took off. The interview was done, the warning delivered. If it was not sufficient, then it would play out as the future samples had shown. This was not at all a bluff.

They made a camp not far distant so as to be able to keep watch on the BEM army. Bird and Terza agreed to watch the five paths, he flying quietly by them several times in the night, she questing telepathically as they did to be sure no BEMs were there. Between checks the Companions and their girlfriends would have time for each other. The roc made a quick trip back to Shee Castle to fetch Birdie and Ruby for the occasion. That way they all could make a night of it.

So did Goar and Incident. "It was awful having Bezoar paw me," she confided. "There was a time when I didn't much care, when I was ugly, but now you are the only one I want to paw me."

"Thanks, I think."

She laughed. "Maybe I could have phrased that more politely. But I think you know what I mean. Come on, paw me." She kissed him, and they proceeded to making love.

In due course the roc flew over them in the darkness. *Terza here*, her thought came. *All quiet this hour; no BEMS on the move.*

Good to know, Goar thought back to her. *Go make Turtle happy.*

Oh, I shall.

It was a good night. But Goar could not be quite certain they had saved Xanth from the BEMs until they actually departed.

In the morning Goar and Incident spread their wings and checked the BEM camp themselves. And discovered it empty. The BEMs had broken camp early and departed. He heard the sound of their big drum beating out their marching cadence: BEM BEM BEM BEM, BEM **BEM BEM**! It was retreating toward the border. They were definitely going home.

"Let's celebrate!" Incident said.

"I thought that's what we did during the night."

"That was passing time while waiting for the outcome of the engagement. This is celebrating victory."

Goar wasn't sure of the distinction, but hardly cared to argue. The two of them went to the junction where the five paths diverged, so as to keep an eye on it just in case the BEMs tried to return. They took off their wing packs so as to have more freedom of motion. They had not done so during the night, for fear that they might have to get into action at any moment.

"That reminds me," Goar said. "Why was the King so interested in your wings?"

"He was just baiting me any way he could manage." She paused. "But now I think of it, it is curious. He said those packs have very special properties."

"They enable us to fly," Goar said. "What else?"

"I wonder." She put her pack back on, then took it off again. "There is something. I feel it."

Goar did the same, and felt it too. "It touches the mind. I never noticed before. Maybe to better respond to our directives."

"Maybe. But now I'm suspicious. If it touches our minds, can it be telepathically traced, the way Terza was, once Doris Dragon touched her mind?"

“Now that makes me nervous,” he said. “Could we be traced while wearing the packs? Maybe by the BEMs?”

“Maybe we’re just guessing, and there’s nothing. But let’s not risk it.”

“Let’s not risk it,” he agreed.

They set the packs aside. Then, completely naked, they made love again. It was delightful. Goar suspected that though Incident was now stunningly lovely, she had not forgotten what it felt like to be ugly, and reveled in the new power of her body.

“As you revel in yours,” she murmured, knowing the parallel nature of his own thoughts.

The roc appeared as they were finishing. They did not bother to cover up, as the bird and turtle were well familiar with their leisure activity, from both physical and mental observation.

“Any activity?” Incident asked, her speech sending her thought. She expected a routine report of nothing new.

The BEMS have returned, in part, Terza thought. *Not to the five paths, which they know we’re watching, but to a chasm we thought was impassible. They seem to be constructing two bridges. We remained out of sight.* She sent them the specific location, which was not far distant.

“The sneaks!” Goar exclaimed.

Should we bomb them?

“Hold off on that,” Incident said. Now she started dressing, and Goar did too. “This could be decoy effort, to distract us while their real activity is elsewhere. We’ll investigate quietly ourselves, while you continue watching the paths.”

Good enough. Bird and turtle departed.

“It’s amazing how well those two get along now,” Goar said. “Terza’s fear of birds is truly gone.”

Incident smiled. “Fortunately Turtle and Birdie know that it is purely a work relationship. Unless they’re into sharing partners.”

“Oh, are we into that?”

“Not even in your dirty male imagination.” She reached for the wing pack, then froze. “Uh-oh.”

He had almost forgotten too. “We can’t use the wings. If the BEMs are tracking them, that will ruin our effort to spy on them.”

"We'll just have to scramble. You can move faster than I can, across level ground. Maybe you should carry me."

"Agreed." He bared his treads, picked her up and set out for the chasm.

They raced for the place, Incident orienting on the location. They came to the far end of it, and he guided along the left side because the tread support worked better there. Then between the trees ahead they saw the activity at the chasm.

The BEMs had loosed arrows trailing lines, across the gulf, to catch in trees, and were now using those lines to guide heavier lines. When those were in place, they would be able send some BEMs across to firmly anchor stout ropes and fashion bridges for armies to march across.

The BEMs were on one side of the gap, while Goar and Incident were on the other side. That meant he couldn't simply wade in with saws buzzing. Bleep! He missed the wings already.

He set her down and they paused, considering, while they remained hidden. "They never showed us their bows," Incident whispered. "Only swords and clubs."

"They are canny monsters," he agreed. "We didn't know they could do construction, either."

"If they have bows and arrows, they can shoot at the roc and stop him from bombing their bridges. We don't want to put him at such risk. He's invulnerable, but getting stuck with hundreds of arrows wouldn't be much fun. It would be a job to pull them all out later."

"Which means we'd better try to stop this ourselves," Goar said. "And soon, before those bridges are completed. But we're on the wrong side, and we don't want to wait for them to complete the bridges and come across to meet us."

Then Incident noticed something else. "One passel of BEMs is male. The other is female. The cunning monsters must have figured I'd show up, and sent a contingent that would not freak out."

"You can flash the males so they drop into the chasm."

"And you can do the same with the females."

"Me?"

"Strip dance for them. They'll freak out when you get down to your underpants."

He was uncertain. "Does that work on females?"

"They have to be pretty stupid, and the male has to be exceedingly handsome. Fortunately you are, now, when you have your socks on. It's worth a try."

"So be it," he agreed grimly.

"Here are some pointers. Move your hips; those are called grinds. Move your groin back and forth; those are bumps. The fact is that females go for that sort of thing much as males do: they imagine that they are making out with the performer. Smile continuously, as if you have just discovered the woman of your dreams."

"I will imagine you."

She smiled and kissed him. Then they separated, and advanced to the two construction sites. But as Goar arrived, he discovered that somehow they had gotten mixed up, and he was approaching the male passel. It was too late to switch places; they had seen him. Bleep again.

What could he do but go into his act and hope for the best?

"Observe!" he called as he came to the brink opposite the BEMs. They paused in their work and gazed at him, maybe relieved that he couldn't get at them with his weapons.

He went into his act, bumping and grinding. The BEMs watched, their eyes bugging. Then they burst into laughter. It was so violent that they lost their footing on the edge of the chasm and fell into the depth. In barely two moments all six of them were gone.

Well, now. This wasn't exactly the way he had planned it, but who could argue with success? He walked to the lines that led to the trees, yanked their arrows out of the trunks, and tossed them into the chasm. His job was done.

Then he headed for the other crew, ready to help Incident if she needed it. Rather than mess up her act, in case it was working, he stopped behind a tree and watched and listened. And was amazed.

The BEMmies were not freaking out at Incident's panties, but they were paying close attention. In fact it had become a kind of class. Incident was demonstrating bumps and grinds, and the BEMmies were imitating them. Then she demonstrated the most effective flashing technique, and they were copying that too. But there was a problem: they lacked panties.

Incident walked to a nearby pantree on her side of the chasm, and harvested a nice fresh ripe blue panty. She put it on over her original one. The females did the same on their side. Then they sported panties of six different colors, and Goar had to admit it made them a lot more interesting. The panties made their bulbous bodies look significantly more slender and shapely. It was evident that just as flesh shaped panties, panties shaped flesh.

They followed with bras, which further enhanced their torsos. Then light robes, which concealed most of their torsos while exposing strategic parts. It was effective; Goar was almost getting interested himself.

The six BEMmies danced in unison, following Incident's lead, becoming a chorus line. Suddenly, they all whirled and hoisted their robes, just so, flashing their panties. Goar clapped his hands over his eyes just barely in time; he had almost freaked out.

Then Goar came up. "Congratula—" he started, to Incident. Then she whirled and flashed him.

He woke to the applause of the BEMmies. Incident had demonstrated how to do it. She had used an extra flirt of her skirt to make it that much more surprising and effective. Had the BEMmies done it that way, they would have caught him, because he would not have seen it coming in time.

Then a passel of male BEMs charged forward, from the forest, ready to cross the bridge in case it had been completed. It hadn't; work had stopped when the class started. They stopped, glaring at the females for their failure.

And the BEMmies whirled and flashed, exactly as Incident had, getting that last little skirt flirt in. The males freaked out.

Goar realized that this bridge, too, had been stopped, because the females had learned something more important: how to freak out their males at home, so their males wouldn't go raiding for human girls with more effective panties. In fact as the news spread there would probably be no more panty raids. The day had been saved in a completely unexpected way.

The six BEMmies bowed together to Incident, who returned the bow. Class was over, and they had graduated.

It was time to go home for both sides. The BEMmies did not snap their fingers yet; they simply picked up the males' feet and dragged them along the path, away from the chasm and the possible sight of Incident. Goar and Incident walked away.

"We'll have to fetch some stink bombs and other discouragements," Goar said. They would keep their eyes on the five paths and two bridge sites, just in case, but this was probably academic at this point. The fact was, the BEM invasion had been halted. Maybe they would continue to raid Mundane conventions and the like, but Xanth was off the list. It was too well defended.

Chapter 16

DANCE

They boarded their flight to return in good order to Shee Castle, ready to relax and unwind. All of them were a trifle better looking than they had been, though they really didn't need it. They had, after all, just saved Xanth from the BEMvasion, a good deed. Goar loved Incident and she loved him. Happiness awaited them. They could retire at any time and enjoy it.

But Goar was wary. He existed under a cloud. He had not yet earned Squid's forgiveness, and until he did, his life was not his own. This was not merely Squid's judgment; it was his own. He could not forgive himself for that dreadful crime.

"Cent for your cognition," Incident said as they rode the roc, referring to an obscure and largely worthless Mundane unit of currency.

He was reluctant to remind her of his private horror, as it affected her too. "It's nothing."

"Nothing for your noesis? Two imaginary cents."

She was bargaining? "It's not worth discussing."

"Three cents. That's my limit."

"Incident, I really don't want to bore you with it." Or horrify her. His life since he met her was a completely different thing.

She sighed. "I see I will have to invoke the next level." She leaned in and kissed him.

His resistance turned to mush, as it usually did when she addressed him seriously. "That's not fair!" he protested.

"All's fair in love." She made as if to kiss him again. It was a potent threat. "Now will you talk?"

He saw there was no help for it. She would have it out of him one way or another. She was amused, but that could change. "What if she never forgives me?"

Incident instantly sobered. There was no need to clarify whom or what or how. "Oh my."

Now that the ice was broken and they were in the freezing gulf of his guilt, he couldn't stop talking. "Why would she ever forgive me? I don't deserve to be forgiven. I don't deserve happiness with you."

She shook her head. "Ordinarily, I'd argue the case. *But you killed her*. How can you ever earn her forgiveness for that?"

"That's my thought, all three cents of it."

"Yet there must be a way, or she wouldn't have given you the chance. Her friend Fornax wouldn't have helped you."

"Unless I owe her my life in return. They may be waiting for the perfect moment. But if I pay that—"

"I'd be a widow." They weren't married, but the sentiment fit.

He faced the pain. "Maybe we should break up, so you won't have to suffer on my account when the time comes."

"I am already suffering."

"But—"

She kissed him again. "That was my way of saying no."

"I didn't mean to eavesdrop," Terza interrupted. "But your minds are overwhelming. Yet I also sense that there's a way."

Both turned to her with forlorn hope. "How?" Incident asked.

"I don't know. But there's something in Squid's mind. She's coming within my range. She's not trying to tease you with the impossible. She doesn't hate you. There really is a way. That's all I know."

"She must be coming to Shee Castle," Incident said. "That's curious."

"She means to talk with us. With all of us. It feels deadly serious."

"Not just Goar?" Incident asked. "The rest of us too? What do we have to do with her forgiveness of Goar?"

"It's complicated," Terza said. "I can't tell how the rest of us relate, only that we do. She'll be waiting for us at Shee Castle." She paused, surprised. "Or maybe it's Laurelai, whoever that is, speaking for Squid."

"Her friend," Goar said. "I met her in passing. Lovely girl."

Now the others joined in. "What could this Laurelai have to say to any of us?" Beetle Bunny asked. "We didn't even know Goar when he transgressed."

"We are nevertheless involved," Terza said. "Incident, her three Companions, and their girlfriends. Seven people in all. Without Goar, we would not be together. He is an integral part of our present lives. We have to do something special."

"If it's to help Goar," Ruby said, "We'll do it. He may have been evil in the past, but he is good now."

On that they all agreed. He was touched by their loyalty, uncertain whether he deserved that either.

They circled Shee Castle, and came in for a landing. A servitor came out to meet Birdie. "Your Highness, there's a visitor. A woman."

"Laurelai," Birdie said. "We'll meet with her in the main audience hall in fifteen minutes. Set up refreshments and then give us privacy. Oh, and yes, we did save Xanth from the BEMs. Spread the word. Our innocent maidens will be safe from their depredations." She made three and a half fifths of a smile. "No four-handed groping."

Wordlessly, he retreated.

As they walked, Goar saw a young woman turn her back on another, and flash her panties—and the other froze in place, freaking out. "What?" he asked, confused.

Birdie laughed. "I am an equal opportunity employer. Some of my serving girls are lesbian. Sometimes they tease each other."

"Panties can freak out a woman?"

"And pants can freak out a man, if he is of that persuasion."

Goar shook his head, amazed.

They made for the restrooms for natural functions like quick mirror primping, then went to the main audience hall. It had been set up with a table of delicacies and chairs to accommodate all of them, facing a small stage at one end.

Laurelai was there. Goar went up to meet her. "You look improved, since I last saw you, golem," she said.

"I managed to do some good deeds, and was rewarded with better looks. We understand you have something to say to us."

"I do indeed. Take your snacks and form a seated audience. I will address you from the stage. You can eat while you listen."

There was something about her. "Are you—?"

Her expression changed briefly to something awesome. "Fornax, borrowing my usual host," she agreed. "But I will let Laurelai handle it unless there is reason for me to manifest. Honor my privacy."

So the infinitely powerful Demoness was present. This *was* important. Like the servitor, he departed wordlessly. He saw Queen Birdie approach Laurelai, and the two conferred briefly. Then Birdie nodded and separated. She had evidently been given the word also.

Soon they were all seated, facing the stage, munching their mini meals.

The young woman took that stage. Her blue-black hair and eyes were striking, and she had a remarkable presence. "Hello, all. What I say here will not be shared with others who are not here; a magical geis, or obligation of honor, has been applied that you will feel if you attempt to break it. Just so you know." She took a breath. "I am Laurelai, speaking for my close friend Squid, an alien cuttlefish phrased as a human girl.

"To reprise briefly, Goar Golem murdered Squid and her human fiancé Larry. Two Dwarf Demons," she pronounced the words so that their capitalizations were evident, "were responsible for putting Goar together, assembling him from several diverse parts including a human soul, and charging him with this foul mission; it was not strictly speaking his fault. Therefore Squid elected to give him a chance to earn her forgiveness for that brutal act. Larry will follow her lead."

She paused, smiling. "Larry is my male counterpart. Just as Ruby can change her form from rabbit to human, being a crossbreed, and Terza Turtle can appear as a human woman, and Incident Oma's three animal companions can change their forms, so also I can shift from female to male. Larry looks like this." She changed to a handsome young man, complete with appropriate clothing, something no ordinary shape shifter could manage. He glanced around and smiled, and there was something about him that made girlish hearts pulse. That was apparent in the reaction of the younger ladies present. Goar suspected that it was the ambiance of the Demon Chaos.

Laurelai reappeared. "In case you wonder how we can appear before you, having been murdered—because of course I died, too, when Larry did—it is because the Demoness Fornax brought us here from a distant parallel Xanth where we were not murdered, at least not yet. So we are impostors, not of Larry and Laurelai, but of their presence in this reality. We are emulating their lives as they would have been, had they lived. The same is true for Squid, who came with us. Once our business here is done, we will return to our own reality. I assure you that we do take the murders seriously. But that is only a portion of our story."

She paused again, her penetrating gaze seeming to spot each member of the audience as though she could see into their minds and souls, as perhaps she could. "You see, while the two Dwarf Demons were behind the crafting of Goar Golem to perform the murders, we believe there was another power motivating *them*. We exposed and dealt with the Dwarfs, but the real culprit remains hidden and free. That is the one we want ultimately to nail. Only when that one is brought to justice will we feel that our mission here is done, that vengeance is complete. The problem is, he is anonymous. We can't deal with him if we don't know his identity."

She paced a little circle on the stage, as if pondering alternatives, then resumed. "This about Demons: they are to us ordinary mortals as galaxies are to grains of sand, virtually infinitely more powerful, and they control the fundamental forces of the cosmos. There is no challenge for them in the mortal realm, only in dealing with each other. Their main interest is Status. Some are dominant, some intermediate, some relatively inferior." She paused again, giving her audience the chance to assimilate the magnitude of the situation.

"They indulge in constant games of chance to gain or lose status among their kind. Chance, because only pure luck is fair to all. They may intervene in mortal affairs to a limited degree to set up those games, wagering on their outcomes. It is as if two may bet on whether a given ant will turn left or right when it encounters the next fork in the trail. They do not touch the ant in any way, merely watch it. A staggering outcome can depend on that seemingly random choice."

She smiled again. "I happen to know of a case where a male Demon sought the input of a single nondescript girl, the fate of the entire universe at stake. If she, with her puny mind and experience, could persuade him, who had all the knowledge of the cosmos, that it was worth keeping, the universe would survive. If not, it would perish in chaos. In fact it was the Demon Chaos and the girl Squid. Not only did she persuade him, she was so innocently appealing that he fell in love with her. So he spared the universe and she became his girlfriend. That was why she was deemed the most important person in the universe: because without her it would have ended."

Laurelai paused again to let that sink in. It was apparent now why Squid herself was not present: she would have become the cynosure, perhaps distracting the narrative. Then she resumed. "In fact we suspect there is a connection between that decision to keep the universe, and the murders. Because in the course of that decision there was a side effect. The two Dwarf Demons were stopped and their attempt to collect valuable magical items, such as a traveling castle and a boat with a fire sail, was stifled. We suspect that a higher-ranking Demon was behind them in both cases. In fact, that the murders were retaliation for Squid's participation, never mind that it was overwhelmingly beneficial to the universe as a whole."

She paused yet again, playing it for clarity and drama. "So who was this murderous power behind the scenes? We want to smoke him out so we can deal with him. By we, I mean the other Demons, especially Chaos, who lost the girl he loved, at least in this frame of reality. But a Demon who is hiding can't be spotted by anyone else, not even other Demons. He has to expose himself." Another brief pause. "So it has been a waiting game, as we searched to discover whom it might be. It is a kind of Demon game, and it has a time limit. If we don't identify him in another day, the Demon statute of limitations will expire and he will no longer be accountable for his actions. He will win by default. All he has to do is wait. Even if he does appear, he could still win by outplaying us. Demon game rules have no relationship to niceness or justice, only to the standards that exist for their play. But if he does appear, at least we have the chance to take him down." She paused again, and smiled. It was not a nice smile. "So we have, we think, found a way around this particular problem. If we can identify him on our own, through research and logic, we can shame him before the other Demons and change the default so that he loses if there is no actual contest. The deadline becomes our advantage. He will have to manifest or lose. This is what we are about to do." She walked another little circle on the stage. She had a very nice walk, as the reactions of the men in the audience indicated. "If we call him out by name, and we turn out to be incorrect, we lose. If we are correct, we force him to compete, or lose by default. Demon rules. But let's wait just a bit on that."

She gazed at the small audience, whose members had mostly stopped eating, distracted by the monologue. Certainly, Goar was frozen: he had had no idea that such things were behind his action in killing Squid. It was part of a Demon contest!

"Here is the arena we have established for the finale," Laurelai said. "It is a dance. A square dance, to be precise. To occur here, in this hall, tomorrow. For this we need four couples. I will select them now. First, Goar and Incident." She looked directly at them. "You have the right to decline."

Suddenly Goar knew it: this was to be his chance to earn forgiveness! He had no idea how, but now he knew when. Tomorrow. At the dance.

Incident knew it too. "We accept." She had picked up on Laurelai's other identity, and had not forgotten that her own present beauty stemmed from Fornax's intervention, enabling them to stop the New Clear blast.

"Beetle Bunny and Ruby Rabbit in human form."

"We accept," Ruby said before Beetle could say something stupid like updoc.

"Birdman and Birdie."

"Of course," the Queen said. It was clear that her rank was not an issue here; she understood the importance of the coming event.

"Larry and Squid will appear tomorrow to make the fourth couple." Laurelai looked around. "And Ninja Turtle will call the dance, while Terza Turtle tracks the four couples mentally." She smiled enigmatically. "Because there may be an intrusion tomorrow. Now we will have a brief private, rehearsal, a walk-through, with Ninja and Terza substituting for the fourth couple while I call it."

They got to work and cleared the stage and chairs, making space for the square. They were not dressed for dancing, and there was no music, but this was practice, not demonstration. The four couples lined up in the manner Laurelai directed, as only Queen Birdie was familiar with this type of dance.

"Set in order," Laurelai said. "As you can see, it forms a rough square, with a couple forming each side. In the other frame we have what amounts to a professional dance group, which is why we selected this form for this occasion. You need have no concern about unfamiliarity, as you will learn the moves now. This one is called Partners, because in the course of it, the partners swap partners."

Goar wondered how a mere dance could settle a Demon wager, but knew he would find out tomorrow. He was sure Incident and the others were similarly curious. But most of them had witnessed Fornax's power when they visited alternate Mundania, and none of them would question her now.

"Everything fits the pattern of the square," Laurelai said. "Always maintain it. Now swing your partner." She used Goar and Incident as a sample couple, showing them how it was done. Then the three other couples emulated them. She continued with the other basic moves: the honor, which was a formal little bow, the do-si-do, the balance, the promenade, the allemande. "When the command 'Men, Change Partners' comes, you will each walk from your present side to the side of your left, leaving your partner behind and taking a new one. The girls will remain in place." Laurelai quirked a smile. "This possibly might relate to the tendency of men to take any girl within range, regardless of their commitments elsewhere. He will do the next round of moves with that girl, until the Change command comes again, when he will make another move. The fourth such move will bring him back to his original partner, and the dance will end."

They walked through it, and Goar found himself beside Ruby, then Birdie, then Terza, and finally back to Incident. She frowned. "Well, you had a time of it, you letch," she said curtly, but couldn't hold the mood and had to laugh. There were similar laughs with the other couples.

"Tomorrow you will be in costume, and there will be music, and one other couple, but the dance will be the same," Laurelai concluded. "However, it may be interrupted. In that case, hold your places and wait for the action to play out, whatever its nature. Now take your seats again."

The square disbanded and they put table, chairs, and platform back where they had been before. Laurelai ascended the stage. "Now to prime the pump." They might not know what a pump was, let alone how to prime it, but they understood that this was to be the finale of this presentation.

"I now name the guilty Demon who set up the murders of Larry and Squid," Laurelai said. Actually, it was Fornax speaking now, not a mere mortal. Only Demons really counted, for this. "You are to be called to account for your crimes when the grace period ends tomorrow. If you do not appear for the hearing to defend your supposed innocence, you will lose your case by default." She paused, and Goar doubted he was the only one holding his breath. "Demon Oma."

Demon Oma! The one Incident and the animals served. The one dedicated to killing innocent people via planted cancer seeds. Goar was surprised, yet unsurprised. It did make sense.

The woman's aspect changed. "I, Demoness Fornax, charge you, Demon Oma, with the unwarranted killing of my host Laurelai, so it is personal." There was a timbre that shook the hall.

Then she changed to the male form. "I, Demon Chaos, charge you, Demon Oma, with the unwarranted killing of my host Larry, so it is personal." The voice differed, but the timbre remained. Oma had made enemies of two of the most powerful Demons extant, those of antimatter and of chaos. No wonder he had hidden!

There was no response.

"So be it," Laurelai said grimly. She glanced about once more. "Dismissed." She walked off the stage and out of the hall, alone. Her job here was done, for now.

The croup dissolved into animated reactions. "What will happen to us, the Incidents, and our partners, either way?" Incident asked Goar rhetorically.

Terza stood. "If I may have your attention, I do have the answer to your question. You will all be freed of your obligation to deliver the seeds of destruction, but will maintain your powers. I was given the word telepathically."

There was almost a whoosh of relief. They did not like their job, but did like their powers.

Then the servitors returned and resumed their activities, none the wiser about the content of the meeting. No one was about to tell them, either.

That night, Goar and Incident reviewed it together. "Oma forced me to obtain anonymous revenge against Chaos," he said, awed by the implication.

"And he did it by killing the mortal woman he loved," Incident agreed. "This was dastardly indeed."

"But how can Oma hope to escape? He is not in a class with either Chaos or Fornax."

"I don't know, but I don't trust him not to come up with something even worse. His whole career has been devoted to making others do his sneaky mischief."

"And why are we somehow involved?" he asked. "Couldn't they have used more effective mortals?"

"It's like the Good Magician's Answers. It has to make sense in the end."

Tomorrow they might well have the answer.

In the morning, they rendezvoused with the companions and girlfriends, reviewing the dance steps and arranging for their costumes. None of the companions had ever attended a dance before. Fortunately, their girlfriends had, though Terza only mentally. They were a steadying presence. Birdie had her tailors fit the suits and dresses, with appropriate footwear, along with colorful sashes for the men and neat tiaras for the ladies, and they really looked quite fetching.

The dance was scheduled for the afternoon, because that was when the Demon deadline expired. The personnel of the castle were invited to attend as an audience. If things worked out, they might then get to dance, themselves, once the real business of the occasion had been accomplished. "They will dress well," Birdie said. "Not because they have to, but because they love to. Most of the time they are servants; for this, they will get to be like nobles and ladies." She smiled. "Some of them might even take an interest in square dancing, after they see how the full circle skirts rise when they twirl."

Ruby, Terza, and Incident looked thoughtful. There had been no twirling during the rehearsal. That might change.

The time arrived. They entered the hall. It had been transformed. It now looked like a forest garden with all manner of colorful plants, and even a sparkling pool in the center, fed by a meandering stream with a small waterfall. The multiple entrances appeared to be doors in the trunks of larger trees. Brightly plumaged birds abounded, of course, perching on numerous branches. Some of that had to be illusion. It was nevertheless impressive.

The audience was seated around the outer edge, facing in toward the center pool and stage. They were indeed well dressed, the men in suits, the women in evening gowns and high-heeled slippers. Goar's only regret was that the skirts were so long that when the women crossed their legs, absolutely nothing showed.

"Have you no shame?" Incident murmured. "They're *peons*."

Goar was startled, until he realized that Terza must have read his thought and relayed it to Incident. Sometimes the girls seemed to get along entirely too well.

"The men, on the other hand, are interesting," she continued teasingly.

"Their legs don't appeal to me."

She laughed. "Just as well."

The dance floor was now the stage, with the musicians of the orchestra seated around it, next to the stream and pool. Oh, how those twirls would show fair legs, on the raised level, because the dancing dresses were not gowns, but rather were designed to rise when they were supposed to.

"Of course," Incident agreed.

"Sets in order," Ninja Turtle announced.

The four couples ascended and took their places as they had the day before, except that now the fourth couple was Larry and Squid, looking handsome and lovely, respectively. It was hard to believe that she was actually a land-bound cuttlefish shaped into the form of a woman. But then it was similarly hard to believe that other members were a rabbit, a bird, and a turtle.

Ninja spoke to the audience. "We are now going to perform a sample square dance, which you may emulate later if you wish to. It consists of four couples who will perform the steps as I call them out. There is no danger of losing your place in such a dance: it is choreographed, and all you have to do is follow the calls. The lead-off couple on the north side, of course, is Queen Birdie and her partner Bird Man, whom you know."

There was a muted chuckle in the audience as Birdie and Bird Man bowed to them. Of course they knew their Queen and her recent consort. They applauded vigorously.

"Next to their right on the west side are Beetle Bunny and Ruby Rabbit." They duly bowed, and the audience offered token applause.

"Next, on the south, are Goar Golem and Incident Oma." They bowed to more token applause.

"And finally, to the east, are visitors for this occasion, Larry Human and Squid Cuttlefish." The audience laughed, thinking it a joke, until Squid transformed into her natural form, showing a bulbous head and tentacles in her dress. She re-formed as human before that dress could fall off. “You may think of her as human,” Ninja continued. “She will maintain that guise for the dance.” Now they applauded more sincerely. They thought her a shape changer, though actually her human form was mostly emulation. She actually formed her tentacles two by two into humanoid limbs.

Ninja addressed the square. “This dance is called Partners,” he said. He glanced at the orchestra, and the music commenced. “Honor your partner.” Goar bowed formally to Incident, and she to him, her low décolletage proffering a peek at her breasts. “Honor your corner.” Goar turned and bowed to Ruby Rabbit on his left, who flashed similar software, while Incident bowed to Larry on her right. “Do-si-do with your opposite.” Goar advanced into the center of the square to meet Birdie, clasping his own elbows as he circled her, back to back, then backed back to his original place. They had to position themselves just so, so as not to collide with the other pairs doing the same maneuver. “Swing your partner.” They joined and swung together in the square dance manner, the rear hems of the skirts lifting. “Promenade the hall.” They linked arms in the prescribed manner and sashayed counter-clockwise once around the square.

Now came the unusual calls. “Dialog with your partner.” The music went to a low repeating cadence as if talking. Goar faced Incident and spread his hands as if addressing her, while she nodded as if agreeing. Actually their words were more serious than the show indicated. “It’s coming,” she said. “I feel it.”

He felt a chill, though of course they had known this was approaching. “The showdown of the Demons?”

“Yes. It’s just a nervous feeling. For Terza, it must be horrible.”

Because Terza was the full telepath. “At least it will soon be over.”

“Yes. But you’re in the center, Goar. I fear for your life.”

“But I’m not central to the showdown.”

“Yes you are. I know it.”

He was central? He had assumed he was peripheral. All he wanted was to somehow earn Squid’s forgiveness and retire with Incident. Why should Demons, those galaxies to grains of sand, care about him? His grain of sand?

The caller intervened. “Kiss your partner.” The music returned to the dancing mode.

What? This had not been in the rehearsal.

"You heard him," Incident said, stepping into him.

He embraced her and they kissed, and it was immensely sweet. The music made an enhancing surge, and there was an appreciative "Oooo," from the audience. They liked this hint of romance. But he felt her alarm, her fear for him, as though it might be their last kiss. Could that have been why it had been added?

"Men, side left," Ninja called.

They separated, and Goar sashayed to his left, around the corner, to join Ruby Rabbit as her original partner Beetle went north. She smiled at him. She looked stunning in her dress and tiara; he was suddenly more conscious of this, now that she had become his temporary partner.

"Honor your partner." They bowed to each other.

"Honor your corner." Who was now Birdie, resplendent in her feminine crown.

"Do-si-do with your opposite." Who was now Squid. She smiled just as if she were enjoying it. Dancing with her murderer.

It continued as before, until the Dialog. The music went into its hush.

"I hope the finale doesn't break up the Oma group," Ruby said. That was right: it was Demon Oma they were out to punish, and Oma had been responsible for the institution of the Oma groups. His fate could indeed affect them.

"I hope not too," he agreed.

"Rabbit needs to make the holes to transition Sarah Spinel between Mundania and Xanth," she continued. "To see to Baby Dinosaur Spinosaurus. We need Bird to take us from the hole to Queen Smote."

"The sexy Dragon Queen," he agreed again, remembering.

"I like her. We're both smart animals who can assume human form. I am sure she'll take good care of Spino."

"She surely will."

"So the group needs to stay together."

She was right. "Yes."

The command came. "Kiss your partner."

But Ruby was Rabbit's girl. Now he remembered freaking out when she had eaten the mushroom and become fifty feet tall and he had looked up at her bare torso. That was now an embarrassing intimacy. "Uh—"

"It's just a dance move, silly," she said, and kissed him.

That set him back in another manner. She did know how to kiss. He had thought that only Incident or the Goddess Tiamat could have serious impact on him, but Ruby was proving otherwise.

"Men, side left."

Halfway relieved, he sashayed on to the north side of the square. There was Birdie. She had looked beautiful across the square; up this close she looked ravishing. "Hello, Goar," she said confidently.

"Hello, Queen Birdie."

"Just Birdie will do, here in our privacy. We're friends, after all."

The privacy of being the center of the audience's attention? Yet, oddly, it was true. The dance was its own environment.

"Honor your partner."

They bowed to each other, and she was every bit as curvy as Incident and Ruby. It seemed to be something about the costumes.

The dance continued until the Dialog. "Bird of course will stay with me," she said. "But he also values and loves his friends of the Oma group, and doesn't want to lose them. You are included in that number, Goar."

"I have the utmost respect for Bird."

"But you see, there is a problem. The group has its mission of performing Good Deeds and making Xanth a better realm. That will require it to travel much of the time. Bird is needed there, and I think not merely for transport. But I need him too. I do love him; that's not just pretense. He freed me from more than that tower. The thought of constant separation from him mortifies me."

"I appreciate that." Where was she leading?

"The only solution I see is for the group to reside at Shee Castle, so Bird can be with both me and the group. I will make a nice garden section for it, with facilities for humans, rabbits, and turtles as well as birds. Does that seem suitable to you?"

"Yes."

"Then I hope I can count on your support, when the time of decision comes."

That was easy, because she was correct. "Yes."

"Thank you."

"Kiss your partner."

Again he hesitated. She was a queen! Dance or no, it would be presumptuous to kiss her in public. But as with Ruby, she did not waver. She took him in and kissed him ardently. And he had to add one more to the list of women who could half stun him when they tried. She was evidently grateful for his support, so she had tried.

"Men, side left."

You are indeed the key to this event, Terza thought to him as he moved to the next position. *You transformed the Oma group into a force for good.*

No, Incident did that, he demurred, *because of the conscience cloud.*

Well, at least you are one stone in the arch. Every rock is vital.

I suppose.

She laughed mentally. *You don't want to take any credit. You have no selfish motive.*

He had to demur again. *I want to obtain Squid's forgiveness so I can be at peace.*

She nodded mentally. *That selfishness I find acceptable. But brace yourself: the showdown is incipient.* She withdrew.

Now he faced his nemesis, Squid. She was fabulously lovely, and still smiling as if she were enjoying it. He danced with her, and followed the commands, and she was perfect in every move. The consummate girl. What would she say to him in the dread Dialog?

All too soon it came. The music hushed. He blurted out his thought. "If I had known you, Squid, I would not have killed you. I am so sorry." As if that clumsy apology could make up for slaughtering her.

What she replied surprised him. "Goar, you were crafted as a golem for one purpose only: to kill me. Otherwise you would not exist."

That had to be true, but it did not make him feel justified. "It would have been better if I did not exist!"

"Not so. What you were crafted to be is one thing. What you subsequently crafted yourself to be is another. You are a good man, Goar."

"Not nearly as good as the one I killed along with you."

She shook her head. "You did not kill Chaos. He was not here at the time. He borrows Laurelai's male form Larry as his host. It is Chaos I love. I don't know why he loves me. He is the most powerful Demon of them all, and I am only an imitation girl."

Now they were in it, and somehow he found it fitting. He spoke again in a manner he had not anticipated. "You don't know why Chaos loves you? I do. It is because you are a truly lovely girl."

She laughed, marvelously well. "But I'm not even a girl. It is only a shape I form." She became the cuttlefish, her dress hanging awkwardly.

"I was not referring to your physical aspect."

She turned human again, blushing. She had been caught by an unexpected compliment. "Thank you."

"But this showdown of the Demons. How does it relate to me? I am just a grain of sand. My purpose ended when I killed you."

"As I understand it, my murder was set up to provoke Chaos into acting rashly, and making an error. The trap was for him. You were the instrument then, and remain so now. Oma will somehow try to make Chaos make the first move."

"Move?"

"This particular Demon game relates to status, as they usually do. The rule is that he who moves last, Demon style, moves best. So if Chaos moves first, he loses. But we managed to change it by naming Oma, who will now lose by default if he doesn't move first. Unless he finds another way to make Chaos move first. So this whole thing is a tryst of fate, a coming together to decide who is to be dominant. We are merely tiny instruments."

Goar found that tricky to visualize. "I suppose if I tried to kill you again, Chaos would have to move to stop me. But I am not going to do that."

She smiled, her sincerity animating it, and somehow that moved him more than the smiles of the others had. "I know. You're on my side now."

"Kiss your partner," Ninja called.

Somehow it seemed as if they had been in dialog longer than the moment allotted for the other dialogues, but perhaps that was just his subjective impression.

He faced her, suddenly deeply uncertain. "Squid, I don't deserve to touch you, let alone kiss you."

"Brace yourself. I do believe the crisis is upon us." She put her arms around him, drew in close, and kissed him. For an instant it was excruciatingly sweet. She, too, could wow him when she tried.

There was an explosion of darkness. It was not the kiss. They jerked apart.

There was a torus of darkness around them. It was expanding outward and inward. The turf of the garden was disappearing into it as if falling into an absolute void.

"Oma has taken over Ninja Turtle!" Terza exclaimed, manifesting as human. She was plainly horrified.

Ninja spoke with the Demon timbre. "By Demon practice, the second one to make a power move is the victor. Now the choice is upon you, Chaos. You have the first move. You can take me and preserve the existing order, or you can save your beloved mortal girl. You cannot do both."

"Oh, bleepity bleep!" Squid swore. "The utter tumor figured a way to make Chaos waste his move on me."

Goar realized that the threat to Squid did not count as a Demon move. Only an action directly against another Demon counted. Squid was mortal. Stopping Oma's attack on Squid—*that* would count, by Demon protocols.

The circle was closing rapidly. It would soon engulf them. But what was it? Goar reached out to touch it with his socked hands.

His hands disappeared. His arms now terminated in severed bones.

"I have found the secret of Nothing," Oma continued. "There is no explosion, merely the emptiness that occurs when the positive and negative aspects of matter, the positrons and negatrons if you will, join and cancel out. It has been asked why is there something rather than nothing? Because the positive and negative aspects are kept apart by the invisible forces for the universe. The original Big Bang generated those forces and thus enabled matter to exist. Eliminate those forces and the two aspects come immediately together and are gone. The original state of quiescence returns, without energy, matter, or rules. I can destroy the universe merely by invoking the force-nullifying process. But in this case, I have limited it to a single spot. *That* spot. The closing torus, designed to progress inward until it meets itself in the center and ends, along with whatever matter is in that center.

"What say you now, Chaos? Your power can stop the process, because the opposites can't come together when chaotic. But by the rule of this engagement, you can act only on one site. Me or Squid. Choose now, or she perishes by default and I win and will become the highest status Demon, immune to any subsequent retaliation." He rubbed Ninja's hands together in evil glee. He seemed to relish his enemy's discomfort as much as his own impending ascent to Dominant Demon, the one with the highest status. He knew Chaos couldn't let Squid be Nothinged, so Oma stood to win either way. He was a truly nasty being.

Goar whirled, facing Squid as their spot became a quickly diminishing island in a blank void. "I will need your help. Change form and cling to my shoulders. I will carry you out."

"Goar, you can't walk through that," she protested, frightened. "You will cease to exist from the feet up."

"Trust me."

"Oh, I do! But—"

"Now!"

She relented and changed, flinging out a tentacle to wrap around his thick neck and haul the rest of her up and in to him. She plainly believed they both were lost, but did as he asked.

Goar mentally flipped a chaos bomb into the torus. There was a cloud of confusion as the disappearing matter turned chaotic. Positive and negative were trying to come together, but were being randomly diverted, so existed as inanimate pandemonium.

He stepped into it. He could feel his feet dissolving into confusion. But he still had control of his legs, and kept them moving, striding onward. He grew shorter as the invisible pit became deeper, or maybe as his legs dissolved, but he kept going. Only a few steps were all that were required.

A splash of the fog of confusion hit him on the face-plate, melting it. But one eye patch remained, and most of his painted mouth. He ignored the pain and plowed on.

He reached the shore of remaining matter and fell forward, putting Squid onto firm material. They were through!

Now Bird Man and Beetle Bunny followed his example and flipped their chaos bombs into the seething void. Overwhelmed, it shriveled to a point and ceased to exist. Nothing had been vanquished! Or would have been, had it not been self-limiting.

"You are safe now, Squid," Goar gasped. "Oma's ploy has been nulled."

Squid re-formed as the girl. "Goar, you saved me! And you saved the existing order! The Demons owe you!" She was so excited that one hand and one foot turned tentacular.

He could see her with his remaining eye, and was able to make the mouth speak. "I just had to do right by you, when I could. I owe you more than that."

She calmed, re-forming. "Thank you, Goar."

"No she isn't safe!" Oma screamed, seeing his victory lost. "She's still doomed, and so are you, golem! So is everything else! After me, Nothing! The Torus was designed to be self-limiting. The main Nothing Bomb is designed to progress outward, with no limit, as long as anything remains to be consumed. That includes space itself. The universe! It is the opposite of the Big Bang. It is the Wee Whimper! Behold your doom!"

He extended his hand, holding a globe labeled N for Nothing. Then before anyone could react, he emerged from Ninja Turtle. He assumed his natural form, which was a giant tumor with arms and legs, somewhat like a BEM, and charged directly at Squid. The globe expanded in his hand as he moved, consuming that hand, becoming a larger ball as it ate the arm below. Oma was committing suicide rather than suffer the survival of his enemies. By the time the globe reached Squid, it would be man-sized, ready to eat her in a single toothless tongueless gulp. Goar knew that even if she fled from it, it would continue to expand, inevitably taking her in, and then the universe. Even Chaos might not stop it, if it got established in the next few seconds. It would swallow everything, leaving Nothing.

Goar did not act without thinking. He acted *with* thinking. That was the point. He filled his mind with the Idea. Then he used his limb stubs to hurl himself forward to intercept the charging Demon before he reached Squid. Goar took the bomb into himself as the rest of Oma disappeared into it.

And the bomb faded out with, yes, a wee whimper. Goar remained in place, unaffected. The bomb and Oma were nonexistent.

Squid stared. "What just happened?"

"I nullified the Nothing," Goar explained, pleased that it had actually worked. "Nothing is stronger than the Universe, but one thing is stronger than Nothing. That is the Idea. If the Idea exists, then so does its pyramid: Mind to think of it, Brain/Body to generate Mind, food, water, air to nourish that body, Environment to provide that necessary sustenance, World to provide that environment, and Universe to form the matter to make the stars and planets that become worlds. It all starts with the Idea, and with the Idea there is everything. I nullified Nothing with Everything."

"I won't pretend to understand that," Squid said, shaking her head. "So I will simply say thank you, again. You saved me twice. Now it is time to get you back together." She was being practical rather than philosophical, a trait Goar had noted in other women.

Goar looked down at himself. He existed to slightly below the waist. There was nothing beyond. The chaos bomb had done the job on the Nothing Torus, but some Nothing power had remained. Enough to take out half his body. "You're welcome, Squid."

She got down to his level. "We didn't finish our kiss." She put her mouth to his face-plate and kissed him, heedless of the ugliness of his damaged head. "And I forgive you," she concluded.

The audience burst into applause. He had forgotten it existed. That it *still* existed.

Then the impact struck him. *She had forgiven him!* Goar was overcome by sheer joy. He had taken her life, but now had given it back, and she had returned his life to him. "Thank you," he said, and lapsed into oblivion.

He woke an indeterminate time later. The audience had become the dancers, and they were indeed trying some squares. Laurelai stood before him. "I harvested some items for you. Lie flat." She pushed his shoulder and he rolled over. "Some fresh limbs." She removed his terminated forearms and applied new ones complete with hands. Then she did the same for the stumps of his legs, fitting whole new ones. "Now sit up."

He discovered that he could do so. In fact he was able to stand again. The new limbs worked perfectly. His arms had functional hands with five fingers apiece, and his legs had regular human feet with toes. But how could this be? The new limbs had to be inanimate, tree limbs in fact, but he could feel them perfectly.

"A new face." She removed the plate and slapped something soft onto his head dome. Suddenly he could see perfectly, and his mouth felt whole.

"Thank you," he said, in part to verify that his face was really working.

"And one other minor detail," she murmured, setting something at his crotch. He felt that too. It was male anatomy!

"But—" he started.

She efficiently put trousers on him, protecting his privacy, then reached in and tweaked the final addition. It sprang to life. How was this also possible?

She put her face close to his, and he recognized the Demoness Fornax. "Do not question, merely accept. It is my private thank-you for the deed you did, saving my friend," she whispered, then turned away.

He realized that she had fixed him, in the process making him completely human. He could not openly thank her, because she really wasn't supposed to intervene in such manner. But he thought it. *Thank you!*

She continued walking away. *You earned it.*

Then Larry, the male form of this body, appeared. He approached Goar, and his Demon visage flashed. This was Chaos. "You saved me some mischief today, as well as preserving my beloved, and I think I owe you an unofficial favor or two. Your original equipment, the saws and treads and invulnerability, will manifest when you need them. And of course you'll have a renewable supply of chaos bombs."

"Thank you." It was of course inadequate, but he was getting used to that.

"I believe you have learned why I love Squid. She is more than just a girl, regardless of species."

"I love her too." It was no exaggeration. She had forgiven him!

"I would have saved her, of course, though at the expense of the existing order. Oma had counted on that. But your intercession meant I didn't have to. I appreciate that."

"I owed her. Instead of abolishing me, she gave me a chance."

"She did. I would have destroyed you, but she demurred. Now I appreciate what she did."

"So do I," Goar said ruefully.

"Some perspective," Chaos said. "This track is one of millions, insignificant to the larger scheme. One dead couple here is virtually unnoticeable to the infinite cosmos. But the involvement of Demons, who spread across all realities, made it affect the entire tapestry of reality. You killed two people on one track, then saved the existing universe in *all* tracks. Squid was right to believe in you. She phrased your assignment as protagonist as a punishment, but she really wanted to give you that chance.

That is a quality hardly to be found in any entity, mortal or immortal. She is that kind of person."

"She *is* that kind of person," Goar echoed appreciatively.

"How can we not love her?"

"How can we not," he agreed.

"And you came through. All else is incidental."

"Oh yes!" Goar said, thinking of Incident.

"We understand each other." He walked away.

So Goar was now both human and killer golem, depending on the situation. The soft sensitive flesh and the hard weapons. That was extremely satisfying. Chaos, too, knew how to render a favor,

Birdie and Bird Man approached. "Did you hear?" she asked in her pre-gossip tone. "Now that Oma is gone, there will be no more cancer seeds. The Mundanes will love that, even if they don't realize who's responsible."

"What will all the other Incidents and their companions do?" he asked, surprised.

"Good deeds. They're not nearly as pretty as you folk are, but they can get there in a few decades if they focus on doing the best for others that they possibly can. They will also retain their powers, to better facilitate that good work."

"That does make sense."

"I am expanding the dance, in honor of what has been accomplished today. I invited everybody who counts. You must do another square."

"Not like the last!" he exclaimed alarmed.

"Not at all," she agreed. "No Nothing bombs or evil Demons. Just a brief interaction to wrap things up."

Goar tried to demur. "I really don't—"

Incident came and took him by the arm. "Only one dance, dear, hidden midst all the other squares. It won't take long."

She wanted this? He had to comply.

They formed the square. Goar's mind was so occupied with the recent events, including his acquisition of a fully human body, that he didn't notice the other couples. Until the dance began and he saw them. King Bezoar BEM with the Goddess Tiamat. Telepathic Doris Dragon of the Sea Kingdom with Queen Smote of the Smoker Dragons, both in resplendent human form. And ugly King Gustave Goblin with his fabulously lovely fiancée Gusta.

He danced in a blur, following the calls more or less mindlessly. Then he found himself with Tiamat, lovely as only a goddess could be. "I fear I will not win you for a paramour," she said with token regret as she flashed her magnificent bosom.

What could he say? He changed the subject. "You're partnering with the BEM king?"

"Why not? I love his grabbiness. Maybe I'll take him home for a night."

How could Goar question her tastes? He owed her a lot.

Then came the kiss, for that dance call had come. She plastered herself against him reminiscently. His new anatomy responded powerfully, as she mischievously intended. He hoped it wasn't evident to others.

Then he was with Queen Smote. "I see Mother impressed you."

So much for concealment. "How is it you have a female partner?"

"Time was too short to round up a male. But Doris will do. She's a dragon, too, and favors the ladies as well as the men. She enjoys this opportunity."

"Opportunity?"

"To do this with the girls." She kissed him in a way that only made his problem worse. She, too, could be mischievous.

And with the once ugly goblin girl Gusta. "I see the dragon ladies are working you over."

Goar's new face blushed. "They are," he admitted.

"I truly appreciate what you did for me. I will be a queen, thanks to you."

"You are welcome."

"You and your companions are still invited to the wedding."

"Thank you. We'll be there."

She kissed him delicately, without illicit passion, and let him go. He appreciated that.

And at last he was back with Incident, and the dance was finishing. When the square broke up, they went to exchange pleasantries with Sarah Spinel Mundane. She was holding the baby dinosaur Spino, and the ladies were all oooing over him, patting his head. He was probably under a niceness spell for the occasion, so that he would not bite off their hands. Sarah looked supremely happy.

Finally, Incident led him out of the hall. "You have had a day," she said. "You need some rest." She led him to their chamber. "After we test out your replacement equipment. It seems to be in good enough order."

Had everyone at the dance noticed? He found himself blushing again.

"No, we're only teasing. You have become suitably anonymous."

That was a huge relief.

"Now for the finale."

"There's more?" he asked warily.

"Nothing much." She stepped out of her clothing.

Oh. Goar realized that he had a very promising hour ahead, and indeed, a life.

What followed was more like Everything than Nothing.

"Curious thing," she remarked as they lay, temporarily played out, on the bed, having given the equipment a thorough workout. It was top notch, and very responsive. Especially the new lips, and the nether addition, quiescent at last. They had feeling like never before. The Demoness had not stinted on her gifts. "Larry and Laurelai are going home now, with Squid and her male aspect."

He was surprised. "Squid has a male aspect?" He had known that Larry/Laurelai was a gender changer, but must have forgotten about Squid.

"Yes. They can switch back and forth to be he and she, or she and he, or male buddies or female girlfriends. But that isn't what's curious. It's that I overheard them privately talking. They are eager to return to their own reality frame. But then she said 'But it may be tricky getting used to being children again.' And he agreed. What do you think they meant? They've been an adult couple throughout, and I suspect they could show us some tricks in bed that we have yet to catch on to. What's this about children? I'm pretty sure they don't have any yet, here or there."

"I have no idea. I have a mystery of my own."

"Oh?"

"The Demon Chaos gave me back my weapons, in case I ever need them again. Then he was almost, well, friendly."

"Why would the most powerful Demon of them all want to be friendly with a golem?"

"Exactly. It's a mystery."

She focused. “I have a notion. You are both males. That means you don’t understand women, especially those you love.”

“True,” he said ruefully.

“Now you have Squid in common, because he loves her and you saved her. You are closer to her nature than he is. When he can’t figure her out, you may be able to advise him.”

“Me!”

“You did well enough with Bird. Now he is betrothed to a queen.”

“I just applied *Managing Women 101* that Tiamat taught me.”

“Yes, I am aware of her impact on you. And you used it on Squid, too, when you complimented her.”

“Maybe I did,” Goar agreed, surprised.

“Chaos let Fornax carry most of the setting up of the trap for Oma, because she’s female and knows what’s what. But Chaos can’t dialogue conveniently with Fornax, in mortal form, because they use the male and female aspects of the same host. So he may want to talk with you, sometimes, when he can’t figure Squid out. It’s bound to happen.”

“I am to be friends with a Demon?” he asked in wonder.

“It just might be. Keep your mind open.”

“Wide open,” he agreed, bemused. He had never anticipated anything like this!

But they didn’t dwell further on the minor mysteries. They had good lives to expand into, and a lot of good deeds to perform.

AUTHOR'S NOTE

In FeBlueberry 2018 (Ogre months are better than Mundane months) when on my morning exercise run, I came up to Ogre Corner and saw a big pine cone in the drive. So without pausing I went to kick it off the drive with my left foot. That was a mistake. My foot stubbed into the pavement and I crashed down on my face. There's a picture of my mangled face in the Marsh 2018 HiPiers column file. Since then I have not kicked a pine cone while running; I do learn slowly from experience.

I also bashed my hands, arms, elbows, knees and my right rib-cage, which stopped me from taking a deep breath, and the idea of a cough was sheer horror. I was eighty-three years old, and falls at that age have consequences. It wiped out my exercises for a couple of weeks. All because of a pine cone. My doctor had me get an x-ray to be sure my ribs were not broken and were healing okay, and they were all right. But there was a spot that showed on my right lung. As I happened about the same time I read an article that referred to such accidentally discovered spots as "incidentalomas." There were, the article said, three kinds: the birds, which meant you were doomed already, the rabbits, which you could catch and treat if you hopped right to it, and the turtles, which were so slow they never got anywhere. Well, mine turned out to be, as my lung doctor put it, a dead turtle. Just dead tissue, not cancer. Maybe from asbestos inhaled as a child. In my day they didn't know asbestos was dangerous. So I was okay.

But anything that happens in my life can be grist for my fiction. In this case, grist for *Tryst*. Now you know where four of my main characters came from. I just thought you'd be interested.

The notion that the Idea is the beginning of existence is not original with me. In the Bible, the Gospel According to St. John 1:1 says "In the beginning was the Word, and the Word was with God, and the Word was God." I submit that the original could as readily have been translated "In the beginning was the Idea." Start with the Idea, and the rest follows. What is a story or a novel but an Idea clothed in narrative? Even in the relatively recent history of mankind, accepting evolution, the word was fundamental to man's shaping. When the first ape lifted up his front end and walked on his two hind feet, the babies could not follow in the manner of animals, and had to be carried. But the mother could not forage and weave baskets and sew pelts for clothing and gather wood for the fire and cook the food and do the myriad other family survival things while constantly carrying her baby. Even when the child started to walk, there was no relief, because children are perpetually getting into mischief. I'm a father; I know. She needed a babysitter, and a teacher, so that the child would be safe while she got everything else done. That was where the Word came in, the Idea. A storyteller would talk to the tribe's children, entertaining them, educating them, teaching them. We owe our sapient minds largely to the art of story telling. To the transmission of ideas. Today we still depend on the Idea, whether it is the Idea of Family Unity, or Democracy, or the vast collection of Ideas in books, television, or on the Internet. Without the Idea we would have nothing. Which is what Goar concluded.

I made 20,000 words of notes in 2018, then wrote this novel in the first three months of 2019. At this writing I am eighty-four years old. The average American man at this age is several years dead, and not all the living ones have all their minds remaining, so I can't be sure there will be future Xanth novels. But I plan to keep writing as long as I am able to do so. My wife and I have been married sixty-two and a half years and live quietly on our little tree farm. When not writing, I read books of all kinds, and watch DVD videos of all kinds. We don't go out to see movies anymore because my wife is housebound and not up to it, but we continue to putter along in our fashion. I still exercise, eat right, and try to maintain my health, but of course age crunches on. I keep hoping for a movie made from one of my books; I believe it will happen, but I'd like it to happen while I'm still alive to appreciate it.

When assembling this novel from the assorted chapter files, I came across a reader notion I had meant to use but didn't; the onrushing text can seem to choose its own directions, just as individual characters can seem to develop their own roles regardless of the author's expectations. And I thought, why not use it in the next novel? In fact it could be the nucleus of that story. It may not work out, but it gives me something to work on, tentatively titled *Six Crystal Princesses.* Young Prince Ion and his sister Hilda set out to rescue the other princesses whom a dragon has preserved in crystal, the way their mother Princess Ida was long ago, per a passing sequence in Xanth #15 *The Color of Her Panties.* Why should she be the only one rescued? Soon it gets complicated, as these are not ordinary princesses. But no need to bore you further. Stay tuned.

If you enjoyed this novel and want to know more of me, you can check my website at www.HiPiers.com, where I do a monthly blog-type column, have news of my new projects, express my ongoing opinionations, and maintain an ongoing survey of electronic publishers for the benefit of aspiring writers.

More anon, if.

And of course when asked where I get all my ideas for my books, I answer "From the readers." I have many more reader suggestions than I have used here; I try to use ones from new contributors before using several from folk who are already represented. The others remain on file, for consideration for the next Xanth novel. It's an ongoing process. Now for the reader credits for this one, in approximate order of appearance.

The title *A Tryst of Fate*—Leigh Anne Harre
Eye of the Bee-Holder—Matt Britt
Safety pins—Alexander Sellers
Grisly Bear, Gal Wires, Lightening Bolts (also used in *Fire Sail*); reminder of the Mundanian Round Tuit; Square Meal; Slow Gin; Fast Gin—Richard Van Fossan
Misty Demon-Angel; Heaven Scent—Misty Zaebst
Housewife, Hornswoggle—Mary Rashford
Next to No Time—Richard Keenum
UFA (Unwanted Female Attention); Falling between cracks—Sharon Young
Talent of telling obscure truths—Jill C.
Tessellation—I learned this from an article by Abby Godon, math

specialist, in the June 2018 issue of freep newsletter by the School in Rose Valley, which I attended in 1945–47, fifth through seventh grades. It discussed mosaics, the fitting together of tiles or other fragments to make a larger pattern. So I formed a mosaic or tessellation in Chapter 7, as you have seen.

Time Flies like an arrow; Fruit Flies like a banana—unknown author, in general circulation.

Time Flies make time fly back or forward—Darrel Jones

Hedge Fund—Laura Kwon Anderson

Sneak Peak—Robert Judas Brown

Jemma—Jema Schunke

C-Weed—Tim Bruening

Tiamat's Dragons—Clayton Overstreet

Boxer puts things in boxes—Richard Davenport

Mints: Enlighten, Accomplish, Advertise, Excra, etc—Jeff Ramsdell

Gators: Alley, Investi, All E—Jim Smith

Pop Rocks—James Beardsley

Spin-ache—Naomi Blose

Melons: water, earth, air, fire = elemelons—Eric Gjovaag

Talent of getting ducks in a row—Sara Cornelius

Sue Nami (tsunami), Min Tu Bi—Randy Gardner

Token Appearance—Eric Bausch

Talent of combining two magic objects—J Ellner

Timbre Wolves—Brandon Roberts

Kaola-t bear—Joshua Davenport Herbst

Mary Wana—Ken Senft

Spellbinder—Cliffton Lyses

Panties freak lesbians—Crystal Farmer

And my credit to my proofreaders, Scott M Ryan, John Knoderer, and Douglas J Harter. I wish I could do error-free manuscripts, but mistakes are like biting flies, always sneaking in no matter how many I slap.

ABOUT THE AUTHOR

Piers Anthony has written dozens of bestselling science fiction and fantasy novels. Perhaps best known for his long-running Magic of Xanth series, many of which are *New York Times* bestsellers, he has also had great success with the Incarnations of Immortality series and the Cluster series, as well as *Bio of a Space Tyrant* and others. Much more information about Piers Anthony can be found at www.HiPiers.com.

THE XANTH NOVELS

FROM OPEN ROAD MEDIA

OPEN ROAD
INTEGRATED MEDIA